The amputated memory: a song-novel
F WEREW   39106002021780

Libbie Cass Library

DISCARD

LIBBIE CASS LIBRARY
757 MAIN ST.
SPRINGFIELD, NH 03284-0089
763-4381

THE AMPUTATED MEMORY

THE AMPUTATED MEMORY

A SONG-NOVEL

WEREWERE LIKING

Translated from the French by Marjolijn de Jager
Afterword by Michelle Mielly

The Feminist Press
at the City University of New York
New York

Published in 2007 by The Feminist Press at the City University of New York
The Graduate Center, 365 Fifth Avenue, Suite 5406, New York, NY 10016
www.feministpress.org

Translation and glossary copyright © 2007 by Marjolijn de Jager
Afterword copyright © 2006 by Michelle Mielly
All rights reserved.

Originally published in French under the title *La mémoire amputée* by Wéréwéré
Liking. Copyright © 2004 by NEI Abidjan. ISBN: 2-84487-236-0 NEI. All
rights reserved for all countries.

No part of this book may be reproduced or used, stored in any information
retrieval system or transmitted in any form or by any means, electronic,
mechanical, photocopying, recording, or otherwise without prior written
permission from The Feminist Press at the City University of New York, except
in the case of brief quotations embodied in critical articles and reviews.

Library of Congress Cataloging-in-Publication Data

Werewere Liking, 1950-
[Mémoire amputée. English]
The amputated memory : mothers Naja and aunts Roz : a song-novel / by
Werewere Liking ; translated from the French by Marjolijn de Jager.
p. cm.
ISBN-13: 978-1-55861-555-7 (trade cloth)
ISBN-10: 1-55861-555-5 (trade cloth)
I. de Jager, Marjolijn. II. Title.
PQ3989.2.L54M4513 2007
843'.914—dc22
2007021440

This publication was made possible, in part, by the Carnegie Corporation of
New York, the Rockefeller Foundation, and by public funds from the National
Endowment for the Arts.

NATIONAL
ENDOWMENT
FOR THE ARTS

Text and cover design by Lisa Force
Printed on acid-free paper in Canada by Transcontinental

12 11 10 09 08 07   5 4 3 2 1

To All my Loves
From yesterday to tomorrow
My natural, spontaneous or invented, recreated Loves,
For, before all else,
We must first learn to create Love

For all my Friends in Madness, born that way or rendered mad

My Master Injectors of anguish,
For, before any wisdom gained,
We must all experience madness

To all my grandchildren, all the Yi in my Village
Who will never cease seeking the Ki
I dedicate what follows here. . . .

So, trying to pretend with eyebrows arched
That they were keeping calm
Each one wondered privately
What was coming next. And what is actually coming next?

Hey! I muttered behind their back
What is next is a novel, of course, you silly fools!
That is to say, fabrications or stories
But intensely lived or to be lived
If only in the imagination of the tale of love
Hey, hey, hey, that was your Grandmama!!!

—Werewere-Liking Gnepo

TRANSLATOR'S NOTE

My deep appreciation goes to Judith Miller who read the manuscript of this translation in its early stages and, as always, contributed greatly with her invaluable comments and suggestions, most of which I gratefully accepted. I always learn from her! My warm thanks to Michelle Mielly for her fine and thoughtful Afterword, once again carefully read and edited by the inexhaustible Judith Miller. I am deeply indebted to Jean Casella for her meticulous editing and her finely tuned ear, which certainly improved the final version of the text. I am equally grateful to Anjoli Roy, Assistant Editor of The Feminist Press, whose generous help and constant vigilance go beyond the call of duty. To the multitalented Werewere Liking go my boundless admiration and gratitude for yet another beautiful work, for her devotion to helping the flowering embodied in all children, and for reminding me that she began writing *this* book at the kitchen table in our home in Astoria, Queens, some ten years ago. As always, my work—and life— would be diminished without the concrete and emotional support of my husband, David Vita. And last but certainly not least, profound gratitude to Florence Howe herself, without whose lifelong dedication to publishing the wisdom and talents of writing women, works such as these would not make their entrance in this country.

Marjolijn de Jager
Stamford, Connecticut
June 2007

The Amputated Memory takes place in an unnamed West African nation, clearly representing the author's home country, Cameroon. The central story focuses on the Bassa people, and is set in their part of this unnamed country and in a city called Wouri, a stand-in for Cameroon's largest city, Douala.

MOVEMENT ZERO

1

I am Halla Njokè.

My family affectionately calls me Fitini Halla—little Halla—to set me apart from my paternal grandmother, whose namesake I am, and who was known as Great Halla or Great Madja. I am in my eighth decade. Tired of pursuing a thousand different professions, I am, more than anything, a singer. At one point in my life I became a writer, thinking that's what I would always be. But I grew weary of vainly writing words or marks that none of my own people could read. It's discouraging to describe emotions that only you seem to have, and all they ever say to you is: "Now, where did you get that?"—especially when you are surrounded by family every day of your life.

So I tried looking elsewhere and with different eyes, creating simpler things: food, clothes, jewelry, and especially songs, since they are more likely to make people happy and bring them closer to at least a modicum of lasting contentment with life, whether times are tough or trouble-free. From then on, the folks around seemed to be more in tune with me.

So it had been a long time since I'd written anything at all, and then one day, on my seventy-fifth birthday, the same desire came to me again. It happened when I was watching the peaceful face of my Aunt Roz, the third one of that name and a distant cousin of my father, whom I found again in Laguna, the town where I retired.

"Auntie Roz," as everyone here calls her to tell her apart from the other two ("Aunt Roz" and "Tata Roz"), was on the terrace resting on a Senufo bed that served as our couch. She had to be a good fifteen years older than I, and yet her gaze breathed the innocence of happy childhood.

Every day she rises between four and five in the morning to visit the inmates in Laguna's large jail, as big as a whole city neighborhood. Working as a volunteer, she prays for and with them, runs errands for the imprisoned pregnant mothers, and helps their children. She walks miles and miles just to go back and forth. In the afternoon she visits those who are confined to hospitals. And still she finds time to remember birthdays, prepare cookies made with peanuts or cucumber seeds, and bring us her good wishes, as old as we are! All of it in complete serenity. I wanted to pay tribute to her.

Auntie Roz is single and has no children. But she has a thousand children all across the globe. She has so many that taking care of them has become more than a profession; it is a vocation, a calling. . . .

She never arrives anywhere with empty hands, and when she leaves, her hands are filled with things for the next person. Here, she may have brought some smoked fish given to her by a brother pastor, and she'll use the money she receives for it to cover her return transportation, or to buy medicine for the daughter of a sister domestic worker who cannot find the time to take care of it. Clothes she receives as a token of appreciation from another sister go straight to some hospitalized female prisoner, and so on. All by herself, Auntie Roz embodies the entire circle of women through whose solidarity Africa will be reincarnated and restructured.

She prays here, intercedes there, and brings hope, comfort, and a zest for life with her wherever she goes. And when, exhausted, she is all alone again in the evening, the only purpose of her tiny television is to link her up once more with the other children for whom she had no time that day. The clichés that politicians spout remind her how political prisoners are forced to endure the despotism of these men, and how the populace is turned into beasts of burden. Perversely violent movies make her ponder the people upon whom these crimes are inflicted, and in her nightly prayers she has a word or two for God about perversion, violence, and their innumerable victims— prostitutes and delinquents, her other brood, who have been dumped into the street and for whom her heart bleeds in compassion. Even in her delayed and furtive sleep, Auntie Roz is never cut off from her thousands of children: In her dreams she fights the crooked cops who, on every corner and for all to see, rip off her poor little public transportation drivers and street vendors and get away with it! She fights and fights, surrounded by angels with swords of light, striking the evildoers and liberating the virtuous, healing some and feeding others, until she wakes up, always with a start. And once she's up, the first prayer is a new surge of inspiration to serve her youthful thousands. For them, Auntie Roz imagines a better world made up of small certainties, a world just livable enough for all of them as they wait for the Eden that's far too long in coming and impossible to foresee honestly, at the center of a world that's worse than hell and not even truthful enough to call itself by that name.

With each rising day, Auntie Roz creates new pieces of advice for all her sons and daughters. For an all-too-silent girl, she suggests rebellion: "Ask God and be more insistent, protest strongly with all your heart, and he will hear you. Sometimes God is distracted because he is so absorbed in the untold number of his creatures in distress on the earth, deep down in the water, and in the air. You may have to persevere to get his attention, stand up for yourself, and also plead with others—men and women—but especially yourself, as you wait for God to make a move."

To a boy who is quick to be impatient, she says: "Hey, do you really think your problem is the only important thing in the world? It's because you have no imagination and creativity, and you're too lazy and self-centered. What if you were caught in a flood or buried in the lava flow of a volcano or gripped by the winds of a hurricane? Can't you find anything else to do while you wait for divine intervention?"

Alternating between God and people, she asks for clemency and revenge, generosity and thrift, forcefulness and patience. She doesn't believe there's any situation to which you can't comfortably adapt if you are one with your God. In short, Auntie Roz is in the service of her children and of God at every moment of her life.

When my decision to write about her and pay her tribute had fully gestated, I told her about it and tried to get her to tell me the story of her life.

"How did you manage to have such a fascinating life?"

"Because of everything that has happened to me—or at least, what I remember of it, " she answered with a smile. And instead of telling me about this mysterious life of hers, she turned the question back to me.

"Look at you, for instance: What has happened to you to make you what you are? Delve back into your own memory. What you'll draw from that will allow you to know me thoroughly, and then you'll be better able to talk about me and appreciate why I am as I am."

"I don't see the connection between you and me, Auntie Roz. We haven't had the same life. . . ."

"How do you know? Sometimes we don't really know what's happening to us. Our only truth is the memory of our memory. Actually, we often perceive what happens in a light that's totally opposite from what's really going on. An important lesson may become a torment or a joke. An exit door may become the bars of a prison, a dead end, or the underpinning of success. We are marked by the things that stay engraved in our memory. So try to remember. . . ."

"Where the confusion of memory is concerned I agree with you, Auntie Roz; but I still don't see where you're heading. Just tell me this: Will you give me permission to write your life, yes or no?"

"Yes, my little Halla, but if you really want to honor me, you should first unearth what your own memory holds. Track down its transformations and metamorphoses in its double game of surfacing and receding. Pull out some snatches of our Unwritten History. You know we've been living in a context that made us choose oblivion as a survival method, a secret of life, an art of living. And surely you know what a colossal joke, what a farce Africa's history is, especially when they try to refer to 'records.' The civil registries don't list who we are, who was born where and when, who are siblings or husband and wife, who has died, who is alive, who is son or daughter, and on and on. More than ninety percent of the data is made up in wild and perfectly fiendish confusion."

"Yes, but who or what's to blame, Auntie?"

She argued that our ways of identification had not been able to withstand the global assault on African spirituality and cultures by the dominant civilizations. That it was no longer really a question of identifying who or what might be the cause, but of surviving, climbing over walls, and attempting to escape the ghettos.

"So they're happy to forget to register a birth or a death. To the living without any papers they give those of the dead, they claim to be the wife of an unmarried brother, or the sister if not the daughter of what is actually a husband.

"And the thickness of the layers of silence became shamefully tangible, since the governments had total control over the records and made sure that every trace of every deed that disturbed them disappeared. Once so-called democracy made its entrance the journalists were in on it, too, reporting opinions rather than facts. Under such conditions, when the atrocities a person has lived through are passed over in silence for lack of any trace or archive, paying tribute to someone would be a hoax. How do you convey Africa's silences?"

Then Auntie Roz stopped talking, absolutely refusing to have her story told. It was a wasted effort. And so I was obliged to begin exploring my own memory, as distant images actually began to emerge. Bits of stories, and the emotions that accompanied them, increased in number every day. Finally I had to admit that my aunt was right: If I were to truly get hold of my share of both individual and collective memory again, it was through myself that I would discover *her*. Then I would be able to pay her a well-deserved tribute and, through her, honor all the women of my clan, who, in spite of all the vile acts perpetrated against them, had nevertheless managed—and were still managing—to remain cherished, indispensable, and self-possessed.

But for this homage to be truly worthy of their sacrifices and battles, of the gift of themselves they had been forced to make, I needed to break the silence myself, to wrench from my personal memory some harrowing secrets. I needed to shake loose the silences about experiences that should have been told, seeing them as facts of life if not test cases, and at least force my own people to say, "Never again!"

Thousands of memories flooded in. Yes, at all cost, I would have to shed light on all the swallowed and forgotten words. I wanted them to brand the memories, indelibly imprinting these reminiscences on the spirit, so that at the moment of death, that great leap toward greater perfection, the memories will be ready, fresh, at any time in any place.

I wanted to raise my voice and set a new path, as firm and trenchant as that of a Gandhi or a King, and just as nonviolent, before our pierced eardrums would forever erase from our memories the true exaltation of a word at the door of perfection.

Then, in my memory, three images rushed forward—three kinds of images of women:
The image of my namesake, my paternal grandmother, Grand Madja,
The image of my mother, Naja,
And that of my Aunt Roz.

From the depth of and all through my earliest childhood, I have images of women, beloved or rejected, scorned or confronted, but always inseparably planted on the edge of my destiny like road signs, luminous signals that drivers could not ignore without impunity, without dangerously exposing their own lives.

So I resolved to write down what my memory would release, without imposing on it any order or priority, and certainly no exterior rhythm.

MOVEMENT ONE

1

The moment of first words takes us back to early childhood.

Childhood, innocence, luck—the marvelous luck that protects the steps of the beginner and the innocence that becomes a formidable rebuttal to malice.

We speak of an unhappy childhood when someone hasn't been this lucky and, with precocious insight, discovers the pettiness of adults; when someone learns to feel fear and abhorrence for growing up; when the child is caught in the web of condescension. Yes, I, Halla Njokè, was really lucky.

My luck is all the more miraculous because I was born insightful, my eyes like magnifying glasses wide open onto the lies, the thievery, and the violence of adults. But I always told myself that they acted out of fear. Never once did it occur to me that it was out of malice.

Malice is revolting, and, had I discovered that, it would have contaminated me. I would have been filled with hate and, without a doubt, become a killer. I would have murdered my father and every man like him. I would have murdered my stepmother and every woman like her. To this day, more than seventy years later, I still don't understand or tolerate viciousness.

But even though my adult years led me to encounter a great deal of malice, if I never killed anyone, it is because the luck of my childhood stayed with me. I discovered I had been correct right from the start: It really is fear that causes despicable actions, and someone who is afraid actually deserves compassion. And I sensed that I would not be able to express my compassion with greater feeling than through song.

SONG 1

And so I want to talk not only to my clan's women,
But to people of the future, too,
Speak of some men in my life and of you, Father, above all,
Lament rather than blame all the fathers who,
By wanting to deny their failure, through their offspring loathe themselves
And, like perjurers, end up demeaning even their own children,
May even stoop to killing them just to survive, drinking their cup of
shame down to the dregs,
One hell of a dirty little life that has no soul, that has no goal. . . .

But, Father, as I tell your story, it is my passion, too, of which I'd like to
sing
My passion for life, its troubles, its hard lessons, and its joys.
I'd like to unveil my devotion and my gratitude to those who, like you,
Like the stepmother throwing the orphan out into a wanton world,
In the end provided a better initiation than loving mothers might have.

I want to speak to you of genies and great men of action,
Like a legend,
Born straddling two eras and two worlds,
Quartered, with all their driving forces quelled
Fighting like lions in spite of it all.
Allow me then, men of mine, to testify for you,
Express my gratitude to you who have at least bequeathed me passion
for what is beautiful
And the thirst for a great opus.

• • •

How I loved you, Father! How handsome you were in the photo you sent to Aunt Roz! In your austere khaki outfit, with long wide pants and long-sleeved shirt buttoned to the chin, you look like a prince in a fairy tale.

On the back of the picture you have traced marks that only Aunt Roz knows how to read, and she tells us what they say: "Teacher at Maloumè." I gaze and gaze at them, and will always know how to write them, even if I do not know the alphabet.

Not a day goes by that I don't touch the photograph to make sure I haven't forgotten the marks written on the back. Aunt Roz is beginning to complain that I'll ruin the picture, but it makes no difference. I always come back to it.

Then Aunt Roz has Grand Pa Helly make a frame from woven rattan, decorated with openwork like lace, a true masterpiece. Very carefully she glues your photo in the center and hangs it on the wall facing the work table in her house. As she strings beads and creates the necklaces she sells at the market at the end of every month, she often raises her eyes as if to ask for your opinion or advice. I follow her gaze with surprise—it doesn't seem to bother her that she can no longer read the marks. But for me, they were part of the photograph, and now that they've been spirited away I find it a bit flat. I report my disappointment and surprise to Grand Pa Helly, my father's father, and tell him how sorry I am that I didn't copy and save these marks in some other place.

"But how would you have done that?" he asks in amazement. "You don't even know how to write yet."

"Maybe I would if I knew what to write with, and if I had such a tool," I say in my most serious manner, desperate to convince him.

He bursts out laughing, although I don't understand why. Seeing my wounded expression, he goes off and opens the largest of his wicker suitcases, the one that is always locked away and doubly protected by his stool crowned with the word Mbombock. Grand Pa takes out a package, from which he extricates some things that were then still unfamiliar to me. He gives me my first notebook and a soft lead pencil, telling me teasingly that he's waiting for my first letter.

Thinking he is challenging me to copy the marks, I promise myself that one day when my aunt isn't home I'll take the picture out of its frame, although I know in advance it will certainly get me a good spanking.

Luckily, Father, you sent another picture, of you in a police uniform as white as that of the "guardians of the peace," as the men who passed through to take the census were called. On the back of the photo, according to Aunt Roz, it did actually say: "Guardian of the Peace in Victoria." I decide to copy all of it in my notebook before my aunt glues the photo into another frame. Every day, I use her absence to begin my copying on a new page, trying to make the marks as small and neat as they are on the back of the picture. Sadly enough, the harder I try, the fatter they get. I don't dare show them to Grand Pa Helly; I'm too scared he'll make fun of me! Half the notebook is already filled with my scribbles. Still, I'm quite sure they really are the marks on the back of the photo, but I honestly don't understand why I can't get them to be smaller.

As I apply myself, I'm intrigued by the fact that some of them return again and again or appear in double sets, as if to repeat or insist on something. I'm dying to unglue the other photo to see if it is the same. Only my fear of a spanking holds me back; how long will I be able to resist?

Then a new photograph arrives.

On this one you are wearing an apron and a tall white hat above an equally white uniform. Aunt Roz says: "Maître d'Hôtel of the Regional Commander of Eséka." This time I count fourteen differences among the thirty-eight little marks, and I tell myself that perhaps ranks are measured by the number of different marks. As you are moving up in rank, they increase the marks. I try to add up all the ones my father has already had since he was at Maloumè, not forgetting there are doubles, too, and I come to the conclusion that he's a very great gentleman. The proof is that his costumes are growing ever more complex.

As a result of devoting myself to recopying every mark on both pictures, I manage to transcribe them from memory, even in the sand. One Sunday at church, as I follow Aunt Roz's finger in the hymnal, I am astonished to recognize some of the marks that I already know how to write. Unfortunately, I still can't read them. But I'm very excited to know that the same marks are used for saying everything and writing everything, even songs. I entertain myself by writing them in every direction and mixing them up in different ways: *Insàloum, ienixria* . . . beginnings, endings, middles. I show my notebook full of scribbles to Grand Pa Helly and Aunt Roz, beside myself with excitement. She laughs so hard she is holding her sides. "Your imagination is going to kill you yet," she tells me. "Just be patient, two more years and perhaps they'll let you start school." After skimming my notebook from the first page to the last, Grand Pa Helly hugs me very tightly: "You are a character, my dear little wife," he exclaims. His golden eyes sparkle with affection. I clutch his neck.

Since there is no new photograph coming to let me practice more marks, the lovely lace of the rattan frame directs my attention toward wickerwork. I ask Grand Pa Helly to help me frame your last two pictures, Father.

SONG 2

Your beauty,
The beauty of your body and of the spirit that dwelled inside
Was manifest in everything you said and did.

For me, Grand Pa Helly, it was what lay at the foundation of every-
*   one's respect for you,*
And lay, above all else, at the foundation of my own.
You'd hold high your slender body with its infinite extremities,
Muscular and firm despite your more-than-ninety years;
Your torso, almost always bare, displayed tall blue palm trees
Proudly tattooed in front and back and on your arms as well,
A grayish blue backlit by your light brick-red complexion,
As the blue-green of your veins rushed restlessly along the full length of
*   your arms.*

Your beauty,
The beauty of your soul and the experience gathered,
Though to be sure not one tooth had resisted time;
Your high cheekbones hollowed by the veritable trenches of your cheeks,
While your pure golden eyes threw lightning flashes of every rainbow
  color,
Depending on the facets and the intensity of your emotions,
Depending on environment and its vibrations,
And they'd light up those trenches like cozy little nests;
Your ears flamed red when you were angry,
Grand Pa Helly, you, my rainbow man . . .
And the beauty of your art made you the very center
Of creation in Massébè, and of what was raged for me, too,
The closest-to-perfection man.

● ● ●

Grand Pa Helly is a planter, as are all the other men in Massébè. Every head of household here has to be a planter. More than anything else, it is the size of his plantation that decides his importance. A head of household is anyone who has a sizeable number of descendants—grown children, grandchildren, and great-grandchildren, all of whom live together and work the same piece of land. The men do the planting and take care of the cocoa, coffee, or palm oil groves, while the women and children cultivate the food crops that feed the family. Living together, they form what is known as a compact family, which does not strain kinship. The combined fields of every man and woman of a single compact family form the "plantation" that makes the head of the household into either a great or a small planter.

Massébè, at that time, is a minuscule village consisting of about thirty compact families. The largest of these comprises a hundred people, sometimes more. Our own family has no more than thirty-five members, yet Grand Pa Helly is considered the most important head of household, and he would be the chief of Massébè had he not categorically refused. All he feels is disdain for the role of chief, which the colonists imposed on a profoundly democratic people whom they contemptuously saw as lawless. The present chief has become a lackey in the service of a government the colonists put in place. His only task is collecting taxes and identifying and informing on any independent spirit among his own people. Grand Pa says that if that role were his he would not be able to eat or sleep, or look at himself in the mirror.

Even though he is not the chief of Massébè, he is by far the most respected of all family leaders. First of all, he is the oldest and the best informed in his social world: He followed the ultimate initiation known as the Curved Cane. He is also the best informed on the culture of the colonists because he studied at the Roman Catholic boys' school in Bibia and was supposed to be ordained as a pastor when he resigned, figuring he already was a pastor in his own tradition and seeing no real reason to hold a double office. What's more, his plantation is the largest of all those in Massébè. My father sometimes arrives with hordes of servants that he brings back from deals he has made with other tribes, no one knows how. For about one to three months these people work with him at a hellish pace to push back the virgin forest and enlarge our plantation. Then they leave again without worrying about the upkeep, to the great exasperation of the whole family, now doomed to doubling its efforts.

There is another reason why everyone respects Grand Pa Helly: The village square belongs to him. It was he who gave all the grounds needed to build the public places: chapel, school, and market. And it was our family that conceived of, proposed, and realized their construction, and that also graciously provided the community with its catechist and schoolteacher.

Every family in Massébè lives on its own land, at a distance of one to five kilometers from each other, depending on the property's size. However, lured by the location, each also asked for and was granted a dwelling on the square, which had become the center of the village. They baptized the square Bondè, which means "to begin," in recognition of Grand Pa Helly's initiative.

Bondè Square looks like a rectangular garden, evenly divided into multicolored, flowering patches that are the dwellings with their Bantu-style four-sided roofs, whitewashed with kaolin, and made of brick-red clay or the black clay of the swamp. Here and there, encircled by small enclosures of shrubs blooming like a *demure pagne*, a colorful skirt, they charmingly line the main road that links Massébè to the other villages. During the week the square is populated only with nursery-school children and members of those families who are responsible for looking after them and feeding them. But on Saturdays and Sundays, on holidays or market days, you would think you were in a swarming anthill—even the oldest woman of the nearby village of Pan will abandon her fields to come and have a good time in Bondè Square.

Our family is the only one that does not own a dwelling on Bondè Square. My father gets all worked up about that, for Grand Pa decided that this is the way it will be as long as he's alive. He dreads that the human congestion would make my father's escapades too easy. And every man in Massébè is grateful to Grand Pa Helly for his good sense, generosity, and tact, since most of them have already been cuckolded by my father.

Still, if Grand Pa Helly is the most respected of the heads of household in Massébè, it is above all because of his talents as a cabinet and basket maker. He makes remarkable furniture that everyone wants for his home, all the more so because it is displayed in the marvelous mail-order catalogue *La Redoute à Roubaix*. Depending on his needs, he barters some of the pieces for merchandise to be selected from the same catalogue. Often the regional commander sends prisoners, well-guarded by armed men, to transport Grand Pa Helly's furniture to the station. It is first shipped to the harbor of Wouri and then sent to France by boat. The pieces can be seen in the following year's catalogue: armchairs, stools, chaise lounges, and beds made of wood, rattan, or a combination of the two.

Our bit of forest contains a few hectares of semi-marshland where Chinese bamboo grows, as well as rattan creepers, raffia palm trees, and a red wood that is perfect for making sculptures, furniture, and utensils such as spoons, plates, mortars, and pestles. When my father is there, he always makes sure to cut as many creepers and as much bamboo as he possibly can, so that the stock doesn't diminish, and Grand Pa Helly won't be forced to get the supplies himself and thereby interrupt his creative work.

To show his gratitude, Grand Pa chooses from the *La Redoute* catalogue—in addition to the tools he needs, such as planes, saws, knives, and chisels—some objects that my father covets: an organ, an accordion, a guitar, or a Telefunken radio.

Grand Pa Helly also barters in Massébè and neighboring villages—his furniture and utensils in exchange for cattle, poultry, fancy *pagne* fabric, and so on. As a result, he has a large pig pen on the edge of the swamp, and there are always at least a hundred sheep grazing in the fields. Sometimes our hen house cannot even hold all the fowl, and the surplus of chickens, guinea hens, and ducks sleeps in the cocoa and coffee trees. Clearly, Grand Pa Helly is thought of as a very wealthy man. Yet he never has money. For reasons unknown to me, he always refuses to keep any or even to touch it. All the money he makes from the sale of what he produces serves to feed and look after the family.

It is Aunt Roz's responsibility to divide the money among the different households, and she always goes about it in the same way. First she gives what comes to Grand Pa Helly as head of the family to Grand Madja, who manages it. Then the share allocated to my parents, my brother, my younger sister, and me, is given to my mother if she is there. If she is not there, Aunt Roz holds on to what is ours and gives only a fifth of it to my father despite his protests, which she always ignores, for everyone knows that my father always has holes in his pockets. No matter how large the sums of money he earns, he can never keep from squandering them in a single day. Then Aunt Roz gives a share to the households of each of my father's other three women. Although he had never married them, they had arrived with the twenty or so children—all girls—they had by him in the course of his travels. The final share goes to Aunt Roz and her husband, Ratez.

Grand Pa is also respected because he is the only one here who is unimpressed by money. The only thing that impresses him in other people is any know-how that he does not possess himself. For instance, when he sees furniture in the *La Redoute* catalogue made by others that he considers more beautiful than his own, he swoons with admiration and won't rest until he has created something at least as stunning.

Obviously, Father, during the times of your absence I couldn't have been better placed to learn how to weave rattan as finely as lace and to create handsome frames. It seems that a long time has gone by since you sent the last photograph, and I'm beginning to fear I'm losing interest in my weaving, too. What's happening to you and when will you be back?

● ● ●

And then one day, Father, like an apparition, a miracle, you arrive, and in your white shirt and midnight blue pants you are so much more handsome in real life than in the pictures. You are the only Black man among all those White men, who are with you for reasons I'll never really know. They are all wearing various kinds of gray or greenish khaki that accentuates the washed-out look of their skin—as if lately they had been ill fed.

And you, the Black man, you are luminous, dazzling, striking. You get busy with a pot of boiling water that Grand Madja brings out, and drop large needles and some strange-looking tubes into it. You break small glass bottles filled with water and suck it all up into another glass tube, to which you then attach a thick needle. You go into a bedroom with grandfather, followed by a great-uncle, another one, and yet another. They all come back out holding one buttock, trying to hide their grimace. What can you possibly have done with your uncles' buttocks? How can an old man be made to show his behind to his nephew in secret? And who do you think you are, father, to dare force yourself upon your fathers with needles and hurt their buttocks? And what is the role in all this of the White men? (Years later I was to learn that at the time of the great epidemics, your White people had provided you with medications for distribution in several villages, and that you arrived to allocate these as a preventive measure. But at the time, none of this made any sense to me at all.)

No one ever thinks of explaining things to children, who just see people coming and going, and events unfold. Like ants, they are threatened and sometimes crushed by the indifference of the violent and inexplicable actions of giants, and no one ever explains a thing. But since children are more garrulous than ants, they have a tendency to ask embarrassing questions. Then they are sent packing with a "Oh, do be quiet! Don't you see your father is talking?"

And I pretend to be silent. Inside my deepest self, though, at that moment I am more talkative than ever. I do believe I actually asked every one of life's questions in that single day: questions on beauty and ugliness. Yes, indeed, there were human beings who were beautiful and terrifying, with eyes as green as the forest and as blue as the sky. There were nasty ones with fingers and noses as crooked as fish hooks. I had questions about skin and its colors, white like fresh peanuts with reddish capillaries, or red like copper as in the ceremonial bracelets of Aunt Roz and Great-Aunt Kèl Lam. Skins as black as polished ebony like those of my mother, Naja, or Grand Madja Halla, or else the brick red of russet gazelles like those of my father and all his daughters, who came from one and the same mold. Then I also had questions about the course of life and the deportment of men. Where were they going, some gangly like wading birds, some scampering like goats, or heavily dragging their feet like the giants in legends, their thoughts concealed from the outside world? Who was the true creator of all this, what were his goals and afterthoughts—why, how? Many answers entered my mind as well, some of which have stayed with me until the present time. That day I understood that, in the end, happiness comes from the ability each of us has to come up with convincing responses to our own questions.

After chattering like rain that rushes down the rocks during a tornado, the White men were all slumped beneath the large mandarin tree in the courtyard, drinking foamy beverages they had taken from their bags. Aunt Roz, who'd been busy in the kitchen, had served them golden chicken and fried plantains. While they enjoyed their meal they started talking faster. I figured that with such fine food and their big appetite they would soon regain some color and not want to go back home at all. My father would certainly be happy to keep his friends around a little longer.

Throughout the day all the men of the village came parading by. You, Father, scribbled on a piece of paper signs like the ones on the backs of the photographs, but they kept me too far away so that I couldn't tell whether there were any I already knew. Finally you came and joined the White men, drank the same thing as they did, and spoke with them as if they were part of your family. They took out a Telefunken radio like the one Grand Pa had, only smaller. While you were listening, you all kept on talking more than the radio did. Grand Madja asked you what you were so worked up about. You said that the Arabs were refusing to hand Palestine over to the Jews and that horrible things were happening in Israel.

I was barely able to stifle a cry of surprise, because Grand Madja opened her mouth wider than mine and exclaimed: "This box tells you things that are going on in Palestine, in Israel, in heaven where God and his angels dwell?" You laughed, laughed so hard that my mouth closed in shame over the whole mountain of questions I was about to ask, which in your eyes might seem even more stupid. And then all of you left again, with bags on your back the same way we carry our little rattan baskets, only yours were made of fabric.

In the evening, sick and tired of my questions, Aunt Roz told me that my father had been responsible for preventing an epidemic. She might as well have said nothing: Not one of her words made any sense to me yet. What I did understand was that you, Father, would be gone for a long time. Strangely enough, I didn't feel sad, just impatient for you to return, convinced that it would bring new and exciting experiences. Oh yes, I loved you so much.

2

I became unhappy about not being a man. A man is free. He shows
up, makes decisions, gives orders, and women and children obey.
The women stay, and the men leave. And like you, Father, I wanted
to leave, to leave with you.

Our oldest brother went away with Grand Pa Helly to be treated by the Pygmies. When they brought him back they said he was
better, although we didn't know what had ailed him. It occurred to
me that it might have been a trick to teach the boys all sorts of different things and let the girls stupidly slave away in the kitchen
without even allowing them to eat what they felt like eating. Men
could eat snakes, turtles, crocodiles, even cats, while the women had
to make do with leaves and manioc tubers. It's no surprise, then,
that they're not smart enough to deserve going elsewhere.

It did, indeed, seem to me that my brother had become smarter
than my sisters and myself—since he was back from the Pygmies he
knew an awful lot! First of all, he now had a room all to himself in
our aunt's house. He had widened a hole in the wall between his
bedroom and that of Aunt Roz and her husband Ratez. He invited
us in, my little sister and me, supposedly to tell us about his Pygmy
adventures. But in reality he wanted us to help him with his newest
activity. Trembling, he would look through the hole, then put his
ear right on it and with his mouth reproduce the noises we could

hear—it was a kind of swallowing sound made by a mouth holding too much saliva. Then he asked us to play flood barrier—pulling up our dresses and standing with our legs apart, rolling our behinds around—while he reproduced the same sound.

I would have never dreamed up such a game by myself. It's certainly very clever, but I don't care for it. No matter how much I rack my brains, I can't associate that horrible sound with anything I know. It must be something my brother saw at the Pygmies, something that only boys can see, since he refuses to let us have even a glance. True, I'm not a boy, but I swear I'll take a look through that hole some day when my brother is not there to make us foolishly roll our behinds around with our *pagnes* bunched up while he makes mysterious sounds with his mouth.

Unfortunately, he is always there when the noise begins. "When will I become a boy?" I ask Grand Pa Helly. He just laughs.

Time passes, and now we accompany Grand Madja as often as possible to make real flood barriers. Once there, we obstruct the brook's flow with a main dam made with the trunks of dead trees, branches, and mud we've dug up from the banks with hoes. We actually do bunch up our *pagnes* and dresses. We open our legs, arch our back, and begin to let the water pass between our legs over the little secondary dams, while we roll our hips to the beat of songs and drums. "*A koum a koum, a koum ndam ndam koum, koum hitok hi koum, ndam ndam!*" Tirelessly, we sing without stopping until all the water is gone and we catch the fish, crabs, and crayfish hiding underneath the mud and roots.

No men are ever present at this fishing trip or at our dance, a dance that is strictly reserved for women. It's all about who rolls her hips the prettiest, who can keep the beat the longest and best while tossing out the water. It is so beautiful! I love fishing and dancing this way, and I'm surprised that my brother, who is a man, would even know about it. How did he manage that? Could he possibly be spying on the women the way he spies on Aunt Roz and her husband Ratez? I wouldn't like that at all. I have to conclude that men, before they become men, obviously learn women's things first. Soon I will, too, without any doubt.

One day my brother asks us a favor: He'd like us to hold him tightly between our legs. Why? He tells us that if we go along with him he'll let us look through the hole. But then he warns us that it's dangerous; we might become men. My sister has no desire to become a man, but I certainly do! I agree to lie under him and squeeze him any way he wants as long as he lets me look first. After some lengthy negotiations he consents. We wait for the appropriate day. When he notices the sound of the floodwater and calls us to his room immediately, my sister and I rush to the hole. Aunt Roz is thumping against her husband, who is burying himself between her legs. She lets out screams that he stifles by sticking his tongue in her mouth. My word, he makes her swallow his saliva! I feel like retching. Ratez rises and turns her over, white foam covering the hair on his lower belly. There's not enough time for me to turn around before a spurt of vomit escapes from my throat, and my brother drops the clump of earth that he's rigged up to close the hole. Uncle Ratez catches sight of us and screams with fury.

They gave all three of us a terrible spanking, sprinkled chili pepper between our legs, and made us lie down on a mat in the sun. My brother growls: "You saw, didn't you? It's all your fault, you little witch! Couldn't you have been quiet at least, like your little sister? No, of course not, you always have to stand out with your outrageous reactions, and always at the wrong moment. Now we won't be able to watch anymore."

"So much the better! What's wrong with you, how can you stand looking at such ugliness," I say to him, sincerely shaken and profoundly disgusted.

He looks at me with as much surprise as anger. He's really very upset with me, and I don't know why. If his jet black eyes were swords they'd slice me in two.

"You idiot! What's your problem? Honestly, I wonder if you're really a girl and will ever become a woman. If so, you'll never have any flood lands between your legs for others to go fishing in! Stay away from me and leave me alone."

I feel his attack on me as an unfair rejection and something inside me closes up.

"If that's what it means to be a woman, then I'm very glad not to be one. I don't want any foaming floodwaters between my legs or any of your saliva in my mouth. I'll never have you on me, and you'd better not talk to me anymore either, you nasty boy."

We stay cold with each other until an uncle comes to pick him up. Still, when we see him disappear around the curve in the road, my little sister and I weep bitter tears. He was sure to learn things, whatever they might be, to surpass us once again with further knowledge. But I console myself by saying that there are some things I'd rather not know. Never again would our relationship be close enough to talk about our private lives, in spite of my spontaneous outbursts and the efforts I'd make, although Aunt Roz claimed that men are quick to forget what they don't like, while most women never forget what has hurt them.

Actually, if it were only my brother and my aunt's husband Ratez, I would have lost any desire to become a man. But there was my father—far away and yet so close, so strong and brilliant—who always knew how to impress not only women but everyone else, too, except Grand Pa! Even Grand Madja and Aunt Roz couldn't stop getting together on Sundays to talk about him as if it were a second worship service. They would admire his photos, complain about his escapades and whims, but always regret his absence and pray to God to protect "their man" and bring him home soon. The other three mamas would come and join the conversation. Their chattering was interspersed with what was to me very irritating, wild laughter, as they rambled on about his great exploits. In a peculiar blend of pride and resentment that only brought the man more honor, they would tell and retell the tales of his seductive arts and his epic fights with their parents or former husbands.

But the person who most inspired my wish to be a man was Grand Pa Helly himself.

Although he was quite old, his tall, slender, and muscular body was always half naked, while the women were forced to be wrapped in layer upon layer of cumbersome *pagnes*. He exuded freedom, nobility, and wisdom. People came from far away to consult him, and his words were scrupulously heeded.

I am Grand Madja's namesake and, as custom has it, I'm also her double, so that Grand Pa Helly is "my husband." He converses with me in the same way he does with my grandmother. He tells me things I think I understand. He takes me with him into the bush to reset traps, collect game, cut willowy rattan, and look for medicinal plants. When we come home he tells me he's hungry, reminds me that I'm his wife and should prepare his meal. I rush over to my little cooking pots, crush some sand, kaolin, herbs, use oil to make a mixture, and pick fruit. Lovingly I serve him, and he has a feast. Was he a magician or did he actually eat my dishes? It remains a complete mystery.

In any case, with him you don't talk about other people as you do with women. He and I talk about ourselves, the earth, and the sky. He knows the constellations and shows them to me, and every night he asks me to find and name them: Ngwén Hônd, or Ax Handle; Bon ba nyû, or the Orphans; Hiôrôt hi honk, or Southern Star; Hiôrôt hi gno mbock, or Northern Star; Makas ma anè, the Pillars of Power; and many more.

To him I reveal my desire to become a man like he is.

"For what purpose? You'll never need that. You are a complete being, better than a man, better than a woman, and you should thank the Creator."

"Does that mean you don't want to be my husband anymore?"

"No, it means there'll be moments when I'm your wife, and you're my husband."

I don't quite see how, but for now I'm the happiest woman on earth because I'm his wife.

• • •

It is the women of my clan who manufacture macho men. They always want their man to be the tallest, the most feared, the most handsome, the most respected, "the most, most, and most"!

My husband covers distances in a day that it takes others five days to cross. When he comes back he's carrying merchandise that five men would have trouble lifting: six tubs of shea oil, four bags of *mpum* peanuts, four bags of sweet massô yams, fowl, pigs, and sheep. All of it is suspended from two long poles he balances on his shoulders. . . .

When Grand Pa Helly returns from his maternal uncles, everyone comes running. When he speaks, everyone listens. They whisper that he doesn't walk on his feet, but that his spirit carries him on its wings. I ask him to confirm what they say. As is his wont, he bursts into crystalline laughter, looks at me tenderly, and says: "That's a good one. Actually, it's less tiring for old bones to take advantage of the wings of the spirit and, besides, it obviously is faster to fly than to trot around on aged legs, don't you think?"

"Yes, I do. But, tell me, then, can women fly as well, is that allowed?"

"Whatever the case may be, you, my little wife, are allowed to take any flight you can muster by yourself."

With a husband such as this, you don't feel a great need to be a man anymore. I'm beginning to appreciate being a woman; the only problem is food restrictions and all the other taboos imposed on women. I, for one, don't like manioc leaves. I confess this to my husband.

He then simply and secretly puts my share of snake, cat, or turtle aside for me. He keeps me company while I'm enjoying my treat so that no one will suspect or mistreat me. Not a soul would ever dare think that he might violate any taboo for my sake alone. There's absolutely no reason anymore to want to be a man; I am a woman, I know and do man's things, I am fine.

Still, inside me there's the awful memory of the battle between the legs, floodwaters and foam, the saliva of others; but a strong sense of modesty overcomes me every time I think of it and I can't talk to my husband about this. So I decide to watch and see how he acts with my namesake.

I discover that they're always underneath white sheets, gently swaying face to face, as if welded together. They caress each other's neck, they murmur sweet things, they call each other's name, and they breathe together in the same rhythm, first fast, then gently, very gently. Afterward they talk for a long time, about the past, about today and tomorrow and beyond. I always fall asleep before they do, even though I really want to listen to the end. In any event, I can't hear very much because they speak so quietly, sometimes muttering, sometimes whispering. When they talk they seem eternal.

I'm grateful they don't fight. My husband doesn't make my grandmother cry, he makes her murmur. And in the morning everything is tidy: not a trace of foam anywhere. I really am very lucky: My husband is a "most, most, and most." "When I'm big enough to have another husband, one of my very own, he has to be another 'most and most,' and my sons, too," I say to myself.

Sadly, now that I'm willing to grow up, I'll probably die without any man close to me. Very few men accept having great women beside them. Those who are daring or crazy enough to want it often pay for it very dearly: They become the laughing stock of others and end up living outside the mainstream. I console myself by remembering that between Aunt Roz and her husband Ratez and their noise in the dammed-up floodwater, and Grand Madja with her husband Helly in their sweet whisperings, there is no middle road that I find acceptable. Merely a recollection of refusal or total abandon, no more, no less. I also console myself with the thought that this way there won't be any man to see me completely decrepit when I'm about to die. You can only die nobly when you are alone, and do so quickly, in a blinding moment that leaves no time for self-pity.

3

SONG 3

Naja, my mother, thank you for my life;
And Grandmother, thank you for my education above all,
For without education a person is nothing, a void.
Humans are not born divine or even human;
They grow into it, achieving it by choosing to transform,
Achieving it primarily because of education.
What is the mystery, then? Enormous work;
The very mystery of the divine is work.

Naja, my mother,
The guitar player isn't born playing;
The blacksmith isn't born blowing;
The physician isn't born healing.
Humans become what they learn,
What they practice with passion again and again.

No, Njokè, my father,
The murderer isn't born killing,
Nor is the soldier born shooting other human beings;
The politician isn't born telling lies,
Nor is the trader born cheating;

The wise man isn't born holy.
Humans are transformed by thought and word,
By actions and realizations,
By time, but by education above all.
What is the mystery, then? Enormous work;
The very mystery of the divine is work.

●   ●   ●

Unfortunately, for most of us work is contradictory to pleasure. I thank God that he granted me the good fortune to weave the two together. A slave cannot make that connection. My namesake, Grand Madja Halla, always told me, "You, you'll always know whether you are free or not as long as you're able to link work and pleasure."

Then she revealed to me that she was a caramel woman, and afraid of the sun. And so, at the crack of dawn she'd gather embers, put machetes and hoes in the baskets we carried on our heads, and off we'd go to the field. She'd light a fire because it was still quite cold at that hour. We worked in silence with twice the usual zeal just to stay warm and to keep the insects from stinging us. Sometimes Grand Madja struck up a song and created a rhythm, which my little sister and I would then join—a kind of regular, irresistible motor. In this way, we always accomplished a huge amount of work that earned us our husband's praise.

We stopped as soon as the sun became too hot. We'd harvest tubers in the last field, pick leaves, fruits, and vegetables, and then go home. Our husband wasn't like the one in the folktales who forced his caramel wife to work in the sun just to prove that she wasn't lazy, as the malicious neighbors claimed when they sneered at her. Instead of protecting her, that husband had forced his wife to prove them wrong, something so unnatural to her that she melted completely, and her husband lost the love, sweetness, and wealth she had brought him while working in the shade.

Grand Madja, Caramel Woman, you told us:

"Sheltered from the burning sun, you can take your time,
And if you take the time to do each thing well,
Each thing well-done will provide you with its own pleasure:

"In the shade of the cocoa trees, take your time to crack the pods neatly:
You'll be rewarded and able to remove the beans without the frustration
of sand and dirt on poorly maintained machetes.

"Take your time to choose carefully the most beautiful and juiciest pods by
separating them from the second-rate ones, and you will be doubly
rewarded. First, the cocoa wine you can extract from them will be of high
quality, as will the chocolate for which your pods are used when it's time
to sell them in the market.

"In the shade of the palm trees, take your time to slice the palm leaves
evenly, and you'll have the esthetic pleasure of making prettier piles.
When it's time to pick the mushrooms growing there, you'll have the pleasure of work well done: All you need to do is reach out and run your hand
through the piles as if you're sauntering in a dream. Then, when the
mounds are completely dry, burn them carefully and again you'll be
rewarded with extraordinary compost that you'll use to plant onions or
potatoes, which will grow like a miracle.

"Take your time when you're gathering the palm tree fruit; select the best,
and the best palm oil will be yours. Keep the lesser ones dry and pound
them gently to obtain half-dry cabbage palms, the only ones that produce
lan, the magic oil that protects babies' skin and the soft spot in their skulls
from a thousand different ailments. Once you've extracted the oil, be careful to stack the bikagang, those round husks now emptied of their oil;
other mushrooms will be your reward, that no waste scattered to the
winds will ever produce.

"I cannot list the endless pleasures that extra effort toward perfection will
bring you, my 'little doubles.' But you have to take your time. And, alas, when
you are caramel as I am, it is difficult to take your time in the burning sun."

Of course, our everyday experience taught us all the advantages of working this way, of transforming one activity into thousands of creative possibilities, joys, and infinite delights. But I wondered about the real story behind the caramel.

For twenty years or so, I tried to live by another one of her sacred theories: "I have no law; I make adaptability my primary law." And so I turned myself into water, condensing with the cold, melting and evaporating with the heat, like dripping rain in bad weather, leaping in free, tumultuous waterfalls from dizzying heights into unfathomable chasms. It was good, of course—everything had its place to which it always returned, and there is no better situation for any spirit than one with so much flexibility. Still, there are those thousand deaths you die without ever knowing the end. You die as an ice cube to be born a few moments later as vapor, and hardly have you become vapor when you die again to be reborn as dew or drizzle, only to start the process all over again.

Start over or continue?

That is precisely the problem: It lies in the perception of time and in the continuity of that perception, always ephemeral, a restlessness going every which way.

That is when I thought I discovered the story of the caramel woman, who must preserve her form at any price so that her action can move toward a real continuity, and endure beyond the time it takes vapor to turn into drizzle.

Yes, a woman who chooses to lead her life inside the home, for instance, needs a certain amount of time to build, give life to her children, and raise them to be men and women.

If she doesn't safeguard her life or her form she will melt; yes, life will go on in other forms, but she, in her form as a woman, will not have the time to bring her endeavor to fruition.

When caramel melts it will, of course, continue to be caramel, but it may run and mix with the sand; ants, flies, and bees may eat it. It may even be forgotten right there in the sun where, with luck, it will stay intact until the night's cool air restores its solidity. But it won't find the whole of its former shape again. Of course, life goes on, all is well, but the woman cannot raise her children, and they are orphans.

"You who care so much about seeing your choices through to the end, about going to the finish line of what you want to realize here and now, you who are bounded in time, be very careful of your present form, which is so precious to your action, for you are a caramel woman."

At almost eighty, I pronounce myself caramel: I need a little time; I refuse to expose myself to the burning sun; I am still needed, if only to sing the remembrance of you, my father.

4

SONG 4

It was twenty years ago,
And maybe more, but it seems like yesterday,
That you departed, Father, falling by the wayside, alone, disowned,
*   exhausted,*
And I, who was not present at your funeral,
Must see to it that, liberated and forgiven, you shall sleep in peace.
For if not I, who would think of offering you compassion, to
You who aroused so many troubled passions:
Jealousy, desire, hate, and admiration.
Can we bestow compassion on those we deem to be superior?
Can we feel compassion for the suffering of a Lôs?
And besides, does anyone suffer who is "ultra-powerful"? Does he have a
*   heart, a skin like all the rest? Is it really blood that's running*
*   through his veins?*

● ● ●

In those days we would hear people talk of two Lôs, two ultra-powerful beings. Nothing like this had ever been seen before in a single sector. It seemed that in earlier times they might anticipate one per century, certainly no more. In addition, the coming of a Lôs was not necessarily a good thing. Everything depended on the actions of the tribe—the arrival of a Lôs could be either a blessing or a disaster.

And here it happened that of the three ultra-powerful men the country knew in a single generation, two were located in the sector of Nyong and Kellé, and both were persistently referred to as legendarily bloodthirsty: Bitchokè and Dimalè! As soon as you committed a slightly unusual act, Father, you were told that you were taking yourself for Dimalè or Bitchokè. You found this intolerable and unacceptable, for you merely wanted to be your own unique benchmark, to be compared only to yourself, Njokè. What had the others done that they should be talked about constantly? Were they, too, not born of a woman? Or did their mothers feed them something of which yours had deprived you? You decided to go and find them, to pierce their secret. Soon you would be the third ultra-powerful one, the greatest Lôs in the district. And if that was too much, so be it! It would be what the Bassa people deserved.

One evening you came back in the company of a little bit of a man with a very dark skin and a tiny, smiling face, but with fearsome eyes—small slits from which darted looks as quick and lively as the motions of a serpent's tongue. You introduced him to Grand Pa Helly in the presence of the entire household.

"Father, this is my friend Pier Dimalè. . . ."

The name dropped like a knife in spite of the word friend—or more likely because of it—and was followed by a long and pregnant silence that seemed to last forever. Was this the ultra-powerful one of whom the whole country spoke? The one who lay down his law and personal will upon entire populations, even though he was not a wise man or chief, not strong or handsome, and had not been mandated by any moral or spiritual authority? Was this really he? Where could he possibly have acquired the power that inflicted his will upon the land?

He smiled. He stood up and warmly extended his hand to a few people, but when he reached Grand Pa Helly, he couldn't extend his hand—oh, mystery! Grand Pa scrutinized him coldly from head to toe, and then cried out to you, Father: "This is so reckless, my son. Is it mere foolishness, or could it be a bad omen? You arrive in a region somewhere and find a man whose own parents named him 'Catastrophe,' you bring him with you, and claim to have turned him into a friend? Can you be friends with catastrophe? Is that not a mystery?"

"Power begins with mystery, Father," you answered before rising and turning your back on us.

When you were about to leave, Grand Pa Helly shouted at you once more.

"Catastrophe is bad luck, and your power won't turn it into anything else."

I'm desperately trying to remember what happened next, but it's impossible. It is as if time froze every movement.

Your friend and you turned to Grand Pa; you were tense and open-mouthed, but not a sound came out.

We—Grand Madja, Aunt Roz and her husband Ratez, my mother, my sisters, and I—were riveted to our stools, sitting as if our necks were nailed to our shoulder blades, looking at you, the Lôs whose nature it is to defy laws and destiny—for that is the way they are.

How many days or weeks went by? Or did time actually stand still? I hear a long scream and rush over. Aunt Roz and my mother are bustling about around Grand Madja, who has collapsed. She is weeping quietly, small monotonous moans that grate upon your heart like the sound of a saw. . . .

Where shall I now place my heart,
My heart; what shall I do with my heart?
What have you done now, my son? You've forgotten my heart.
The earth has already swallowed eight of my sons, has broken my heart;
The earth has left me with only one son, and he has no heart.
How foolish to have affixed my own heart to his.
It is finished, it has happened, and here is my heart,
Burning me, piercing me, crumpling up inside my belly;
What shall I do with a heart that has run aground in my belly?

Huge commotion! A man comes out of the guestroom. Grand Pa Helly comes out of his bedroom dressed for one of his great journeys, his ceremonial machete in its sheath tied to his hip, his crossbow and arrows on his back, a rattan bag and his Mbock cane in hand.

When he sees Grand Madja weeping, Grand Pa Helly stops for a moment and closes his eyes. He takes a very deep breath and then says in his nighttime voice: "If nothing else I'll bring you his body, but I swear that I'll bring him back to you."

And he goes off without another word.

I don't recall his ever before being absent for such a long time. Grand Pa Helly was a husband who was present, not some draft of air perpetually gallivanting around like my mother Naja's husband or Aunt Roz's husband Ratez. They always had to run after those two, inquire after their whereabouts, use a weathervane to investigate where the wind had blown them. You also had to protect yourself against these drafts of air when they came home, or they could cause mumps or a stiff neck. Those two husbands were truly rough!

Even when absent, our husband was always there. We'd wait for him serenely, and he always came back, equally warm and considerate.

This time, the wait was not as serene as usual. At night, my namesake, I saw you getting up with a start, taut as a bow, and you waited, holding your breath. You stayed awake until daybreak. Sometimes you prayed out loud—you who always told me that God is like the elephant who hears silences and whispers more clearly than words uttered out loud. You really were much too anxious, and I still don't know why because you didn't tell me anything.

Soon I understood that my father had committed yet another one of his transgressions. All along, on any given day, someone might arrive to tell a tale, which meant agony for you and my mother, anger for Grand Pa Helly and Aunt Roz, and incomprehension for my sisters and me. Nobody explained anything to us, but through sentences we snatched and laments we heard, we learned that he'd taken another man's wife, fought with some chief, or abducted someone's daughter. Sometimes he himself returned with the booty of his raids. Aunt Roz and Grand Pa Helly would bawl him out relentlessly, while my mother fought with her new rivals, ripping their clothes to shreds, throwing the contents of their suitcases in the latrine, and always coming up with new insults and new tricks until she won him over. You, my namesake, you bewailed your heart.

But this time around, I knew it really must be very serious.

Aunt Roz and her husband Ratez left after Grand Pa Helly. My mother collected her things and departed, saying she wouldn't come back anymore. But it wasn't the first time she had done this.

She'd always come back, ranting and raving ever more loudly, as she did when my father had gone to kidnap my youngest sister from her. She arrived with a delegation of uncles and cousins armed with machetes and arrows. It took three days of negotiating, three slaughtered sheep, a large pig, and several chickens loaded inside *mintets*, woven palm leaves used to wrap provisions. Then the armed men turned around and, after accompanying them to the end of the road, my mother came back on her husband's arm, both of them laughing uproariously. They immediately went into their hut, forgetting that we were all waiting for them before we would start eating.

Yes, she often came back on his arm, laughing wildly, her belly rounded with a next sister that my father always managed to deposit surreptitiously in her womb when, tired of his newest conquest, he would go off to get her back again. So for her it wasn't serious; my father would undoubtedly take her back as soon as he returned from his latest adventure.

What was worrisome, however, was the long absence of our husband, magnified by that of Aunt Roz. Even more worrisome was the return of her husband Ratez, who came back for three large rams. Then I learned that the Pygmies had demanded them as a sacrifice to snatch my father from the hands of death. More on edge than usual, you, Grand Madja, waited like an impatient fiancée.

5

Tonight my youngest sister and I linger very unobtrusively in the back of Great-Aunt Kèl Lam's courtyard, where she repeats her newest epic, singing the praises of our ultra-powerful father who, they say, is coming back soon. My namesake gave Great-Aunt Kèl Lam nine chickens so she will sing and dance the Nding and pay homage to the ancestors if her son comes home safe and sound, and if her husband and daughter come back with him. She sings and repeats certain refrains.

He has returned,
He has become,
Njokè has become more of a Lôs than Dimalè.

Mere mortals have always been told
That the noncompliant one does not die,
But will see the consequences of his deeds.
Now, the ultra-powerful needs these experiences;
He will not become fire except by burning,
Will not become a genie except by drowning,

He has returned,
He has become,

Njokè has become more of a Lôs than Dimalè.

Njokè had the audacity to confront Dimalè,
An ultra-powerful man they call "Catastrophe";
To surpass the Master of catastrophes,
One has to find greater power than that of fate itself.

One goes off to deride the unspeakably famous Dimalè where he lives,
Abduct his eighth wife, the most beautiful of them all,
And not bring her back until she's birthed a little girl that
Is her spit and image,
And strut about with her at the market of Mbébè Libông,
The very kingdom of Dimalè!

He has returned,
He has become,
Njokè has become more powerful than Dimalè.

Thereupon Dimalè saw red;
He ordered his men to destroy Njokè
And to never let the name Njokè be heard again.

But Njokè fought back, sent all the market men running,
Splitting hairy hides with dried salt cod,
Slashing faces with splintered bottles,
Gashing backs, arms, and calves with his machete.
Did he not become more of a Lôs than Dimalè himself?
So sang the women at the market of Mbébè Libông.

He has returned,
He has become,
Njokè has become more famous than Dimalè.

Then Dimalè grew doubly enraged,
Belched in humiliation and spat excrement;

The very essence of fury rose up inside his skull,
Awakening the genies of his catastrophic power.
In an ambush,
Njokè shattered, his spine broken;
Njokè sewn up inside a sack stuffed with stones
Before he was thrown into the Sanaga from the top of the great
*   waterfall.*

Let us sing of Njokè, let us praise him.
He has become more of a Lôs than Dimalè,
Whose fatal power he snuffed out,
For Njokè lives, oh sons of the Bassa people:
A pair of White men picked up a loaded sack,
The stuffed sack that washed up on the Pygmies' beach;
The Pygmies swore they'd look after Njokè, the chosen one among the
*   strong;*
His father came home holding his hand,
Having offered three rams to be sacrificed to the Pygmy masters. . . .

Song, myth, epic poem. What could be more fitting to remember forevermore the daily facts, embellish and purify them, give them breadth and immortality.

All your daughters, Father, were made to learn the song by heart at the ceremony of your return. Women and children sang and danced. The young and old came together in their exhilaration. Yet, your parents seemed drained and distant. The faces of your closest family members seemed covered by a veil—and perhaps their hearts as well—while their short and furtive smiles alternated with equally short and furtive scowls.

No, really, Father, your parents were not happy.

• • •

Hearing that you had been officially recognized as the third Lôs of your generation and that you would soon be home again, my mother came back on her own so she wouldn't miss the celebration of

42

your new status. But she was not happy, undoubtedly because she could well imagine what her new life as the wife of a myth would be. And what a myth: ultra-powerful and an inveterate seducer besides. First of all, what should she do to rid herself of the unwanted rival who had entered the myth together with you, Father? But then, on second thought, this—the anonymous number, the "eighth" wife of Dimalè—would not be her greatest worry. Celebrity chasers posed a more serious problem, the entire swarm of curious females that would prowl around day and night from here on in. All the fool-hardy, adventure-seeking minors who would arrive without delay, baskets on their backs and infants in their arms, claiming to have been seduced, invited, or deserted—and in her role as the first wife, mother, or stepmother of all the others, she would have to take them in.

She would never tolerate it. Perhaps she ought to leave right now with what still remained of those memories that were good, before the coming hell would erase everything from her recollection, including the happiness of a past when mad passion had bound you to one another.

Aunt Roz was not happy either, thinking of the waste.

Of the ten children born from Great Madja Halla's womb, only two survived. As a woman and the eldest, Father, Aunt Roz had been raised to be your second mother, to do everything for the two of you. It was also because of you that she hadn't been able to marry the man she loved, because he had never understood why she'd asked him to come and live with her at her father's house.

Nothing like that had ever been done in Bassa country! A man who, rather than bringing his wives back to his village, would go and live with the family of one of them, even if she was his favorite? It would mean relinquishing his masculinity, his honor, his free-dom. And wasn't the woman who dared suggest such a thing to a man trying to be a man herself, thereby insinuating that he was not a real man? Wasn't that an insult to be taken to the court of Ngué, where it could be punishable by death? For truly it was a crime, and the court of Ngué had to be heedful that no crime go unpunished.

Fortunately, the man had loved her very much and hoped to be loved in return, so that their devotion had wrought the miracle of sympathy: He did not take her to court. Nevertheless, love wasn't blind enough to let them forget their respective responsibilities: He had to think of his male rights and she of her duties as the older sister-mother. They each thought the other's love wasn't strong enough but, swayed by their own deep feelings, they decided to understand and forgive one another.

In the end, Aunt Roz saw that if she wanted to remain true to her education as a woman of honor, she would always have to abstain from loving a man. And what is a sense of honor if not respect for one's commitments, carrying out one's share of the responsibilities through one's own actions, no matter what the cost?

Thus she had to make do with a man who couldn't be bothered with these kinds of considerations and who based his life on personal pleasure. His name was Ratez—the failed one—what a joke! She married him, and never had any children—what was the point? Her son-like brother was sowing his seed in all directions; not a year went by that one or two women wouldn't come to deposit a child Njokè had left in their belly, not counting the ones my mother had every other year, regular as clockwork. Aunt Roz was married and the mother of this whole brood. She felt she had sealed her woman's destiny.

So Aunt Roz could see the mess these new offspring would create, a brood that would fall on infertile ground; that would succumb to abandonment and abuse. The previous year, one of the women my father had deserted was thrown out by her own father after he'd badly beaten her just a month before she gave birth. She came to the village with her bundle on her head, her skirt wet from the waters of a premature delivery of stillborn twins. Aunt Roz wept and wept for a week. She started to drink palm wine and snort powdered tobacco, which flushed the pale skin she had inherited from Grand Pa Helly. Even her eyes turned red. Her husband Ratez took advantage of it by having her twice as much at night and every morning, too. Aunt Roz washed the sheets.

Grand Pa Helly wasn't happy either. He was thinking of the sleepless nights he would have to devote to comforting my namesake in her anguish, the anguish you were causing her, Father. Whole nights in which he would have to come up with funny stories about children who were just as awful as you, but who saved themselves thanks to some miraculous feat because at the last moment they'd remember a piece of advice their mother, their father, or their grandparents had given them.

"There was Nzinga, mischievous to the point of silliness, but when a monstrous leper tied her up in a burlap bag and forced her to lick his wounds, she became aware of her flaws and learned such a hard lesson in obedience and respect for her elders that she turned into a model for the others. Barely had the monster ordered her to lick his wounds when she set to it, gently and seriously, humming a lovely song that cured him in the end. Then she discovered that he was actually a very handsome prince, bewitched by a sorceress, for which the only cure was to meet someone who would love him just the way he was. The prince married Nzinga, brought her back to his kingdom, and invited her parents so he could pay them homage. No doubt your son, too, one day will . . ."

"Yes, but Nzinga was a woman, and women always end up growing wiser, while men . . ." Grand Madja replied.

So Grand Pa Helly had to come up with other tales about male heroes who rediscovered the equilibrium they'd lost through their actions. How many stories would he have to invent, and for how many nights in a row? Would he manage to turn some of these anguished nights into nights of love, during the risky performance where imaginary tales merge with the storyteller's wishes, and in the end turn his own head inside out? Perhaps an old man like him was filled with hatred for his last and only legitimate son, and wished him dead—something Grand Madja bitterly accused him of, Father, on days that he exploded with anger toward you. On the day of your glory, for which he sacrificed three huge rams, Grand Pa Helly was thinking of all the trouble you were bound to make for him in the time to come. He had no difficulty imagining the rages he'd have to suppress, the pain he'd have to soothe, and all of this out of love for my namesake, that plump bit of a woman with her gift for stripping him of all rational power, logic, and decisiveness, and moving him to tears.

No, Grand Pa Helly was not happy at all.

The worst of it was that Grand Madja Halla wasn't happy either, and with good reason, for the mother of a Lôs is like the mother of a boxing champion. The blows that were bound to pour down on her son's head prevented her from giving free rein to her pride in his victories. Mothers would rather see their sons happy and cheerful, even at their apron strings, than dead and buried, covered by the national flag.

What greater Lôs would come and depose you, the way you had just deposed Dimalè? What affront, what shame, what dishonor would he make you suffer? She would be better off dying now while you were idolized and at the peak of your fame, even if it was disastrous. What would she do with her heart when the inevitable fall into the abyss ensued? She put her head in my mother's lap and exhaled, keeping her lungs empty, determined to stop breathing, but my mother was not paying her any mind and didn't notice. This indifference triggered Grand Madja's lungs, and she told herself that if she were to depart here and now it would be the end of you, Father: No one else would devote such complete attention to her miracle of a son.

"My God!" she exclaimed.

She was shaking with horror, stood up, and went to her bedroom—where, Father, she began to pray for you.

6

In spite of the unspeakable agony, the ceremony was really lovely, and everyone had something to contribute.

So as not to blame himself later on, should things turn out badly, for giving blessings without believing in them himself, Grand Pa Helly delegated the task to his cousin and initiation partner, the Mbombock Tonyè Nuk. This man was dying with admiration for your daring and good luck (which he called insolence), although he considered them arrogant, Father. Uttering his blessings upon you, he asked that the power you had just snatched from the esoteric forces of nature be productive for you and for the entire tribe. He recited a series of highly symbolic proverbs, and concluded that, no matter what, you alone were responsible for deciding what to place in your bag, riches or rags.

Grand Madja forced herself not to meet her son's gaze so that she wouldn't cast a shadow over his happiness. She moved from a group of Mbombock initiates to a group of Kindak initiates, serving them kola nuts, kola bitters, flavored bark, and Guinea pepper—ingredients that, when measured in a particular way, are supposed to wrap the spoken word in very special power. People chewed them while uttering incantations.

In spite of the huge number of guests, Aunt Roz went out of her way to cook beautifully prepared dishes, as if she were merely making dinner for her husband Ratez. She took special care with the presentation, and every time she served a new dish the crowd gave her an ovation.

Even my mother joined the party! She smiled at all her known or presumed rivals, seating them affably and showing personal concern for each. She'd chat with one and laugh loudly with another. She exuded charm, and was so attractive that many of the guests couldn't hide the fact they were mesmerized and captivated by her.

In the end, the sorry sight was you, Father! It happened when you saw my mother chatting warmly with your cousin Gwét; he was telling her how incomparable she was, assuring her she'd always be the queen of this family if not the tribe, that the men of your clan would never abandon her if you were to be foolish enough to neglect her. Had it not been for the presence of mind of Great-Aunt Kèl Lam, who immediately began to hum the praise song of your superiority, we might have seen you run after Uncle Gwét the way you once went after Uncle Ngan, bat in hand. Aunt Roz burst out laughing, took my mother by the hand, and led her away, saying: "Bravo, Naja, well done! Now that you've decided to listen to me nothing will throw you off anymore, you'll see. Let's go and have a drink."

They went off together serenely, supreme in their complicity; and you left, peeved, forced to follow your man's destiny. My apathy in the face of this male status, which had once impressed me so, came as a big surprise to me. I began to think that perhaps this status was no more than appearances. Might Grand Pa, my super husband, be right? Maybe I was in the throes of acquiring something finer than what a man had.

Perhaps it was because that day I was the only one to watch you without fear, without any specific attitude toward you, that you came to me and addressed me for the first time as one human being to another, honestly and openly. Or so it seemed to me, at least.

You asked about the school I'd just begun. You talked to me about White women and the Yellow women of the People's Republic of China, who were involved in the same things as men: warfare, politics, trade, and technology. Some of them actually commanded battalions and flew airplanes. You told me that only the school of the White people would liberate Black women, because then they wouldn't be compelled to marry and become submissive to a man out of habit.

"Take your mother, for example. She shouldn't be in a position to need me; she is much too intelligent for that. But she believes the contrary out of habit, because that's how she was raised. If you continue to be serious about your studies at the White school, you'll acquire new habits and won't need to slither around like a snake, the way she's doing right now for no good reason."

I didn't understand what you were alluding to, but I remember that you said you would help me study at the White and Yellow universities as long as I passed all my exams without failing. You told me you'd be going away for a while, but that you'd come back in time to keep your promise.

I was so thrilled that I danced the Nding behind Great-Aunt Kèl Lam for the first time, copying her steps and her mysterious cries. She announced she had found her replacement, and everyone congratulated me. I don't know why, but at the end of the ceremony I had the impression that it was actually I who had been honored more than my father, for my bliss was greater than that of all the others put together.

• • •

Because I wanted to know so much more about the Lôs, I still remember that you, Father, told me this by way of explanation the next day: "A Lôs is someone who, without any special training, seizes enough power and strength from the forces of nature to change the course of his life. He can speed up the evolution of things and people in time and space, and he can impose his will on human beings and on the elements. He can also slow them down, impose his own rhythm on time and people. For example, Dimalè, or 'Catastrophe,' as his name implies, really is a disaster for the ordinary man who runs up against him, because for the ordinary man the unexpected is always catastrophic. The ordinary man loves his habits, his tranquility, and his routine. The relatively exceptional man, however, who sees all of life as a pathway of initiation, is always interested in coming up against the unexpected. Catastrophe is the sign that renewal is underway. And the Lôs, the 'Ultra-powerful' who is necessarily exceptional, greets catastrophe gladly, for it will allow him to evolve."

I then remembered that they said Dimalè had a genie inside him that gave him the power to impose his will on people ten times stronger than he. He would even put the village chief to work to carry out every one of his new desires: a piece of land he liked on which he wanted to establish new plantations, a new woman he'd seen somewhere whom he wanted to marry, a new friend with whom he wanted to join forces, even if he lived more than ten villages away. All the men who lived along that route would have to congregate, along with their wives and children, to install roads, lay out and dam up new paths, build bridges, work his new lands and those of his new allies. Obviously this was catastrophic, and turned everyone's life upside down.

But Dimalè was generous enough to let the land of those he forced to work for him be cultivated by the collective members of these new communities. As a result, and in spite of the fear and humiliation of forced labor, everyone ended up by having a share in the interest; everyone wound up with large plantations, while the bridges and roads were beneficial to all. A whole new way of life was thus born from the actions of an ultra-powerful man named Catastrophe. It was the reason why, in spite of his unsettling appearance, Dimalè had the support of a large section of the community, which found him more worthy of their admiration and respect than the "great and grand chiefs," as they were known then, who looked like scarecrows.

"Some of these heroes stand out because of the power of their mountainous muscles and the strength of their steely nerves, like Bitchokè. Others because of the tenacity of their desire, the strength of their conviction and will, the wealth of their dreams and aspirations, like Dimalè," you concluded, Father.

In contrast to Dimalè, you, Father, were tall and physically strong. You were handsome, and people were inclined to approach rather than withdraw from you. The Lôs, however, should always have something a bit repulsive about him, and you had nothing of the sort. You could permit yourself to unite strength and charm, and alternate between them as you wished. Why, then, did you create that need for those fits of brutality, which terrorized women and senselessly humiliated men? No doubt you were already trying to figure out how you might surpass Bitchokè, whom they called a ferocious animal, and in so doing you practiced to gain power by means of the absurd. If your father had ever dreamed you'd be a Lôs, the way Dimalè's father surely had foreseen, he would have named you "Absurd," instead of giving you a name as ordinary as Njokè, "The Elephant."

What can I say today about your life as a Lôs? Did you slow down or accelerate the evolution of the world? Did you suspend or erase time? I'd give anything to hear your own perception of yourself, you whom I never heard express regret about anything at all— not about the worst of your blunders, or about any sorrow you may have endured. I wonder if you ever experienced remorse.

I could convince future storytellers, Father, that what guided you was the desire for beauty and greatness, a thirst for the absolute. It doesn't really matter where it leads us; we all decide what we want to keep in our bag, rags or riches. The truth is not always pretty or merciful.

• • •

The new woman preceded you like ground hot pepper cast to the wind of a whirling harmattan, making one weep, sneeze, and cough: You came back with a White woman snatched from her husband. She owned cars, and so she had to have a paved road at least twenty-five kilometers long to go from the district's central town to our village. Everyone knew that now the problems would really begin. Some decided to go and visit their maternal families where, in our tradition, one would be safe. But when you arrived you brought them back by force, and didn't stop at whipping and recruiting their maternal uncles, a violation of the taboo that had never before been committed. From then on, no one anywhere would be safe.

You emptied out the fields and schools; you compelled women and children to clear the earth. And so Aunt Roz, my mother Naja, my sisters, and I found ourselves building a road to accommodate the arrival of your White wife and her vehicles. Your parents were the only ones who didn't come to the construction site, but at least you didn't have the nerve to beat them. They sat down on the ground in front of their house, legs stretched out in front of them, and they covered themselves with ashes as a sign of mourning. They kept a semi-fast for as long as the work went on, neglecting their own labor so they could devote themselves to prayer.

Once again I was infinitely lucky, since I was grooming myself to be like a White woman but had never seen one in the flesh. I wanted the road to be finished soon so that I could become enlightened. As a result I was the only one who, of my own free will, worked on the road with enthusiasm and zeal in order to attain my goal, and therefore I was the only one who actually enjoyed working there. For everyone else it was forced labor, slavery, and pure hell. They suffered insults and were whipped, felt humiliation, anger, hate, and ill will.

That is why all of them endorsed Mpôdôl when he stood up in the National Assembly meeting that was to consecrate our country as an Overseas Department of France, and said: "Down with colonization, down with the colonizers and their collaborators, down with forced labor and exploitation, long live liberty and our rights, long live 'Independence!'" It was broadcast live on the Telefunken radio. Everyone stopped to listen because you had raised the volume, impatiently waiting for the moment that would make you a French citizen and break the barrier you'd been feeling between your White wife's fellow citizens and yourself. It was a dreadful shock to you, who didn't understand "that a Negro could stand up right there in the Assembly full of White men and question the already established rule." You rose and declared that Mpôdôl was an outlaw and should be thrown in prison for the rest of his life—and at that very moment the voice from the Telefunken box repeated the same words, as if you'd crawled in to possess it the way a *bissimè* spirit possesses a woman in a trance.

We heard a huge hubbub inside the box.

"Where did he go? How come he's 'disappeared'? He's not some spirit, after all! Get him back and bring him here dead or alive, even if that damned Elephant Forest has to be combed in its entirety!"

A loud noise followed, and then the box fell silent. You gave it a terrible kick, and it cracked open into a dozen pieces. All the people in the crowd took to their heels, scattered in different directions toward the forest, including my mother and Aunt Roz, while you, the "ultra-powerful" one, were unable to follow sixty adults taking off in sixty different directions at the same time, like the rays of a black sun. Only the children stayed, frozen, overcome by the sudden speed of the events. Time seemed to have set out on a madly accelerated course toward an unknown destination, where a trophy that should not be missed stood waiting.

How disarming you could be, Father! You didn't seem concerned; you picked up the smallest children, one on your back, one on your shoulders, one by the right hand and one by the left. They clung to you like little monkeys. "It's all over, children, we're going home," you said softly. All the other children followed your lead. You dropped each of them off in front of her or his parental home, and only my sisters and I were left, right behind you, when you arrived before your parents, who were in prayer and covered in ashes. We stood in front of them for what seemed like an eternity. Finally, Grand Pa Helly raised his eyes and seemed to recognize something. You calmly told him: "It's war, father, I have to leave. But don't worry, I'll be back soon."

You went to get a bag from your bedroom and then departed from the village. A silent tear etched a path of its own through the ashes on Grand Madja's right cheek.

You were the only one, Father, who used the word war. Nevertheless, a huge massacre followed, and cost the lives of more than a hundred thousand Bassa and Bamileke men, women, and children. Entire villages were burned and pillaged, women were raped, entire populations deported and confined to what they called "relocation camps," where they were subjected to brainwashing sessions meant to convince them that Mpôdôl was their personal enemy, the enemy of their own evolution and global development—in short, the enemy of their happiness. A large part of the Elephant Forest was cleared and ravaged. None of this appears in official discourse or history books, which occasionally and only vaguely allude to "the events of independence." Sooner or later, however, all of us had to count our dead and try to describe what had happened at home. Here is my account.

7

The first event, in Massébè, our village: We hear a car motor. People come running because there is no passable road here, so how could a car come through? All the same, a motor revs up, a blast of hot air blows between the legs of the assembled people, the grass flattens, but we see no car.

Having reached us over your passable road, Father, the phantom car leaves tire tracks! Everyone is yelling in bewilderment and fear. Now every villager is following the tracks of an invisible car, in a frenzy of motors and voices, as far as the thirteenth kilometer, which is where the roadwork had come to a halt twelve days before.

The motor stops. A woman in a trance says that she sees a red car driven by a skeleton. The car is filled with all kinds of scythes and forks covered in blood, but only she can see them. Even the Mbombocks, Grand Pa Helly and Tonyè Nuk, don't see the red car. What is certain, though, is that everyone has seen the tire tracks and everyone has heard the motor cut off.

The men begin to berate the invisible car: "You won't come through here again, whoever you are, not without showing and introducing yourself! We order you to explain yourself! Or else you'll be sorry you were ever born! You're on the soil of free men, and if you want to hang on to your own freedom, you'd better be on your way and never come back!"

The Mbombocks Grand Pa Helly and Tonyè Nuk use their fly-swatters, drenched in rapidly prepared potions, to sprinkle the place where the red car was supposedly parked. The motor suddenly starts up again and revs very loudly, flattening the grass and people with hot air. Did the car take off? The motor's noise moves up into the sky like that of an airplane! Making an effort to be first, people stand up in baffled silence and go home single file.

• • •

Second event: A Sunday morning with everyone already in their Sunday best, as is proper, some for the Catholic mass and others for the Protestant service. In Massébè it is one or the other, just about half and half. Of course, everyone is animist as well; they have already been purified by the medicine man's Lilan Liliaceae, a plant in the lily family, and have made offerings to the ancestors. You never know. . . .

After breakfast, just when everyone is ready to leave the house, we hear a loud noise coming from the north. We go out and move in that direction, but when we reach a neighbor's house, the noise seems to be coming from further away. Again everyone arrives at the thirteenth kilometer, right where your road stops, Father. Now the noise is coming from the South. We retrace our steps, following the sound, and walk until the day is half gone. Now the noise is coming from the north!

We all sit down and wait for this sorcerers' meeting in bright daylight to come to an end. It lasts until sundown. The same woman in a trance claims she hears a meeting where the end of our world is under debate. According to her, the ancestors are pleading on behalf of Massébè, sketching out some visions of its evolution and renewal. But the spirits don't want to hear any more; there are too many sorcerers striving to make time stop.

"In the name of heaven and earth," the woman shouts, "stop obstructing the course of life." And she collapses in a faint. She is so heavy now that it takes four men to move her. Again we go home single file, unable to resist, as if each of us felt the need to fall into line.

• • •

Third event: This time the news arrives like a thunderbolt, and terrifies everyone: The Whites have decided to comb the Elephant Forest to flush out Mpôdôl, known as the Great Resistance Fighter.

But all the roads that lead there have become very dangerous because the majority of the inhabitants of the villages bordering the terrible forest have joined the resistance, and in effect form a guerrilla force that prevents the army from reaching the Great Resistance Fighter. The Whites consider burning the whole forest down with napalm, but a few "converted nationalists" implore them to consider the environment, and suggest that they find more accessible paths. They see the village of Massébè as an ally, because of you, Father, the friend and brother-in-law of the Whites. They call you in as a consultant, and you reassure them: Indeed, if they spare the mythical forest of your ancestors, you yourself will guide them in, going through your village, where you are sure nobody will resist.

Yes, indeed, the news comes like a thunderbolt, proving to the men of Massébè that you are bragging about having emasculated them all. If they were to let you through, it would be the only thing History would remember!

The reason why people submitted to your will doesn't matter: It might have been out of respect for your father, compassion for your mother who had already shed so many tears, love for your sister or your wife, or perhaps out of fear of you and the myth of the Lôs you had created for yourself. However, the men of our village decided that the Whites were not going to penetrate the Elephant Forest via Massébè, except over their dead bodies. It would never be said that Massébè was the gate through which Mpôdôl—the eyes and the mouthpiece of every Bassa—had been handed over to die, thereby transforming an entire people into deaf-mutes!

They hold a meeting in front of your parents, and ask them to talk you out of it—or else to urge you to come with all the battalions of the White army stationed in the land of the Bassa and the surrounding regions, if you could. But you should be prepared to face the fact that you and your friends wouldn't pass through Massébè without first slaughtering its entire population, including the women and children. And even so, the spirit of the land had made up its mind that you would not pass through.

Grand Madja decides she'd go and catch her son herself and hold him down until he either trounces her first or else gives up. As she doesn't know exactly where he is, she goes to lay siege at the gate of the headquarters in the district's main town, positive that they'd pass by there. Alas! At the advice of Aunt Roz, Grand Madja's three illegitimate "daughters-in-law" leave with their children to find refuge among their own tribes. With her most recently born little girl in her arms, and once again almost at term, my mother leaves for her people in the city: If everyone in Massébè was going to be massacred then at least these few would survive.

Aunt Roz announces she is ready to bar the road to the Whites, even if she has to do so with her teeth! She lends your old hunting rifle to the men, Father, but unfortunately there is only one cartridge of bullets left, meant for hunting partridge. Never mind—it is decided that this one cartridge would be shot only as a last resort at the commander of the Whites himself.

"Who other than Njokè knows how to use this rifle? Nobody!"

"What do you mean, nobody? Of course there's someone! Minkéng Mi Ndjé, an uncle, asserts that he once used this same kind of rifle to kill a buffalo on a hunting trip."

Aunt Roz expresses her surprise, never having heard this story, and all the more skeptical because her cousin is extremely myopic. He protests vehemently and demands that Aunt Roz prove him wrong. The rifle with its single cartridge has to be entrusted to him.

Many other suggestions are made: setting elephant traps on the road to prevent the Whites from advancing; capturing some of them and diverting others; bringing in some Ngangan Sunkan with their magic powers to have them place poisoned warrior ants and prepare lightning, and so on. While they are putting the finishing touches on their thousand defense strategies, we hear a *nkou*-drum announcing your arrival, Father, accompanied by a commando unit of some fifty soldiers.

Now, there are barely thirty people in attendance at the strategy meeting. The rest of the village population has not yet been alerted. What should be done?

"Go on the attack right away," Uncle Mingkeng orders, and the fearful herd follows its nearsighted and panic-stricken leader into the bush.

Grand Pa Helly puts on his Mbock dress and rushes into the bush as well, but in a direction that was his alone. I never did know his intentions. I am now in the house by myself, in charge of all the homes—those of my parents, my grandparents, those of the three mothers, and of Aunt Roz and her husband Ratez, who always manages not to be present when problems arise, like a cat when death approaches. In addition to this, I am responsible for my little sister.

I lock all the doors, and bring the cooking pots and the food to my grandparents' house where we lock ourselves up.

The sound of an explosion awakens me. My little sister was sleeping quietly. I go to take a look outside—nobody. I gather up my courage and venture as far as my father's rear courtyard. Not a leaf stirring; there isn't a bit of air—all of nature is holding its breath, as am I.

Suddenly everything moves—wind, shouting, people running. Aunt Roz comes out of my grandparents' house with my little sister in her arms and, after motioning me with her head, is swallowed up in the bush. I follow on her heels.

Aunt Roz should have been a man, she is so fearless, always ready to take the initiative, avoiding obstacles but never deviating from her goals. While the others flee from danger, she returns to it. She hides behind a shrub, and we can see the battalion of White men buzzing excitedly. One of them is lying on a kind of bag, his left shoulder bleeding profusely. My father is busy with him, holding a knife that from time to time he'd run through some flames. Water boiled on a blue-tinged fire that came from a kind of bronze-colored stove. I later learn it was a camping stove. A team of White men return, holding on to five of my uncles, all tied to one another.

My father pretends not to know them, shaking his head in denial at every question, as my uncles did, too. Unfortunately, I can't understand the questions.

Another group of White men come back, holding Grand Madja, Great-Aunt Kèl Lam, and another dozen women, fastened to a rope. One of the Whites brutally strike my great-aunt, but she doesn't flinch. The soldier pushes her even more violently so that she falls, pulling all the other women to the ground with her.

Aunt Roz holds her breath, her body rigid as a tree trunk. Her ears are as red and transparent as those of Grand Pa Helly during his rare moments of rage. Although my sister and I are just as rigid, ours came from complete lack of understanding.

A different group of White men arrive, followed by at least twenty of my uncles. How had five small White men been able to tie up twenty of my very solid uncles? Oh yes, they had rifles. . . . But when I saw about twenty of my cousins, children like me, bound up and whipped, I almost let out a scream. Holding me in a vicelike grip, Aunt Roz puts her hand over my mouth. Our eyes are bulging like a snail's antennas.

A whole crowd of people, all tied together with rope, is now standing around the White man on the ground, who'd been temporarily forgotten. Now he is wrapped up in white bandages and placed on a makeshift stretcher. A few of my uncles are forced to carry him. They hoist the four handles of the stretcher up on their shoulders, and the procession moves toward our village. Aunt Roz waits until they are gone and then we turn back, using a shortcut to get to the house before they do.

Aunt Roz acts as if we were returning from the fields, mud-stained and carrying hoes and baskets with vegetables. We'd seen and heard nothing; we know nothing. We even wait to see them appear before we begin to unload. Right away about ten of the White men surround us and rip away our baskets and Aunt Roz's machete. She begins to yell and confront her brother, asking him what is going on—in Bassa, as if she doesn't understand French, thereby making it possible for all of us to follow my father's explanations.

"Resistance fighters fired at Captain Râteau. They're wrong if they think they can stop the battalion from entering the Elephant Forest and catching that outlaw who claims to be Mpôdôl! Furthermore, they must know there'll be retaliation: If the captain dies, sixty men from Massébè will be shot. You'd better pray that he doesn't die, for then only twelve will be shot."

Shrieking comes from every side. Many other people arrive to hear the news, and are all arrested, bound, and pushed to the ground after being hit with rifle butts or machetes.

My father had stated that the men from Massébè would never shoot at White people—first, because they all respected White authority, and second, because they didn't own any rifles or ammunition. He had been willing to swear to this, because he knew them so well. Now he urges every man to attest to this himself, loud and clear, so that he can intervene and convince the White men to search elsewhere. But no one utters a word.

The White man in white bandages is placed in my father's bed. A team that returns from the neighboring village announces that the Ndog Béa have dug trenches barring the evacuation of the captain by that route. They'd have to cope here for the time being, and figure out what to do next. The Whites make a radio call and arrange for a helicopter to evacuate the injured man.

"While we wait," my father tells the villagers, "we have to feed the whole battalion. Therefore I'm asking everyone to contribute poultry, pigs, sheep, so we can feed the fifty White mouths that are now here, as well as those who are with them."

That is when Grand Pa Helly, whom no one saw approaching, very calmly says: "There's enough here to feed all these mouths for nine days without depriving the people; they've been through enough already. Let's hope the White men won't stay any longer than that. Tell them to set our young people free so they can slaughter the animals, and the women, too, so they can prepare the food."

The three slaughtered pigs are more than enough to feed the whole battalion. These gentlemen decide that everyone has to be tied up again before going to sleep. More than sixty men and several hundred women and children are bound together, one arm attached to the person in front and the other arm to the person behind. This way we form one very long line that soon changes into a spiral, and so we spend the night, like an enormous snail of prisoners. Some people, like Aunt Roz and her cousins, don't sleep a wink.

In the morning two helicopters unload a veritable medical team, and enough equipment for an entire clinic. They listened to the captain's chest and declare that my father has done a good job. Just imagine, a single cartridge meant to hunt a bird, a miserable bit of lead, had lodged in a shoulder, and my father had extracted it with ease. The captain's life was never in danger, and that same evening he had eaten lustily of the pork cooked in tree bark, asking for more at breakfast time. No matter! They brought in an alternate captain ordered to carry out the promised retaliation and continue the mission to the Elephant Forest. They deem it wise to send my father back to the capital. He disappears into one of the helicopters.

The snail of prisoners slowly unwinds and the long line is taken to the bush. Five very flushed and confused young White men are assigned to kill twelve Black men whose wives had cooked the pork in tree bark that was to be their last meal. One of the young men, the puniest of the five, named Private Marteau comes to a halt in front of me. Our eyes lock for what seemed like an eternity to me. A voice thundered: "Come on, Private Marteau!"

He jumps, and puts his gun to the head of my Uncle Ngan Njock, whose arm is tied to my right arm. One side of his head explodes, the blood spurting out. My uncle slumps to the ground, as did Private Marteau, who started to vomit violently. I tried to stay upright, but the weight of my uncle forced me to bend over in two. I see several other uncles of mine fall not far from me, and the ones who collapse pulled the rest of us to the ground with them. Nobody screams or cries.

It seemed as if death had immobilized everyone. Soon the buzzing of fat green flies is heard and, little by little, like the throbbing of a motor, a whole swarm latch onto my Uncle Ngan's head.

Even after the battalion had been gone for several hours, we remain still on the ground, some in their eternal sleep and others drugged by exhaustion, fear, or despair. Still others with their eyes open, obstinate in their determination to look death right in the face. As for me, I can't keep my eyes off the swarm of flies laying tiny white maggots on my uncle's head.

Even today, I still wonder why an entire village population, alive and welded in death, lay motionless for hours. Perhaps we thought there were a few White men left, watching us to see if one of us might budge, and ready to blow his head off. Or perhaps we preferred to die together, and not be one of those who would some day have to describe something this grotesque. Undoubtedly, that was the reason why the event wasn't spoken of again for another five years, and even then only in half-whispers, under breath and in veiled terms, like a distant nightmare. It took five years of waiting for the deported inhabitants of Massébè to come back to their land and for a purification ceremony to take place.

On a tourist trip to France, we visited Oradour, a small village in the Limousin, whose population had been slaughtered by German soldiers during the Second World War. Although they had already lost the war, they still locked innocent women and children in a church, burned them alive, and in the name of their glorious fatherland shot unarmed men like pheasants. While visiting such places, where signs provided many details, the memory of the Massébè massacre brutally invaded my consciousness. I wondered if a soldier named Marteau had visited there the way I was visiting here, and had then remembered his own actions. Recalling the scene in his mind, did he tell himself he'd served his country, as these mad officers had done? But then, France was not at war with the land of the Bassa! There had never been any war, proved by the fact that there is no record of it anywhere. Private Marteau must have been wholly convinced he was achieving his mission of civilization and salvation.

In some way, for the man whose life is a perpetual path of initiation, he would be right. As my father used to say, catastrophe is a sign that life is evolving, and this is salvation. But for Massébè's ordinary women and children, it was a sordid and unspeakable massacre, a catastrophe that even someone like Dimalè would not have unleashed.

As night fell, Grand Pa Helly, who certainly had the skill of vanishing and reappearing, seemed to emerge from nowhere in the company of the Mbombock Ton Nuk and Great-Uncle Mbon Minyèm. Silently they untied everyone's arms. Completely numb, the people painfully rose. Twelve bodies remained on the ground for all eternity. Women undid their *pagnes* to cover the dead.

Great-Uncle Mbon told us that every hut was burned down, and that the three of them had spent the day following the battalion's trail, trying to salvage what could be salvaged after it departed. They wanted everyone to recognize they'd never see their village again the way it once was, and they'd never again own anything at all.

"Yes, we do! Now we own combativeness and a vastly increased determination," Aunt Roz said. "They won't enter the Elephant Forest via Massébè. The blood spilt here must stop them. So, everyone stand up!"

And everyone remained upright throughout the years that the repression lasted. The healthy men and women joined the resistance. The rest of the population was deported to a kind of concentration camp they called the Relocation Camp of Bondjock. Grand Madja and Aunt Roz went there at Grand Pa Helly's insistence. But Aunt Roz was the link with the resistance fighters, collecting half of the dried cod, the chocolate, sugar, and milk they gave us and depositing them in the shrubbery. She always managed to convince some young military guardsmen to let her look for traditional medicines for her aged father or fruit for her children. Her accomplices then passed the provisions to the fighters through the camp's fence—to the enormous disapproval of her mother, who dreaded another retaliation, another massacre, if her daughter were caught red-handed as a supporter of the resistance. But nothing could stop Aunt Roz. She always answered that it was her duty to try to put right the ills her brother had created.

She was the main resistance organizer in the region. Her husband Ratez had settled in the district's main town, where he had found a job as an assistant to the local commander, and so she had free rein. She had made the food supply and rationing service completely subservient to her by becoming its director's mistress. She could therefore collect all the leftovers from the officers' mess and have the women make them into meals again before she deposited them outside the camp for the resistance fighters to pick up. Indeed, for three years the battalion of Bondjock unwittingly provided the resistance with sugar, milk, smoked fish, beef, and vitally needed medications. Aunt Roz figured it was the least she could do. She also organized small teams to sabotage the machinery intended for opening the road to the Elephant Forest. The children would pour a bit of sauce in the motor oil, a bit of salt in the carburetors, in tiny quantities—just enough to slow down the work, but keep anyone from figuring out the reason.

The road never went beyond Massébè.

And elsewhere, nobody knows the name of the village that today has a hundred inhabitants at best. Better that it remain anonymous than it enter the history books under the name "gate of the death for every future."

8

There was nothing but alarming news about my father: He had become a consultant to the Whites, a "collaborator," as this new class of people was known from that time on. Or we were told that he had returned to Douala, where he had seduced and instantly married a midwife who worked at the maternity clinic of Eseka, Bitchokè's stronghold.

"Couldn't he ask his White friends to post his midwife-wife somewhere other than in this cursed place, where a certain Bitchokè, mad with hatred and contempt, decapitates his brothers?" Grand Pa Helly wanted to know. What irresistible destiny was driving his son Njokè to run so permanently with danger? Was it recklessness? Ignorance?

Grand Madja wanted to die of shame, and implored the ancestors and the spirits to open the earth beneath her feet and swallow her up. Alas! Not a month went by that we didn't hear talk of Bitchokè: He had caught some patriot in the resistance with his own hands and delivered him to the White soldiers. He had set fire to the house of someone suspected of being a resistance fighter or one of their accomplices. He had abducted the wife of another fighter and had her raped by all his men to humiliate the husband. As a reward the Whites had given him hunting rifles with bullets meant for elephants. Then he had promised to kill Mpôdôl himself with

an elephant bullet "to squash his dirty traitor's skin and send it flying to the four corners of the world, so that the earth will forget he
ever passed through this life."

Bitchokè couldn't tolerate hearing that another Black man was
on the trail of Mpôdôl: It was his private hunt, as he reminded anyone who would listen. When he caught a resistance fighter and
delivered him, Bitchokè was careful to behead him and have his
head exhibited on the square for two days so that everyone would be
sure to take note of his own power. Once and for all, he wanted to
destroy the myth of invincibility that surrounded the famed patriotic resistance fighters, which so exasperated him.

"What ill fortune has generated this 'nameless era,' this non-era,
saddling me with White soldiers and commanders, thereby over-
shadowing my power as a Lôs and relegating me to the despicable
role of a 'collaborator' or, worse, of a mere underling?" Thus he
would lament, in places where he had done his damage, according
to the accounts spread by innumerable witnesses. "It's the fault of
that lousy Mpôdôl and his whole gang of gutless Mbombocks who
could find nothing better to do than hide out like rats in the bush!
Why didn't they take up arms and organize a true resistance? Why
didn't they call upon the deities Ngué, Um Nkora Ntong, and all
the other Lôs powers to liberate them?" he kept on moaning.

In fact, they said that Bitchokè utterly despised White men, but
since he found them to be more shrewd and much more powerfully
armed, he'd told himself that as long as he had to ally himself with
someone, it might as well be them.

"I'm infuriated by every pretentious Black, I feel nothing but
contempt for those so-called patriots, incapable of getting along
with each other, who've allowed the colonizers to come in by taking
advantage of their divisiveness! These Black pseudo-intellectuals
and politicians know nothing about their own traditions anymore,
and forget to call upon Lôs like myself to rid the country of these
invaders. I'm especially angry with Mpôdôl, who, if he were worthy
of the name, would obviously have called upon me, the greatest of
all the Lôs! I swear I would have purged the Bassa land of all these

cantankerous pigs, even if it meant eating them raw," he never failed to add.

"One doesn't necessarily catch mange the same day one eats a leopard's skin," as one of our old proverbs says. That is why on the day my father met Bitchokè for the first time, he never could have imagined the slew of misfortunes he had just unleashed.

Indeed, sometimes it is as if a higher power subjugates even our innate free will. Every act becomes an involuntary function, just like digestion or perspiration, and that's fatal. To be sure, that fate is generated by prior acts, but when it starts moving you can't escape it anymore, for each act must find its recompense. And only my father knows what actions he committed to set this peculiar destiny in motion.

Grand Pa Helly had to go in search of the news himself, and when he returned we were given the most recent, very colorful information. "The name of Njokè's midwife is Naja as well," he told us.

My mother took great offense at this, wondering why he couldn't at least have found a midwife with a different name. She could understand that her incorrigible husband wanted a midwife, just as she could understand that he'd taken a White woman as a wife, since she herself was not. It was a craving like wanting sweets and was always very short-lived. The last time, the deserted White husband had simply sent his runaway wife back home, proving that it wasn't just Black women who had to suffer the laws made by men for men. Although it was sad it was nevertheless a consolation.

What really bothered my mother was that her husband wanted to disregard her to the point of changing wives without changing names. This willingness to merge the two women shocked my mother to the highest degree. Ranting and raving into the wind, she called upon various witnesses—her father-in-law, her mother-in-law, her sister-in-law, and anyone else who was willing—to listen.

"Am I not right? On top of it all she's a 'sista' Jehovah's Witness like myself! If only she were a daughter of Babylon I could at least assume that she must have used Beelzebub's methods to take away my man for good. But no, Njokè saddles me with a mind-boggling

MOVEMENT TWO

9

In the "relocation" camp I decide to divide my time between the White school, the more or less esoteric teachings of Grand Pa Helly and Grand Madja, and the resistance teaching of Aunt Roz who repeats all Mpôdôl's words—his ideas, his patriotic vision for the country, its revolution, and its rebirth.

Of all these lessons, I much prefer those of the White school, undoubtedly because there I am the best in every subject. The teacher has me do two years in one. I take the exams to finish elementary school and the admission test for secondary school, and pass them at the top of my class. Unfortunately, the results don't count because my file is not valid. My parents continue their court case, one appeal after the other. They have new birth certificates with new names made for each child, so they can each prove the children are theirs, since the other "parent" doesn't even know their names. The court of appeals has confiscated every birth certificate, and upholds the demand that my father submit to the testing.

I wonder if I'm supposed to give up my White and Yellow dreams. What is my father up to? He'd promised to help me pursue my studies as far as my aptitude would let me go, and for that reason I made it to the top of my class. Has he forgotten both me and his promise? Or is the promise beyond his financial means, so that he is no longer able to keep it? Or is he just another show-off, as his cousins claim?

Strangely enough, Grand Pa Helly defends my father, the only time I ever heard him do so. He cites "the events" that are so long in being resolved, the dangerous circumstances. He advises me to take the final year of school over again so as not to forget what I learned while I wait for my father to keep his promise. It was sweet to hear my faith confirmed: Grand Pa Helly wouldn't lie. Soon my father would come and take me to a White and Yellow people's school, and I'd become a test pilot just like the idol he had chosen for me in a magazine, Wou-Tchou-Ti, the little seventeen-year-old Chinese (or Korean) girl who led an entire squadron. I was in a hurry, but at the same time I felt ready to wait by taking the same class over again, at least for the three years I'd gained on the others.

Grand Pa Helly didn't lie; my father came the following year.

A few days earlier, Aunt Roz had acquired official permission to take Grand Madja, who was very ill, to the district clinic. Actually, it was a pretext to attend a very important meeting. Some activist women wanted to study a new strategy for helping the resistance fighters, since "the events" were going on longer than had been expected, and the backlash was increasing.

SONG 5

When the devil, catching up with you, unexpectedly
Wants to see your private parts,
He causes you infernal diarrhea.
Yes, all the forces of nature are at the service
Of the destiny that is to be fulfilled,
When it is forbidden to forbid,
When fate and chance are bonded by a pact signed in blood.

When my time came to receive the blow of fate,
A thousand "accidents" occurred that caused my mother and my aunt,
Even my grandmother, not to be present
To surround me with at least a word that would have changed
The direction of my path.
Yes, when the devil, catching up with you,

Wants to see your private parts at the wrong moment,
He causes you infernal diarrhea.

• • •

While repeating my last year at school, I was more a tutor than a student. At recreation one day I discovered my legs were dripping with blood. Both embarrassed and terrified, I fled into the classroom and refused to leave my seat. Baffled by my sudden and inexplicable insubordination, my teacher questioned me in vain—not a word would break through the lump in my throat. First of all, I wasn't hurting anywhere and I couldn't understand where the blood was coming from; and second, I was afraid of my own explanation.

Two days before, a classmate had gone into a wild trance and was needlessly making trouble for me because she was jealous. She claimed I'd cast a spell on her and was squealing like a wounded dog, threatening to take revenge on me if something were to happen to her. Her parents had to take her to a medicine man to quiet her down. I knew I'd done nothing to her, but the mysterious blood flowing between my legs disturbed me profoundly. Surely they would now take me for a sorceress, a soul-eater.

To ward off this disaster, I swore I wouldn't leave my seat until everyone else was gone; but a few of them kept insisting, which put my nerves on edge. I was like a cornered wild animal. As soon as anyone came near me, I showed my teeth as if I were going to bite; finally, I myself wondered if I were in the process of turning into a jackal or a panther, right there in the bright light of day in front of the entire class. My fear and shame soon reached their peak, all the more because my anger at my classmates was growing, and they were certainly not showing any understanding as far as I could see.

They were whispering idiotic things.

"You should give her a spanking, Sir, or else she'll never stop trying to be 'interesting' and taunting us with how brilliant she is."

"She already thinks she's the teacher, Sir, and she's always in your place in front of the classroom. That's why she's getting to be so arrogant."

The teacher finally had enough of my stubborn refusal to respond, and pulled me roughly from the seat I clung to; I had to let him haul me out of class. Very excited, all the students applauded.

Outside, the teacher at last understood what was happening to me. He made all the children go back to their classroom, picked me up like a baby, and quickly brought me to his house, where he handed me over to his wife. "Madame," as we called her formally, looked at me the same way my grandmother would, with a trace of both mockery and tenderness.

I asked her a thousand and one questions to be sure this was no sorcerer's blood. She had a hard time keeping herself from bursting out laughing, but assured me that if this were sorcerer's blood, I, too, would be in a trance just like my classmate. While she taught me how to wear protective cloths, Madame explained that I had just become a woman and from now on would be seeing blood with each new moon, that every woman in the world went through this, and that it was the great difference between us and men.

"You certainly are quite precocious, but you were that way with your studies, too. It's in your nature; don't worry about it," she reassured me.

Unfortunately, she was too succinct. She said nothing about the connection between this blood and pregnancy, or about possible precautions to be taken. Did she even know herself? And had she known, would she have burdened my little head with it? I don't think so. In her place, no one would have thought of alarming the frail and childlike little girl I was, without the slightest sign of a bulge on her chest or without any awareness whatsoever of her femininity and seductiveness, always half-naked among the boys as if I were one of them. I truly wasn't aware of sexuality yet. There's no doubt that in that area I was very backward.

A few days later, when Grand Madja and Aunt Roz returned, I had already forgotten the incident and therefore did not mention it to them. I went back to class without the other children knowing what had actually happened. They no longer dared say anything against me, fully convinced that I was under the protective wing of

Monsieur and Madame. At last they all left me in peace, and I served as their tutor with greater patience and good will, waiting for my father to come soon; that was what Grand Pa Helly himself had said would happen, and he never lied.

SONG 6

My father, double human of a giant tree,
His feet at least as gigantic and threatening,
Roots buried deep down in the riverbed,
Dousing himself in the waterfall.
His arms, lianas and boughs,
Sometimes wrapping around my body and holding it imprisoned,
Sometimes defying heaven with their splinters, broken shards in the face
of God,
Held up high to the sky, the knife shimmers reflections of clouds and of
water,
Turbulent witnesses that, even so, will keep forever silent,
The hair of his Kamsi priests, Bami Mediums with their defiant manes,
Dense foliage of lianas and boughs protective of our secret ceremony.

• • •

My father does, indeed, come back, although in deep despair, and only three days after Grand Madja and Aunt Roz return.

He explains that he couldn't keep his word to me in spite of his willingness to do so. In fact, he's afraid he'll never be able to keep it, because the court wants to deny him his paternity and demands that in the next few days he take us to a special institute for a blood test. If not, the police will come and get us and hand us over to our mother for good, assuming that his refusal is an implicit admission that she is right and that he has always known he is not our father.

"I swear to you, my little mother," he says to me, "not only did I never doubt it before, but I'm still completely sure that I really am your father—yours, in any case. I won't tolerate even the idea of any doubt, because I know it in the depths of my heart. You resemble me down to your very soul. Of all the dozens of children I've sired across the land, you're the only one who awakens this feeling of certainty in me, and I find it diabolical that your mother's family wants to destroy it."

He explains to me that the test results can be contested if there is the slightest doubt, whereupon my mother's family will make sure to have the scales tip in their favor.

"I don't want to run any risk at all, not where you're concerned, at least. You are my mother, my soul, the pride of my life, my only real hope for survival. I don't know or feel for the other children the way I do you. I might be able to console myself if they were to separate me from them, but not from you. So I've found a solution: I'm going to put my blood into your body and then the test will have to be positive. Of course, this must remain a secret between the two of us."

You knelt down before me, Father, and even so you were still taller. You asked me to swear I'd keep the secret. You seemed to be suffering, you seemed so frail, my heart was breaking to see you so unhappy, the victim of unbearable injustice. I hugged you tightly in my arms and for the first time felt really angry with my mother. At that very instant I thanked heaven that she was far away from me, for I could have been disrespectful to her and risked the wrath of God upon me, as Grand Madja Halla had taught me.

Yes, at that very instant I felt I inhabited Grand Madja's skin; I was her namesake, after all—Halla, like her. I felt it was my duty to protect you as your mother, poor man. I told you that nothing could separate me from you and that I'd drink your blood; if necessary, I would bathe in it, or open my veins to infuse them with it, as you saw fit, provided that in the eyes of the whole world I be recognized as your daughter, unequivocally and forever.

"That's good, my love. I knew I could count on you. Early tomorrow morning we'll go to the river together for the transfusion before we leave for town, where the tests will be done."

"Why not get it over with right now? We'll avoid any possible problems in the morning: It might rain, or the authorities could come to check the number of people in the relocation camp, as they often do. I'm ready. . . ."

"You're right. But we'd better wait. It's a strange ceremony that might even seem unpleasant to you. First you have to be sure you're brave enough and can withstand and truly want this transfusion. I want you to be sure you won't regret it and, above all, that you won't hold it against me later. If I hurt you, you must always remember that I love you very, very much and that I don't want them to separate us. Will you remember that?"

He worries me with all this thoughtfulness. He doesn't usually talk to me this much. The transfusion is bound to be dangerous. I recall the tales of sorcerers who drink the blood of disobedient and jealous children. I tell myself this doesn't hold true for me and that, in any case, I'll accept any pain so that my father and son will never have to suffer the way he is suffering now, here at my feet and before my very eyes. Still, I have one last question for him.

"So it will hurt a lot?"

"Not much. Perhaps you won't feel any pain at all if you'll just trust me and do exactly what I tell you to do."

I can hardly sleep that night. I get up at the first cock's crowing and slip outside. My father is already at the wheel of a jeep. I'll never know what pretext he used to convince the head of the brigade to lend it to him. I wonder how he manages to have such a noble bearing even when dressed in a military uniform, although under normal circumstances these always look frightening to me. A double-barreled hunting rifle stands beside him and another very short rifle hangs from his right hip, suspended from a belt complete with bullets, just like the soldiers of the local command of our relocation camp wear around their hips. He drives off immediately. I'm happy and very proud to be by his side.

He quickly leaves the camp by the gate that comes out into the district's main road and drives very fast. Then he veers off onto a road that has just opened, and is supposed to go to the Elephant Forest. The Caterpillar combines are parked on the side, obviously waiting for the workmen to arrive that morning. I'd heard about these machines, whose droning reaches as far as the camp, but I'd never yet seen them with my own eyes; absolute monsters they are, with gigantic blades and wheels taller than our car. Then we leave the road and enter the forest by a small path my father seems to be familiar with. He must know where we're going. I'm careful not to ask questions or make any comments. I trust him, and I don't want him to have any doubts about that or think I'm afraid.

The path stops at a dead end consisting of a pile of wooden logs. Apparently, an enormous, highly prized tree was chopped down and cut up into several pieces. They must be planning to use the Caterpillars to lift and transport these massive chunks. My father cuts a path around the log pile and parks behind it. We get out and continue on foot in silence. My father looks in every direction, stopping from time to time to listen. A thousand birds are singing. I'm trying very hard to distinguish the ones I know, thanks to Grand Pa Helly, Grand Madja, or Aunt Roz. Then we hear the sound of a waterfall. My father lifts me up and carries me on his back to move along faster.

He puts me down at the foot of another huge tree whose roots sink deep into the immense river and asks me to get undressed. I do. He hands me a small *pagne* to wear for the river bath, as is customary in Massébè. My father stands on the other side of the enormous roots and has also taken off his military garb and his belts with the ammunition. He, too, is wearing a *pagne* in which to bathe, as is proper. He places our clothes in a hollow of the tree and takes me by the hand, holding a small knife in his other hand. I say nothing, but, already thinking about the pain and imagining my opened veins, my heart is beating very loudly.

We go upstream along the river and reach the great waterfall. When the water is up to my neck my father lifts me up and carries me on his belly with my legs spread; they enfold him tightly. This makes our progress in the water a little more difficult because the current pushes us with great force, and I'm trembling both with fear and the water's chill. We move forward until we reach a small waterhole between two rocks. A spray of water comes down on us like the pump that's used to wash the cars in the military camp, but with much greater power. I'm afraid the water will carry us off, but my father plants himself like a tree in the riverbed. I feel his powerful legs gripping the rocks beneath us.

Now the water reaches up to the middle of his tall body, so that the lower part of mine is fully submerged as well. Still, the current weaves its way sharply between our two figures. I raise my eyes and look at my father, but he is gazing up at heaven as if in fervent prayer. The branches of the giant tree make zebra stripes, shadows threatening the milky white sky, the same color as the early morning clouds that whirl around softly and silently.

When my father's eyes finally settle on me, they lock as if to close I don't know what sacred door. He asks me to close mine and not to open them again until he tells me so.

"You must obey these orders strictly so that the blood transfusion will be successful," he tells me somewhat breathlessly.

I'm dying with fear and cold, but never in the world would I let my father suspect it and have him deprive me of his trust.

I surrender to him, to the sounds of water and wind;
I try not to feel anything,
Sure that I shall suffer less that way.
And, indeed, I do not feel any real discomfort,
Not as much as I had feared, at least.
Certainly, a flash of fleeting pain cuts straight across my body
In the space of time it takes a lightning bolt to cut across the sky,
But the water, ever faster and more forceful in this time of floods,
Quickly eases it, erasing it as if by magic,
In its battle against my father's liana arms,
Now trying to tear me away from him,
Then forcing me again flat up against him.
Our pagnes *float around us everywhere,*
Like the multiheaded hydra's tongues in our ancestral tales.

My father, a tree immutably planted in the riverbed, does not move other than to keep himself in place and resist the force of the current. But some part of him has planted itself inside me like a hard living root, and vibrates somewhere inside my belly. My imagination tries to find a first sign of understanding: Perhaps his arm, made longer by the knife, seeks to deposit his blood somewhere.

Perhaps part of his hand opened earlier,
Already lets his blood flow into my belly.
Could it be that he is pouring out all of his giant tree's sap
To make me his irrefutable double, I wonder.
I'll have to show him everlasting gratitude for life.

For a moment he trembles as violently as I do, then he pulls me away from him, lifts me up, puts me on his back like a basket and goes back to the water's edge. Phew! I can't wait to get out of this hellish and terrifying riverbed.

"That's it, my little sprite, well done, you may open your eyes now. I hope it didn't hurt too much. In any event, you were very brave. We'll win the case, you'll see."

I hug him tightly with all the strength of my love. I'm so pleased that he's proud of me and, even more, I'm proud not to have disappointed him.

A warm liquid spurts from between my legs when my father puts me down on the riverbank. I'm terrified at the thought of jeopardizing the test results, but he reassures me. Still, I close my legs very tightly so as not to let this precious blood get lost. I wouldn't want to have to start the harrowing ritual all over again.

We arrive at the relocation camp with the back of the car loaded with huge papayas, guavas, and mangos we have picked on our way back, in what was once an orchard. My father goes into the house and comes out with a basket that he fills up, then places in front of Grand Madja, who is sweeping the courtyard.

"That's for Papa and you," he tells her. "I don't know when you'll see such fine specimens again, because I don't know when I'll be back."

Grand Madja clasps her son to her breast as if to keep him from leaving. It is barely half past six, but already spirals of blue smoke are escaping from every rooftop and mixing with the early morning mist, as fleecy as the low-hanging white clouds that enveloped us in the forest.

What a magical morning, and how different everything seems. Is it because of my father's uniform? Strangely, even the looks given him by those people who normally throw hostile glances seem new to me, almost supportive, like the approval of a clan for its wrestlers when they bring home a hard-won victory. Their looks are filled with fear and admiration. They greet us with lowered gaze or a slight bow. Even my Aunt Roz looks at me with a touch of envy in her eyes, the way one looks at initiates who have come through their ordeals with flying colors. I take this to mean that she is well aware of the ceremony, and approves. She has prepared a bag with my things and those of my little sister. Apparently she supports her brother in his battle with my mother and her family, she who has always been my mother's friend, and it surprises me a little.

My father goes straight to school to alert the teacher that my sister and I will be absent. The teacher is distressed to release my little sister, who is repeating the third grade and will now risk failing again. But there is no other choice; these are court orders.

As for me, I didn't come anywhere close to making a connection between what had just happened to me and what I thought I knew about sexuality, through Aunt Roz and her husband Ratez or Grand Pa Helly and Grand Madja. Maybe it was because of our position in the middle of the river. I honestly believed it concerned a blood transfusion to make the tests work out. In fact, they were successful. I spent all my time in prayer and contemplation until the court session where we were told the results. God had to have heard my entreaty: I had obeyed my father and, what was more, I had been brave, for it is written: "Honor thy father and thy mother: that thy days may be long upon the land which the Lord thy God giveth thee."

MOVEMENT THREE

10

The court clerk opens a sealed envelope.

He places some of the documents to his right and others to his left. My father's hand in my left hand and my sister's in my right are tightly clutching mine. We hold our breaths. An incredibly long silence follows, as if all are still waiting and not believing their ears. The end result is that only two of the six daughters (the youngest one and I) and my oldest brother are my father's; the others turn out to be the offspring of a different sire.

Timidly, my little sister lets go of my hand. Her sobs rip through the room as if she's been given a death sentence, or as if her soul has been damned. I feel all the more helpless as I look at her because her grief doesn't quite manage to disturb my personal delight, our delight—my father's and my own. Our hands stay welded together, and our eyes beam as we glance at the others, without really being able to imagine their feelings. Happiness makes us inattentive, superficial, and self-centered.

I cannot remember my mother's eyes or those of the rest of the family that day. Looking back, I still tremble at what they might have thought, perceived, or said on my account. How did we separate, how did we travel? What happened until the day that the trial's outcome was decided? In my memory there is only the sense of a period of victorious bliss.

All the children are present at the new trial. The court decides that my father's children will be in his custody and the rest will stay with my mother. Then she begins to shriek the way a dying dog howls. Not knowing what to do anymore, the judge requests that with the exception of the two youngest ones the older children select which of the two parents they prefer to live with. They all choose our mother—other than myself, of course.

For I, Father, remember that I am everything to you; just before the trial began you repeated that again. I don't have the courage to abandon you. Still, I suddenly feel a very strong urge to align myself with all my brothers and sisters, to change my home address, and, more than anything else, to be with my mother again, who, something tells me, will never come back to you this time.

The last one to be questioned, I proclaim categorically: "I want to stay with my father, and nobody can stop me."

Right away, my little sister comes back to me and clutches me like a little monkey clinging to its mother. That is how we find ourselves alone with you until the next verdict—for you appeal the decision again, of course. Having come to court at Grand Madja's urging, Grand Pa Helly wants to take us home, but you, Father, decide to keep me with you. My little sister screams like a pig about to be slaughtered, but it makes no difference, and Grand Pa takes her away without me. And I cling to the idea that now I'll be going to school as promised. Clearly the second trimester is very busy, but I'll be able to start up again without fail when the new academic year begins, you repeat. In the meantime, you ask me to lend your midwife-wife a hand; she's just been promoted to assistant director of nursing at the Great Hospital for civil servants and is pregnant again as well!

So it is that both your wives and almost all your children are together in the regional stronghold of Bitchokè, as if tied hand and foot and at the mercy of fate.

● ● ●

Father, you introduce me to my new mother and instantly leave us alone, without bothering to find out how we'll get along. It doesn't much matter to you that I'm with a new mother Naja, without knowing what to call her to distinguish her from my own mother, whose name is Naja, too.

"Hello, 'Mam' Naja," I say shyly.

She doesn't answer, but scrutinizes me thoroughly from top to toe and back again, several times, as if to latch on to some details that will allow her to recognize me among the hordes of children she sees at the hospital every day. Her eyes show no hate, no love, no kindness, no malevolence—just a kind of absent-minded curiosity. In the fifteen minutes of our first encounter she asks my name two or three different times, and then she warns me that I will have a lot of work to do, won't have any time to be bored or do anything foolish. Matching action to her words, she shows me laundry in an enormous bucket that apparently, judging by the fetid smell of rotting soap it emits, has been sitting there soaking for several days. It's going to take much thorough rinsing to get rid of the stench. Thinking that she's done with me, Mam Naja picks up her bag. Where is she off to? Undoubtedly to her hospital. At barely one o'clock in the afternoon: What an eager beaver, I tell myself.

Who could ever explain what made me follow her? Perhaps the sudden fear of being left all alone in this unfamiliar house and neighborhood made me feel like a stranger. Or perhaps I was already complying with fate. Today all I can do is go along with the second hypothesis, for in my mind nothing else could explain my behavior that day.

She walks the way others dance. A very rolling dance, very rhythmical, with highly pronounced rotations. I copy her rhythm and entertain myself by exaggerating the rolling of my already well-defined hips.

As a result, of course, I hadn't been paying attention to the road we were taking or to the passing time. Out of the blue, she turns around and looks carefully behind her, before she dives surreptitiously into a courtyard. She glances over me without recognition, for she certainly would not have expected me there. In a panic, I quickly hide behind an old parked car and then notice a large intersection I hadn't seen before. I wonder what direction I came from. How do I go home? At this hour of blistering heat, there's no one in the streets who can give me any information. I stay crouched behind the car until my legs cramp up. Whatever is Mam Naja doing inside there? Perhaps I should take a closer look. But then I have to get back to my hiding place very quickly: My own mother Naja and her oldest sister Tata Roz are standing at the door and questioning an old guard. The desired information must be extremely important, for it seems to literally propel them forward, all excited, with lots of silly giggling, and without even saying goodbye to the dumbfounded old man as they jabber away without listening to each other. They pass by me on the other side of the car at such close range that they would certainly have seen me had they not been so self-absorbed. I have often wondered what would have happened then. Our fate would undoubtedly have been different. But the die was cast.

Paddle your own canoe, Halla, keep paddling;
What matters is to paddle your canoe of Love.
Paddling the canoe of Love grants intelligence;
Paddling the canoe of Love grants strength and elation,
Justifies life and all its tribulations.
Paddle your canoe of Love, little Madja Halla.
You'll be done with despair;
You'll relinquish pride and impatience;
Paddling will turn into love and nonviolence.
No matter if you do not reach the other shore;
Your promised one will meet you on the waves one day
And bring you to a new world.
Paddle your own canoe, little Halla;
Paddle your canoe of Love.

The age-old lullaby comes bubbling into my head, a lullaby of my old namesake Grand Madja Halla, sung to me at an age when I was the only one to enjoy the luxury of her full attention, before all the other sisters were born.

There is always that recourse to past happiness, and always the miracle of recreating and updating it. Confronted with my present deadlock, with my mother Naja and her sister hiding in a street watching Mam Naja, who is taking another road, I have no other choice but to go in the opposite direction, the road of the unknown. And I want that road to be happy. That is why Grand Madja's lullaby springs up from the depths of my memory and bursts forth over my senses, infusing them with its sweet hues, sounds, and vibrations. I want to flee from what I see of my mothers Naja: the pettiness that Grand Madja so frowns upon. Until now I've managed to keep myself far away from that, and I fully count on continuing to do so. I'm already happy. I walk along humming the lullaby, which now finds support from some drums. Yes, indeed, drums are calling me, and I start running; I run, singing, toward the drums. They lie at some distance, but my rapid forest-girl's stride gets me there quickly. There is a crowd in a square. I squirm through the legs of the spectators who are blocking me from getting closer. Finally I'm in the middle of the circle! Tiny men and women are playing and dancing in the square.

Because my question escapes from me out loud, a mature lady explains: "It's the Pygmies! The 'authorities' have extricated them from the resistance fighters. They won't be allowed to work as guides for the resistance anymore, and, killing two birds with one stone, they'll make this an opportunity to educate, civilize, and integrate them. In the meantime, the government says they must dance in the square before every important event."

"That's right; and there's going to be a great event right now," a supposedly well-informed gentleman adds. "The ultra-powerful Bitchokè has decapitated one of the last and closest collaborators of the Mpôdôl and will be escorted by the French military to display his head throughout the weekend. Everyone has to understand that the events will come to an end the moment that Mpôdôl's head is nailed to that same 'billboard'; those intractable types should stop doing the foolish things that so needlessly prolong these stupid events."

A full squad of White soldiers comes out of a black car and gets busy around a black box, which I later find out is a hearse. The drums have fallen silent. So have the dancers and spectators. You can hear the green flies' wings. The soldiers climb back into their car, and the crowd slowly moves forward toward the center of the circle. A head is impaled, like a pumpkin, on the top of a fork stuck in the ground. Only this pumpkin's eyes are rolling backward; the dangling tongue is covered with a swarm of green flies, whose buzzing now seems as unbearable to me as the helicopters' engines on that cursed day in Massébè. My whole belly shudders, and my stomach explodes into a bright yellow surge of bile in my throat. I clutch the fork without knowing why. My body is clearly functioning beyond my control today.

A thick hand comes down on my head and yanks me off the ground by my ears. My feet are fluttering in the air pathetically. Suddenly my eyes are at the level of an enormous male face that in a wild and frightening way is quite beautiful: His teeth are oddly white and prominent, and his almost golden eyes flash with many flamelike sparks. As if arising from a cave, a deep voice wells up from this massive whole: "You know him, don't you? Is he your father, your uncle, or your brother?"

Terrified or fascinated, I answer idiotically: "Yes," though I don't know to what.

"Fine, then you can keep him company. I'm going to kill you. Just let the other members of your family dare try to come and get you. Put this thing in there, Bitchokè's orders."

A White man lifts me up like a twig and carries me to the black car. No one in the crowd moves a muscle, other than a middle-aged lady, who asks me softly whose daughter I am. I answer: "Of the husband of the assistant director of nursing. I am Halla Njokè."

I disappear into the darkness of the hearse, of my obliviousness or my steadfast refusal. Or both.

•   •   •

My father used to love telling the story of his first encounter with Bitchokè. According to him, it was truly an emotional shock, a flash of lightning. Even though they'd never met face to face, a serious disagreement had already developed between them. Having announced himself as the father of the girl who had been kidnapped that very morning on the main square, my father expected to be confronted with an enraged and veritable ogre, as this famous ultra-powerful one was reputed to be.

It turned out to be one of the rare surprises of his life, for instead he found himself before a human being whose magnetism sincerely overwhelmed him—even more than his first meeting with my mother, the only woman who had shaken him from the very first, he would add.

The man's provocative look and smile, his royal bearing, the silken hair that seemed to be inviting caresses—it all had the same effect on my father as the most attractive female charms. He felt both ashamed and confused, to the point that he remained standing there, staring openmouthed, for countless minutes. Just as surprised, Monsieur Bitchokè burst out in self-conscious laughter, for he had been expecting a furious reaction. They recovered at the same time and in chorus uttered the same words—"Well now"—then nervously burst out laughing together. Then they stretched out their hands and genuinely laughed at the unexpected collusion.

My father ended up speaking his first coherent sentence: "I am Njokè. I've come to fetch my daughter. I believe she's been mistaken for someone else."

"Yes, indeed," Bitchokè responded, and ordered someone to set the prisoner free.

As my father tells it, they had nothing more to say to each other for the time being, but they still managed a final choral reply: "See you soon, and thanks for understanding."

Laughing loudly, they left each other, and my father led me away, whistling all the way home with interim bursts of solitary laughter and unintelligible monologues. I don't recall having seen him that excited very often. It really is true that you don't catch mange on the same day that you eat the panther's skin.

11

In those days, the children of Africa's urban centers were truly God's little sparrows, who had neither field nor granary. And these children no longer had a clan to back them up, but sometimes only a gang. Yet people were astonished at the violence and delinquency running rampant.

Some parents no longer even wondered how their children lived, as if everything always went of its own accord, as it had in the days that the parent was secondary, and the entire community took responsibility for all its children. Now, the basic rules that used to allow for such solidarity—respect for taboos, for the dignity and general interest of the clan—had been completely flouted. One was under the impression that in this new society, only riff-raff would manage to get somewhere. The family circle was growing narrower and narrower. Systematically and on every level, the population was being materially and spiritually impoverished, while all the essential values of the local cultures were made less and less practicable, especially among the elite.

That is undoubtedly why, having lost their sense of initiative and responsibility, it wasn't hard for men to grow accustomed to not worrying much about their offspring. So the children lived by their wits in every way possible, and it actually became an ever-growing trend for parents to send their children out begging or into prostitution to feed the rest of the family.

To my great surprise and confusion, my father adopted the same attitude, the way one catches an epidemic disease. He would go out in the morning and come back at noon or later and later in the evening. He'd find his meal on the table, his clothes freshly cleaned, starched, and ironed. He no longer cared who had done this, when or how, or what had happened in his home all day long. I tried talking to him, communicating with him if only with my eyes, but all in vain. Even while he ate he wouldn't take his eyes off his notebooks or newspapers. He no longer had any ears except to listen to the newscast on every radio station, or to his friends or party comrades, with whom he incessantly discussed politics. Then he would leave with them on propaganda tours or to politically oriented cultural activities, and nothing else existed anymore.

Here, mealtime was no longer the moment of happiness and sharing that my grandparents had made us love and respect so much, like a sacred and festive ceremony, one that inspired us to love cooking. On the contrary, mealtime became a moment when I'd reluctantly dredge up old aggravations and frustrations, a moment that drove me toward some demoralizing conclusions.

I had become the servant in my father's house without him even realizing it. And so he couldn't even derive any pride from having an industrious and virtuous daughter who was well brought up, according to custom. He should at least have thanked his mother and given her credit for the fine work she'd done. Our Grand Madja Halla had trained us well, to be responsible in the household from the age of nine, the age of the first female initiation.

Therefore it was completely logical that at age eleven I mastered the skills needed to run our home. Every day, I'd clean the house from top to bottom, do the dishes, wash and iron my father's clothes and those of his midwife-wife and their three little boys, too. I'd also go to the market that, fortunately, wasn't very far, barely two kilometers, come back, do the cooking, and make sure everything would be ready at one o'clock at the latest, the time that my husband might be coming home from work and my children from school, the time that my father and stepmother usually came home for lunch and their nap.

Having thoroughly absorbed my lessons as a caramel woman, I always got up very early and finished a good part of the chores—laundry and dishes in particular—before dawn, before anyone else was up. Sometimes I preferred doing these at night before falling asleep. Then I washed and fed my little brothers before my parents left the house in the morning, after their breakfast. In my home I wasn't going to have to worry about laziness and incompetence. I was always proud of being ready on time. It was my one pleasure, and guaranteed me some serenity.

As a reward for all my efforts there was never a single remark or any encouragement from my parents, especially not from my father. I began to wonder why it had been necessary for him to be assured of his paternity through a ritual blood transfusion, only to ignore it so completely afterward. I figured that even a machine deserved a bit of attention every now and then, a kind of maintenance check. What had happened? Perhaps something very serious had happened to my father, and he was steering clear of me.

Sometimes my stepmother mocked my cooking for being too sophisticated, calling it "grandmother style," and asking if it was New Year's Day. Then she'd run her hand through my hair as if I were a cat, make fun of me, and call me "mother-in-law." It was her way of letting me know that she enjoyed it, but that was as far as it went. In her defense, I realized how worn out she was when she came home, and knew that she, too, could surely use a little more affection; but I couldn't find the right words or gestures with which to ease the tension and thereby bring us closer.

Poor Mam Naja! Often she'd wait for her husband, checking her watch every few minutes, an atmosphere not conducive to chatting. The new man my father was turning into seemed truly determined to add to the already-tense atmosphere, and thereby made it more frightening for me.

Not able to take it any longer, Mam Naja would sometimes eat alone, stuffing herself like a pig. She'd only leave the table to flop down on the couch, where often she began to snore almost immediately, sometimes until early morning. When he came home, my father wouldn't bother to wake her up to take her to their bedroom. Such indifference, I thought, could really kill just about anything: love, childhood, and hope.

In the end, what was my father up to?

I decided to try to find out, and one fine morning, having done all of the housework beforehand, I followed him. Gracefully he went through the streets, greeting everyone with a kind word or a personal remark, the way he'd always done. He went straight to a garage in the valley section, where for hours on end I watched him take an old engine apart in the burning sun and then, with true zeal, put it back together again in the body of a different car.

Why, then, was he so withdrawn when he came home? Did he feel some special resentment toward his family? What terrible things had we done to cause such a profound change in him the minute he returned?

What did my father really want? He had explicitly wanted me with him as his daughter, and he had me there. To what end? I didn't understand anything anymore, and a kind of mute rage began to beleaguer me.

When my spirits were at their lowest, and I would begin to lament my lot, Grand Madja's voice would come into my head to straighten me out: "Always feeling self-pity combined with negative thoughts about the rest of the world inevitably leads to holding others responsible for your own failures. In that state, it's better to set your creative and inventive mind in motion and come up with an acceptable explanation for the behavior of those you incriminate. Promise me that you'll at least try!"

And of course I promised, but out of context words like these don't contain any concrete reality. If you're lucky, you might hear them surface again from the depths of your memory when you're confronted with problems; only then do they reveal their full weight.

Fortunately, I was that lucky, and because I heard them I was finally convinced that my father must be involved in ever more abstract and thorny battles, and that I couldn't ask him to turn his attention away from those for the sake of my trivial desires. If I wanted to be worthy of him, I should be struggling as he did, silently and unobtrusively, and be as lighthearted as possible. True, I no longer had any clue about the stakes in his battles, but it was of the essence not to feel judgmental toward him anymore.

"You don't judge your parents. You should only get to know and accept them, for they will always be ours, just as they are, and there's nothing you can do about that," Grand Madja used to say.

All I needed to do, then, was be patient until I understood what my father wanted, what was to become of us, and how we could improve if I myself participated in the effort.

Thus I had to manage as many African children must—in other words, live like the birds scratching about left and right and being just as happy as King Solomon was, according to the Bible. At the market I bargained long and hard over the prices of every item. I endeared myself to some of the saleswomen, who started to save additional pieces for me out of kindness and friendship. This way I managed to obtain some solid discounts, and with my little savings I would buy the clothes I needed secondhand. My stepmother must have thought that my father was spoiling me, and my father that his wife was being very good to me. And because they never had any time to discuss it, they never knew the truth. I went on living without either my father or my stepmother ever buying me anything at all. After the constantly increasing recriminations from Mam Naja, I understood that "he spent all his money on his party and on parties with his friends and mistresses while she alone went out of her way to keep the household going." I didn't know whether she included me in this household for which she so exerted herself.

12

Popular wisdom says that everything comes to those who wait. For some unknown reason, my father begins to show renewed interest in me, and although it takes a different form it's better than nothing. He takes a growing pleasure in introducing me to his old highly placed or affluent friends, as a way to reinforce their relationship. I especially remember the first and last on the long list of these introductions, no doubt because each marked a critical turning point in my life. Because of the first one I began to judge my father, see him as a sick man; and the last one convinced me that it was my stepmother who was at the root of my father's internal sickness. And so the first one signified a noteworthy evolution in my usual feelings of affection, tolerance, and incredible admiration, which I now attribute to my undue naiveté, my feelings, and my view of the world as inculcated by my grandmother's teachings. The last one unleashed my first impulses toward rebellion and the desire to fight with all my might against what I thereafter saw as an obstacle, even if that meant forgetting my grandmother's teachings, as long as I could change our life. The first to the last was merely a progressive, almost normal, and rather predictable development.

First introduction: An old, very red-faced, freckled Swiss man. He was a planter with acres and acres of coffee and cocoa beans not far from the city, houses with several stories at the center of his plantations, electricity, and running water—the ultimate in luxury at the time.

One night, invited by the old Swiss man to his very beautiful colonial house in town, my father takes me to dinner there. A red brick house with huge stones and a tile roof on a frame of rafters as massive as the trunks of young iroko trees. Here and there on the walls of the enormous living room are terrifying masks, hunting rifles, animal skins and heads, family photographs, and portraits of a young man in military uniform, probably the owner in his youth. There are also maps of Africa and Switzerland framed beneath glass, and beautifully dyed fabrics in heavy gilded frames, which in their own way tell the story of a man who has spent time in many places and knocked about a bit. All the furniture (armchairs, low tables, enormous armoires) are made of massive, slightly buffed and undecorated wood, giving the impression of power and weight and, at the same time, revealing that they have been handmade by people who like to do everything themselves.

After showing my father a chair to his left, the old gentleman invites me to take a seat in one of the enormous armchairs across from him, and for a very long time looks at me in silence. His gray-blue eyes, cold as steel, literally turn me to ice and make me feel as tiny and lost in the chair as in a coffin!

"Pretty, really very pretty, but perhaps too thin yet, no?"

I make myself even smaller. In the end they forget about me completely. The two of them spend what seems to me like an inordinate amount of time in the cold living room, emptying an entire bottle of alcohol as they discuss the family vineyards and wine cellars left behind in Switzerland, something that saddens them so deeply that at moments their voices almost break with stifled sobs.

Finally, we go into the dining room where immense posters of almost life-sized palm trees cover the walls, creating the illusion of being inside a palm grove. At least five giant irokos must have been cut down just to furnish this one house, made entirely of massive wood. Long, heavy, straight-backed benches and an endless table, about ten meters long and thirty centimeters thick, stand imposingly in the center of this "palm grove," flanked by two enormous sideboards placed like pillars at the gates of paradise—or hell, as I imagine them. The table is resplendently set with silver-plated cutlery and countless platters of food worthy of a banquet: pigeon, guinea hen, braised chicken and duck, sautéed sweet potatoes and bananas, salads, fruit, and several bottles of wine. I can't believe that all of this was prepared merely for our three modest stomachs.

Now as red as a grilled crawfish, the old gentleman seats me right beside him to his left, and my father around the corner of the table to his right, as if he wanted to keep him somewhat removed from me. He coughs incessantly, enough to crack his ribs, and turns even redder when he catches my eye, then tries hard to cough less.

Perhaps he has tuberculosis. I try in vain to find an answer in my father's eyes, but he's avoiding mine. Is he trying to put on an air of self-assurance? Then the old gentleman lights one cigarette after another, putting them out almost immediately. The ashtray fills up repeatedly, and the houseboy regularly comes by to empty it. My father picks up the conversation again.

"I still don't believe you'd really just abandon all of this."

"I told you, it's becoming untenable for me. These so-called patriots, overly ambitious as they are, ask nothing other than to replace their bosses. So they take out all their frustrations and bitterness on everyone else, without any differentiation or recognition. And I really don't feel like being a scapegoat for anyone. I've served this country for a quarter of a century now, investing all my intellectual and material resources without ever thinking about my native land. I think it's dishonest to judge everyone by one standard this way, and I truly don't need to be taught any lessons in nationalism by freeloaders who have no vision whatsoever for this country and who think they can get away with anything just because they were born here. That is the reason for my decision."

"In any case, you don't have a thousand alternatives," my father replied. Either you make the first move by dealing with a partner of your own choice, or that madman Bitchokè will take everything away from you. He's sure to find a way to either accuse you of something and have you deported, or to have you assassinated somehow."

"Don't talk to me about that monster, or you're going to spoil my evening, and I'm not particularly in the mood for that today. And don't worry about me, he can try anything he wants, he's not going to put his hands on my property. I know he'd like nothing better, and the best way for me to take revenge on him is to deprive him of that chance. He's already stolen everything from me, even my love for and faith in this country. Better to set everything on fire than let him have any part of it. That way I'll force him to pay for destroying my house."

"You'd better say 'all the houses' he has destroyed," my father says sharply, in a sudden rage that makes us all shudder and stops the conversation for a moment.

The old man looks back at me and brushes me lightly with his foot.

"Excuse me," I blurt out.

He begins to cough and light cigarettes again, putting them out one after another.

A moment later, when the supply is gone, he calls for his employee, but finds that he has quietly gone home. Extremely annoyed, the old man staggers up, determined to go and get more himself, but my father stops him and sends me in his place, without considering the lateness of the hour. I'm so afraid in this unfamiliar part of town that I run to the store as fast as I can. I run faster than I ever have before and am back so quickly that I catch them in a conversation that stops me in my tracks.

"You'll see, my dear Njokè, you won't lose in the exchange. True, your daughter is very pretty, she's a thoroughbred, and she pleases me a lot. I'm convinced she'd be the joy of my final days in my native Jura Mountains. She would always remind me of the sun here, and I wouldn't have many regrets. Still, don't tell me that the two coffee and cocoa plantations and the houses that come with them aren't enough."

"That's because you don't realize how dear my daughter is to me and how intelligent she is. You have no idea how much she can do for you that she wouldn't be doing for me any longer. This house and the cars in your parking lot must be part of the deal to make up for my loss."

"Let's not exaggerate; it's not a loss. I'm not going away to eat her alive, after all. She'll always be your daughter and within your reach. Think of the vacations you can come and spend with her, with us. Besides, you know perfectly well that I don't have much longer to live. If that turns out to be so, she'll be back with you in no time, and she can still be of use to you, with the new knowledge she's bound to gain over there if she is, indeed, as intelligent as you claim."

"My dear friend, in my opinion your offer is unacceptable, so let's not discuss it anymore."

"Fine, listen here! I can't give you this house or the three cars. The house is practically sold already. There will be many expenses connected with my resettlement in Switzerland and my health care. That's why I have already sold or promised to sell a number of things. But I do want to make an extra effort by throwing in the truck as well, which doesn't have a new owner yet. That is the best I can do, take it or leave it."

"Agreed, it's a deal. I . . ."

I cannot help making a sound, and they turn in my direction.

I come trotting in as if I have just arrived and hand my host the packages of cigarettes, making my traditional little curtsey, well-brought-up girl that I am. Then I sneak off to the toilet, claiming it's urgent. I am reeling. My father is bartering his daughter who, so he says, "is everything to him," without ever mentioning what the conditions for her welfare are. It's enough for him to acquire an old car, a plantation, and some houses, things he had already acquired on his own at another stage in his life. How his daughter is to live with a senile old man already on his last legs, what would become of her if he died, and who would protect her—none of this is of any concern to him. Suddenly I have no further doubts: He must have lost his mind; he is a sick man.

From that day on, I catch myself watching his reactions the way you watch the reactions of the family madman.

Oddly enough, we never speak about any of this. What is there to say, anyway? When would you bring it up? Where would you begin? What tone would you take? Life seemed to be moving faster and growing more cumbersome with every passing day.

I have to force myself to struggle, alone, for greater understanding and tolerance—the only option I have if I want to sustain some sort of balance; and in return, we maintain some semblance of family life. I'm wholly convinced that if I give this up, everything will explode.

Something new: On Sundays I go with my father and his elderly friend to his very beautiful and impressive estate. Before the two of them disappear into the plantations, my father gives me specific instructions concerning household tasks and cooking in a White man's home. Upon their return, they have a good time eating, drinking red wine, refining their moneymaking plans for the coffee and cocoa in a private system of direct exchange, which they want to establish with Switzerland. They rave about the profit they'll make after the country's pacification, and never talk about me anymore, as if my case were unquestionably arranged.

Maid from Monday through Saturday at my parents' house, on Sundays I am now the White man's maid.

Sunday evening I go back with my father. We stop at the house of Adèle, a fat woman with many children, two of whom are mixed-race. She serves my father a copious meal, which she surely spent all day preparing. Then he goes to her bedroom with her and spends a good bit of time in there while I play with the children in the courtyard. We don't come home until very late. Mam Naja always makes nasty remarks, and just as systematically my father beats her up and throws her on the bed, slamming the door in my little brothers' face. Her sobs wear away at my heart like the tapping of water drops eroding a rock. In the end we always hear my father's voice become more gentle.

"Please, stop crying now! Look—I didn't want to hurt you. But you really exasperate me with your stupid scenes. Come on, come now. . . ."

The sobs grow less intense and less syncopated. Then we hear her hoarse voice: "What spell is it that makes you forget our love, my darling? Whose spell is it? Tell me who you're spending all your time with now, and I'll find a medicine man to release you from her permanently. It's so wonderful when you're your old self again."

"And whatever makes you think there's someone else? Do you feel I'm losing my strength or that I'm less attentive than before?"

"No, my darling. You're wholly with me, close and so marvelous, my loooooove. . . . But I don't know why you change like this! Are you sure you're not bewitched?"

"Me? Never! Why wouldn't you be the one who's bewitched? Don't you see that you're the one who's changed, who's always making scenes, complaining all the time, as if I weren't enough for you anymore?"

"Never in my life, my darling! How can you doubt me like this, doubt us, doubt our love? Have you forgotten our vows?"

This is followed by all kinds of mewing in every tone of voice, until finally snoring takes over. Mondays and Tuesdays are relatively calm and peaceful, as if they are still lethargic after Sunday night's passion. On Wednesday nights Mam Naja takes my little brothers and me to Kingdom Hall, to the Jehovah's Witnesses, as if to ward off the misfortune that won't be long in coming to poison the week. Sometimes she even manages to convince my father to come along with us!

13

At Kingdom Hall you learn about a really strange God, a God who needs humans to bear witness to other people about his grandeur and kindness, as if they themselves might not be affected directly by his presence. The very intolerant way in which these "witnesses" speak in his name—my parents first and foremost—seems very far removed from the image of the immanent, immensely magnanimous God my grandfather used to tell me about.

At Kingdom Hall, we run into my mother and Tata Roz. They exchange venomous looks with Mam Naja during the obligatory greetings between "fraters" and "sistas" that always close the meetings. I wonder whether they scratch the palms of each other's hands the way little girls do when the teacher forces them to shake hands after they've had a fight and are whipped in punishment.

One day, when Mam Naja is on duty, my father agrees to drive the little ones and me there alone. My mother grabs the opportunity to come and play her own Naja role in the presence of Tata Roz. Their necks swell with such vituperative words directed at their "sista" that I wonder what they're actually bearing witness to.

"Hey, Brother Njokè, always on duty on Bible study day, isn't she, that midwife-wife of yours? What a recurring coincidence, don't you think?" my mother insinuates.

"Coincidence, or is it by design, so she can be free to meet the man who runs the Forest Service and who just happens to be Bit-chokè's younger brother?" Tata Roz quickly adds. "He picks the most select women, cuckolds their husband, and gets away with it, knowing full well that nobody would dare attack the younger brother of the most terrifying of the ultra-powerful, certainly not a 'frater' Jehovah's Witness. So your wife goes off to see him quite shamelessly, while everyone laughs at you. And to top it all off, I'm sure that hypocrite claims to be a 'sista' only to prevent Naja from getting her husband back, since she knows that a true 'sista' Jehovah's Witness would never try anything like that to hurt another."

"Drop it," my mother says. "God is watching and surely has found a solution already: Bitchokè's sister-in-law has decided to make her pay, and has told the whole town about the loose whore that hides behind her nurse's uniform. She says she'll send a bailiff to catch them in the act. It's only because of the shame that will come down on your head, Brother Njokè, that I come to pray God to stop her from keeping up this masquerade. I really wish none of this had ever happened."

My father puts on his most derisive air: "You think I'd feel humiliated because a woman lets herself be taken by just anyone? Isn't that what every woman does? Isn't that what you yourselves have done and keep doing? I sure hope you're not expecting to push me into some stupid confrontation this way, because I really have better things to do!"

He tells us to follow him and leaves the two women standing there, the wind taken out of their sails.

That evening at the dinner table, in the most offhand manner, my father tells my stepmother straight out what my mother and Tata Roz had said, word for word. She goes into a wild rage, protesting up and down, and in declaring: "Poor gossipmongers! They've nothing better to do than to go peddling their disgusting imagination. What I really feel sorry for is your ex-wife's lack of personality. At her age she still needs her older sister to give her yamlike existence something resembling stature. How sad!"

My father howls with laughter. That is when I begin to understand that he probably already knew the story, a plausible explanation for his recent behavior. In my eyes he has nothing but contempt
left for women, and I, undoubtedly, am part of that group! The idea
is repugnant to me.

Yet, if the truth be known, each of my two mothers gives me
the distinct feeling they're as dangerous as a bona fide *naja* serpent.
Sure, one secretly gives me doughnuts and French toast that she
makes especially for me, hoping to persuade me to choose her side
at the next court session, as my other sisters do. The other one
speaks to me only when she gives orders, like a mistress to her servant. The doughnuts are sweet, but not sweet enough to help me
swallow the slanderous words that always come first. They almost
leave me with the same impression of harshness as the other one's
indifference. I'm beginning to see too many comparable traits in my
two mothers, Naja. I think I understand why their own mothers
gave them the same name: Naja, "Fear."

I'm starting to feel truly sorry for these "sistas," and once again
I'm uncomfortable inside my female skin.

Why is it that women must always tear each other apart because
of men? Men, after being with the same woman another man has
had, just go on thinking about the future—like the Swiss man and
my father, who each had his turn with Adèle, and those after Bitchokè had her, if I have that straight.

Why couldn't my two mothers have a trusting conversation and
come up with a joint strategy for my father and the children? Was it
because no one had ever educated them at all on this topic? Still,
Grand Madja, the mother-in-law to each of them, was extremely
voluble when it came to advice on female strategy toward what she
called "the innate instability and irresponsibility of men": "Man is
born unstable and therefore very weak; foolishly, it's our society that
makes him conceited, because it insists on his being strong and taking care of women at any cost. Women are naturally responsible for
life. If they'd take that role on conscientiously, they could settle their
problems in solidarity with one another instead of fighting because

of men's inborn instability, and then they would shape a different breed of men."

They were not aware how they foolishly harmed themselves by creating such a petty atmosphere around their children. As those "by nature responsible for life," did they ever think of the psychological impact of their behavior on their offspring's future? Did women even have time left to think that way? Were they not too busy now, with unanticipated new circumstances, which demanded they prove their professional competence as well? Who would pay the price for this new battle? The children—which is to say, the future of all life, without any doubt.

SONG 7

A naked Master covered in clay,
A serene Mother quite comfortable inside her skin,
A clear-sighted and kindly guide,
A rigorous priestess brave of heart
From whose gaze sorcerers and liars flee.
Dignitaries grow ashamed inside their clothes before her nudity,
And the sages the shame of their knowledge before her madness.
My Master, my Guide, my Mother, my Priestess Némy,
Némy the naked madwoman, her body soaked with clay,
My first question mark on Nothingness and Chaos,
The point of departure toward personal experience with Divinity.

• • •

It was then that I realized something was moving around in my belly, kicking me now on the left and then again on the right side. Suddenly my breasts had grown larger. I wondered in which of my two mothers I should confide. They were so busy radiating fear that they didn't notice the physical and mood changes in me, so that neither of them would be able to try to comfort me, at least about the movement inside, which I couldn't for the life of me explain.

I figured that my mother, my aunt, or my stepmother, and perhaps all three, had sent me the *hu*, the malevolent thing, a kind of contagious evil spirit that is passed on to children to turn them into sorcerers. It wouldn't surprise me, considering the dark thoughts that more and more frequently entered my mind when I was in touch with my mothers. I needed to get back to my grandparents, or else find someone to purge me.

As I was waiting for this to happen, a person came to Kingdom Hall one day whom I shall always consider a great master, who allowed me to question myself more seriously about God and his creatures, and begin to recognize what Grand Pa Helly used to call "a complete being, better than a man, better than a woman."

She came to Kingdom Hall completely naked, her hair thickly coated with red clay. While all the "fraters" and "sistas" prayed to their father who is in heaven, she entered soundlessly and stood right at the center of the lectern, her hands stretched out to the side, gazing toward heaven. When the people opened their eyes after saying their "amen," she was there like a vision, the revelation of the God whom they had invoked. For an interminable moment, they all stood there gaping; then one of the brothers began to choke with rage.

"Back with you, satanic devil, in the name of Christ the Savior! You'll be thrown down into the deepest abyss for a thousand years, and God has said that you will never leave there again."

"My name is not Satan; my name is Némy. Calm down, poor brother. You may be troubled for no reason. God may have spoken those words, but that was a very long time ago. Since then he must have changed his mind. What do you expect? He created life and human beings, who evolve with such speed that he himself is forced to change as well, or else his creatures might reach a point when they surpass him. So let's calm down. I've come to wish you a fine day, my brothers, and may God bless you."

She lowered her arms to bless the bewildered crowd. My mother Naja moved forward with a *pagne* to cover Némy's nudity and gently pulled her outside, with me closely behind them. Once outside my mother said: "Goodbye, my sister. Keep the *pagne* for the next time you want to come again."

"Goodbye, my daughter, but take back your *pagne*. There is no *pagne* that can hide the poison that we exude—that's secreted through every hole in our body. Do you think that the *pagne* you're wearing now prevents me from seeing the fear, the hate, and the confusion that grip you? If you were to present yourself naked before God, he might bring you some relief. Go, my daughter, and don't worry about me."

My mother brought her hand to her face and began to weep.

"That's right, yes, weep a little; it will make you feel better."

And she went away. I was hesitating between consoling my mother and running after the naked madwoman. The latter won out. After wandering around for several kilometers she suddenly turned around and asked: "Why are you following me? What do you want from me?"

Throughout the long walk, I had never even asked myself that question; my thoughts were suspended in time, and I was really caught off guard. I needed to come up with an answer, if only for myself: "I. . . . There's something walking around inside my belly. Since you can see what's behind *pagnes*, can you tell me if it's the *hu*?"

"Absolutely not. He wouldn't find any room inside you or, at least, he wouldn't feel very comfortable there. You are too much of a visionary and too open."

"Open? Then tell me what this is."

"A baby, surely."

"A baby? But that's impossible."

"Why? You're not sterile."

"I'm just a child, and I don't have a husband yet."

"Well, then, it must be one of the three."

"Three what?"

"Either the Holy Father, the Holy Son, or the Holy Spirit."

At the word *father* I stand rooted to the spot as a massive veil of naiveté is ripped apart before my eyes. I leave a world of blissful certainties to walk straight into the world of excruciating questions screaming for answers. And not one of the dozens of questions that are stuck in my throat, unable to leave my lips, seems to settle the very first question I have: How can a blood transfusion be transformed into a baby?

No doubt because that blood was deposited in the belly.
My father had the wrong point of transfusion
or else was wrong about the thing to be transfused.
Perhaps he deposited a child instead of his blood.

Maybe, though, the child and the blood are one and the same thing. Maybe blood placed in a belly automatically makes a child. In that case, my father had to have known! But then, was this allowed? Did a father have the right to do such a thing to his daughter, even if she was adopted? Had the famous ritual transfusion been nothing but an enormous lie, intended to give a baby to me instead of my mother, and thereby force me to stay with him? What about the ritual oath—was that just intended to keep me silent? Were we about to catch the disease of incest?

The memory of a ritual to treat incest suddenly comes back to me from way back when I was seven, at the dawn of a distant morning, the earliest hours of daybreak.

Drums yank me out of bed. I run to the river, where the sound is coming from. I come upon a scene that stuns me; slumped on the hillside I am voicelessly present.

A crowd stands in a circle around a cousin of one of my father's three wives. She is completely naked and awkwardly tries to hide her nudity with her hands. Dressed in red, the medicine man unleashes an ugly, mangy dog from a shrub where he lay sleeping, and ties it to the poor girl's nude body.

Drums and bells invite everyone to a war dance.

The voices howl more than they sing:

"Dog, take your bitch,
Take your bitch
And let go of our daughter.

A dog knows neither his mother nor his sister,
But the child of mankind is fully able
To differentiate his mother and sister from all other women.
Dog, take your bitch and take your paws off our daughter,
Leave our daughter pure."

How shameful to see them gazing upon a naked woman
Attached to a dog that thrashes about
On top of her as she struggles back,
Both of them linked by terror alone.

I notice Aunt Roz close to the medicine man, her eyes wild as if she were drunk. I feel such shame that I would die if anyone saw me watching all this. I run back to the house and almost knock down Grand Madja, who's coming out of her kitchen. She holds me very tightly in her arms because I'm shaking like a leaf. All my body's tears cry out at her, letting out my anger at what appears to me as collective malice and cruelty, like a dreadful nightmare.

"Explain! I want to understand why you allow such horror to take place and let Aunt Roz be present there. You, who always tell us that we must flee from wickedness as from a monster, for it is the primary energy of sorcery—you uphold such humiliations done to a woman like yourself, one of your own granddaughters. Don't you see that you're supporting sorcery, too?"

"Calm down, my little namesake. Now then, I understand you're beside yourself with rage. You see that I can't bear watching such things, and that's why I'm here and not over there with everyone else. If you think that I'm able to stop this ritual, you attribute more power to me than I have. Since time immemorial our people have practiced this, and they find their own explanations and reasons to justify it."

"Well! Fine! I'm listening, Grand Madja."

"After all, it does no more than shed light on what people do in the dark, and it's a good thing to look it right in the face. Don't think that what is obviously ugly in the light is any less so in the dark. If you find them ugly in the light, there's no point in doing them in the dark. This girl was convicted of incest. By sleeping with her brother she behaved like a bitch, and it's only normal that they make her sleep with a dog in public; dogs know no shame and make love publicly, even with their own mothers."

"But she isn't a dog. . . ."

"That's why she must cleanse herself of this shame in public, and together with that public, discover the horror and shame of her act. In public and with them, she will become human once again. Then they'll untie the dog. They will take care of her and, with her, the whole community. I guarantee you that after rituals such as these there will be no more incest in the community for at least two or three generations! So it's well worth the trouble, don't you think?"

"But Grand Madja, how do they know that she actually committed incest with her brother? Did someone see them?"

"Nobody has to stand behind us to supervise and prevent us from violating the most sacred taboos of our tribe. Our spirit should be our only guide and our own judge. Just remember that if you do something shameful in the dark, sooner or later it will be uncovered and seen in the bright light of day. As for this woman, she has just lost a third child in the same way: Her babies don't fall ill, but their four limbs swell up and gradually grow cold until they die. It's the irrefutable, the unquestionable sign of incest. She really had to confess, for otherwise she wouldn't be taken care of and not one of her children would ever survive."

"And where is the brother who committed this act with her? Doesn't he have to share the humiliation? Or are men exempt from it?"

"No, nobody is or can be exempt from the shame of his actions. But her brother died a few years ago."

With appalling accuracy, the mere word "incest" brought back images that had been entirely erased from my memory.

This is when I felt my first profound panic—the kind that stops your heart, anesthetizes you, gives you amnesia. And, with an instinct for survival, it was the very first time that I sensed in myself a feeling of duplicity: I had the firm belief that, seen from this perspective, this thing inside my belly wouldn't make either my mother or my stepmother happy, or my father for that matter, and that I must absolutely cover it up and persist in keeping it a secret.

But who would help me now, counsel me about what to do? The madwoman Némy, certainly. I look back at her. She is gone.

I don't know where I am anymore. I roam the city all night long and don't get back to the house until early morning. My father is standing on the terrace, ostensibly worried.

"Where are you coming from at this hour?" he asks me curtly.

"From the house of the Swiss man," I say coolly.

"That old crook! He helps himself without having finalized our agreement!" and without any further questions he goes grumbling back into the house. Phew!

14

"Don't ever eat a panther's skin, it's taboo," Grand Pa Helly, my very great husband, always told me. "If you eat the panther's skin you'll catch mange."

"Why?" I'd ask him every time, but he wouldn't answer.

One day he finally told me: "The panther is the cruelest of all wild animals. If one could call any animal a murderer, that would be the one. We're afraid that the marks of what is too sordid will stick to our skin, and that's why we avoid eating the skin of frogs and many other ugly animals whose flesh is delicious, nevertheless. So, I think that all the aversion attached to the panther's skin to set up the taboo just indicates our denial of the ugliness that lies behind some things, even when they're as beautiful and fascinating as the skin of the panther. Unfortunately, gluttony always leads some people to violate the taboo."

You, whose every physical and mental aspect is so ravenous,
Tell yourself there is no taboo of the unknown,
Turn your fiery temperament toward every good and unknown thing that
    tempts you, even if it means that you may be unexpectedly tainted.
At least you'll open the realm of experiences for your people.
But you're wasting time if you allow yourself to be tempted by taboos
    that have already been established.

The violation of a taboo is extremely harmful, and kills slowly and treacherously. Sometimes, through the sheer desire to convince your conscience there's nothing wrong, you forget. And you certainly won't catch mange or leprosy on the same day that you eat the panther's skin.

The first mange or the first leprous spot that appears after the surreptitious eating of a panther is always so concealed, so unlikely. You don't link it to your original act. Time passes, and you forget. And then you blame your neighbor's liniment, which you borrowed the night before, or the heat, or the brambles, or whatever else.

After our violation of the taboo, it is Némy the madwoman who reveals the first sign of mange.

It happens the first time that my father and I go to Kingdom Hall without all three of my little brothers. Mam Naja has said that she has an emergency at the hospital, but the oldest of the little ones clings to her so tightly that her husband tells her to take him along, and we will keep the other two.

As we are leaving the service, mad Némy stands rooted in front of the door, still naked and muddy like a pig after rolling in the mire. Ever since her first nude appearance at Kingdom Hall, and the way in which my mother had dealt with the incident, everyone has opted not to speak with her. Some greet her inconspicuously and carefully skirt her as they leave. Others retreat to the back of the hall in the hope that she will go away on her own and thereby clear the exit. I wait to see my father's reaction. He stands up and says: "Let's go, the children are hungry, and so am I. Move over, Némy, I'm in a hurry."

"Too late," Némy answers. "What had to happen to keep you from eating tonight and perhaps for several days has already happened. When people should hurry up and act to avoid the unforgivable, they're never in a rush. In earlier days, someone who claimed to be a true Lôs would take power and change the world. And since the chief should set the example, he became a flower to inspire his people with the desire to pick flowers. He became a cloud to force his people to look up, or a jewel to make them love beauty. But you, who call yourself a Lôs—what did you expect when you used the looters of this town instead? No doubt you're waiting for them to finish gnawing away at the dignity of all this country's people, aren't you? Sullying your family, too, and even breeding with them? Well now, that was done a long time ago, and yet you weren't in any rush to react. All that was missing was the cry of your blood, wasn't it? Well, you poor cuckold, Lôs of my ass, it is here now! Really, you shouldn't leave this place before saying nine Ave Marias first."

"You've got the wrong church, Némy. Get out of the way or else. . . ."

"Or else what, you pathetic man? I feel especially sorry for the men and women of this country, these washed-up people who accept everything without rebelling against adulterous chiefs and notorious sorcerers, who have nothing but the dismal land they deserve. What are you all waiting for, to publicly reject these mealy-mouthed Lôs, to tell them the true reason for your refusal to cooperate? What are you waiting for, to throw them out, deny these spreaders of discord, these embezzlers of the heritage who proclaim their supreme indifference to the future, and allow themselves to humiliate the earth itself, deep down to its very roots. Come on, help me, you band of cowards—throw this worthless Njokè on the ground so I can spank him properly."

To the great glee of everyone there, she grabs my father, clearly determined to give him a spanking; but he merely picks her up like a feather and carries her outside, where he gently puts her down. She begins to laugh wildly, pointing to my father's now mud-spattered white shirt. He pretends to chase after her, and she bolts, still laughing. All his "fraters" and "sistas" laugh as well, which doesn't exactly please my father, who quickly hauls us off.

He insists on going by the hospital, to pick up my little brother in case Mam Naja is still on duty. I follow him reluctantly because it's a considerable detour, and with the small plump boy on my back, really. . . .

An unusually large crowd at the hospital entrance catches our eye. We quicken our pace, our hearts tight with fear without quite knowing why. A woman recognizes my father, lets out an awful scream, and then faints. The onlookers recognize us, move aside, and we find my little brother lying at the bottom of the main stairs, blood trickling from the corner of his mouth, the right side of his skull crushed. He must have fallen on his head from the top of the banister, which he loved to clamber up on; someone must have turned him over when they found him. The midwife on duty is uttering puppylike squeals.

"His mother brought him to me to watch, but I had a patient in the room. I actually forgot about him. My God, my God," she keeps wailing incessantly.

"Where is she?" my father shouts.

"I have no idea. Probably where she usually goes. . . ."

"Where's that, for God's sake! Where? Speak!" my father shrieks as he grasps the poor midwife by the hair.

"I'm telling you, I have no idea."

My father charges out, and some men race after him, begging him to come back. Then what happens? My memory recreates nothing for me but short vignettes:

• People sit beneath an enormous veranda that is unfamiliar to me, around the small body wrapped in a sheet and placed on a huge bed.

• The police commissioner has a private conversation with the midwife under a flickering light bulb.

• The rooster crows and I look for Mam Naja in the crowd, but it's no use. The silence weighs heavily, and the night seems endless.

• Some men motion to the commissioner, who gets up and runs out, followed by the men, although no one else moves.

• We're glued to our seats. I hear snoring.

I must have fallen asleep! I wake up at home in bright daylight, my two little brothers crying with hunger. My daily grind takes over, and I think I've had a nightmare. Surely Mam Naja had another night shift and will soon be home with the oldest of the three, and I should make sure that her breakfast is warm and ready for her.

But she doesn't come. I stay there with the children, not even daring to go to the neighbors or the hospital, afraid to have to face the reality of my nightmare. I stay there for three days and two nights without any relative coming to see how the living are doing. Without anyone else thinking of coming to inquire after us. I can't believe it! What if my parents never come home? What if I were sick and couldn't get up to open the door and take care of the little ones? What if we had no provisions, as so often happened? Could we possibly die of solitude, right here, in the heart of the civil servants' residential quarter, just because everyone else is busy with her own affairs? They are party to some serious negligence. In this new atmosphere, traditions, too, seem to have gone underground!

I don't know why, but my conscience linked the loss of my little brother to the words of Grand Pa Helly about the panther's skin, and to those of mad Némy. Under these circumstances, his death seemed to herald a veritable scourge. But my father didn't approach it the same way, or else he would have reacted, and taken measures to protect us. Unfortunately, instead it seemed more that he was going numb. He was now continually seen in the presence of Bitchokè, participating in his political propaganda, and in bars where they went for their frequent alcoholic binges.

Everything seemed clear to me: Since the taboo that I didn't dare name anymore had been violated, this was the punishment, which had now begun to make itself felt. If my father wasn't going to do anything to purify us, he would inevitably dive down into the depths of the hell he had initiated and perhaps even die.

According to the logic of Grand Madja's teachings, my father would soon be deprived of any great motivation, his creativity would stagnate and fade, and the power he had accumulated until now would be turned against him and against all those who loved him. But hadn't it always been like this since his childhood? Perhaps he was born that way, and his quest for the Lôs power was precisely the same as his desperate desire to reverse the hazy direction of his life.

But, "he who associates with pigs always ends up by falling with his nose in the mire" as Grand Madja also said. There was no choice but to conclude that since my father had "fallen under the spell," as he himself described it, of the predator Bitchokè, he was foundering more and more, slithering into a kind of character disintegration. True, considerations of good and evil had never been his strong point; but never before had he paid so little heed to his own dignity, and been so lacking in personal and passionate goals as to waste time in endless wandering. It occurred to me that his relationship with the man who ceaselessly killed and violated sacred taboos was hastening what I thought of as my father's "moral degradation." In any event, something had already defused his search for the true Lôs power; in my humble opinion, he was forsaking the destiny he had begun to forge as a a builder. Now I thought he was merely turning into an "indecisive dreamer," an expression that Grand Pa Helly often used in reference to his son, and that I finally seemed to understand.

I wondered what I could possibly do at least to lessen this misfortune, if not wipe it out altogether—I, who didn't even know exactly what had happened on that day. All I could do was pray.

Even now, after all this time, I still don't know exactly what had happened. My parents came home in silence on the fourth night and didn't talk to each other for several days. A woman at the market told me: "Your father was right to beat up that presumptuous Forest Service man, who thinks he can get away with anything just because he's a cousin of that thief Bitchokè. But he should actually whip Bitchokè himself. It's because of him and people like him that our ancestors have turned their backs on us. It's a pity there's no other, more powerful Lôs with a kinder disposition to oust him and give some hope back to this region. Well, his arrogance has taken a beating, at least, if only because someone had the nerve to punch his cousin in public. From now on your stepmother can keep her superior airs under her skirts, since the whole town knows she was caught red-handed in the act of adultery and is pregnant as well, while her abandoned child cracks his skull!"

Later I learned that my little brother was buried in the municipal cemetery and that the veranda was part of the house of my Uncle Kon, who had just been named as prefect and who'd had the funeral moved to his home to stand by my father in his ordeal.

15

Months went by—rough and disturbing months.

The old Swiss man died very suddenly, without having had the time to carry through on his verbal contract with my father. A distant nephew arrived from Switzerland and put the whole property up for sale to the highest bidder. Bitchokè offered more than anyone else, even more than a minister who came from the capital city, which must have made the old man turn over in his grave, while my father protested: "That Bitchokè is really getting on my nerves, and one day I'll lose control and . . . let's hope that God won't ever let that happen, because it'll be a disaster!"

Farewell to the Sundays on the plantation. Farewell to the escapades and meals at fat Adèle's with her swarm of kids. Perhaps my father even left her with a tenth one in her belly.

Mam Naja has gained at least twenty pounds since I arrived, and her belly is simply massive. I'm forced to prepare separate salt-free meals for her. My father no longer beats her, and her sniveling has stopped.

As for me, I've plumped up a bit and am beginning to look like a woman, but I still can't believe I'm pregnant. Besides, no one pays any attention or speaks of it. A twelve-year-old girl is blossoming a little early, but in our family that's normal, so apparently nothing strange is going on.

• • •

My Uncle Kon's new position as prefect seemed to have produced renewed hope and fresh energy among the population. At the market I heard the word "rebirth" used for the first time in the women's songs. There was talk of the courage required for reconciliation, and the Bon Ba Long, the Children of the Land, were mentioned once again. People were asked to persuade their families to leave the resistance and register with the new party of national conscience, whereupon all else would be forgotten.

The new prefect was coolly solidifying his reputation as the "converter of the resisters," to my father's great exasperation. He called him a traitor.

"Must there always be someone in the family to stand in the way of my vision and destiny as a Lôs? What sort of peace with the resistance does my cousin have in mind? They're lying in ambush and have just one thought in their head: Stab us Lôs in the back because we can substantiate their panic, their cowardice, and above all because we remind them of the bad political choice they've made."

My father would shake with fury when he talked about it.

The new leadership created posters showing the steps to be taken toward rehabilitation and placed them on the big square to help obliterate the photographs of decapitated heads. They planted trees and flowers, too. They said that the influence of the Lôs's terror was disappearing already, because all they were doing now was drinking in bars and nostalgically discussing the past. There was talk also of the "legality" of their behavior—what they were and were not allowed to do, and the boundaries they ought not to cross in their hunt for resisters.

Some spoke of victory, but they didn't know over whom. All they knew was that the Great Resistance Fighter had been brought down, although to everyone's deep distress not by the expected Bitchokè, or any other supposed Lôs, for that matter. Every one of the people maintained strict silence, as if they wanted to remain unnoticed. The women's songs insisted that their Mpôdôl wasn't dead, but waiting for the reconciliation of his brothers and sisters in all the camps so that he could luminously reappear and continue to serve and develop his country. Everything would gradually come back to order without the Lôs, to the latter's great dismay.

Unfortunately, something inevitably pushes the powerful to extremes. Apparently, power does not readily adapt to a harmonious existence. As soon as one power seems to achieve some measure of harmony, someone emerges to launch the action that will humiliate the defeated and rekindle feelings of antagonism—and then it begins all over again!

An ill-advised counselor made my uncle decide to go on an official visit to Bitchokè's stronghold and convince the people in his power that he no longer stood for anything. The news was even transmitted through the national press and on the radio, with commentaries that treated the Lôs as "small worn-down spears" and "aged roosters." Jeeps came from the capital to enhance the luster of this "New-Style State Visit." Flags were flying everywhere, even in the palm and coconut trees.

That day my father didn't leave in the morning, as was his wont. After washing up and dressing, he unfolded his chaise and settled down on the terrace in front of the house. He had just gotten comfortable with a newspaper, a fashion catalogue, and a calendar—I told myself he must be looking for samples of clothes and a pretty name for the coming baby. He'd asked for a bowl of warm milk and some bread. I had gone into the inner courtyard to attend to my usual chores, and had just about forgotten he was there when I heard him scream! I rushed over. . . .

• Some neighbors are already gathering!

• Mam Naja is on her knees next to my father, trying to calm him down and hold onto him.

• Civil servants in our neighborhood, suddenly returned as if fleeing a catastrophe, offer incoherent and contradictory explanations, and everyone is talking at the same time.

• The upshot of it all is that the new prefect, my Uncle Kon, was found murdered in Bitchokè's house, where he had spent the night during his tour of the region.

"No doubt he was killed by the last of those disgraceful, hateful resisters, who wanted to sabotage the honor the prefect himself was doing Bitchokè!" the partisans of the Lôs suggested. "Indeed, to show the respect due to a patriot and an ultra-powerful to boot, the prefect chose Monsieur Bitchokè's home as the official residence for his honorable mission." "Who is to say that it wasn't Bitchokè himself who assassinated the prefect in cold blood in his own home, so that the 'sons of the people' would be crushed, relentlessly slaughtered in the resistance forces as well as at home, while the others get away with it?" the partisans of the resistance fighters volunteered.

One of the market women, who thinks it her duty to come and tell my father the news herself, says: "Whoever they are, this time they've gone too far, and we've had enough of their violence! The prefect died with his eyes open, and the image of his assassin is imprinted on his retina."

"They say that a photographer is on the way to get a hold of that portrait and enlarge it. They'll be exposed yet, those villains," another woman adds.

My father starts to shriek like a madman again, as undone by his cousin's death as by the suspicion that weighs on his almost-friend: "They're all the same, they're all scum, Bitchokè as well as the resisters! But I'll take it upon myself to clear the earth of whoever is found guilty or is even an accomplice in my cousin's death, and that will benefit the entire human race!" my father yells.

Perhaps he is having a vision of Bitchokè as a rival, or of Bitchokè's cousin, the presumed father of the child inside Mam Naja's belly; or perhaps he wants very much to be free from the stranglehold that she, crouching at his feet, has on him, undeniably delaying his mission as avenger and savior. No one will ever know what image it was that unleashed his destructive energy.

With lightning speed, my father shoots a violent kick into his wife's lower belly. Like an earthworm she twists on the ground in pain before losing consciousness. Astonished at his own violence, he immediately calms down and begs the people to help him get her to the maternity clinic.

Petrified with fear and incomprehension, I let the crowd literally drag me off to the clinic, where I collapse behind the chair of the head midwife, whom they all affectionately call Matron Chris. Transfixed, I keep an eye on the whole labor process. After what seems like an eternity to me, a large, completely limp newborn comes into the world, after which Mam Naja utters a long scream— a scream similar to what I imagine the last cry before death to be. She faints a second time. Again, my memory restores only its frozen images to me, some of them accelerated, others in slow motion:

• The big dead newborn weighs ten pounds, according to the scale. Mucus oozes from its mouth.

• My father beats his head against the wall for so long that I'm amazed it doesn't explode before the nurse manages to quiet him down.

• My father wraps the big newborn in a towel, then in bonded paper, and takes the package out. On the way he greets people as if nothing were wrong. In his hands the package looks like a bag of yams. He puts it on the back of a bicycle and heads toward the house, riding as slowly and naturally as possible.

• I follow him at a distance, my lower belly hurting as if I were the one he had kicked.

• Suddenly, at the edge of our neighborhood, my father turns off and takes the path toward the bush.

• The weatherman watches him leave and checks his watch. What time could it be? Is it morning or evening? I have no idea.

• I take the same road, but lose sight of my father. I walk through the bush aimlessly, unaware of my movements and thoughts.

• My father almost knocks me over on his return. When I see his tear-filled eyes, he smacks me.

• I hurt for him and cry with him, but also from the unbearable pain in my lower belly, which I can't handle anymore except by hugging it with both hands.

• My father helps me up on the back of his bicycle, the same place where the big newborn was before, and takes me back to the maternity clinic.

• Mam Naja snores in her sleep in the recovery room, and Chris, the midwife, has almost finished cleaning up the place. She looks at me holding my belly and turns to my father:

"Njokè, you're not going to tell me you also kicked your daughter in the belly, are you?"

"Oh no, really now! That's what worries me. I don't know what her problem is. Maybe the shock was too great for her, and now she thinks that she's the one I hit. Why don't you take her into another room and try to calm her down?"

In the delivery room, where there is no further sign of the previous birth, Chris notices that my dress is wet and that I'm shaking all over. She asks me to lie down on the table for a quick examination. Surprise!

"Well, I never! Your waters broke and you're about to give birth. So you were pregnant as well, and didn't even know it. Do your parents know? My God, what a family, what a day!"

I remember Grand Madja's scornful laughter when women cried during their delivery and I hold back my screams deep down in my throat.

"Push, little Halla, push! Good job, you're a very brave girl. Push one more time. There we are. . . ."

Chris catches a tiny little infant, cuts the umbilical cord, and, holding it by the feet with its head down, shakes the baby vigorously. It thrashes wildly and finally utters barely audible little sounds. She puts it on the scale.

I can't help crying out when I have another contraction, stronger than any of the earlier ones. Chris comes running.

"Easy, easy now, you're not going to cry over the placenta when you were so brave while the baby came out. Wait, let me help you. . . ."

She presses my belly in a downward motion, and I push as hard as I can.

"Incredible, you've got twins in that little belly of yours! Well, there are plenty of mysterious things going on in your house, that's for sure."

Utterly exhausted, I close my eyes for a moment. When I open them again I see my father in intense conversation with the midwife: "I'm so sorry, Njokè, it's a bad day for you! This one was stillborn. There was nothing I could do."

"It's all right, Chris, I'll deal with it. It's not your fault. You take care of the living; I'll be back."

• On the scale the tiny infant is still fluttering its limbs.

• My father wraps up the stillborn child the same way as before, and leaves again.

• Chris brings me to the ancient shower after helping me with the expulsion of the placenta. She washes and bandages me, then helps me get dressed again.

"Rest a little, right here in my office. I'll take care of the baby and then I'll be back to help you into your bed."

• My eyes, my mouth, and even my heart are dry. I'm unable to weep. I'm unable to speak. I feel nothing.

• Still, I cannot stay still. I get up and go to the delivery room. Just as I'm about to cross the threshold, I freeze in place: Mam Naja is bending over the baby, looking at it in bewilderment and talking to the midwife. . . .

"Chris, how's this possible! My huge belly and nothing but this little mouse inside? I can't get over it! It must be my mother's fury that blew me up like that, there's no doubt. And a boy, to boot. I thought it would be a girl this time; she'd have my mother's name, and I could have appeased her that way, get her to understand me and forgive me for my stubbornness. Now I don't know what to do anymore."

The midwife wants to say something, but Mam Naja interrupts her.

"Too bad, eh, Chris? I'll give my little boy my mother's name anyway. When he's grown perhaps it will be fashionable to have genderless names, and he'll thank me for it; or else he can just change it. For now, and to avoid any curse, we don't have any other choice, do we my little Guerredelies! That's quite pretty, and fits you like a glove!"

Unbeknownst to me, my father has been standing behind me; he, too, has heard the strange baptism. He goes into the room, closing the door in my face, then comes back out almost immediately with the midwife, whom he preremptorily takes to her office.

She comes back a few moments later and tells me: "Your father is waiting for you outside to go get the baby's clothes. Give me enough time, at least, to tend to the infant!"

I did not go back to the clinic again. My father brought me to his fat Adèle, who took care of me for three weeks to remove any trace of the birth. He made Mam Naja believe that he had sent me to the village with the good news of her delivery! And she believed him.

Thus, that Sunday only one birth was registered at the clinic, and only one assassination in the town's death records.

16

In my mother tongue, the woman who loses her husband is Yik (widow), literally meaning "forsaken." With a slight intonational change, one can hear it as "who knew or thought she knew."

The man who loses his wife is Nkus (widower), "moulting," or with a slight intonational change, "wealth."

What a strange difference in these two states—but no matter! They exist, for sure, since they have been named.

The child who loses one or both of his parents is Man Nyu (orphan), which means "child of the body," without any other nuance, to indicate the absence of the *mbu*, or soul that gave him life. Nonetheless, he exists as the child of a communal or social body—an environment, in any case. He has a status that has been thought of and named, and therefore he exists.

The parent who has lost a child has no name, not in any language that I know. Either that parent's status is so special and so grievous that people chose to ignore it, or else it is so inconceivable and unacceptable that it has been unconsciously forgotten. In either case, it doesn't exist because it has not been named. According to the documents and vocabulary that give names, I do not exist for having lost my children, or never having them. Yet, I live, I speak, I work, I eat with other people and share countless moments and all sorts of experiences with them. This one experience, however, is unique, uncontrollable, and has no name. Yet, it is the compass of my destiny. What am I—who am I, then?

More than two thousand years after Christ, the Judeo-Christian religions still avow that their God punishes children for the sins of their parents until the fourth generation, and only God himself knows why it is not longer or less long. I believe that God forgives a great many faults of the parents through the grace and innocence of their children, and over the course of several lives. This explains why some people who ought to be burned alive on the spot for enormous and reckless mistakes live to be as much as a hundred years old and die quietly in their beds. They are given extravagant burials, posthumous funeral orations, and interminable eulogies. Mountain-high wreaths are placed on their coffins and their portraits are enlarged to put the recreated hero-grandfathers on display for their grandchildren. Really, if you see a man who dies alone when he has children and grandchildren, it is only because he has mistreated God himself.

There is no doubt that a Lôs is doomed to mistreat God, and is therefore prepared to die a "bad death." But I, who am *not* a Lôs, I don't want to accept your having died on the side of the road, Father, without my being there to at least have gently closed your eyes on the absurdity of your life. That is why—and this is the gospel truth—I will pass into posterity, so that you may survive! It is for you that I'll try to be a mother and a grandmother who survives time, ashes in a reliquary, in a sanctuary, an ancestor watching over several generations of your grandchildren without their having to fear the slightest divine retribution. For you I shall do everything not to mistreat God, so that God will forgive you for your quest to be a Lôs.

• • •

Not a single one of Mam Naja's family came to visit her after the birth was announced: not her mother, whom my father had specifically invited, not any of her brothers or sisters, although there were more than half a dozen of them.

When her maternity leave was up, Father couldn't find anyone to take care of the child or keep the household going with some semblance of family life. The only one available was me. To persuade me to stay with them, my father said: "As soon as the child can walk and talk I'll finally register you at school, and you'll see how easily you'll catch up with the others and even pass them by, for you won't have lost any time."

"I see! I haven't lost time, even though the three years I gained in primary school are now gone? What will I do to catch up with my classmates, who are already in eighth grade?"

"You are very smart and you're certainly learning more important things here with me than you would at school."

"You think I'm learning things from you by being with you? We never see each other."

"Yes, we do, we see each other every day. One of us is always looking at the other and learning a lot that way. You see it when I hurt, and that puts your mind to work. The same thing is true for me: Thanks to you I'm learning a lot. I don't know what would have become of me if you hadn't been with me. Just because we don't communicate with words doesn't mean that nothing's going on."

"But at school I'd be allowed to express myself with plain words, like all my classmates. I'd hurt less and be a happy child like the rest, like everyone else."

"But you're not everyone else. While your classmates were still playing in the sand, you had a child without anyone knowing or treating you like an unwed mother. You've learned to run a home like the finest wife and mother. When you go back to school you'll be on the level of the teacher. You'll progress as fast as you did in primary school; and later on you can lay claim to a husband who'll think you're a virgin and will respect you as such, according to our customs. In the meantime, you can secretly watch over your child as over a precious treasure."

"But maybe this child won't survive. His limbs might swell up, and he'll catch his death of cold one fine day. His twin was stillborn. . . ."

"No, believe me, nothing bad is going to happen to this child. You should know that his twin didn't die because of what you think. And that's why it's important to keep the secret. If people knew he's your child they could ask questions, be suspicious, and your fear would hand you over to the revenge of the violated taboo."

"But I didn't violate anything at all, I didn't know. I . . ."

"I know you didn't know and I did. But I'm a Lôs, and that means I resist fate or conquer it, even when it goes against taboos. Didn't we win? The child is here and he's a normal boy, born from a legitimate couple. Even the mother has no inkling. Our child will live, you'll see."

"A child who won't even know that I'm his mother."

"What does that matter? You're already taking care of children who aren't yours and who love you more than they love their own mother. Thanks to the fact that your child is seen as belonging to your stepmother, a civil servant, he'll have child benefits that will allow us to raise him in the modern way that you yourself could never have managed. And finally, you won't have to suffer any shame or sarcasm, as you would if there were even the slightest suspicion."

"But the midwife might talk."

"Never, she swore an oath to me and she won't break that, I know. She's my friend and my accomplice. But even if she were to talk, she could only say what she knows, and she doesn't know anything that's really dangerous. If you go along, if you keep quiet and accept this, I promise you that your child will grow up sheltered from any harassment. Besides, I'll always consult you when an important decision has to be made concerning him. You're quite lucky, actually, for in the end you'll have every advantage and few inconveniences. You can't blame me for not protecting you and for not having tried everything to get us out of the mess I got us into."

Indeed, we never spoke of it again, although his promise to consult me regarding my child's future was never kept.

Sometimes I had the impression that Mam Naja knew something, either because the midwife told her what she knew or because my father talked in his sleep or insinuated something in one of his rages, but nothing was ever openly said. It has been a good forty years ago that the midwife died, twenty years since I became a fatherless child, and about fifteen since Mam Naja joined the stormy love of her life. Soon I'll be visiting them.

Who will speak of Africa's silences? Who will know where the work of true excavation must be done?

• • •

And what if there were only silences?
But then there are the places they call "oblivion,"
Into which consciousness retreats,
Like instruments of magic,
Like a distortion of life
Or perhaps a different art of life,
Perhaps a secret of survival.

I don't remember what came of my Uncle Kon's assassination, or the results of the implausible investigation that followed after the photographs of his retinas were taken. Still, the idea of those miraculous photos-as-witness kept the people excited for a long time. In markets and big squares, as well as in churches, an outrageous amount of time was spent constructing various hypotheses. A new version was born every day, a veritable saga in which my father incited Bitchokè to one-on-one combat in front of his house. They wounded each other seriously and both needed medical treatment; both were permanently scarred. I believe that my father's desire to become a Lôs suffered a mortal blow that day. The Lôs facing him no longer inspired him with fear, admiration, or fascination. He no longer saw any reason to try to take his place; this was of no interest to him anymore. You don't recover from the death of a hero or the values he represents. Bitchokè no longer terrified him, and the new model, Kon, had died before he could even sketch an outline of the kind of hero the future suggested. And no one knew who had destroyed him.

I don't know when people stopped skimming the book of Kon, when they closed it, or who followed the final chapter. Later, not one of the few people I was able to question, who had been living in the town at the time, could remember the events. A close friend, who was the town's administrator fifteen years later, confirmed for me that not a single archive dealing with these "events" had been preserved. So many "events" lost and forgotten!

As for me, I stopped following the saga as soon as I had to take care of my child. Nothing else mattered anymore, not even the famous school of White and Yellow women, which until then had continued to be the only thing that motivated me. Now, the only reason I had to follow my path was to give this little creature, who was lost to me in advance, everything I was capable of giving him in the unforeseeable period of time allotted to us.

That is when fate chose to help me turn a new page, as if it were a personal favor, perhaps an answer to my silent prayers.

MOVEMENT FOUR

17

Mam Naja was appointed head nurse in a different village, "far from this cursed town," as I told myself. Perhaps I was too prematurely excited, for the place in question was none other than Libôn: the birthplace of Dimalè! Taking my father and his family away from the stronghold of Bitchokè, the Lôs who had been so envied and had so fallen, and throwing him into that of the defeated and spiteful Dimalè, seemed like a new book written just for me, to allow me to experience other facets of our history in a different landscape.

The clinic was brand new, and the arrival of the new head nurse made it possible to have a solemn inauguration at last.

Monsieur Sub-Prefect gave a long speech about rebirth, development, and new perspectives for the district, which had suffered so much. "It is only a small first step, but one that signifies the Government's willingness to dress the deep wounds inflicted upon the peoples of Libôn. Pier Dimalè, the soul of Libôn, is in prison for fifteen years, and I know how much his family and his village need him. But we cannot ignore the fact that this valiant son of Libôn also abused his power as a Lôs; he had to understand once and for all that the government would no longer tolerate so many excesses. But along with the government, I hope to console the people of Libôn by sending them this woman, worthy of acceptance in the heart of the region, who will help bring new lives into the world, heal wounds, and bring solace to our hearts."

The sub-prefect overstepped the line of subtlety to say a kind word about my father when introducing him: "Another well known Lôs, who will certainly protect the village from the greed of the few depraved resistance fighters still around."

The people gave my father a standing ovation. You would have thought he'd just been named head of security of Libôn. It's true that people only love the strong. Nobody in Libôn had forgotten the Lôs who had humiliated Dimalè on his own ground a few years before.

A new house was built for the head nurse: two bedrooms, a kitchen, and a living room. For the first time in my life, I had a room! Papa set up two beds and whispered to me: "One for you and your child, one for the other little ones." We didn't have to sleep in the living room anymore.

Libôn was very much like my own village. The houses stood closer together, as in an expanding city, but there was just one main street. The arrival of a car was always a real event, except on Saturday, market day. Then the little sheds around the central square were covered with a thousand colorful *pagnes*, towels, scarves, and piles of secondhand clothes. Dried cod and fat prawns filled the shelves, spreading their smell of salted smoke, which attracted the flies.

Children from the interior of the country thought they were in the big city, a heaven. They'd run all over the place, chirping like the small birds in the fruit and palm trees that would spirit away everything edible they could find: manioc or corn fritters, fried yams, the smoked little pink fish called *gougeons*, and so on. Alcohol-filled chocolates, the color of multilayered beads, had to be carefully kept in closed jars to protect them from the covetousness of the little thieves.

The whole animated scene disappeared as if by magic once the rays of the sun turned toward their bed. Everyone was in a rush to leave so they could reach home before nightfall. Then only familiar faces were to be seen, like the members of a large family of whom you might grow tired. You lived your week looking forward to the following Saturday.

In the clinic, though, there were always people, more than a one-nurse clinic could handle, even if she was a head nurse. She had no assistants, and all by herself she was obliged to do consultations, clean up, sterilize syringes, give injections, dress wounds, and assist with about three to five deliveries every week. I did all the housekeeping at home and even at the clinic, including all the laundry and cooking for the family.

After three months it became clear that Mam Naja needed help with bandaging wounds and giving injections, because patients were arriving in ever greater numbers and from ever greater distances. Some had to sleep at the clinic and go home the next day because they were too exhausted from their long trek. Then my father would insist that I prepare additional meals, for he couldn't bear seeing patients go to sleep hungry.

So I become a nurse's aide on the job, and soon I even do night duty when Mam Naja is too tired. When all of that is done I must still do the housework and the cooking. Fortunately, on such days my father is quite willing to tend to the children. He washes them, changes them, and feeds them without any argument. Sometimes he tells us funny stories or folktales. As soon as I finish cleaning the living room and the bedrooms, I go to the kitchen, where he follows me with the children. Their presence in the kitchen always forces old Rebecca to get up. She is a half-blind old lady whom my father picked up across the river. She sleeps in the kitchen by the fire, which she never allows to die down. Clearly she can't help with the cooking, but when we're with her she does her utmost to be pleasant, ask questions, and tell entertaining stories, too. Sometimes she surprises us with extremely relevant, often portentous remarks, and my father says she must occasionally be visionary. The children love her, most of all my baby, whom she holds in her arms much too long for my taste. I'm afraid she spoils him to the core. We stay together until the meal is ready and served. Then we go back to the living room after giving a share to old Rebecca, who is like a grandmother to us.

As far back as I can remember, my father had never spent so much time at home. There was nothing for him to do there, nothing to see, nothing to produce. No garage where he could poke around in old engines, trying to make new ones out of them, as was his passion for a while before Bitchokè took up his time. No large crowds to harangue, as he did during the short period of the multiparty system that had preceded the "independence," when resistance fighters needed to be "reconverted" or comrades recruited. So he had plenty of time for us and, in the end, I believe these were the only moments in which we enjoyed a true, complete family life.

Some days, when it was my turn to get some afternoon rest, he'd leave to lend a hand with the intravenous injections and even with some consultations, if Mam Naja was in the delivery room. It was too good, too unexpected, coming from him. I wondered how long it would last. Sometimes I caught him looking at the patients and the children: Suddenly he would lose all motivation and be overwhelmed with boredom. He'd go off inappropriately, leaving the children by themselves. From what I knew of him, it wouldn't be long before he'd come up with a new passion. It was a question of life or death for him: My father could not tolerate monotony or live dispassionately.

This had only just occurred to me when he found a new interest: fishing. At first he'd come back before mealtimes, very cheerful, with a fine fresh and gleaming threadfin or a pink carp. He thoroughly enjoyed preparing it himself, presenting it with great care, like a true chef. I was very envious of these kinds of apparently exciting outings, and dying to go fishing with him.

One afternoon, when my two little brothers are sleeping next to old Rebecca, I put my baby on my back in the hope that he will fall asleep, and begin to follow my father from a distance.

What is the spirit that always moves me to follow people without any truly conscious, premeditated plan, without any adequate preparation or safety measures? I tell myself that one day I am bound to find myself face to face with someone who will not at all appreciate my behavior.

Such thoughts must have distracted me. Just before reaching the river, I realize I've lost sight of my father. Perhaps he has spotted me and is hiding to get away from my ill-timed shadowing. My heart is pounding wildly: What if he comes out from behind a bush and asks me where I'm going or what I'm doing? I'd better have an answer ready. I don't dare turn around to look behind me anymore. I feel as if an entire army with studded boots is on my heels, running frantically! I walk faster and faster to the little beach that I had often gone to when we first arrived in Libôn. All the village girls would come to swim and play in the water here. Someone is always there. Oddly enough, it is empty now. The solitude increases my anxiety and fear; it's too much for me, and I finally force myself to turn around, expecting someone to call out to me: Surprise—there is no one! It takes me some time to understand that my heart is making all the noise. Fear really does create monsters inside us. I plop down heavily on a huge dead tree trunk, which has been there for some time; I used to stretch out on it when we first arrived. My baby is sleeping peacefully on my back in his nest of *pagnes*.

I don't know how much time it took for my pulse to get back to a more or less normal rhythm. I don't think I fell asleep, but I believe I simply lost any awareness of time, seeking refuge in one of those states of perception when past and future are merely a fusion of unsanctioned and immaterial instants, a kind of compact whole. A state you only become aware of after the fact.

18

And when I emerge, I come back with my head and heart filled with a
  voice,
A voice such as you can only hear coming from inside yourself,
A voice that sings and speaks to the soul in silence,
A voice that scans rhythms ruled by the spirit alone,
A voice from the depths of a body or a space,
Formless, faceless, and yet leaving indelible traces.
Later I'll be able to forget your scent, your image, even your eyes,
But never will I forget your voice, Yèrè.

• • •

A voice that recreates the nameable: "At last, you're back. In my
heart I've called you so often. Didn't you hear me? Why did you
stop coming to this creek to swim? Before, you'd be here at least
three times a week. I'd watch you beat the water like a drum with all
the other girls; you looked like a new sun, and I thought that God
had created this delight for me alone, because until then he had surrounded me with nothing but sorrow and misery. Perhaps I'd managed to find a way to redeem myself in his eyes, to deserve your
coming. Do you know you're a genie? And I thank heaven for having put you on my path, if only to make it known to me that the

world is not just a hell. Welcome, my genie."

He is a stocky boy, gleaming black, with eyes so deeply black that in their incessant sparkling they are constantly turning to a raven blue. I've never seen him in the village and do not realize he's talking to me. I think he's saying a prayer or some sort of litany, an invocation to a goddess behind me. I turn around to look at her, but see no one. The boy smiles at me sweetly, and there's something like compassion in his eyes.

"Are you all right? Are you back with us again, awake?"

I jump and straighten up immediately. The tree trunk has made deep indentations on my chest, and it hurts. I can't hold back a grimace, and I twist to stretch my muscles. On my back my baby sighs and stretches, too, but continues to sleep peacefully. Time and space abruptly become real again. I stammer: "What? I wasn't sleeping. I just got here and have to get back home before my parents realize I'm not there and start to worry. What are you doing standing there, looking at me like a halfwit? Why don't you help me get up? The child is getting to be very heavy."

He holds out his hand to me, smiling even more, and helps me up from the old tree trunk. His hand is firm and warm. I loosen the *pagne*, and he takes the child in his arms, as if he were receiving a newborn, his stunned gaze seems to suggest. We walk in silence. At the village entrance he hands the child back to me with a touch of solemnity in his movements. He certainly is a strange boy. Maybe he's a *bissima*, a genie from the river, as in the folktales. Suddenly fear engulfs my heart again. My throat tightens, and I can't speak anymore. I take the child and leave, speechless. He jumps in front of me and walks backward. His gestures are truly those of a child, and he looks happy. What is it, then, that frightens me so?

"If you don't sleep so long the next time, I'll teach you how to fish," he says with a laugh. "Call me Yèrè, but you don't need to tell me your name because I already know you're Halla. I'll always be waiting for you down there by the creek with the drummer girls. Take your time, but don't forget that I'm waiting for you."

He runs ahead of me scampering like a playful goat, and goes into a shrub behind the large kapok tree. He's either a water genie or a forest genie, I say to myself, now convinced. I won't go back to that beach anymore; he might abduct me, and my parents would never find me again.

When I arrive at the house, Mam Naja looks at me suspiciously: "Where did you and your father go off to? You leave me in the lurch all afternoon, with all those patients on my hands, and then you calmly come home, each from a different direction to make me think you weren't together. If you've decided not to help me anymore, just say so, and I'll insist that the sub-prefect hire at least one competent nurse and a nurse's aide for me."

My father leaps from the bedroom like a spring. "So you do admit we're competent as a nurse and aide. I thought you hadn't even noticed all our efforts. If only you would show you're satisfied with our help or, at least that we relieve you from a good bit of work. But no, never a thank you, never a single sign of appreciation or encouragement. Everyone owes you, but you, you don't owe a thing to anyone, right? Well, in my opinion I don't owe you anything anymore, either; so go ahead and ask for more personnel from whomever is in charge. I'm finally going to have some time to think about my own life again."

My father's scathing response apparently catches Mam Naja off guard, because she opens her mouth several times to say something, but no sound comes out. And, to tell the truth, I'm bewildered as well. I didn't know my father was wallowing in so much anger. So he, too, knew one needed a word of encouragement, a sign of gratitude, every now and then? I thought I was the only one! When she was annoyed at me for stopping in the middle of an activity under the pretext of not getting any response, Grand Madja used to tell me: "It's your weakness that's at fault, and your all-too-many impulses, always so foolishly hungry for a response. How many women do you think would manage to love their children and help them grow up if they expected something in return? Do your piece of what's needed and let that be enough satisfaction in itself, or else you won't be a real woman."

Just as I'm growing accustomed to the idea that these superficial emotions exist only to make me bemoan my own life, complain about my lot, and therefore justify my state of mind, here is my father taking me back to a feeling of doubt and disrupting my progress toward Grand Madja's wisdom and serenity. So many new beginnings!

From that moment on, it seemed to me, everything fell apart very quickly.

My father left every Saturday in one of the cars that had arrived for market day. He would be dropped off in the administrative center of the district, and wouldn't come back until Wednesday, only to leave again—in search of paid work, so he said.

The sub-prefect arrived on Saturdays as soon as my father had left, and did not go home until late at night. He took Mam Naja I don't know where, but I could well imagine why. The truce and the dream of a normal family life didn't last more than six months because of my parents' fickleness. The nightmare we had experienced in the big city was returning right here before our very eyes— and nothing was being done to prevent it. I didn't want to stay there any longer, holding together, by myself, a household in which its founders had no faith. A kind of nausea and a feeling of injustice drove me away, for I, too, was in revolt. I didn't exactly know against whom I held the greater grudge: my father, whose unbearable instability I couldn't keep myself from judging, or Mam Naja, who in my opinion was incapable of holding on to her husband and at the same time working as a modern woman.

So I suddenly began to find my way to the river as soon as my parents turned their backs. I left my little brothers with old Rebecca and, with my baby on my back, I sat on the old tree trunk near the creek of the drummer girls. Yèrè, whom I now called My Bissima and who called me his water genie, always joined me right away. It seemed as if he sensed my presence there; even when he was in the village, I never had to wait more than fifteen minutes before he came running. He told me about his life as an orphan without any close relatives, his working in courtyards of various people to find a transient sleeping place and some food, here today and there tomorrow. He was preparing for his primary school diploma and his entrance to the Protestant secondary school in the village, hoping to study far away and become a doctor. He wanted to know if I'd wait for him, and then we could get married as soon as he had his high school diploma; we'd go to the capital where he would study medicine. He taught me to recognize plants that some of the old people in the village had shown him. He was extremely obliging and respectful toward all his elders, and had the gift of getting them to divulge all their secrets of wisdom.

He was the first one to direct my attention to the differences between what he called the knowledge of the Whites and the knowledge of our ancestors. He made comparisons that left me openmouthed. I couldn't follow the rhythm of his thought processes. He was truly the most intelligent young person I'd ever met. He told me ancient tales and myths, and sang epics to me like the one that the great poets in Grand Pa Helly's courtyard used to sing during the Feast of the Dog, in the last week of December.

His voice was extraordinary, almost not human, with modulations that created successive echoes, like those inside a cave. Sometimes my fear of him returned, but I think he understood, and then he would become as gentle as a lamb and start humming. He would capture my gaze and hold it, and we'd look at each other for unbelievably long periods of time. He would take my hand and clasp it loosely for a very long time, gradually tightening his hold until I told him he was hurting me. Then, with a laugh, he'd let go.

"So, I'm not dreaming—you really are human and right here next to me. I'm so happy, I'm afraid there's nothing else left for me to discover on this earth."

One day we caught a speaking fish, a fish that printed words into our heads without ever uttering a sound. We looked at each other to make sure each of us had heard the silent words. The fish told a story about a united land called Atna, or Atlana.

"It can only be one or the other, but not both names at the same time," My Bissima answered, "since one is the opposite of the other.

Atna means 'union,' and Atlana is 'to take apart, to divide.' A single country cannot have both names at the same time."

"If you wish," the fish replied, "not at the same time, but alternating.

Atna at night when all must be merged;
Atlana in the morning when things must be apart.
Specify each thing, name each being differently.
But don't evening and morning belong to the same time?
The time in which you misused your part of knowledge and power,
Or the time in which you shared with others.
Atna or Atlana, call it what you choose,
Within the same time.
That is what I came to tell you."

The fish pulls from our hand the line we have been holding together, and crosses the river like a shooting star. Our fishing-line traces his path like a luminous trail. Enraptured, we watch, and then suddenly My Bissima kisses me on the mouth. A flow of memories of my Aunt Roz and her husband Ratez surges up from deep down in my belly, and I vomit a long spurt of yellow saliva. For a moment of utter bewilderment he looks at me, then with a laugh he tenderly takes my hand, still capering in his inimitable way.

"I'm happy, so happy! Come, let's go, I'm done."

The next morning he didn't come to the river. Nor the day after, either. Then I saw some people pass by carrying a body wrapped in a white sheet. An old woman said a litany for the end of an orphan's life. For weeks I roamed along the river without so much as a sign. I didn't dare ask any questions about him. I only knew that he had left for good. To me it was the fish that had come for him. Did I weep? Did I suffer? Did anger or bitterness build up inside me? Did it have any role to play in the rest of my life as a woman? Consciousness immured, oblivion, great escape toward survival. But the intense presence of his voice remains:

"Yèrè Mbèi Ngock grew beneath the phantom tree
Like a mushroom, Yèrè son of the albino stone;
Yèrè will live like the squirrel of the ancestor Sénd Biok,
Scrambling and jumping along the branches
Without building a nest, without digging a hole;
Yèrè is just a passerby astray on the earth.
If you are looking for Yèrè, son of the albino stone,
Look beneath the phantom tree
Where the mushrooms of rediscovered genies grow."

This was his favorite song, the meaning of his presence on earth, which I could not understand. But the period of ignorance and unconsciousness doesn't matter: One day a mushroom grows beneath the phantom tree on the albino stone. May the intensity of your voice guide me along the branches, Yèrè, until the day that genies reunite.

19

I no longer left the house, and so had more time to observe the evolution of my parents' behavior.

One evening, when he plainly had been drinking a great deal,
my father approached while I was clearing the table, yanked at me
as if I were a puppet,and pushed me up against the sub-prefect, asking him: "You know my little mother? Oh no, I didn't introduce her
properly? Well, take a look at her. She's a genius. She finished all of
elementary school in just three years, making it possible for her to
devote the three years she saved to me. Now I'd really like to have
her attend high school as I promised her, but I have no work. I'd
like to find something interesting either in mechanics or in modern
agriculture. Surely you have something for me, don't you?"

"Of course, my friend. All you had to do was ask. I've got something that's perfect for you."

Having turned into a "friend of the family," as he puts it himself, the
sub-prefect loses no time in finding my father an apprenticeship in
the district's biggest city, where he will be trained in the maintenance of industrialized plantations and their equipment. In addition
to a substantial grant he is to receive for this, at the end of three
months my father will be in charge of the maintenance of agricultural machinery throughout the region. He is so thrilled to be head-

ing out and feeling independent again that he doesn't even try to see what's afoot in his own house—or perhaps he chooses not to see it.

In my father's absence, the sub-prefect visits us at least twice a week, bringing bread, chicken, sweets, and all kinds of treats—"as your father would if he were here," is the way he likes to put it.

Mam Naja takes it all, gives us whatever she feels like giving us, and often offers some of it to the children of our village and of neighboring villages, undoubtedly because she wants to buff up her image and renown, which have been in decline. She no longer devotes herself to her work the way she did at first; the crack in the family, highlighted by my father's departure, has really destabilized us, even if we all try to hide it in our own fashion.

Some days, when the sub-prefect brings chicken or guinea hen, she insists on cooking herself, although she certainly has no talent in that area. She prepares floury sauces that immediately thicken as they rise in the pot. The sub-prefect automatically asks: "Who's created today's delicacy?" My little brothers answer in chorus: "Mama did!" After a laconic "Very good," he comes up with all sorts of tricks to have as little as possible of it, and serves huge portions to the little ones or old Rebecca.

When I make the meal, however, he eats with obvious pleasure and pays me many compliments. Mam Naja resents this, and decides to send me away from the table to eat with old Rebecca in the kitchen. Pretending to give a portion to the old woman as usual, the sub-prefect takes advantage of the opportunity to court me explicitly and insistently. He probably has come up with the idea of using me to get rid of a mistress who has become too clingy and bothersome and is a bad cook to boot.

As soon as my father comes back from his apprenticeship, the sub-prefect asks him for my hand in my presence, just as Mam Naja is called away urgently to assist a woman in labor.

"You're sure to hear very soon that during your training period I visited your family very often," he says in a confidential tone. "Trying to make their life a little easier while you were absent, I had a chance to observe your daughter closely. You were right: You've got a very special creature here, a real treasure. She would make a fantastic wife, the last grace that God and you yourself could offer my waning days on this earth. Would our friendship warrant your granting me her hand in marriage?"

My father looks at him with his usual mocking smile and keeps silent for quite a while. Nervous, the sub-prefect keeps checking his watch as he looks at the door, as if afraid that someone else might come in and hear a possibly negative response, which was taking a long time in coming. Having enjoyed the fun of prolonging the suspense, my father finally says: "I promise I'll at least give it some thought while my little mother grows up. Don't you see she's still too little? In any case, for now all I can think about is the new job you promised me. Until I've tried that and proven that they can count on me to be responsible for them, there's no room in my head to think about marrying off my little girl to Monsieur Sub-Prefect. But in principle you may consider yourself accepted. The sooner I can start, the sooner we'll be able to talk about this again."

Surely this was a persuasive argument. Less than a month after he came back from his apprenticeship, my father receives his orders and an old Land Rover for his travels through all the plantations of the district.

Once this happens, we only see him on the weekends. He arrives at the same time as all the city merchants. He brings barrels of oil, yams, and game in his company car and sells it all in no time flat, buying what he wants to bring home as his fair share. He seems absolutely delighted to play the master of the house, who arrives as a lifesaver with piles of provisions: packages of cod, popular canned goods (corned beef, mackerel, sardines, condensed sweet milk, and so on), and enough breakfast rolls to last all week.

Goodbye to our traditional sweet yam breakfasts, bits and pieces of reheated manioc, and the deeply black fruit of the *safoutier* tree, fried until golden brown. Goodbye to leftovers au gratin and the other dishes we argued over because we wanted to scrape the crusts from the bottom of the pot. Now the tendency is to throw away what remains, but luckily there are always ravenous patients in the morning, all too happy to take advantage of our leftovers. That makes double work for me, however, because I now have to prepare the "modern breakfast" our parents can't have us do without anymore, in view of their new social status, as well as the traditional breakfast I insist on making so I don't have to waste any food. Grand Madja always made us collect even the manioc that had already been tossed, wash and reheat it, or cut it in tiny pieces to be soaked in water for several days, from which we made another very sophisticated dish, called *kousèt* in the folktales; she would never forgive me if I forgot this: "The ancestors punish waste. There's always someone around to whom you can offer the food that the spirits are gracious enough to grant us. Throwing it out is a sign of negligence, laziness, and deplorable self-centeredness. Always put your creativity to work to nourish life the same way it nourishes you," she would endlessly repeat.

On weekends the house is a joy. In the evening, Mam Naja asks me to heat water for my father, and she then lovingly massages his feet and back. They're calling each other "darling" again, as they did in the beginning. Love has returned to the house. I think this is the period in which my brother Helly is conceived.

On Monday morning my father leaves again to go back to the opportunities his new status as provider gives him. Monday or Tuesday evening the sub-prefect arrives, takes Mam Naja out for a walk, and joins the family for the dinner I prepare. Mam Naja doesn't even try to cook anymore, but she always has something negative to say about my food. Perhaps that is why anger is beginning to raise its head inside me, unless it is because of what, in my eyes, is her unwarranted infidelity.

Today I realize with some alarm that she is jealous of me, and perhaps I am jealous of her as well. In fact, we have been rivals all along, although neither of us ever utter the word, even in the most secret corners of our heart. Still, it must be said that we are rivals, even if things go unnamed, even though we secretly avoid each other.

As soon as she is in love, she suffers from pathological laziness, and I have to do most of her work again—to be nurse, wife, and even lover, although not in bed. People know it, although we don't speak of it. On top of this, there are plenty of unanticipated comments and suggestive songs. Not only does she never show me the slightest kindness, but Mam Naja manages to grab every opportunity to insult and humiliate me in front of patients, my father, and the sub-prefect. She increasingly enjoys being nasty to me in public. Slowly but surely, my anger escalates, and one extraordinary Sunday it explodes.

My father and the sub-prefect are at home, and I decide to cook separate meals to anticipate their not always compatible tastes: chicken with a creamed peanut sauce for the sub-prefect, who loves that, and grilled chicken for my father, who doesn't care for sauces very much. I'm so eager to have both dishes come out well and please both men that I'm having a hard time also satisfying Mam Naja, who is having a drink with them and keeps on calling me for a bottle opener, a corkscrew, another glass, and who knows what else, as if she were nailed to her chair and couldn't drag herself away for a single moment to help herself.

After performing half a dozen such "errands" and almost burning my chicken several times, I decide not to respond to her calls anymore until my two dishes are finished. Old Rebecca comes in with her gentle smile and curls up on her bed next to the main hall. There's something knowing in her look, and I'm trying to understand what the old woman wants from me. That is what they call having your head run away from you—my body keeps cooking, but my head is preoccupied with old Rebecca, so much so that I actually no longer hear Mam Naja calling me. Then, tired of calling without getting any reaction, she finally pulls herself out of her chair. She cuts a piece of sugarcane in the courtyard and comes into the kitchen, where I'm bustling about with my child in my arms, peeling yams and checking the meal on the stove. I don't hear her come in. She beats me with the sugarcane, first on the head and a second time on my right knee, so hard that it feels like an electric shock. I'm thrown backward, as the child flies toward the pot with boiling peanut sauce!

Both of us witness a miracle: Old Rebecca leaps up with incredible speed and just manages to catch the child in her arms. But the little one's left hand goes into the peanut sauce, and he shrieks with surprise, fear, and pain. Old Rebecca throws me a quick look of compassion. I rush forward to gather up the child so I can take care of him, but the old woman orders me to wait. She quickly pushes her hand into her vagina, pulls it out again, and rubs it over the injured part, just as Grand Madja Halla always used to do, which eases the burns immediately. When the child starts to calm down, the old woman turns to Mam Naja, who stands crying against the kitchen door, and in a rage that makes her already quavering voice shake even more, the old woman says: "I thought all along that you hated this child, that perhaps it isn't even yours. Now I'm sure of it—you just want to kill him, burn him alive, and for all to see. For goodness sake, I've never seen anything like it!"

A moment of astonished, icy silence ensues. Mam Naja suddenly turns around, throws the piece of sugarcane into the sauce, and rips the child from the old woman's arms: "You old witch, you're not going to get me!" she screams, on the verge of madness.

I never do find out what she says then. What I do remember is that I hear my father answering her: "In any event, the child can walk and eat on his own. If you no longer need my little mother for your work, she's coming with me to the plantations while she waits for her fiancé to come and marry her properly."

Apparently, this is the first time Mam Naja hears about the marriage plan. There's no doubt that my father has not told her before, but he now comes out with it as if to stun her. At that exact instant, I'm convinced my father knows about his wife's newest infidelity, and in her eyes I see that she, too, has just begun to suspect him of revenge.

The sub-prefect is profoundly embarrassed, and excuses himself under the pretext that he has forgotten he is expecting guests himself: "Clearly, my heart is already much too comfortable in this house," he says, "and I'd be happy to get married very soon so I can take my wife with me and be quietly at home again. At the end of the month I'd like to meet the family so we can set the dates for the various ceremonies."

He doesn't look at Mam Naja or shake her hand. He gives me a forced little smile, and my father sees him out.

All the time that they're outside, Mam Naja is in shock, neither looking up nor speaking a word. I feel almost sorry for her, but then I think of my baby, whom she almost burned. I recognize she's forcing me to distance myself from him and that, while I'm roaming around the cocoa plantations, she might suffocate him or drop him from a rooftop. My throat tightens.

What drove old Rebecca to speak up that way? I never divulged anything to her. How could she have guessed? And how was it possible that Mam Naja didn't ask for any further explanations, when she was supposed not to know anything about it? Anxiety was killing me, and I was trembling from top to toe. I hated these moments when I felt as if I were exposed down to my insides, completely naked under the sun. I knew I needed to find a semblance of calm at once to confront a delayed reaction from Mam Naja. She gave it to me herself. As soon as my father came in again, she stood up with my child in her arms and said to me, sharp as a knife: "Forget this child."

I decided I must do it immediately. Yes, as of the very next day I would devote myself to forgetting my child. It was for all of us a question of life or death. Moreover, officially I had never had him, and that was something I needed to remember forever— or, at least, try to live as if it were so.

Némy used to say: "When our consciousness starts to be locked inside its walls, it creates oblivion, even of ourselves, our state of mind, our desires and contradictions, erasing all questions and answers in the mere name of survival. That art of survival at any price probably hides the secret of our resistance as Blacks! Having suffered centuries of being traded, of being treated like cheap merchandise, of being tortured, morally and physically, during countless periods of slavery and colonization, we thrive with such serenity that the world keeps talking about our fine childlike spirit."

Ah! My blessed mother, Priestess Némy, run over by a train that very year, may you rest in peace and oblivion!

20

So here I am, right behind my father on the cocoa and coffee bean plantations. He shows me how to prune a cocoa tree, not only to give it a prettier shape but to make the remaining branches stronger and more prolific. He explains the mixture of products that help kill parasites and prevent plant-pod disease. It's a whole new world.

We walk dozens of miles every day inside the plantation, living like the birds, without needing to sow before we harvest or cook before we eat. Heaven provides. The family of the owners of the plantation takes care of our meals, and will even have them brought to us when we're in the farthest reaches of their property. We are offered food that equals that of great chiefs: *masso*, the sweet yellow yam; *nkônô ngond*, made of squash seeds; *hikok*, wild leaves; *manga*, tarot; and game simmered the same way grandmother makes it.

We're treated with love and respect, and people look at us with admiration and even envy. We are the new models of service and competence: "Beyond any borders of clan and tribe, beyond merely personal gain, we are working for a greater and more prosperous nation, for a rich and noble continent that is in charge of its own destiny," my father repeatedly tells people. He proves to be extremely meticulous and patient with the planters, as he teaches them what will transform their fields into truly modern plantations, which can compete on a global level. In every village we pass through, boys and girls ask us a thousand questions: What course of study should they follow to become a professional in this field? How long will it take? How old must one be to start?

My father has time for each one, offers personal answers, and explains the various agricultural career possibilities and prospects. He believes in what he's doing. He radiates happiness and is growing younger before our very eyes. Although he has, since the death of my little brother, smoked three packs of cigarettes a day, he now suddenly decides to quit. He tosses the last package into the river and will never smoke again through the day he dies. I'm discovering a new man, as passionate, brilliant, and fascinating as ever, but attentive to others, even to me—he is someone really new and beautiful.

Also new, he's starting to talk to me about my mother, every day, nostalgically, remembering her love of perfection, her insistence that he be perfect at all times.

"I now miss what used to exasperate me," he admits to me. "I should have met your mother at this point in my life, and I'm sure we would have been very happy. You see, it took another Naja for me to realize that I prefer the first one, and that in my heart she'll always be very special to me."

At that moment I decide to do everything I can to bring my parents back together again.

"Why don't you try to win my mother back and redeem yourself in her eyes? She's loved you too much not to want to forgive you when she actually realizes how sincere you are," I tell my father.

"Forgive me for what and redeem me from what? Don't you think your mother also needs to be forgiven and redeemed? It's precisely because she would come up with words like these, just as you have now, that I don't even want to see her. What I said is that we would have done fine had we met now, because then we wouldn't have to talk about the past and forgiveness, but about love and what we might build together. Don't you see the difference?"

Of course I saw it, but it wasn't so much for their sake anymore that I insisted on wanting to get them back together. It would simply be the easiest way to get rid of Mam Naja, who, I was sure now, was vicious poison for my father—a poison that transformed him into an ever more indescribable monster.

All these decades later, I regret having had such thoughts about her. True enough, she didn't help him improve, but it wasn't she who poisoned him. It was the lack of recognition of his genius that changed my father into a monster. And in this, each person is first and foremost responsible for himself, something I came to see again and again in different people, starting with myself. A stifled creativity becomes temptingly monstrous and always destroys everyone who is near and dear to you, if it doesn't destroy you first.

Surely what the Bassa call *hu* is such perverted creativity! My own creativity had been blocked because I couldn't attend the school that meant so much to me. I had put it off for the sake of my baby, and in order to please my father and my stepmother. Now that I was making every effort to let go of my child a second time and perhaps forever, I let myself enjoy the beautiful days with my father, but without any great commitment.

It seems to me now that the plan to reconcile my mother and father was the first manifestation of my creativity's perversion. We had heard that my mother was pregnant, and this time it most certainly was not by my father. It meant she had rebuilt her life. My father was living with Mam Naja, who was also pregnant again. What right did I have to set myself up as the restorer of relationships?

In spite of myself, in my head I sent messages to my mother from early morning to nightfall, begging her to come and see us. And I'd tell my father every day: "My mother Naja is coming, and you'll see each other again. You'll explain everything to one another, and all will be well, you'll see."

"I forbid you to try anything like that! Don't you understand? It's too late. I'd have to be ashamed for the rest of my life and I can't live like that! Besides, do remember that I've never said a word to you about your mother. In any case, we're getting all worked up over nothing. What would your mother do in this godforsaken outpost? Even if they paid her, she wouldn't go where she knew me to be, especially as long as that witch of her sister is alive."

"She'll come, you'll see; I swear she will."

"Be quiet and think about something else. Anyway, rest time is over, and we have to get back to work. So, up you go!"

We left the tree trunks we used as seats and began working again in silence, but inside our heads the ideas were brewing. At least, inside mine an unfamiliar voice kept repeating doggedly: "She'll come, she's on the way, she has arrived, she's here." I thought that my father had to be telling himself: "Never, she'll never come back, and it's better that way."

I was right. She was already there. A messenger was sent to Libôn to bring the news to my father personally. He had come the day after we departed and had followed us from village to village, always appearing too late; that was now seven days ago! He walked the one- or two-hour distances between villages that we covered by car. His exhaustion was understandable.

He delivered his message in a hoarse voice: "Your first wife has given birth to a girl and has had a nervous breakdown right after the delivery, crying that it wasn't true, that she couldn't have had a baby because she hadn't seen her love! As soon as they showed her the little girl she began to bang her head against the wall, and they had to take her to the hospital and give her tranquilizers. Since then she's plunged into a profound state of apathy from which they can't seem to release her. So your sister Roz has managed to convince your wife's family to let her take her to a reputable healer she knows without telling them that you're in the region. She sent me right away to give you the message so you can meet them at the home of your mutual friend, the healer Minta. She feels that your being there will help her enormously. Let's go right now; too much time has already been wasted."

My father listens open-mouthed as he looks at me, his eyes as round as a beached carp. I wonder if he'll have time enough to hit me before he has a stroke. But no, he calms down immediately, and without any sign of playfulness in his voice he manages to whisper to me: "Little witch, are you happy now? Get in the car, we're leaving!"

We drive all night. The messenger certainly understated how bad the road was. It is quite simply impassable: We constantly have to replace a plank on a bridge, gather up earth, sand, or stones to fill a huge hole, cut branches to make a deep puddle shallower, and so on. We arrive at dawn, entirely worn out, and sleep all day. When night begins to fall, the drums of the healing ritual pull us from our state of limbo. I wake up first, not knowing where I am, anxious and unsure, as happens so often when life hits a crossroads.

I'm lying on a mat in a corner of a large hut. A fence-high double bed made of bamboo stands at the other end of the room. I can't see very much and am really beginning to panic when I notice my father's huge frame jump up to perch on the edge of his bed. He appears as disoriented as I. I burst out laughing. He turns around and says: "Ah! There you are! Where are we, and what time is it?"

I laugh all the more because he really isn't very awake yet. He looks like a lost child. My laughter pulls him out of his sluggishness. He swears under his breath and leaps to the floor.

"My God, oh, my God, the ritual! Hurry up, in heaven's name!"

There is a crowd in the courtyard. Women dressed in red and white *pagnes*, kaolin smeared on their feet, hands, and faces, beat bamboo branches together and sing. A line of women completely wrapped in red *pagnes* play triple bells, whose sound pierces my body. My legs begin to tremble. I grasp on to details.

Five men are beating drums on the other side of the loop. The dense crowd has formed a tight circle, but my father holds my hand and we resolutely clear a path through the mass. When people turn around and see his tall figure, they make space. Some greet him and call him by his name. Obviously he is well-known here, but he barely answers and keeps moving to the center of the circle. My mother is sitting on the ground, her legs straight out, her long hair completely covering her face as if to hide or protect it. My father dashes over toward her, but several people block his way. Then the Sunk-ang, the healer, comes forward, kisses him, rapidly says something into his ear, and indicates a place for us to sit.

Everyone sits down again except for the healer in his red *pagne*, who stands in the center of the circle and starts to chant. The men and women in red sing a canon, then the women in red and white sing in chorus, and then the whole gathering responds. It is a song I shall never forget:

"My husband, oh, my dear husband,
I'm dying of the ugly way I've acted.
Hesitantly moving forward, sitting down at every stage,
I'm dying of the ugly way I've acted.
My flightiness, my wanderings, my unfulfilled desires,
I'm dying of the ugly way I've acted.
Crime is the son of thievery, in turn the son of lies;
I'm dying of the ugly way I've acted.
He who lies will steal and then end up by killing;
I'm dying of the ugly way I've acted.
My husband, oh, my dear husband
I'm dying of the ugly way I've acted."

My mother irately plugs up her ears, no doubt because she refuses to hear unjustified accusations. I follow her example and plug up mine; I feel that the song accuses her, and I find it crude and hateful to identify her this way for public condemnation. She isn't here to have further abuse heaped on her, but to be taken care of. Why doesn't she look up to see my father's love? That is what would save her; I'm sure of it. But she stubbornly keeps her eyes riveted on the ground, and her ears plugged. I have to try to get closer and talk to her. I begin to move forward across the ground on my behind, the way some legless people do. With every new song I slide ahead two or three times and then freeze.

Suddenly, night falls like a veil thrown by a sorcerer. I begin to shake. What is this fear; what am I afraid of now? Actually, I'm trembling because the trance into which several of the followers of the Sunkang enter, one after another, is contagious. Some of the women in red and white sweep off into the dark forest, wildly beating their bamboo sticks. The followers in red are jumping like kernels of corn in a blazing hot frying pan, working away at their bells with increasing force. Without becoming strident, the sound penetrates everyone's heart more and more intensely and causes such vibrations in all those present that their voices quaver.

Then Master Sunkang begins to sing yet another song, which takes my breath away, for in it a *bissima* is invoked by the name of "Yèrè Baoura." My body begins to take enormous leaps, as in some forms of levitation. I land on my mother like a meteorite. She raises her eyes, and as she recognizes me she shouts my name and faints. Now I go into an irreversible trance, singing the song dedicated to the genie Yèrè Baoura; I rip the bamboo from the hands of a Sunkang follower in red and white, and start to run toward the forest. But fast as lightning, Master Sunkang catches me, pulls the bamboo out of my hands, and replaces it with a copper wire that gleams like molten gold in the light of the fire. A kind of magnetism literally electrifies me, and I lose awareness of all that I've known until this moment.

I am another person in a different world. Yèrè, my late genie friend, comes toward me surrounded by very tiny genies that bow and scrape to him and call him Baoura, the "enormous one." He smiles at me ironically, the way he used to, while my hand passes through his body as if through a cloud. I sense his ethereal yet very warm presence guiding me and showing me plants with which to cure my mother. I pick them with astonishing ease: Just by touching them with the copper wire, leaves, bark, and roots are cupped inside my hand. I bring them to the Master Sunkang, who takes back his copper wire, too, and that empties me of all my energy. I sink into a blue mist, wholly unconscious.

When I come to, my father is in the center of the circle holding my mother in his arms, his eyes filled with tears. She says to him: "So you were there. Then I understand how I could have had a child, and another girl, too. It was you, wasn't it?"

"Of course, my love, who else would it be?"

"Now I understand everything. Well then, where is that bad little child? Bring her to me so I can nurse her."

"You left her in the city, that bad little child of yours, my dear friend," my paternal Aunt Roz, standing behind me, says. "We'll have to leave very early in the morning to nurse her before she starves to death."

"But look at that, the whole family is here, and no one can see the little girl. I'm so ashamed, my dear sister-in-law. Don't be angry with me, though, I'll bring her to your village for the baptism," my mother says in the tone of a spoilt child.

Then I understand that she still doesn't see the real situation, or else she's in denial. Her mind is active again and, to survive, is in the process of inventing an acceptable version of the facts.

It is her version until the end of her days.

"Her bastard of a husband had found yet another way of possessing her without her being aware of it and made her pregnant with a daughter. Since she wasn't the Virgin Mary, and had not received an annunciation, she'd almost gone crazy with worry because she didn't know by whom or when she'd become pregnant. Undoubtedly, that bastard took advantage of her in a moment of great exhaustion. Perhaps he'd made her take a sleeping pill or a hallucinogen."

When I wake up, I can't remember the end of the ritual. Surely someone had brought me back to my mat. Where had my parents gone? I notice that my father isn't in his bed, but my Aunt Roz is snoring peacefully beside me. My fretfulness awakens her, and it is she who tells me the rest of what happened.

"So, my little priestess, I didn't know you were so strong! Did you see everything you brought back from the forest? And hear your voice as you prescribed the way certain leaves were to be boiled to prepare a potion for your mother to drink, how certain bark and roots were to be reduced to massage her for a long time after a sheep was sacrificed for her? The healer followed all your directions to the letter, and when your mother came to in the arms of your father, she began to chat with him as if they'd never been apart, and he had to stay with her. The ritual came to an end with a miraculous cure once again; but love is also a truly powerful remedy, you see. I thank heaven that I had the inspired idea of sending your mother here and allowed enough time for your father and you to make it here, too. Well now, get up, and we'll go and see if all is well."

We can't find my parents, and my aunt concludes this is a good sign. We spend our time helping to cook the sacrificial meats for the evening's thanksgiving. Master Sunkang, the healer, requests to see my aunt, who asks me to come along with her. He receives us in one of his places of consultation.

"Roz, first of all I want to thank you for your renewed friendship and confidence in me by bringing your sister-in-law here when no one else could do anything more for her. I'm very happy that you're not disappointed. I also want to congratulate you on having a great future priestess in your niece, if she is properly controlled. I assume that this same confidence will let you entrust her to me for as long as is necessary. And if you're afraid I'll take advantage of her you can always demand that I ask for her hand, as is honorable."

My aunt bursts into her most sarcastic laughter: "You men, you're all the same, without a doubt, and you'll never change. This little girl, no more than an earthworm yet, has already put you in such a state?"

"Wait, Roz, don't take my proposal so lightly. I made it only in response to your confidence in me. I alone would know how to unfold the genie in this child and offer her the life that her gifts merit, which would go well beyond the ordinary."

"Your argument is pointless. In our family no one has an ordinary life, and she least of all. Although she's still too young, she's a special person, I know that, no old fool like yourself is going to bring her the best she ought to have. If you can't make do with memories of us, then you should have yourself buried. But don't let me catch you looking at my niece in that smutty way again, understood? Or else you'll wake up one morning with a big empty space between your legs, you bastard!" Then, she added, "Having said that, thank you for curing my sister-in-law."

Both of them laugh uproariously. I find their crude way of joking around very strange, but I've noticed before that adults have a tendency to tell each other a few basic truths in supposedly jocular ways.

Early in the evening my father arrives with a demijohn of palm wine that he bought during his long walk with my mother. The news runs through the village in record time. People come into the healer's courtyard with coconut goblets and seats under their arms. Some of them bring their share of wine as well, and very soon the courtyard is swamped. Chitchat and bawdy laughter fuse and mix with sarcastic commentary on the healing ritual. Laughing raucously, a man shouts at my father: "Hey, Njokè! You're something special! Neglecting your beautiful light-skinned wife, a midwife to boot, to come and whimper publicly right in the middle of the healing ritual over that swarthy one you rejected a long time ago, a looooong time, indeed! You looked as if you wanted to eat her whole last night in front of us all, you know? Well, I wouldn't want to be in your shoes when the light-skinned one hears about this, ha ha! You can rest assured that there'll be people more than willing to tell her about it, if only to look good in her eyes and receive better care from her in the future. You'd do better to have some answers ready, my brother. . . . Ha ha!"

In earlier times my father would have made him swallow his words and his tongue, but oddly enough he rises, kisses my mother tenderly on her forehead, greets the Master Sunkang, empties his coconut goblet in one gulp, and says to me: "Let's go to bed, my little mother, we have to get up very early tomorrow morning. My thanks to the whole village, and goodbye to the late-sleepers and all the others I won't see before we leave in the morning. Goodnight to all. Roz, are you staying much longer?"

"Not at all. I'm just going to make sure that Naja eats. I'm coming."

Master Sunkang insists on accompanying my father to our hut

to make his request again, this time to possibly more compassionate ears.

"You know, my dear Njokè, the genies have just made a veritable gash in your little girl's body. Someone needs to take serious charge of her to restore her equilibrium and teach her how to control rather than submit to these genies. I think I'm the only one who can do that properly, or else she'll always be subjected to trances and will spend the rest of her life wandering off in pursuit of the genies. I told your sister, but she's always blinded by her implacable jealousy, as you know. So, I'm telling you: It would be better if you left your daughter here with me so that I can spend the needed time with her."

"Yeah," my father laughs, "or the time needed to bewitch her completely. Drop it, my friend, she's not for you. I've already promised her to someone else."

They both laugh happily, kiss each other warmly, and slap each other on the back.

• • •

The next morning my father and I accompanied Aunt Roz and my mother Naja to the highway to make the regular bus connection to the capital; they were in a hurry to get back to the baby and nurse her at last. My father and mother had seen each other again, as I had wanted for so long, it was true; but as my father said, it was too late for them. In any case, my mother finally had her own version of her life and could explain it to herself; she could now make a new life and a different story for herself.

Without thinking, my father took us back to Mam Naja's, the same way a horse automatically returns to its stable. Once again I would be with my baby, but, sadly, I was more distraught than I'd been when we left, without quite knowing why.

21

SONG 9

How plentiful they are, placed on our path to awaken us,
Coming together at the opening of a breach in our consciousness;
Plentiful they are, these true beings, bringing hardship to widen the cleft
Erasing the blows we suffered without disturbing the scabs of our
    indifference,
Yet constantly relighting the golden thread, like a strand
Between our various levels of perception, like other ways to exist.
Minta, Master Sunkang, if you weren't the matchstick, you were
At least its herald, its prophet.

But how much dead space
Between one feeling and another,
Between a memory and a state of oblivion,
Between a death and a new life—
And then comes the day of a new departure:
A new death or another birth
That truly knows how to make the difference.
Sarah and Isma Mbeï, if you were not its path,
At least you were one of its footbridges.
Death here is rebirth elsewhere,
And being born here equals dying elsewhere.

This time it was a Sunday. That Sunday. . . .

I'm overwhelmed by an irresistible need to isolate myself. Everything seems noisy, irritating, and intolerable to me: The children are clinging to my feet or climbing on my back, reminding me of little monkeys; their squealing is like that of the weaverbirds in the high noon sun. All I want to do is chase them away and escape from them, and although usually they are my energizers, my support, they're smothering me like a weight on my chest.

Sunday at noon.

Having finished the cooking and the household chores, I vanish and retreat behind the clinic into the large cocoa plantation, where I never venture because its density scares me so. This particular noontime it seems to be the only possible refuge, one where no one would think of looking for me. I don't go very far because I quickly find a place I like, which I dust off before lying down.

Soon the memory of my mother's healing ritual comes back to me. A new depth comes to my images and sense of the forest where Yèrè Baoura, the genie with the face of my late friend, and his entourage of small *bissimas* show me plants. But I also remember the words of Master Sunkang when he told my father that if he didn't personally take care of me and repair the "cracks" that the first mystic trance had produced in me, I'd run the risk of being eternally troubled, incessantly wandering. I try to repress a mad desire to set off and break with everything I've known until now. Obviously, the genie Yèrè is flooding my head again. I have a sense of being watched, and jump up.

Indeed, two young people—a boy and a girl—are looking at me through the foliage. Aware that they've been discovered, they flee, singing provocatively, the way children do when they're trying to get a reaction. I recognize the language as Bassoo, old Rebecca's mother tongue. Amused, I run after them, trying to imitate the song and sound. They run faster to put some distance between us, forcing me to exert myself so I won't lose sight of them. A sudden about-face reverses the roles, and it's their turn now to do their utmost to catch me. Finally they make me fall and jump on top of me, laughing in the same tone, with the same expression in their small slanted eyes, which clearly shows they're brother and sister. I try to extricate myself while they attempt to hold me to the ground, and we roll around on top of one another like children, beneath the cocoa trees, for what seems like an eternity. Finally exhausted, we stop and try to make sense of things.

I had never seen the boy before in the village, but I recall having noticed the girl several times at the so-called creek of the drummer girls, where I used to go when we first came to the village. Unfortunately for me, she never dared speak to me, just like the rest of the girls in Libông. I would greet them, and they'd respond with a respectful curtsy, as is proper when faced with one's elders. They played the water like a drum or watched me play, but then they'd leave, very discreetly. Had I been in school with them it would all have been much easier. But since I was a "nurse," they saw me as the older one, the adult, and they wouldn't have allowed themselves to come closer to me. I would have had to take the initiative in breaking down the barriers. With my complicated and busy life, I didn't have the time.

After the spontaneous play we have just enjoyed, I realize that since Yèrè's death I haven't had a single friend among the children of Libông! I'm spellbound by the irresistible innocence and charm of these two. They introduce themselves to me: "I'm Sarah Mbeï," the girl says, "and this is my brother Isma Mbeï."

"We've tried more than once to approach you and offer you our friendship, but each time we were afraid you might dismiss us. And now," the brother continues, "I'm really sorry that we wasted so much time, since we have so little left."

Quite surprised, I interrupt: "Why do you say that? Do you have to leave the village?"

"No, unfortunately, but we've just heard that you're going to be leaving Libông for good," the girl says, instantly sad. "We'd like to have a correspondence with you, at least, after you go. Would you be willing to write us? We've never in our lives received any letters."

"If you're willing to be our friend," the boy adds, "you'd open up the world to us. Of course, we understand that it may seem a bit silly to you, who travel with your father all the time. But we beg you to recognize that we can never even hope to have such an experience, not with parents like ours, in any case. So we must create our own ways of making the dream of traveling come true; it's been haunting us ever since you came to Libông."

"So," the girl picks up, "we've been watching you since this morning, waiting for a chance to talk to you. I've called you with all my powers and, see, you came. Am I not a talented sorceress?"

"You certainly are, my dear. But is that any reason to claim that you know something about me I don't know myself? There's no question of my leaving here so soon. I'm going with my father to the plantations while I grow up and wait to be married; he said so himself!"

"We heard your stepmother tell our mother, who delivers your fresh vegetables. She says you're a witch who's starting to be harmful to her children in her own house. But we know you, and we told our mother that your stepmother is lying; everyone in the village sees it and says so, and even she herself knows. She can't stand your being there anymore because it makes her too ashamed, and so she's invented some reason to send you back to your village. She says she doesn't have time to supervise you and, what's more, that you're too brazen and already looking at men, even though you're only thirteen and a half! So you're supposed to go back to your grandmother, who's the only one with any influence over you, or else your fiancé won't find you to be a virgin."

I hear them, but I am not listening anymore. The spell is broken, and I'd like to be somewhere else, where I would know nothing about the plot they've so brutally revealed to me. My stepmother has really made up her mind, then, to get rid of me for good, sending me away from my baby once and for all. I am overwhelmed with despair.

I've lost Yèrè, the only friend I ever had. Now, barely do I meet some young people my own age when I hear that I will be taken away from them. Foolishly, I begin to sob, and they start weeping with me. We cry so much that in the end, huddled on top of each other beneath the cocoa trees, we fall asleep; when we wake up, we are surprised to find that it's afternoon. I run home, praying to heaven that my father won't be home yet. Thank God, his car isn't there. Just as I am about to enter the kitchen without being noticed, Mam Naja pulls at my back and begins to hurl insults at me right there in the courtyard, calling me a vagabond and a tart just like my mother. A loudly honking horn keeps me from leaping at her. It's the sub-prefect, trying to be more jovial than usual to lighten the atmosphere, which he recognizes is about to explode. Then my father arrives, parks his Land Rover, and the two men draw us into their false cheerfulness as they take us into the house, each one holding his woman by the hand. Just before we cross the threshold, I pull the gentleman back and beg him to follow me. A kind of soundless rage crawls up my spine.

What strange coincidence brings all these people together? What moment was it that I conceived of what was coming out of my mouth?

"I just heard that my stepmother's going to send me back to the village and I know the reason—she wants to take revenge and get rid of me. I also know that you're using me to cover up your affair with her. You pretended to ask my father for my hand just to delude him. But you can't fool me: I'm going to tell him everything now, and I'm just letting you know so it won't take you completely by surprise."

"You're not serious, I hope. You'll provoke a tragedy, and I don't believe that's what you really want."

"The tragedy rests in your lies and your duplicity toward both my father and me. All I'm doing is bringing them to light, because I refuse to be the only one to pay the price. But you might be able to prevent all that."

"How, pray tell? I'll do anything to avoid the worst."

"Well, then, you'll have to help me do something important in the next two days. I need money, a lot of money. I'm going to find another wife for my father to marry, and I'll need to pay a dowry for that."

"Is your father aware of this? Is he sending you to trap me this way? How could he drag such a young daughter into such wheeling and dealing? Speaking of duplicity!"

"You're wrong. My father knows nothing about it for the simple reason that I only just came up with the idea myself, when I heard about my stepmother's cowardly plan to send me away, catching all of us off guard—you, my father, and myself. I want to act faster than she does, and it is God himself who wants to spoil her plan by letting me know about it beforehand. So, will you give me the money? I'm warning you, if you refuse the only thing left for me to do is tell my father everything."

"Wait, calm down. How much do you need?"

"I don't know. Enough to pay a complete dowry: *pagnes*, a sheep, tobacco, beverages, and cash. Weren't you supposed to pay a dowry for me sometime soon?"

"Yes, of course. I agreed with your father that I'd go to your village next month to present them with your dowry."

"And how much did you expect to give as my dowry?"

"Oh, a most respectable one, maybe three hundred thousand, at least. . . ."

"Good, let me have half of that."

"What, right here and now? But I don't have that!"

"Well, too bad for us all."

"No, wait, I beg you. I'll see what I have on me. I've just received a sum of money from the district chief, I don't know exactly how much."

He goes through his pockets, pulls out all his money, and quickly starts counting as he glances around, panic-stricken. He counts out a hundred and thirty-five thousand francs and hands them to me. I take them and wrap them inside my shawl, then run to hide them under a pile of old palm trees in the cocoa plantation. The whole transaction has taken no more than fifteen minutes. We go back to the house where my father had set up a turntable and is playing a record. I'm enchanted, relaxed, beaming, and perfectly content. So is Mam Naja. She has used my absence to set her own transaction in motion: She's convinced my father to send me back to the village. She looks radiant, like someone who has managed to accomplish a desperate mission, and throws me a triumphant look. But my serenity worries her, and in the end her pleasure is marred, while I patiently wait. My father takes the floor.

"Your mother wants you to be with your grandparents to better prepare yourself for your marriage, and I do think she's right. You'll go with your cousin, who'll be leaving in three days, so that you won't have to make that long trip all by yourself. Besides, it will be more honorable if your fiancé goes there to ask your grandparents for your hand. What do you think?"

"It seems fine to me. But I'd like to travel with two of my friends, if their parents allow it, of course, so if you wouldn't mind, please come with me, father, to ask for their permission. My friends will come back either with my cousin when he returns or with me when my fiancé comes to pick me up, which won't take too long, I hope."

"Of course, I'll be glad to go with you and ask the parents' permission, but I didn't know you had any friends close enough that you'd want them to come with you."

"Our friendship is very new but very strong. It would be really hard to separate us now, especially because we haven't had time to prepare for it."

In her relief at knowing she will be rid of me in barely three more days, and at getting off so lightly, Mam Naja asks no questions at all. Usually the one to make a scene every time my father opens a bottle of wine, she now generously gives him one. He takes it without batting an eye, just as amazed as his wife that I have been so easily convinced. Their shared relief grows into downright glee as they drink their wine.

The sub-prefect remains silent, something that would have been of concern under normal circumstances; but now I'm the only one to notice, afraid he might say something untoward. Soon he makes his excuses to leave, and I relax at his departure. Not understanding my tranquility and cheerfulness, Mam Naja decides on her own, and to my father's annoyance, to turn off the record player. It's a good opportunity for me to ask him to come with me to meet my friends and their family.

It is one of the most reckless, dazzling ventures of my life.

Along with my father, I land in the middle of a family whose children I've only known for five hours, in a house that's been pointed out to me from a distance and with parents I've never met before. Without waiting for permission, I begin to speak to "defend our friendship, which is much too precious to be sacrificed," thereby justifying our decision to leave together.

"And so I've come to try to persuade our respective families to seal a lasting alliance. I'm asking for the hand of my friend for my father once she is grown up. And I'd like to turn over the dowry as a necessary guarantee without any further ado, leaving it to my father to round it off later on."

My father has had few occasions in his life to be this astonished; he can't find a single word to say. He really is taken off guard today, but my new friends are even more surprised, and also can't find anything to say other than to nod their head in agreement to every one of their parents' questions. With all the formalities included, the transaction lasts exactly an hour. It is agreed that I'll be leaving the day after tomorrow with my friend and her brother. They only ask me to postpone bringing the dowry until the following day, so that they'll have time to alert the family.

My father begins to laugh heartily when we leave. He holds his sides, coughs, and begins to laugh even louder, unable to ask me any of the many questions he tries to articulate. They're all cut off by his irrepressible, mad laughter. The moment he begins to quiet down, and I wonder how I'll escape from an interrogation that may be hazardous to my plans, Mam Naja calls us from afar: "Ah, there you are, you two! May one know what you're so happy about, and why? Perhaps you're planning to party it up under the full moon until dawn?"

We join her, wholly in her clutches again and obliged to change our conversation. At the house, social demands take over, and my father and I have no further opportunity to talk privately before the next morning, when we again meet with the family of my friends.

During the day, I had managed to buy a demijohn of wine, five chickens, five *pagnes*, and a sheep, and drop these off at my friends' place. I have a hundred thousand francs left in cash and give this to the parents.

At the time, a hundred thousand francs was a large sum of money for such an underprivileged family, and to them it was a gift from heaven. Uncles and aunts greet us, and each one of them pronounces blessings and gratitude to the spirits of the ancestors. Finally, the father's older brother speaks more solemnly: "My daughter, your sister who is here with us belongs to you and to you alone, from this day onward and until the day she has reached the age of womanhood. At that time both of you must return here, together with the man in your family whom you have chosen to be her husband, as long as he consents, of course. We don't think it will be your father, who seems to be monogamously married and who hasn't spoken a word since we've been discussing this. It is clear to us that you alone have initiated this affair, and that you have the support of our children in their great desire to get away from the poverty we live in. But we bless our children and we thank heaven for the grace that it is now being granted them," he says, and asks my father with tear-filled eyes for permission to let me sleep one night with his children in their humble home.

To our great joy, my father consents, and so I feel that I have already left my stepmother's home. I won't have to spend another night in the house of the woman whom I will hereafter always see as a traitor and an overt enemy. I know she'll find out soon enough what I've just done, and she won't ever forgive me.

She was to hear it the day after our departure, and until the eve of her death, many decades later, we would remain sworn enemies, always fighting at the slightest provocation.

MOVEMENT FIVE

22

SONG 10

A face never offends its owner;
Everyone thinks he's beautiful, and does not want to hide that fact.
Even with nostrils the size of an elephant's watering hole,
A pockmarked face as in days gone by,
And mangy buttocks like the dry season's powdery yam,
Everyone thinks he's beautiful, and admits it to himself
In the mirror, frontally or from the side;
Everyone names himself, stands upright, and is drawn in,
Lovely as the gnat I am, I want to preach to all the wretched
And invite them to my table of sounds to taste a new and unfamiliar
    word—
Words of pure water, words of fire; words of stones and molten iron.
Come and listen to my word; come and invent a new way to approach
    the world.
Adults play infernal games, play with fire;
Adults love games of domination, of manipulation;
But I direct myself expressly to the child surviving deep inside me, inside
    you,
The child who still does not grasp why
Adults unlearn to play so fast.
To reinvent the world without despairing,

I want to preach to all the wretched, to bring out whatever remains
In the most profound depths of their childhood and their inspiration.

• • •

In the bush taxi that takes us away from Libông, my friends and I
are held captive by a stifling silence. What are they thinking? As for
me, I'm ranting at Mam Naja. In all its wicked meaning, the name
alone makes my hair stand on end and is revolting to me. Moments
later, I would wonder, what on earth has possessed my father to add
it to the whole string of saints' names that he loves to adorn me with
and drive me mad, as he does when he says goodbye. He grabs me
by my hair, rubbing it like a puppy's fur: "Well now, my little Agathe
Solange Yolande Augustine Evelyne, let's see, my Michou Nicou
and all the rest of it, don't make that face. Soon you'll be back holding your head high. You've won a hell of a battle, you know? You
are blessed among all women, my Mary Magdalene Martha Mireille.
When you come back you'll be 'Madame Sub-Prefect' and, should
anyone be tempted to come anywhere near your knees with a sugar
cane in hand, I guarantee you that your husband will have him spend
a few days in prison. So, go on then, my red Mamba Super Naja,
and see you soon."

It is too much. What is making him call me by that cursed name,
Naja, which too many unpleasant people around us already have, that
name that seems to bring bad luck and the whole mess of trouble that
comes with it? From my disastrous stepmother to my mother, and a
slew of cousins and half-sisters in between, no one ever calls them by
that name at happy moments, but always to complain about them or
console them for the innumerable troubles that seem to hound them.
So it has to be a name of misery, a serpent's name.

I catch myself trying to establish a link between each of the
many Najas I know and my fear of the serpent by the same name.
"Fascination and venom," I tell myself, and my mood grows darker
and darker.

Besides my mother, the other Najas I know are actually very
modern, in their educations, and in their ways of dressing and

speaking—social worker, teacher, state-employed nurse, these "intellectuals" who are considered so priceless were literally fascinating to every man of my father's generation. Yet, in their home life with them, these men didn't seem any happier. A few thoughts of Aunt Roz on these new kinds of relationships come back to me now.

"Our men are seeking new situations. They want to present women who do them honor, and for these 'new' women they're prepared to forget their first wives and children, family alliances, our societies' taboos, and so forth. They discover that 'love for two' is supposed to rhyme with always. In its name they clear the board of the past, of ideals, and of ideologies. They only think about 'personal success,' and see their future selves in the image of their former White bosses, who walked hand in hand with their wives at the prefect's evening parties, their shoulders covered with medals, and without any kids to trip over."

Aunt Roz recounted that one of these Najas had seduced one of her cousins, whereupon after twelve years of marriage he deserted his legitimate wife and six children and remarried in France to continue advanced studies in economics. When he returned, he was sure he would become a minister of state and wouldn't know what to do with an uneducated peasant wife. But once there, the Naja in question had found a higher bidder. "Well, our men shouldn't wait to have both the oil and the money the oil brings in. Every cowry shell has its dark side," she concluded.

Throughout the trip, I cannot rid myself of these somber reflections. I see no way out other than picking up my studies again, to avoid being abandoned one day by the old sub-prefect in favor of educated and fascinating women of the Mam Naja type, who are able to take lovers without knowing how to do anything with their hands, and are capable of getting a new husband in every city their careers send them. My father now only lives and moves where his wife's assignments take them, and so, on the eve of my future husband's retirement, I will have to follow that hypocrite of a sub-prefect to any hole in the wall where the last years of his career might take him, in the same way that my new friend is about to bury herself in Massébè by marrying one of the men in my family. Is that fair? Am I right to use her to hurt Mam Naja? "In any event, some lives are doomed to mediocrity from the start, and this won't be any worse than being in Libông with her parents," I say to console myself.

In this savaged state of mind, I am reunited with my grandparents and tell them of my adventures. They listen in amazement, and then Grand Pa Helly merely says: "There's nothing we can do about it, you'll always bring change wherever you go. Take these children's bags to your aunt's house."

"I beg you, Grand Pa, I want to continue school; it's absolutely necessary to assure myself a better future. Help me to convince my father that I have to be spared this ridiculous marriage."

Grand Madja starts to laugh uproariously, and finally says: "Drop your fantasies, my namesake. You'd better think about building your future now and prepare yourself for that in the best way possible; that would be more sensible, don't you think?"

"In any case, wherever you are, you'll do what you have to do, and you will be grown-up; your destiny will find you, never fear," my grandfather concludes, trying to comfort me.

I feel desperate, as if defeated, yet in my heart there is complete refusal: This will be the last man to whom my father will ever try to sell me. All the encounters he'd arranged for me with specific people were nothing but a perpetual attempt to trade me like a piece of merchandise. Now, however, I believe I've bought back my freedom by buying him a "little mother" to replace me. I have the right to try my luck elsewhere. But where and how?

How many lives collide with this same question and never find an answer, placating you to stay there and submit, without daring to envision anything else at all. And you scrape along in melancholy for the rest of your life. You, for instance, you who are reading me at this very moment, can you truly declare that you are where you wanted to be all along? That you have made all your own decisions—where, when, and how you were going to live and why? If so, do you recall how you went about it, and can you explain that moment—surely the most fundamental moment in any life—to your children or your peers? If not, have you tried to understand your fears and attempted to overcome them? For if you cannot manage that, you will have failed to reach what in this life is called "illumination." Yes, I believe that illumination is the blinding moment when you think you've found your path and understood your reason for being in a given life. Even if it is an illusion, at least you have the energy needed for the next stage, which may be the one that will at last reveal the misunderstanding.

Where should I go now? How can I depart from an apparently fatal destiny? First of all, stop thinking about it. Work, keep busy, every moment of the day.

I begin to follow Grand Pa Helly everywhere, as soon as my share of the household tasks and field work is done. I pester him with questions about village gossip, traditions, about his wickerwork and his cabinetry, about everything and anything. I lend him a hand, although he protests vehemently. To get away from me, he often invents work appointments with other Mbombock sages. Then, to the great displeasure of Grand Madja Halla, I carry his ritual bag!

"A girl about to be married doesn't carry the bag of the Mbock anymore," she repeats over and over again. "That ritual bag has powers that may be harmful to a young woman's fertility. You'd do better getting ready for that, instead of acting like someone who should have been a boy! You're not a child anymore, you know."

"She won't mature and become a woman overnight just because her father decided to marry her off to someone who could be her grandfather," Grand Pa retorts. "Fortunately, she is what she is, or else she never could become a woman, or anything else for that matter. So why don't you leave her alone."

They leave me alone for the next few months, and I again enjoy one of those privileged periods in my life that have made me into the happy creature I would eventually become for good. I experience moments of discovery and continuous wonderment—discovering things, discovering the nature of people—that are all the more exhilarating because I have no agenda but to be ecstatic.

My grandfather is once again the great "husband" of my early childhood, and has no problem bending the customary rules to grant me my unconventional requests. He reveals small secrets to me that, had he been there, only my brother would have learned. Thus, under the influence of specific formulas of the male Mbock initiation, I see a piece of bark turn into an antidote for poison, a shield against any White weapon, or a tool by which to read messages of geomancy. I learn formulas to reinforce the magic powers of the bark of the *simgang*, the *yôp*, or the *e badjôb* that, when vigilantly kept in the bottom of a bag or on your person in a *pagne's* knot or in the fold of a garment, will cancel out any effect of the "evil eye," cause all poisoned food to drop from one's hands, and defuse any malevolent spell that is placed on the path. Grand Pa won't eat meat, shakes no one's hand, and sleeps alone for three days before going to gather this bark. And when he carries it on his body and he's angry, he refuses to point at anyone with his right index finger.

One day, when he is on his way back from one of these hikes, looking for bark and lianas, I finally discover why. An uncle who is jealous of my father, blaming him for having made off with Mam Naja, his childhood fiancée, had attacked a whole row of young mango trees my father had planted, laden with their first ripening fruit. Grand Pa Helly, who has no patience with gestures of empty maliciousness, becomes infuriated and almost points his finger at him. Drawn there by the untimely cutting of the trees, Grand Madja arrives before us with many uncles and aunts and lets out such a resounding scream that we are frozen in place. Quickly collecting his wits, Grand Pa Helly instantly points his already-raised right index finger at a young palm tree, which instantly turns brown and withers. The jealous uncle lies shaking on the ground, making little mouselike squeals and inaudible apologies. All reproachful eyes now turn to Grand Pa Helly, utterly ashamed and stunned that even he could have made such a gesture. For a Mbombock may never show anger, especially when it can provoke destructive acts.

Shame and remorse cause Grand Pa violent pain in his lower belly that forces him to take to his bed, where for three days he suffers and groans, unable to control himself.

It is the first manifestation of the prostate cancer that will eventually kill him. From then on he asserts he is unable to carry his Mbock medicine bag, and insists on this until the end. I now have an "official" excuse to carry it for him, and it allows me to accompany him without being the target of any further sarcastic or argumentative remarks.

I become the exceptional female bag carrier that men are forced to tolerate, and in the end they become accustomed to my silent presence even at certain meetings of profound wisdom. Grand Pa has found the only way in which to introduce a girl into this gathering that is forbidden to women, and thereby transmit to her a few snatches, at least, of an initiation that is rapidly being lost.

Thanks to these meetings I find my serenity and inner peace again. My future marriage no longer exists: I've swept it away, to the extent that when my father arrives to announce its postponement until after the end of the year's holidays, I'm convinced that the power of my refusal has scrapped it permanently. I know this marriage will never take place. At the same time I discover that from now on I'll always be able to influence the events in my life, that my refusals will be effective, as will my commitments. What I still need to learn is to detect as clearly as possible in myself what I don't want, and learn to refuse things for my own personal reasons, rather than to please someone or out of fear of another person.

My father tells us that in truth, the wedding has been postponed because of a summons from the court of appeals for new blood tests, required because of conflicting results. I look him straight in the eye to make sure he isn't planning to start his special transfusion again. His gaze is as empty as if no such event had ever existed, or as if he has forgotten it all, erased it from his memory. What is more, I am sure today that he has succeeded. The power of forgetfulness is phenomenal. It is the traumatized who have a hard time wearing the veil of oblivion.

Grand Madja is right: I must try to think of my future without going to school. I'm already getting all worked up when I think of how the next hearing will unfold—we'll go to another Institut Pasteur to have blood taken in the presence of a bailiff, who is assigned to pick up the results under seal. There is a new twist, however: The examination won't take place before the same bench, but in the capital city itself. "At least it will give us a chance to get a new perspective on the world," I tell myself. In spite of this lucky enticement, I can't bear the thought of a new trial. I can't bear hearing the same drivel from the same witnesses recounting in every detail the changes of men in my mother's life, bragging about their direct intervention to help her find someone better than the hypocrite my father is. I can't bear watching my mother lose her voice because of her shouting, crying, and affirming that, sadly enough, she has never loved any other man. "How many times do I have to say it before everyone stops inventing all these stories on the pretext that they're helping me get custody of my children—who, unfortunately, I'm obliged to protect from the most irresponsible man in the world?"

I don't want to see my father leap at her like a wild beast again. I don't want to be present at the endless farce that culminates in a general fight between her family and their witnesses on the one hand, and my father and her on the other. They are so shameful, these guardians of the peace, stupid enough to make you weep, grotesquely minding everyone's business in the mess of sexual game-playing. The blasé judges will obviously ask once again to reflect on the matter, or will quickly pronounce their verdict only to have it immediately appealed by the losing party, so the whole thing can start up again from scratch. All this has now been going on for five years. And, of course, I still can't go to school!

MOVEMENT SIX

23

The capital city is actually an entirely different world. Asphalted roads, glistening stores, luxuriously decorated shop windows, and streets always jam-packed with busy, rushing, frenetic, heaving crowds. In this throng, one madwoman more would never be noticed.

We are staying with a friend of my father's who used to be a garage mechanic in the town where we lived before going to Libông. My father introduces me to his daughter, who is barely older than I.

"This is Deborah, your elder; she attends the girls' secondary school where I had planned to enroll you, and she knows the city very well. I put you in her hands. We have more than a week between the tests, the results, the actual judgment, and the verdict. Try to have a good time and discover as much as you can, because we'll have to get back to the village by the twelfth of January. Don't forget that your fiancé, the sub-prefect, will be waiting to take you back with him, assuming nothing interferes."

As soon as the blood tests are done my father magically disappears into the city with his friend. Deborah grabs the opportunity to go off as often as possible under the pretext that she's showing me around. One day it is the bridge over the river or the harbor, the next day it is the girls' high school, or the former royal palace. She has bought postcards of the monuments in question, which she describes to me in minute detail. All she has to do then is make a detour and rush into a cottage where her lover awaits her. The two of them go into the bedroom where they giggle, then sigh, and finally snore. I do my best to imagine the city by studying the postcards until I doze off with boredom and am released from any further worry. Toward the end of the afternoon Deborah wakes me up and we go home, chatting and laughing about specific features of the monuments. The girl's mother receives us with a fine meal and congratulates her daughter on her generosity and eagerness to show the city's wonders to a younger country girl. She boasts about the advantages of the city, its many available activities and opportunities, its access to a variety of educational fields, thanks to the numerous schools and the contact with people from so many different and complementary cultures. She adds fascinating historical details about the monuments as if she herself had experienced them, and her daughter takes the opportunity to select the next place she will show me. I burst out laughing at her mother's naiveté; she will probably be fooled throughout her life since she's so eager to see only what she wants to see, and that keeps her from fretting.

This trial will be the decisive one—for me, in any case, because that is the premonition I have the minute we walk into the courtroom.

For starters, the capital city's court is a great deal more impressive. It seems to me that any verdict rendered here will be much more difficult to appeal. The walls and desks are covered in massive slabs of wood, veritable logs with the weight of the law. The place reserved for the judges is stunningly handsome. The number of magistrates, all dressed as if for an exceptionally solemn ceremony, is unbelievable. Most surprising of all are the three rows filled with magistrates also in ceremonial dress, but apparently much younger. I tell myself that with so many magistrates present to sit in judgment over our affair the outcome is bound to be definitive. The unusual solemnity will surely have its effect.

It takes me a while to understand that all this is not specifically for us. By pure coincidence, we are witness to the installation of the new prosecutor and to a whole group of young magistrates taking their oath, some as lawyers and others as judges. Our trial is the only one on the calendar of the new prosecutor and the young magistrates, as an interesting case of jurisprudence to be studied by some and to be brought to an end by the others. It is a kind of master class with case study and demonstration.

The young men swear to serve justice and impartiality, to be influenced in their judgments only by the law and by their profound conviction of serving it to the benefit of society.

The prosecutor expresses his thanks for the honor and the trust placed in him by this prestigious appointment and promises to keep his word.

Finally they begin our trial. First there is a long reading to review the preceding verdicts and appeals. At last they come to the one called for by Monsieur Njokè, now brought before this court for a final appeal. They move on to reading the results of the blood tests. Once again they prove that of the seven children who are the object of the litigation, only three are shown to be the actual progeny of the father, two share a blood type with the mother, and the last two are of another blood type. In our ignorance of blood groups and hemoglobin types, we have the surreal impression that blood has recognizable faces.

The prosecutor forcefully attacks my mother: "Marriage is not a creative affair, Madame, but an institution," he hammers away. "It is the business of ordinary women and men in service of society and not a stage for actors and actresses. It's high time to stop this soap opera. I request that divorce be definitively decreed. In view of the infidelity proven by the results of the blood test, I request that Monsieur Njokè be exempted from all paternal duty toward any children that are not his and that the mother keep her bastards. . . ."

He speaks artfully and directly. One can tell that he has learned the game. Everything seems far too rehearsed, even the looks. The only false note comes from me, suddenly standing and moving toward him. No one is concerned or understands what is happening. Roughly I pull at his robe and stop him in his stride. He turns around and his sentence hangs suspended in the air, as does his gesture, like a caricature. I don't know when I have stood up or what has ripped me from my seat. I don't know what I have in mind. I think that, like everyone there, I only realize that something strange is going on at the precise moment of that suspension. For an eternity, our gaze remains as if welded, our throats tight. My father's hands come down on me and tear me from the floor like a straw. He forcibly puts me back down in my seat beside him, under heavy silence.

I am in a black hole; once again there is a huge gap of time, beginning with the prosecutor's frozen look and his suspended gesture, as if in a photograph. The verdict? Not heard. Not a word, not a face, not an interval, not a movement survives.

As if I were dead and buried, then resuscitated on the day my father told me, at his friend's house, that we were going home the next day. The calendar on the wall shows it is the eighth of January. My heart leaps inside my gut. Only four more days and I will be in the arms of trickery! Then a thousand details and close-ups dance inside my memory.

• My friend's stunned look as she finally realizes she will have to submit to a return to her normal routine. A silent supplication flutters on her lips.

• Her father's lewd gaze at me, like a cat who sees a mouse escaping from beneath its paw, which I notice for the first time.

• The mother's look at her husband, of such naiveté that it suddenly seems feigned to me, too close to real stupidity. A smile both of relief and provocation. Has she taken me for a future rival?

• I search for my father's glance, but in vain.

• The tomato sauce in heavy china dishes with roses on their edges.

• The tiny squares of soaked manioc.

• The checkered plastic tablecloth.

• And then my voice. . . .

"What else can I still visit before we leave? I don't know whether there will be any opportunity to see life and discover other people's views through postcards where I'm going."

"I know," Deborah says, hopping up and down, "I'll take you to attend a public radio broadcast tomorrow evening."

"There," her mother says triumphantly, "there couldn't be a better way to end your trip in a festive manner—it's a grand finale!"

The complicit looks of the two men. I bet they have their own plan for the evening.

The mother won't take her eyes off them. She knows more than she wants to let on, I'm sure of that now.

Ah! In the end adults really are no laughing matter.

24

My Wheel of Fortune,
My summit, accelerating my descent,
My abyss, thrusting itself toward the mountain tops,
My eternal effort in the dunes,
Always within hand's reach
And yet so uncertain,
My unforeseen foreseeable,
A bit outdated, déjà vu,
And yet like the certainty of a morning
And the surprise of its innumerable incidents,
Like a gift from heaven despite the violence of accidents,
The same certainty each morning since that furtive evening
When my destiny was in your hands,
You whose name will stick to my skin,
You who will push me toward the huge leap
And affect even my self-perception—
How, in that intense uncertainty, could I foresee meeting you?

• • •

My first outing in the city by night, filled with light: traffic lights,
thousands of headlights, streetlights, signs in a thousand colors;

even people's eyes seem to have taken fire, to be transformed into lights, lights of craving and desire, of lust.

For once I pray that we can actually go to the broadcast, and that I won't have to be limited to postcards. Alas, I have no choice but to settle for the rebroadcast in that sightless room.

This evening Deborah is particularly excited. Her boyfriend has ventured very close, too close perhaps, to our house, and we have to pretend not to know or even notice him. He's holding a large radio, which is playing a popular rumba. He passes us, slows down, lets us pass him, and then it starts all over again. We arrive at his place first, but hesitate to go in. Finally, my friend charges into the cottage and goes straight to the bedroom. Our host gives me a radiant smile and rushes in after her, dancing the twist.

Frankly, I have no earthly desire to go in as well just to hear their chortling again. I'd really like to walk around a bit. But a group of carefree boys passes by very closely and begins to whistle at me, one of them going so far as to touch my behind. I resign myself to going in and literally collapse on the usual chair.

I don't know how long I've been horizontal before I realize I'm not alone. My heart nearly stops when I discover a boy right beside me, looking at me almost nose to nose, for he must have been quite intrigued to see me so upset all by myself.

Astonished at my fear, the boy recoils all the way to a corner of the wall and raises his arms as if threatened by a gun. I start laughing nervously and then burst into tears. Even more surprised, he comes back to me.

"Please—I'm so sorry. I didn't want to scare or hurt you. I . . . I would so much like to help you or console you. What's wrong? Who did this to you?"

"Did what?"

"Well . . . whatever it is that has put you in this state. Who's making you cry like this?"

"Isn't it you?"

I cry all the more, irresistibly, and don't know why. The young man kneels in front of me and takes my hands in his.

"Calm down, I beg you. I'm here now, and you're not alone anymore."

"Really? You're here now. And where will you be later when they're busy marrying me off to my grandfather?"

"Well . . . I don't know."

"You don't know, do you? So leave me alone! I bet you don't know what's going on in the next room, either. You don't even have ears to hear."

"Yes I do, generally I hear quite well! But I'm at the seminary. I'm going to be a priest, you know."

"Great! So all you need to do is pray."

"I'm doing just that so you'll stop being unhappy. But apparently I'm not doing a very good job."

"Well, for God's sake try something else then. Time is running out. I don't want to be handed over to that old vulture unscathed. Do what they're doing in there."

Overcome by I don't know what madness, I grab the young man and pull him on top of me. His weight turns the chair over, and we are on the floor. I feel as if I have eight hands and I don't know if they are mine or his. We carry on like furies, and I feel something like a rip, which makes me scream.

I beg him to stop, but he's in a wild frenzy.

He must be having some sort of sudden epileptic fit.

I'm shaking with an indefinable sensation, between pain and pleasure, and am crying all the more.

All of a sudden the boy begins to yell, yell so hard that our friends in the next room emerge thunderstruck as he lets out a final gasp and collapses in a heap beside me. My skirt is covered in blood.

The boy has a haggard look, as if he were having a nightmare.

Frozen in place, our friends stare at us.

I get up, intending to ask them for an explanation, but I collapse, suddenly dizzy.

"I . . . I don't know what came over me," the boy stutters. "Eh . . . it's the first time and . . . I didn't know . . . well, that she was a virgin. I am so sorry, really very sorry! I . . ."

"Couldn't you at least have been a bit more gentle and less noisy?" my friend protests. "The neighbors must have heard your mooing. And look at her bloodstained skirt, what are we going to do now?"

"I . . . I'll wash it if you want me to . . ."

"Stupid bastard! He's a real find, this one! Where do you dig up those friends of yours?" Deborah says.

"This is my seminarian friend. I've told you about him many times. He's not bad. It must have been a spontaneous thing for them. Let's calm down. You go and help her undress in the other room. I'll wash her clothes and iron them right away while you help her put herself together again. That way you can both go home looking good. You, my friend, follow me if you can still stand up, you deflowered little priest!" He bursts out laughing.

While my friends are busy washing my clothes I doze off, shivering under the sheets. I'm dreaming that a snake bites me in my lower belly. Grand Pa Helly catches him by the tail and tries unsuccessfully to pull him off, but he hangs on by his fangs, blowing a kind of hot air into me that makes my belly swell up so big that I'm going to explode. I'm suffocating and fight back. Grand Pa Helly tries to calm me down.

"Gently now, my little wife. Venom, you know, isn't always what we think it is. But when it truly is venom, then we do not reason with it. Then it's better to enter into the substance and give it form in the hope of surviving and enjoying it as well!"

I don't understand a word of this speech, and my belly continues to swell as the snake keeps blowing. I can't take it anymore. I'm tearing myself away from the impending explosion and wake up. My friend puts my warm and steaming clothes on my belly and looks at me with a mocking smile.

"Well, how about you! You should have told me a long time ago that you wanted it, too. My friend has better-looking buddies than this boor you took on at the last minute. If I'd known, you would have had a better time. . . ."

My throat is constricted, and no sound comes out. The boy is waiting for me in the living room, deeply embarrassed. I throw him a stealthy look and leave without a word. I won't see him again for another five years.

My unforeseeable foreseeable. An outdated déjà vu.

MOVEMENT SEVEN

25

Truly, God wants what woman wants. Of course, she has to want it with all her heart. I got what I wanted: The sub-prefect did not come. A messenger arrived at the same time we did to announce that he had been transferred elsewhere, and thus had to leave to start working and move his family there before he could come to pick me up. Something tells me that the gentleman is too afraid of me and will never come for me. You don't marry a woman who awakens anxieties lurking in your consciousness.

I'm overjoyed, and roll on the floor with gratitude: I will never marry him; God himself has heard my prayers and made this decision.

And so life in the village goes on again in ways to which I am relatively accustomed. Grand Pa Helly, however, is in ever greater pain, and no longer able to suppress his groans when he has to urinate. It's so astounding to see him cry like a child. He can't bear to have me watch him anymore. He's tried every herb and tree bark known to help with this disease, with no result. The thought passes through the family that his illness is the punishment for his almost deadly anger, for which he cannot forgive himself. He locks himself in his room, and only Grand Madja is allowed in to wash and feed him. I'm not permitted to see him any longer unless he himself calls for me—that is to say, only when he has moments of temporary improvement; sadly, these occur less and less frequently. It is very sad for both of us, and we have a hard time putting up with it. He forgives me for a few brief intrusions, during which I gently take his hands and massage them in the hope of comforting him, which he allows me to believe I do.

In the end he agrees to an operation.

My father comes to get him, and they are gone for almost two months. When they come back, Grand Pa has found his serenity again and gained some weight. Everything could have been as nice as before if my father had not, once again, had those absurd ideas that always managed to turn things upside down, to speed up time or transform it into a nightmare. This time he wants to create an artificial lake and raise fish. He goes back to the city in search of the necessary material for his site. Anxiety engulfs the entire family, since we are used to disasters taking place whenever my father throws himself into a new project. Some months go by without any news from him, and we hope he's given up or forgotten his project, as did sometimes happen.

My father chooses this moment to mount a fresh attack. When his Lôs urges awaken, and his passion to act is aroused, no tempest is able to prevent him from executing his plans, all the way to victory or failure. Anyway, for him, victory and failure are part of the same thing, merely two possible results of a journey taken.

When he comes back, he claims he only has three weeks off and says that everything must be done within that time. He is already dreaming of his future annual leaves, during which he'll empty the pond; the whole village won't know what to do with all those fish, and will be thinking of him all year as they wait for the next miraculous catch, which only a Lôs could have arranged. A new Herculean labor is beginning!

No sooner is it said than done. The next day my father begins to mark off the perimeters of his project and dig up the earth. Every living soul in the village is expected to be there. Even the dogs, chickens, and pigs participate. To temper my father's demands, even Grand Pa gets back on his feet. He helps everyone as best he can, constantly going from one end of the chain of workers to the other. As a result his pain comes back, less frequently than before but more violently, and it overtakes him. An uncle who is a doctor passes through and says that Grand Pa hasn't taken enough time to rest up, and thereby has delayed the healing of the interior scar; he would be better off if he observed the full recovery period. Grand Madja decides to slow down all activity so that we can all spend more time at home and keep Grand Pa from jumping up for every little thing all the time. My father accepts that Grand Madja must care for her husband, but refuses to liberate the children; and so, from morning to night, we move the soil in little bowls to build the great dike. It's exhausting. There are times when I'm so tired I feel dizzy. But I have to keep going. If I fall, my father might guess. . . .

Grand Madja had already figured out my secret a few weeks before, when she caught me at night eating a *hikok*, the tough herb from our primeval forests that pregnant women love so much. Here, as soon as a woman begins to prepare the *hikok* on a regular basis, everyone keeps an eye on her. I would never have believed that an herb could arouse such a craving just because you're pregnant. By ruling the unconscious, old customs sometimes manage to turn into laws. In its very foundations, all of life seems to be nothing but a series of practices and habits. Would that be its only way to evolve? A person begins to do one thing, and the others follow, and then still others are born doing the same thing.

So I feverishly pick my *hikok* by day, cleaning and chopping it in secret in the bush. At night, when everyone is asleep, I prepare it and gobble it down, clean the plate, and no one is the wiser. In the morning Grand Madja complains of witchcraft in the village. "Where does that smell of hot *hikok* come from, if not from witch-craft? It is so strong at night, it's as if the dish were under my bed; it's hot *hikok*, but we can't find it anywhere."

I stop for a few days, but the urge is so intense that I go right back to it even more ravenously. One night, Grand Madja catches me in the act. She looks at me with her mischievous little eyes and bursts out laughing: "So it's you, my namesake, who's practicing witchcraft? Well now, that's quite something!"

I don't respond, hoping she'll believe it's just pure greediness. She doesn't insist, but I know she fully understands.

A little while later I feel a terrible craving for pork in black sauce. When the urge becomes too strong, I begin ranting as I wander through the fields. One Saturday I find myself yelling at God himself for making me so wild for unattainable things: "You can't pick pigs in the brush like *hikok*, after all, dear God! How am I going to appease this yearning? Am I going to have to steal pigs in the neighboring villages at night?" I say out loud, addressing the sky.

Then I see a pig lying stretched out beneath some banana trees. I'm so stunned that I think it's a miracle. I check my small machete to see if I might slit his throat with it. I approach the animal on tiptoe, but he doesn't move. I touch him; he doesn't move. He is dead but his body is still warm. I look in all directions and call out, to find out who is around and might have killed this pig, but there's no answer. I decide to remove a haunch, wrap it in leaves, and quickly go home to prepare the black sauce. I'm about to sit down, determined to eat the whole thing and get rid of any traces before Grand Madja returns, but at that precise moment she comes back and inquires where such a fine dish came from. I answer that my cousin Legro gave it to me.

"God be praised," she exclaims. "So obviously, if there is so much solidarity between you, your generation isn't going to get lost like your father's. I'm going to run off and thank his parents for this marvelous gesture."

"Wait Grand Madja. They've gone to Môm and won't be back before night time."

"Ah, well. Then I'll thank them another day."

Phew! I still have a bit of time before my secret is unveiled to all. At the end of the service in church the next day, the church elder announces that a pig who was bitten by a snake has died on the edge of his field, and he invites the owner to come and take him away. However, he insists on adding that one leg has been removed and swears by God in heaven that it wasn't he who helped himself to it.

Grand Madja's eyes seek mine; I pretend to be praying very hard, absorbed in my own request to God. I dread the moment when we'll return home and I'll be forced to offer an explanation. But she seems to have forgotten, and I thank heaven for this new support. The next day, Grand Madja returns from the market with two legs of pork and prepares them with black sauce herself. I'm salivating, and envy the stranger for whom the dish is intended. I wonder if I'll have a chance to taste it.

When the meal is ready Grand Madja calls me and puts it in front of me. "Forgive me, my namesake. You know my gruff nature, my intense shyness, and my reserve in showing my private feelings. Of course, I understood that you're pregnant, but I didn't know how to talk about it and where to start. There are certain things I really dread. Every day I put it off until the next, actually treating it lightly, and I almost lost you without realizing it. Because of a perfectly normal craving, you were forced to hide, and you went to eat pork that was poisoned by a snake. You could have died! And what would I have told the people? It still makes me tremble. So here, eat your fill of it. You know I won't be able to offer you as much as you want later on. But at least I hope we can talk about it freely from now on."

But the days pass, and we don't talk about it. She asks me no questions, and I don't know how to bring it up. Nevertheless, she makes me eat more vegetables and fruit and has me drink certain homemade mixtures, telling me it's good for the baby. It is at this juncture that my father arrives with his new project.

If I drag my heels he will notice it all too soon, knowing me to be a hard worker. The first week is so hard that I start to vomit, then feel dizzy and fall down. My father comes up with a diagnosis: worms! They have to be eliminated. But just in case, he still decides to take me to the doctor of Ékôa, the nearest health center.

The suggestion is less than thrilling to me. I pretend that all is well and go back to work with forced enthusiasm. But a dizzy spell almost causes me to fall to the bottom of the dike, which is reaching an impressive height. My father is concerned, and puts me on his bicycle to go to Ékôa. I tell myself my time is up. Having to endure all the bumps across the many miles on a bicycle, how would my discomfort and pain not be noticed?

I must have wanted so much not to feel anything that I didn't notice either time or distance. My memory has retained not one feeling, not one recollection of this trip of endurance: no face, not even a word spoken between my father and me, nothing, nothing. As if we'd been instantly transported.

After listening to my father explain—according to his diagnosis—my parasites, my malaria, and perhaps my "asthenia," or general weakness, the doctor asks him to allow me to be examined alone. In spite of himself, my father leaves the room. With a look of relief, the doctor locks the door.

"Well, Mademoiselle, what is going on? Lie down here and tell me everything."

"I'm fine, Dokta. I'm just tired. My father doesn't understand that some work can be too much for a person. I'm not a man, after all."

Pulse, stethoscope, blood pressure, looking at my throat, eyes, and ears. . . . I try to return his gaze, but I look away when he puts his hand on my abdomen.

"You certainly are not a man. How many months?"

"What?"

"Your pregnancy . . ."

"What pregnancy?"

"Come now, don't play with me, little one, I'm not your father. You've been carrying a baby in there for at least six months. Open your legs, we're going to do a check-up."

"Out of the question! What check-up? I'm not pregnant and I don't want you to put your dirty hands on my body."

He hits me. The pain and mostly the surprise take my breath away. He takes advantage of it to grab the upper hand in a kind of mute battle.

"Listen carefully. You're going to lie down quietly and let me examine you, or else I'll call your father in right away and I'll tell him everything; guess what's next!"

I lie down. He begins to palpate my body and then, gradually, it turns into something else! I have to think fast. If I resist loudly my father will find out and cause me who knows what public scandal, something I don't want for anything in the world. The only way to shut this bastard up is to keep calm and trick him. But this squealing little pig revolts me. I open my eyes and look at him coldly, as if he were an insect, and say: "I'm not eating any more pork until I deliver." He turns away in shame. He won't dare say anything to my father! He opens the door and pushes me outside, forcing himself to stay calm.

"You were right, she has to get rid of the parasites; and she'll need a quinine cure and some tonics because she's anemic and incubating malaria. She will also need at least three weeks of rest."

"That much? I need her on the work site. Are you sure it's not a trick—did she seduce you into getting her out of having to construct the dike, perhaps?"

"Come on now! What an imagination you have! Take her to the nurse for these two injections and have them give you all the pills I've prescribed here."

The doctor gives him a rapidly scribbled piece of paper. A quick goodbye to my father and then he scurries back into his office without even glancing at me. What I feel is a kind of contempt mixed with pity. I honestly don't see what this sordid and gratuitous act could have done for him. How would he justify it in his own eyes?

I'll never know, since I will never see him again. Nevertheless, I've often thought about it when seeing certain male ways of behaving. Above all, I remember it because on that day I learned something that was to save me from many a false step: A man cannot handle the lucid gaze of a woman. Even the most rabid rapist loses his hard-on before a woman's cold and indifferent stare.

The most urgent thing for me now is to untangle my situation: My father won't be ignorant of my state indefinitely. I am now about six months into my pregnancy, and will soon begin to show. If he finds out about it on his own almost anything could happen. I'll have to take hold of my courage, find a good moment, and inform him myself. Since he's decided to give me just one week off instead of the three weeks prescribed, I'm going to use the time to think this through calmly. Unfortunately, my week of rest goes by without offering me the right opportunity. When I go back to work again I feel even more tired and desperate than before.

What to do? I'm going around in circles inside myself, as if I'm in a cage, I stop talking, laughing, and even lose my appetite. Grand Pa's cries of pain go on incessantly now, and everyone thinks that's the reason I'm so upset. In fact, no one else talks or laughs anymore, except my father, who gives orders and makes fun of "this gang of sluggards; I don't know what I've done to our good Lord to deserve them, when what I need are true human Caterpillars, and a real army of them at that, not this uncircumcised bunch!" His lifeless mockeries fall flat in the murky silence.

26

Grand Pa Helly's cries are becoming veritable death rattles, especially at night, when they keep everyone awake in spite of the enormous exhaustion that follows their hellish days.

One morning Grand Madja comes to the site and, forgetting her usual reserve, publicly rebukes her son: "What kind of a man are you, anyway, Njokè? Are you actually human, or are you an animal or a monster? You make people work like beasts of burden without any consideration for anyone, without any compassion even for your elderly father. It's because of you that he's gone back to work against doctor's orders, and I'm sure that his internal wounds have opened up again. He bays at the moon, and you won't even stop your lousy construction, if only for one day, to take care of him! I swear to you that if anything at all happens to him I will hold you responsible forever. And as if that isn't enough, you strut around swaying your shoulders, thinking you're a Lôs. Listen to me carefully: The actions of a true Lôs are eternal, and immortalized by his admirers. Now, look around you: You are so inhuman that nobody admires you, nobody wants to immortalize your callous work! You're exerting yourself for nothing, my poor boy. I beg you, pull yourself together while your father is still alive and while people put up with you out of respect for him and gratitude for his enormous generosity. Stop running after the wind and at least concern yourself with your father's final days. How many times do I have to tell you this, and in what language, in what tone, before you understand!"

The whole crowd is silent. We're waiting for a disaster to happen. Surely he isn't going to beat his own mother? He moves toward her, his face taut.

"No, no, monster!"

The scream escapes from my throat, and I'm running toward my father. We reach Grand Madja Halla at the same moment; she hasn't moved an inch. She looks her son straight in the eye and says to me, as if speaking indirectly to her son: "Quiet, you! Don't ever forget that you have no right to judge your parents. Who knows what you yourself will be guilty of some day!"

"Give me the key to the cocoa storeroom," my father says very gently, almost tenderly. "You, little Halla, get ready to leave for Otélé with your sister. You're going to sell cocoa there at the market early tomorrow morning. You'll come back with the morning train, and your grandfather and I will be waiting at the station. With the money you bring back we'll go to the hospital of Métèt, where I hope they can operate on him again and take better care of him. Go now, tell your sisters and Fidèle Foulani. You're leaving right away."

Grand Pa Helly comes up behind us.

"There's no point in wasting money on me. I will not go to Métèt or any other place where you will spend mad amounts of money only to come back with my body. If you have any money, prepare the documents for my little wife, who's dying to go to school while you're dragging her around all over the place, any way you see fit. If you have any money, take care of your children; be a father, be a husband at last. How can you be a Lôs if you haven't even managed to be a husband and father, something even a gorilla is capable of being!"

My father leaps up, picks up his father the way he'd pick up a baby, and carries him back to the house, reprimanding him as if he were a child.

"Have you lost your mind or what? Didn't I ask you to stay in bed? The effort is making you bleed, you know that; you must stay in bed until someone treats you, understand? As for my money, I'll decide what to do with it, and the most urgent thing right now is to have you taken care of. And please, do me a favor, don't force me to get you to the station tomorrow morning in the same way I'm carrying you now."

To everyone's great surprise Grand Pa does not resist or try to get down. It is an alarming spectacle to see his tall, lanky body being carried sideways like a puppet by his giant of a son. And most spectacular of all is his smile. Loudly he says: "I dare you to transport me tomorrow morning. If you could do that, then you would truly be a Lôs."

Laughing, my father addresses the gathered crowd that's following them: "You're all witnesses, are you not? Tomorrow my father himself will pronounce me a Lôs, for at last he will recognize me as such! My day of glory has finally arrived! Tomorrow I will carry my father the eight kilometers to the station and take him by train to Métèt for more surgery."

Grand Pa Helly makes the air ripple with his purest laughter, which we haven't heard in a very long time. My father is so surprised himself that he sets him down on the ground. Grand Pa walks very straight, as in the good old days, right into the courtyard. Astounded, everyone follows him. Still laughing, Grand Pa looks at us all, his eyes filled, at the same time, with both compassion and mischief. Finally he looks at his son, who for once is as astonished as everyone else, and says: "Please forgive my son Njokè in advance for his pointless arrogance: He will not be able to carry me tomorrow as he's been boasting, but don't hold that against him, because it isn't up to him. Just tell him that if he takes care of his children like a true father and of his wives like a true husband, he will be more than a Lôs, and I shall recognize him as such, even from my grave. God gave him a progeny of geniuses, and that is better than being a Lôs. I'll pray that he ends up by realizing this some day soon, before it's too late."

Pain shoots through him suddenly, and he folds over. He grasps the wall and literally crawls all the way to his bedroom, followed by my father who does his best not to think about the worst.

• • •

A special day, a day of oracle and omen . . .

Instead of leaving immediately to catch the train, we linger into the afternoon, and we wouldn't have left at all if not for my father's insistence.

The bags are packed: half a bag of cocoa per able child, or four in all. A whole bag for Fidèle Foulani, the Fula man who is in love with my Aunt Roz, and who has abandoned his cattle for her. He lives here with us and takes on all the man's work my father doesn't do and Grand Pa Helly is no longer able to do.

Once the bags are packed, a storm threatens, although it never rains. At noon, when the threat has passed, a messenger from our Great-Aunt Kèl Lam arrives, saying that she urgently wants to see me.

My father is against it. Aunt Roz says that I can't refuse going to my great-aunt when she calls for me. Words, more words, and lengthy discussions. To put an end to it, Grand Madja decides that, as my namesake, she will respond to the call in my place, and we can simply leave. At that very moment, the *kou-bilim*, a kind of two-headed snake that moves in both directions, twisting and turning like a roundworm, begins to cross the road.

This snake is seen as the herald of catastrophes. Several voices rise to demand the children's trip be canceled, but without success. My father insists, and we leave the village around mid-afternoon to cover the eighteen kilometers that separate us from Otélé, with the cocoa on our heads. At an average of three kilometers an hour, we arrive late at night, too tired even to think of eating.

We immediately settle down beneath a market shed, rather than going the additional kilometers to our great-uncle's house, where we normally stay. But we're not the only ones sleeping in the sheds. On the eve of the weekly Otélé market day, there's always a crowd of people coming from distant villages to sell all kinds of products:

cocoa, different oils, palm almonds, yams, peanuts, corn, and even small game. Women set up everywhere to prepare manioc doughnuts or cereals, red beans, all sorts of stews, and corn beer. Men sell palm wine, mushrooms, fish, and crab caught during their nighttime fishing trips. Some come directly to the market at dawn with the products of their catch, hunt, or harvest. To shorten the wait for the sunrise, various clans or newly arrived groups form circles for storytelling or dancing. In short, the evening before market day is a celebration, and the people who arrive generally don't sleep. But we are so exhausted that we sprawl out on top of our bags of cocoa and do just that.

I dream that Grand Pa Helly calls me into his bedroom. I go there and sit down close beside him. He asks me to listen very carefully so I won't forget what he's about to tell me, for it is our last talk. I promise him my full attention.

"Stop once and for all being so preoccupied with what you call school: Your father will never send you there. If you continue to hope for that, you'll waste time and a great deal of energy for nothing. And you'll miss all the important things you must learn in the great school of life that is right here, every day and every moment, within reach of your common sense. Open your eyes wide, your ears, and your heart, and you will know that you are in your own school, the one that God prepared especially for you. You will have a child. Don't try to abort it and don't let anyone prevent you from having it. He will be your school. He will make you go where you should or must go. Hold on to the love, compassion, and sweetness that have always flooded your heart and until now have allowed you to understand other people, and you shall always be protected. Continue to gather the family together, and our tribe will expand beyond the seas. Give me your hand."

He takes it to his mouth and spits in it. Then he has me pass it over my own forehead before he raises it in front of his face, where he keeps it for a long moment while he studies the lines as if to read my destiny, after which he closes his eyes, and his hand falls back down, leaving mine suspended in the air. I keep it there for a moment and slowly lower it to his face. He is completely cold. I shriek: "Help! Grand Pa Helly is dead!" No one hears me. I shout louder and louder, repeating the same phrase. People crowd around us when they hear my cries, but don't dare wake me up. It's my younger sister who shakes me.

"Wake up, you're having a nightmare. Grand Pa Helly isn't dead; Papa will take him to the hospital soon. It's almost daytime. We're going to take up the front spot at our usual buyer's place. Come on, get up."

"I tell you that Grand Pa Helly is dead. He has just died. He spoke to me. I looked at the time. It was five-thirty. What time is it?"

"Five-thirty-three, my girl. Maybe she has had a premonition in her dream. . . ."

One of our aunts, who is in the area, approaches out of curiosity and recognizes us. After dispersing the crowd around us, she asks me to tell her my dream. I do, though I don't say anything about my pregnancy. When I stop she begins to weep silently. My younger sister starts to scream, and now it's my turn to calm them down, assuring them it's only a nightmare. But privately we all know that the crisis has come. We pull ourselves together as best as we can and force ourselves to sell the cocoa as quickly as possible so we can get to the station on time.

When we reach the station of Môm, eight kilometers from our house, we're all glued to the windows, hoping to relieve our anxiety by seeing Papa and Grand Pa Helly. Alas, it is Isma who welcomes us with a smile intended to reassure us: "Papa wasn't able to carry Grand Pa Helly—which we more or less expected, didn't we? So he asks you to take this envelope and this ticket, which will take you to the town of Makak. Go and get Grand Madja's younger brother, because she needs him to help her convince her husband to get treatment. You must come back on the evening train with the things needed, as indicated in the envelope."

Isma Mbeï keeps smiling, but I have already understood. He doesn't want my sisters and me to start screaming here in the station. In fact, they are sending me to my great-uncle to purchase what is needed for the funeral.

I don't shed any tears. I feel calm and almost serene. I think back to what Grand Pa said to me, word for word, and tell myself: "Now you are a widow, little Halla!" But then I immediately console myself: "My husband isn't dead. He left on a journey where I shall join him later. We said a sweet goodbye. He promised to protect me, always. It's up to me to find a way to respect his instructions." I review his words in my head; then a thought suddenly gives me a start.

He said that in the future I would have a child. Didn't he know I had already been pregnant? He, who had always been so insightful—how could he not have suspected what was going on? Perhaps he had vaguely sensed something that he knew he wouldn't be able to endure. His position would have required that he surrender for punishment to the council of elders anyone who violated taboos, even if that were his own son; and in this case the guilty one would unquestionably have been killed by the tribunal of Ngué. Knowing that Grand Madja would have died of sorrow over this, he may well have chosen not to notice. But wasn't this a different way of condoning my father's actions? In the end, it is hell to have an only son!

Indeed, under this land's patriarchal regime, the daughter does not belong to her parents, for later on she will move elsewhere to create another family with her husband's name; therefore she is not considered one of the heirs. The experience of having had ten children—nine boys and one girl—and having buried eight of the boys, with my father the only survivor, had made my grandparents react as if they were the parents of an only child, all the more insecure because they were always afraid they would have to bury him as well! Fear may have turned them into accomplices of my father in spite of themselves, inclined to forget their daughter, who had always been left to her own devices despite her far greater involvement in the family.

In my innermost heart I decide never to be the mother of an only son.

"I'll have a thousand children even if I have to create them with my own hands like God, but I'll never let my child put me in the absurd situations my father inflicts on his parents," I say out loud, startling the other passengers near me on the train.

I am now convinced that Grand Pa let himself go to escape from the perpetual contradiction within himself, and that Grand Madja won't have any other way out either. If she loses hope of changing her son, sooner or later she will let herself die before her time, as my grandfather just did, although he certainly had plenty of time left to live, resembling eternity as much as he did.

In Makak I find out that my uncle has left for the capital and won't be back for another two days. I cannot wait that long. What to do? I feel incapable of going out on the road alone all the way to their village on the edge of the Nyong. I decide to open the envelope and read the message meant for my uncle, in the secret hope that Grand Pa is dead in my nightmare alone. Sadly, my father has written that Grand Pa died at five o'clock this morning, with his hand raised in a blessing. He apparently went peacefully, but Grand Madja is in an alarming state of shock. She hasn't uttered a word, and my father doesn't dare leave her alone. Thus, he begs my great-uncle to take the money enclosed and buy candles, the shroud, and four bags of cement at the Central Bazaar.

I am right in front of this famous bazaar, where everything can be found—from sardines to the antimalarial Nivaquine to soldering irons. I give the letter and all the money to the cashier. She reads it and offers me her condolences. Everyone in Makak knows my great-uncle; he can't leave even for a day without the entire town knowing it. He's been the head of the registry office here for more than twenty-five years, running the office everyone must pass through to register births and deaths.

The lady calls a strong-armed worker and gives him instructions in a language I don't understand. Later on I am to discover it was pidgin. A few moments later the four bags of cement are piled up outside. The lady hands me a kind of rice sack in which she's placed the shroud and three large dried codfish that she asks me to give my family with her condolences. She also gives me five hundred francs, saying it is the change she owes me. I find myself in the street, twenty-five kilometers from my village, with two hundred kilos of cement, an unwieldy bag, and five hundred African francs, when I need three times that much to pay for the transportation and freight. Even if I had to take the train by bribing the conductor with the five hundred francs, there would still be the last eight kilometers left to go. My head stops thinking, and my body starts to function by itself as sometimes happens to me.

A government Land Rover is parked right next to me, its cover down—probably belonging to the sub-prefect or the police commissioner. I have no idea which. The owner or driver must be inside the bazaar. I throw my bag into the car and begin to add the sacks of cement, but have such trouble that I manage only to hoist the first one in. Fortunately, a kind young man passing by loads them in without any great effort and then goes on his way, whistling and throwing a roguish look in my direction. I get into the vehicle and, not knowing if all the seats are taken, sit down on the sacks of cement.

Lucky for me, a handsome man in uniform comes out of the bazaar with cartons of cigarettes and a bottle of Gordon's gin, a drink my father considers a great luxury and always tries to keep in the back of his closet in Libôn for special guests.

Completely taken aback when he sees me perched in his car on top of my cement bags, he first goes around his vehicle to check the license plate and make sure it's the right one.

"Mademoiselle, surely you are in the wrong vehicle. This one really is mine, I've just checked it."

"Is it really your vehicle, sir? Are you sure?"

"But of course! I can prove it to you." A sassy look. He's in a good mood and sure of himself. I take the plunge.

"God be praised, sir! I was afraid I'd see a driver who wouldn't be able to make the necessary decision. Since you yourself are the vehicle's owner, you can help me out of the fix I'm in and drop me off with the cement, which I don't know how to transport."

"Oh, just a moment here. Where am I supposed to drop you off?"

"In Massébè, please, sir."

"What? You certainly have some nerve! With that bad road, and at this hour? I have guests, Mademoiselle, and really cannot do a thing for you. Get down, please, and in the future wait for permission before you get into someone else's car. May I point out to you that this is not a taxi but the vehicle of the commander of the Police Brigade of this district?"

"And are you the commander of the brigade?"

"In person, and I order you to get out of this vehicle!"

"Then you'll be obliged to remove me by force, for I am under your protection, and you are refusing me this. Whom do you suggest I contact?"

I begin to cry, and he is totally stunned. You'd think he had never seen anyone cry. I tell him about my grandfather's death, the reasons for my trip, my great-uncle's absence, and conclude: "God himself has put you here to save me, Commander. But if you don't want to help me, there's nothing else for you to do but put me in your prison with my baggage until my uncle returns in two days. On the other hand, if you're willing to drop me off, I'll give you the five hundred francs I have left."

He bursts out laughing.

"Ah, the people of your tribe, really, God has given you the gift of gab as an affliction or a reward, I don't know which. Look at this little thing with a tongue longer than an anteater's. Ah! If I tell this story to anyone they won't believe me, so I'll take you to the police station for everyone to see for themselves."

He drives off, roaring with laughter. I draw the conclusion that I've failed and will be sleeping in prison. I feel that all my strength has left me. I collapse or faint, I don't know which. Men's laughter wakes me up. Several policemen are looking at me as if I were a weird animal.

"So, are you planning to come down to get into the cell?"

I feel angry and humiliated by their mockery, and answer:

"You'll have to carry me to the cell; that's your job and I'm not going to help you. Of my own accord I will walk only to Massébè."

The commander, who at that moment is coming out of his residence, laughs all the harder.

"What did I tell you? She's a case! Go ahead, get in, we'll drop her where the road permits. I'd be surprised if we make it all the way: I've heard that a bridge has been cut off, but I don't remember which one. Let's go, I have to be back before nightfall to receive the new sub-prefect!"

I'm so happy that I throw my arms around his neck and kiss him on his cheeks, forehead, hands, and I don't know where else. He looks at me with increasing astonishment. Touched, he grumbles: "You're lucky, little one, that I'm very occupied today with official business: I was going to take a closer look at your case because you really appeal to me. But it's all right, today I'll stick to playing the good Lord's messenger."

Each time we approach a river I dread we'll find the broken bridge, and we'll still be very far from our house. What would I do? Luckily, they drop me right at the bridge over the little Massébè River, two kilometers from home. The policemen go to the trouble of taking my cement bags across for me.

"With our apologies, Mademoiselle," the commander says. "We would have liked to take you right to your house and pinpoint the spot, right, friends? But because of the state of the road, it took us more time than expected, so it's already late afternoon, and soon it will be dark. From here you can safely go and get your family to come and carry the cement, can't you?"

"Of course, Commander," I say effusively. "May God bless you, you and all your men. My father will certainly come to thank you after the funeral."

As he moves off, the commander's sardonic smile leaves me with a vague melancholy. In fact, all the time I was with him and his men I had forgotten my Grand Pa's death for a while. And here, all alone on the road with my bags of cement, I suddenly feel like an orphan. And look like a real fool! What am I going to do?

27

The first few houses are located about one kilometer away on the other side of the hill. I cannot take the risk of leaving the cement by the roadside to go and find help. If a Bissoumè happens to pass by, he will steal the cement so that we won't be able to bury Grand Pa in the specific manner that prevents people from exhuming the bones.

Ah, the Bissoumè, those body snatchers, what a curse they are! What do they do with the bones? As soon as someone in our region dies, the Bissoumè begin to roam around and use almost any malevolent skill to exhume the bodies. It seems they're already succeeding in moving coffins long distances below the earth, as if with a subterranean electric drill. They say there is trafficking in bones to manufacture various poisons, powerful talismans, and heaven knows what else. They even say there are photographic film factories in the West where they use nothing but human bones. Yet, no Soumè is known to be wealthy. What do they do, then, with the money they earn? What do our sorcerers do with their knowledge? What do we do with our mystical powers? Why do we choose this kind of gratuitous turmoil, which weighs so heavily on this side of the world?

While my mind is dwelling on these gloomy thoughts, I have the distinct feeling that I am being spied on. My nerves are on edge, and the hair on my skin stands on end. I turn around so abruptly that the person behind the bush doesn't have time to hide again, and I recognize him.

It takes me a moment to calm the shaking inside my belly, and then I call out to him by name, for it's one of my uncles! "Why are you hiding behind the bushes and spying on me, Uncle Minkéng? Do you think I'm keeping one of the policemen hidden inside my *pagne* and that he'll catch you to make you pay your taxes? Get out of there and help me carry the cement to the top of the hill before it gets dark and the Bissoumè make it disappear! Unless you're one of them, as they say, and you're getting ready to attack me. In that case, go ahead and be quick, if you dare."

He obeys my voice, which I made as firm and calm as that of Grand Madja. When faced with an enemy, she always said, calmness and serenity were the only truly protective talismans. My uncle extricates himself from the shrubbery and stammers: "What, me a Soumè? You've got to be kidding? You know yourself that . . . eh . . . the cops and I, eh . . . I just wanted to make sure they weren't going to hurt you."

Then he picks up a sack and begins to climb the hill.

"Watch out, Uncle Minkéng, I've got my eye on you! Don't try to run off with the cement. I beg you to put it down at the top of the hill where I can see it, and then come and get the next one so that no Soumè will be able to steal it without our noticing."

"You, my cousin's daughter, don't you start ordering me around like your father. You could make me angry and that might cost you a spanking! Don't think you've reached the age of impunity yet."

I have nothing else to say but, highly suspicious, I watch him all the same as I push and roll another sack up the hill, finally reaching the top by the time my uncle has hauled three of them. Just then other uncles coming from Pan for the wake join us and help us carry the whole lot to the village.

The last rays of sunshine are dancing on the wall of my grandparents' house like will-o'-the-wisps. I go inside, and people make room to let me through. When I come into the living room, now transformed into a death chamber, I see Grand Pa's tall body hunched over as in his moments of great pain. I stand by his feet and stare at him with dry eyes. Some five minutes later his body begins to stretch out, imperceptibly at first, then more and more distinctly. The people around him stand up, panic-stricken, and look on, ready to take to their heels. Even Grand Madja and Great-Aunt Kèl Lam have risen from their seats. Grand Pa Helly's feet are now beyond the bed. The full length of his body is his once again. The grimace that seemed to clench his lips together has vanished, leaving his face relaxed and smooth. The news has gone all around the courtyard, and everyone comes running. But it is all over.

I don't remember much of the wake other than the chants of the Maoum, the male initiation, sung by a few Mbombock who were there through the night: deeply moving chants, astonishing voices, and mesmerizing melodies, but with completely perplexing texts. At certain moments, you even have the impression they're singing in coded foreign languages. The singing doesn't stop until sunrise. All the village women are busy at the fires scattered through the courtyard. Everyone has left the death chamber. I lie down alone at the foot of the bed in the back of the room. I can see the door, but from the doorway no one is able to see me.

That is when an old great-uncle sneaks in. After making sure that he's alone with the body, he quickly takes a pocket-knife out of a knot in his *pagne* and starts to remove the nails and hairs on Grand Pa Helly's feet. I am so stunned that I leap up at him and grab him around the waist as his knife cuts my arm. Aunt Roz comes into the room immediately; understanding what is happening, she grabs the incriminating relics, which he cannot hide, from the old man's hands. The old uncle spits on my aunt's forehead, although this is a forbidden gesture for a man of his age and standing. My aunt staggers and falls, fainting into the arms of my father, who arrives just at that moment. He gathers up the precious relics, helps his sister into an armchair, grasps the old man, and tries to strangle him. Many people have come running and stop him just in time, but they all shout at the old uncle, who is instantly banned from the ceremony. For Aunt Roz, though, the damage has been done; she will never regain her good health. For another thirty years she will live with constant pain in the very place where he spat at her, and none of the many medications brought to her from the East and West will ever bring her relief at all, nor will any test uncover what is wrong with her.

• • •

The ceremonies of the farewell meal begin.

Women have cooked a variety of animals killed during the night. Maternal uncles have brought yams; paternal uncles, the drinks. Appointments for nine days hence have been made with those who owe debts to or have claims on the family. The moment of burial has come. I stay right beside Grand Madja, trying to emulate her calm and dignity. But when they begin to lower the body into its grave, a piercing scream erupts from my innermost depths— a scream so prolonged it seems it will last until my final breath. The casket slips from the hands of the gravediggers, almost pulling one of them down. The Mbombock Mbondo Libon grasps my arm and takes me far away, followed by a terrified Grand Madja and Great-Aunt Kèl Lam, who as a result miss the end of the burial. When the four of us are in a quiet corner of the backyard, the Mbombock says: "From this day onward this person is never to go near another corpse and, above all, is to avoid attending any burials, is that understood? Some people are meant to accompany the dead, others to welcome the living. She belongs to the second group and will have to make her peace with that; you do understand, don't you?"

Since that day I have not accompanied anyone in my family to their final resting place. Likewise, life has made sure to keep me far from any grave and has always put me at the door of new births. I am ready to respect this mandate until the last day of my life, unless life decides to impose a new directive at the last minute.

All my father's "wives"—traditional spouses, former and new lovers who had had children with him—attend the ritual of the mourning novena with their children and many other family members, with the exception of my mother. From our family's maternal branch only my younger sister and I are present: no aunts, no grand-mother, no maternal uncles. We feel like orphans. Mam Naja comes with two of her sisters and all her children, but not my child. I think she does it on purpose to punish me, knowing how happy I would have been to see him. She says not one word to me, looks at me with obvious hatred, and plainly avoids me when we run into each other in the courtyard.

She is simply enormous with her full-term pregnancy and quite comical when she tries to steer clear of me as she enters a door. I can't help laughing, which really irritates her to no end. I recognize that my laughter is not innocent! I would really like to return the aggravations she constantly inflicts on me, particularly her choice to deprive me of seeing my child. And what's more, I still believe she's the source of my father's malice. When he's nasty to me, it's because she has found a way to make his life miserable. There are so many things that put me in a spiteful mood; I would love to transcend them, as Grand Madja recommends, but I still can't manage it. For instance, I can't keep myself from showing up in her presence with my girlfriend from Libôn who I have betrothed to my father, although I know how intol-erable she finds that. And so, what had to happen happens.

The day of the final ceremony, I plan to show that our clan is not to be ignored. I gather together my little sister, my friend Sara from Libôn, and her brother Isma, and decide to take charge of the yam stew. I choose Aunt Roz's largest pot, careful to present a dish equal to what my mother and all my sisters would have prepared had we been together. I consider my mother the first of the official wives, and it's her clan's responsibility to present the most impor-tant dish; as the oldest one present here, it's my joy to save her honor. But Mam Naja assumes that, since she is now the only offi-cial wife, it's her duty to be the best. Our rivalry goes back to its beginnings, filled with venom, enough to poison everyone.

Mam Naja enters the backyard where I've set up with "my peo-ple," snatches the pot off the fire, and almost scalds us all. This incites a general brawl in which the various clans of my father's wives take sides. And I'm very happy to see that, in spite of her absence, my mother holds the absolute majority. Yes, we all come out of it with black eyes, shredded lips, scratched faces, bitten arms, but Mam Naja gets the worst of it, and is forced to leave immediately with her entourage to make sure that nothing untoward happens to her pregnancy.

We will not see each other again for several decades, until a few weeks before her death. I will visit her in the hospital then, filled with remorse. At that point I will recognize that we weren't enemies, but sisters on the same path of change—a steep, winding path, but a necessary one for learning the lessons we both needed to learn. When our eyes will meet, I will know that she, too, has come to the same conclusion. We will kiss each other tenderly for the first and last time in our life. We will not speak of the past, unable to change anything, fulfilling our destiny. She will depart free of me, and I will remain alone to deal with my fears and my secret, alone in my choice to keep the pact of silence or to move things in a different direction from then on, at my own peril. The tears that will fill my eyes as I leave her will be tears of self-pity, of envy of her, now free, and of fear of the future. They will be tears of profound bewilderment.

We don't realize sufficiently the importance of an enemy. A fierce enemy in life is a thousand times better than a mediocre friend. A true enemy is more motivating, mobilizing, and stimulating. You never bow your head or lower your arms when facing him. You hang on by your teeth and claws so as not to fail in front of him, thereby confronting and overcoming the most dreadful obstacles; whereas a mediocre friend is demoralizing and bloodsucking, a perverse parasite that draws energy and inhibits any drive toward great deeds, that diverts lofty aspirations and pulls you to inertia—and all of it in good conscience, all of it justified by pseudo-loyalty.

Mam Naja's death would create a huge void inside me and impart the awareness of what is called aging. I would find myself without an enemy, without an anchor for my tenacity, rebellion, and daring. Above all else, I would hold onto the memory of our embrace and kiss, of her playful and knowing smile with just a touch of defiance in her eyes.

28

As soon as the ceremonies of the mourning novena are over, my father decides to double efforts to complete the work on his artificial pond. And so the torment begins again.

Grand Pa Helly's permanent absence weighs more and more heavily as the days go by: There's no one left to play the role of mediator between my father and the others, to smooth over his verbal and physical tactlessness, to alleviate the harshness of his decisions, making fun of them and introducing some humor. Everyone bears the full burden, taking everything to heart, while the atmosphere grows heavier each day.

Added to this is the unspoken, shared impression that my father is in some way responsible for Grand Pa Helly's disappearance. Here no one believes that anyone dies a natural death. However, Grand Pa himself never stopped complaining about those who are always looking for a scapegoat; I believe sincerely that he would not have thought kindly at all of people holding his son responsible for his death. Even Grand Madja is one of them; she so obviously stays away from her son that you feel she shares the general sentiment. I wonder whether she is aware that she's dissociating herself from him and for the first time putting him in danger. Her grief is such that she's beginning to lose some of her sense of reality.

So all of us work in silence, putting the full weight of our belligerence into finishing the job as soon as possible. Most likely it will take another week—and not a day longer!

That is when the Ba Touu Pék, the Omniscient One, revs up his machine of surprises. I'm crossing the dike to go to the other side of the pond, where there is some shade, and work there when my father calls out to me severely: "There goes another lazybones, dragging her feet to make time go by! Come back right now and do your work here."

"Papa, it's too hot there. Maybe you didn't notice, but almost everyone has moved to the other side. We'll go back there when the sun starts to go down. We're using the time to make some progress on the other bank."

"Nonsense! What about your sisters—they're still here, are they made of different material? Stay and get back to work."

I keep going toward the other bank, but he pulls me back roughly, and I feel like a plum tree being shaken. Nausea wells up in my throat. I return to my sun-exposed spot. But after three roundtrips with my container of soil I feel I'm about to faint. I rally all my willpower to avoid my father's thunder, but my destiny has already ceased to be my own. I'm nailed to the ground, perspiring profusely, and incapable of any reaction. Grand Madja comes running over to me and reaches me before my father does, preventing him from being the first to speak.

"Leave her alone, will you please! Isn't she doing enough already? Isn't she brave enough for you, in the state she's in?"

"What state? You're the one who spoils the girl. She's not what she used to be, and I'm not at all pleased with the changes in her. She's going to get up and go back to work or else. . . ."

"Or else what? You're going to get rid of her pregnancy?"

"Her preg . . . excuse me?"

Something tells me to get away from there as fast as I can. I gather up my last bit of energy and rush off to the dike. When my father recovers, he charges at me, knocking down anyone in his path. He grabs me by the neck and pulls me back in the other direction, then pushes me toward home.

Since my Aunt Roz has gone to town for treatment, I know there won't be anyone else to stand up to him and that I'll have to protect myself if I don't want to be slaughtered. So I decide to keep calm and control myself. As soon as we are out of view he shouts: "What? You're pregnant? Since when and by whom?"

"Not by you, in any case! This is my business."

I've scored. He lowers his head for a moment.

"What do you mean?"

"May I remind you that I'm engaged and that it's up to my fiancé to ask questions of this sort. Unless you wish you were the perpetrator of this one, too?"

Two smacks in the face send me flying to the floor and stop my breath. Grand Madja arrives with a few other people, worried about what might happen. I feel a rage close to madness rising up. I pull free from Grand Madja's hands and plant myself in front of my father, who is being held back by half a dozen others.

"Is that all you can do with your children, hit them, give them blood transfusions? What else can you do to me? Kill me? Well, don't be shy: You've just about done that already. You did kill me once before, you know."

"Shut up, or I'll cut your tongue into little pieces."

"You don't get it, do you? It's all over. I'm dead and you can't kill me twice. You cannot reach me anymore. From now on I'm a ghost who can only haunt you. Touch me, and I will rattle off your entire life right here in public!"

The bystanders are rooted to the spot. First of all by my voice, that improbable voice that always emerges from me in moments of extreme agitation. And then, they also cannot understand why my father hasn't yet smashed me to bits but, on the contrary, beats a grumbling retreat: "Just pray to heaven that your path doesn't cross mine again today."

Grand Madja comes over to me and murmurs in my ear: "Get away from here. Go to the Mayos or somewhere else, it doesn't matter where, but hide, or else I feel a great misfortune will be coming your way. Ah, my husband! You surely have abandoned me with this monster. Who will help me now?"

She crumples to the ground like a sack of potatoes and begins to weep all the tears she has held back since Grand Pa Helly's death. I run off, weeping, too, for her helpless sorrow, for my pointless anger, for our whole absurd condition.

I cannot walk fast; my lower belly hurts. It's as if the baby is kicking me or bumping me with its head, I don't know which. I feel overwhelming fear. Something tells me to hide in a bush, to rest, but I don't know why it comes into my head that my father could find me there and suffocate me with my baby, still inside. Or else a snake might bite me, and I would die senselessly, rotting away alone in my shrub. It's as if I am riveted to the road; if my father should come in pursuit of me, he will find me here, but at least there will be passersby as witnesses.

An intersection. Where to go? Where would he not be likely to look for me? Or better, where would he look for me first? I need to go in the opposite direction. I decide to retrace my steps and take the longest way to the train station. It is necessary to put at least one train trip between him and me. But I'm dealing with my father, and he's thought of it before I have and sent Isma to catch me. When he materializes behind me like a hunting dog, I'm only one kilometer from the station. I feel relieved, sure that my friend won't hand me over. I start to cry in his arms: "God be praised, Isma! I feared the worst. Please, hide me, help me get away from death. Think of our friendship and have pity on me. Think of your responsibility, too, in everything that might happen to us, to my child and me, if Papa should find us. Why are you so unsympathetic to my arguments?"

"I don't want you to go away, that's all. You're the one who brought us here, my sister and me, and you're not going to desert us now. We'll stay together; your father is not really going to kill you. Maybe he'll spank you, but I'll be there to console you. I love you, you know."

I can't get over it. How can you claim to love someone and not recognize that her life is in danger? While he thinks only about keeping me for himself, he doesn't realize he's in the process of risking our lives. I implore him again, try to pull him behind the shrubbery, promising to have sex with him, right here and now, if he agrees to keep me company in a hiding place so that my father won't find me. Surprisingly, he seems tempted, and his eyes are looking for the ideal shrub when my father appears. Faced with this dilemma, he shrugs his shoulders. I look at him with pity. He would have hidden me to sleep with me, but not to save my life. Really, I've had it up to here with men. When my father arrives he looks calm and asks: "Is it that bastard of a sub-prefect who took the liberty of getting you pregnant before marrying you first?"

Why didn't I say yes? I think he would have settled for taking me home and dealing the old man a blow to make him pay. Alas, I'm too honest and, not given to keeping quiet, my big mouth opens up as if I'm about to vomit.

"Now, that would kill me. Isn't it enough that he cuckolds you with that Naja wife of yours? Fortunately I forced him to buy you a young substitute wife to save your honor. But honor is not something you're familiar with anymore, is it? If they promise you an old car it's reason enough for you to sell your entire family and your own soul as well. If anyone like you were to make me pregnant, I think I'd vomit the fetus out through my mouth."

I can see that every word stabs him and I'm quite prepared to say ten times more when he stops my breath with the back of his hand. I feel the imprint swell up on my cheek as if it were being inflated from the inside out. Blood spurts inside my mouth.

"You little slut! So it's not even your own fiancé who got you pregnant? Where have you been hanging around to pick this up?"

He kicks me in the belly so hard that it throws me more than five meters toward a slope, and I go hurtling down it, punch-drunk. He comes to me, in slow-motion, and shouts: "So that's the way it is, is it? Fine! I'll help you vomit it up; I'll rid that belly of yours from the bastard inside. As long as I don't see the fetus with my own eyes, I won't stop beating you, and that's on my word as Njokè!"

My final hour is here. I take out a small bracelet-watch my mother gave me, enclose it inside my left hand, and swear to myself:

"As long as the palm of my hand doesn't open to let go of this watch, my belly won't let go of my child, a child whom I declare to be the opposite of violence and the world's future, and that's on the word of a future female Njokè." I shut my heart and my whole body, everything except my eyes. I hunch up in fetal position and stop moving. Only my gaze watches the events. I look at my father the way you look at the void.

He hits and hits. Not coming up against any resistance, he grows ever more irritated and, dripping sweat, pulls me over the ground like a sack of cocoa. People arrive and beg him to stop. He threatens them, goes after a few of them, kicks them, then comes back to me, lifts me up, throws me over his shoulders and moves ahead. When he's tired he throws me down like a bundle of wood. I maintain my fetal position, fall and roll and stop moving. The motionlessness exasperates him. He curses me, insults my mother and her whole family: "Ah! Your phony innocence, just like your mother's, is no surprise to me; all I have to do is turn my back for all of you to cheat on me with my own cousins, with White men, and even with Yoruba! Ah, but I'll make you pay for all your mother's whims, and her sister's, and their own damned mother's!"

My gaze is blank—no anger, no fear, no hate, no love—for the simple reason that at this moment I don't feel anything at all. All I hear is Grand Pa Helly's voice telling me not to let anyone get rid of my child, and all my efforts are going into protecting my belly. I'm determined not to waste any energy.

At times he pulls at one of my feet or arms, or grabs me by the neck the way you pick up a puppy or a kitten. But it gets him nowhere. He knows that I won't move on my own feet, that he will either have to give up on bringing me home, which he will not allow himself to do, or carry me the way he had promised to carry his father; this is making him crazy.

He cuts down some shrubbery branches, collects bits of palm from the stacks of branches people leave beneath the palm oil trees along the road, and in utter fury whips me with them until he's exhausted. Then he carries me again. . . .

He would like to sit and rest a while, but the ever-growing crowd behind us prevents him. Finally he sits down with his back against a tree, for my weight is becoming too much for him. I sense that he wants to talk to me, so I clench my jaws to make sure that no sound will come from my mouth, and even less from his.

What would I do if he were to speak to me in that voice he sometimes uses to talk to his mother when trying to mollify her: "Little Mother, have pity on me! Help us out of this situation."

There's no doubt that I would slip down and walk,
That all my strength would leave me,
All my resistance crumble,
And there's no doubt that my baby would be detached from my belly;
I clench my jaws more tightly. . . .

To cross tumultuous rivers
Like the Liéguè or the Yamakouba,
By the only tree trunk that serves as a bridge,
To cross the turbulent waters
On the shoulders of someone
Or with someone on your back
You have to be stark raving mad,
And yet we cross,
But we are not that mad,
For we know full well that the drop would be fatal.
Inwardly we are both trembling;
Alas, our hearts are equally matched,
And no one wants to let the other sense the fear.
We both hold our breaths
And feel the held breath of the crowd behind us.

Bravado becomes our only motivation,
Bravado or courage,
The courage to face ourselves before knowing who we are.
Sometimes we have to brave the world, brave life and death,

To discover and know better our possibilities and limitations,
The real truth is that courage
Is to be fearful and move forward still.

When I think back on this today, I cannot help but admire you, Father, and admire what you passed on to me in spite of yourself. Had you used that tremendous courage to serve a great cause, had you been humble, had you been able actually to love someone, you could have changed the world. Alas!

• • •

Once we escape the threat of a fall into the unruly waters of the Yamakouba and then the Liéguè, your knees buckle, Father, and we collapse on the ground together. You don't even try to get up again. I feel that sleep is about to overtake us; we have been on this road for more than six hours in a violent, hand-to-hand struggle. Even the wildest passions are blunted when fatigue sets in. Your desire to tame me, Father, has disappeared, has crumpled, is dead on its feet.

The silent crowd of onlookers has crossed the rivers, following us; some of them hold hands while others are determined to go it alone. Now they surround us like an army of shadows. Night fell a long time ago. A gentleman emerges from the darkness, points his hunter's torch at us, and bursts out laughing when he sees you fully stretched out with your head on my belly.

"Aha! Here we have a Lôs comfortably ensconced on his daughter's belly right in the middle of the road! Didn't I hear you say that you wouldn't stop beating her until you'd seen the fetus expelled from that belly? Well, her belly still seems quite round to me, and I don't see any blood between her legs! Now then, sublime Lôs that you are, go ahead, beat her, beat her! What are you doing? Sleeping? Might that little girl here have been right about you? Who else will you frighten anymore? Come on, get up and kill her, just so you'll force all of us to tremble whenever we see you!"

You, Father, get up painfully.

"You're lucky I can't see you or recognize your voice, or else I'd make a date with you in your bed tomorrow morning, you bastard! You're not the one to dictate to me how to discipline my daughter. If you don't have what it takes to make your own daughters, just bring your wife to my cocoa plantation, and I'll lend you a hand, you son of a bitch!"

The man leaps up with all his claws out, but you bring him down with a swift kick that propels him into the crowd of shadows. Cries fly through the air and get you excited: You get up and kick a few others, blindly punching them in the jaw or the stomach, creating panic. The noose is loosening a bit.

"Go home and leave me alone, all of you! What I do to my daughter is none of your business, you gang of cowards!"

At that very moment the well-known voice of the Mbombock Mbondo Libon rises from the crowd, calm as only the voice of a Mbombock can be.

"You are right, you can do to your daughter whatever you want. You can even kill her, and no one here will raise a finger to keep you from doing so since you are stronger than the entire tribe, right? But remember one thing: This land belongs to the tribe of the Lôg Sénd. And the Lôg Sénd tell you via my mouth that you will have to eat your daughter after you kill her, for you shall not lay her to rest here on their land."

"Is that so? And who'll prevent me? You, perhaps, you degenerate? If you'd been as powerful as you want people to think you are, you so-called Mbombock, you would have kept the Whites from ordering us around in our own land! Poor assholes! Would you have even said a word to me if my father were alive? Just be aware that I'm not afraid of your band of sorcerers. And if you want, I'll fight you on this very land!"

"Very well, then! Go ahead and kill your daughter. . . ."

You turn around and rush at me like someone possessed, lift me off my feet, and throw me with brute force into the ditch. You are moving forward to finish me off when the youngest son of Great-Aunt Kèl Lam grabs you from behind and pulls at you with all his might. You are flustered, Father, for you were not expecting anyone to intervene. A large moon has come out from behind the trees and illuminates the scene as if by magic. Now your cousin confronts you:

"And you were actually ready to kill your daughter on the order of sorcerers, Njokè? I knew you were dumb, but now I know you're stark raving mad! Well, since you want to kill your daughter, you ought to know that you'll have to kill me first!"

"As you wish, dear brother! That will be one less imbecile in my aunt's house."

When you raise your arm, with all the power that is yours, to grab at your cousin, you bring it down on the razor-sharp machete he has held up as a shield. Blood spurts into the air. The cousin takes to his heels, you and the horde of shadows following him. They have forgotten about me in the ditch. It is Fidèle Foulani, desperately looking for me in the dark and whispering my name over and over again, who manages to pull me from my hole very late that night. You, Father, have lost a great deal of blood and are unconscious. The bystanders would gladly let you die, but your cousin saves your life by asking for help to bring you to an uncle, a healer, who will stop the hemorrhage, tend to the terrible wound, and give you stimulants.

You do not regain consciousness for five days, in your aunt's house where your cousins insist on watching and taking care of you. Grand Madja could not stop them and prefers to stay and nurse me. When they bring you home, Father, we look at each other for a long moment, but you don't say a word to me. I know something has broken inside you, inside us. It's the end of an era, a world. It's a fate we must accept from now on. Nine days later I manage to get away, having decided to go back to the big city where my mother lives.

MOVEMENT EIGHT

29

SONG 12

That thing called destiny or fate
Has been recorded by my memory,
That thing without body or face,
Yet so recognizable,
That arrives on little cats' feet,
Envelops you with its unequivocal presence,
Imprinting a turn in your path;
And from this day forward each choice is made according to the form
And color it alone has previously designed,
For you've already made your true choice long before your birth
With the destiny you yourself created when you chose this body.
If you do not understand, if you do not believe it,
It means there is no choice,
For destiny was here before,
Before your first breath came into your body.

My memory knows how to recognize my destiny, having stored it;
My being relinquishes all resistance as soon as it is manifested.
All I am then is a solid block of attention, scrutinizing, observing,
So as to define the outlines of its features better every time;
I feel surprised again at the twists and turns of its complexity,

And am evermore ennobled before the power of divinity,
For it has created, yes, verily, it has created all of us. . . .
Likewise, is every step not also bound toward a destination,
And does walking every day not guide us to the one true place of
thought and destination,
Our destiny. . . .

• • •

Why this night and not another—the one before or the one after?

I walked the twenty-five kilometers that separated us from the administrative center of the district, knowing my father was too exhausted and discouraged for another pursuit to bring me back.

I got into the night train without a ticket, expecting the conductor to find me out soon enough and make me get off at the next station. I looked for a congested corner where I might hide. Two hands gently covered my eyes. A woman wearing a lovely scent was standing behind me, and I tried to guess who she might be. She took her hands away and embraced me.

"Halla Man, Fitini Halla, what a pleasure to see you! How you have grown! What are you doing here?"

It was my oldest sister! As if by magic, there she was to save me from the conductor, bring me to my mother, to the next turn in my new life, to the next plot line in my future. I had created this destiny long before, and it was incontrovertible. Could I shrink back, get off the train and flee? No, everything was on track; everything flowed from the source; everything would move by itself hereafter. The site of my next choice lay ahead. All I had to do was walk forward to that point.

Anticipation, hope, excitement, imagination—they are all synonymous in my memory, beyond place and time, all inside a single sensation: the foreshadowing of a peaceful life close to my mother.

She had fought for six years to have me with her.

She had lost the trial in the courtroom of men.

Now the courtroom of destiny agreed with her.

We were finally going to live together, rediscover each other, confide in each other, love each other, and be fulfilled.

She is so astonished to see us that she leaves us standing in the doorway and goes to her bedroom without a greeting! I run after her, crying, and literally force open the door behind which she, also weeping, is trying to retreat.

We don't know what to say, how to console each other after so much time lost. We must be quite exasperating, judging by her husband's looks as he watches us, advising my sister and me wryly to take our bags to our uncle's house and come back when his wife has pulled herself together. My sister brings me there, and in the evening goes back to my mother's by herself to discuss my moving in with her. Alas, when she returns she doesn't bring the issue up again. I tell myself that Mama surely has to arrange things first, that I need to be patient and make the most of the happiness I've already found: being so close again and able to see each other every day.

I do this so successfully that I don't notice my uncle and his family's embarrassment, the commotion around me, or the comings and goings of my always-irritated Tata Roz. I don't understand that my mother and her husband are refusing to have me live with them, to welcome an unwed pregnant daughter into their respectable home, the disgrace. . . .

When my ears unexpectedly catch an exchange between my sister and aunt, crudely revealing the reality of my situation, a sudden, acute rectal pain flashes through me. An irresistible urge forces me to spend fruitless hours on the toilet.

It starts to rain, and rains uninterruptedly for seven days and seven nights. When the feeling becomes too strong, I go out and roam around in the rain until the pain subsides. But it comes back, more blinding each time. I no longer speak to anyone. The whole family thinks it's because I am in shock over my mother's rejection, and so no one dares talk to me, not knowing how to console me. Nobody here really knows me. To each of them I am more or less a stranger, if not downright strange. My sister avoids me so she won't have to deal with my questioning looks. And so I am alone in our room to fight off another intestinal thrust that wants to escape from my belly! Perhaps I have hemorrhoids. Poor girl—since I'm only seven and a half months pregnant, I don't even realize I have been having premature contractions! When the water breaks I hurry off to find my aunt. She rushes me to the hospital as the baby's head is already crowning. Five minutes after we get to the maternity clinic he is born with a collapsed right lung. But he cries all the same, and I sense that he will live. I greet him: "Welcome Grand Pa Helly, Junior." It takes a month of care before he's able to breathe normally. Neither my mother nor her husband set foot in the maternity clinic.

• • •

When I reread the documents my mother collected after her husband's death years later, I wondered, once again, what could possibly explain my stepfather's extremely antagonistic attitude toward me. My mother's official explanation was that he suspected I came to try to bring her back to my father, even though I had not expressed any intention of that sort or suggested the slightest move in that direction. How could I want to bring my mother back to my father when I had just fled from him myself? I knew there had to be other motives I couldn't figure out—and I was right.

Passages from my stepfather's prison journal
(which my mother left behind at my house after her husband died):

When she came into our living room, and I saw her for the first time, my heart almost stopped: I thought it was my wife after being treated by a fairy, or after stepping into a miraculous spring of rejuvenation. That is how I always imagined she would be had she been twenty-five years younger. A tempestuous desire engulfed me, arousing me. That girl was not my wife—she was the devil itself. At that very moment my wife came out of our bedroom and stood rooted to the spot when she saw the apparition that seemed to be a reflection of her younger self! Her face lit up radiantly, she had to rub her hands across it as if to check her eyesight, but the image remained. Then she realized it wasn't her reflection. As a result, her thoughts went elsewhere, an elsewhere filled with a thousand feelings and sensations that began to dance a saraband beneath the skin of her frail face. . . . Was it a smile? a grimace? sorrow? pleasure? Or was it all of them at once, the tumultuous, marvelous world of which this face reminded her, framed by the doorway like the portrait of a Madonna enhanced by a delicate molding? A Madonna frozen in time, though I hoped not forever, since the silence and motionlessness were dragging, and I had to get to work. . . .

"Sista Naja, what's going on," I asked her.

She jumped as if stung by I don't know what thorn! Was my voice that offensive? Finally she turned to look at me.

I had the feeling I was transparent, empty, bleak, for she didn't seem to notice my presence. Large tears were streaming down her cheeks. She turned around to take refuge in the bedroom, but then the reflection dashed forward, away from the frame, crying: "Mama!"

My wife's two lives appeared to be merging into one trembling embrace. I didn't recognize her voice anymore or, more precisely, I couldn't tell one apart from the other!

"Dear little 'mother-in-law,' tell me I'm not dreaming! Tell me it's really you here in my arms! And where is your father?"

Then I understood. The marvelous world in which I did not exist was the world of this girl's father. She had arrived with a world from which I was excluded. We weren't going to be lovers!

Their effusiveness knew no end. They emanated a scent of honey and pepper that stuck in my throat. I became harder. I followed them like a shadow into the bedroom where they put down the little bundle that was dangling from the reflection's fingertips. Immersed in their ramblings interspersed with little giggles, they either didn't see me or were pretending not to. I was fuming and wanted to shake them, demand to be introduced, remind them they were in my house, and that I was the father here!

I, the father of an eternally youthful Madonna!

I, the father of a bitch in heat, filling the air with a scent of sex and pepper!

I, the father of a girl blind from birth who would never see my incestuous desire.

Right when I had that thought, her eyes looked at me—or rather, at my rising fly! Shame overwhelmed me, from the tips of my toes to the roots of my hair, and I had the clear sensation that her gaze was coldly following the sudden slackening of my ardor. A slight frown revealed her astonished curiosity and affected me like a slap in the face. I left almost at a run. I heard my wife's voice calling me, as if she had just remembered I was there. I straddled my bicycle and pedaled as fast as I could. Along the way, I remembered that my wife's oldest daughter had been there, too! My God, surely she must have seen me in that state as well. What hurricane had just come into my life? Barely arrived, this, my wife's daughter, had chased me from my own house, at the same time revealing to me my life's hidden thirst. I was already in love and I knew we would not be lovers.

I don't want this girl in my house, that's very clear, I've decided.

30

Naiveté, indifference, intellectual limitation, or pure foolishness—
what illness did she suffer from, the girl I was? She was ignorant of
her first sexual experience, which everyone says is unforgettable;
ignorant of the resulting pregnancy, forgetful of the anguish, unfit
even to recognize the labor pains of a second delivery, and, above
all, incapable of discerning and naming a true feeling. Was I upset,
shocked, humiliated by the rejection of my mother and her husband? Was I angry with anyone? Did I feel sadness, resentment, or
hatred? Certainly I have felt anger in my life, untimely and sudden
anger, but as soon as it calmed down it would always leave me whole.
Is it possible that some people are sheltered from every emotional
and sentimental upheaval?

The most intense emotion I felt in the maternity clinic was
embarrassment. I couldn't get over the fact that I'd turned into a
load of worries for my mother, when I'd come with the simple
dream of having her count on me—of having her, too, benefit
from my small talent as a housekeeper! I so much wanted her to be
happy and proud of me, wanted her husband to be a better father
to me; but no! Tata Roz was happy to explain that, when all was
said and done, I was nothing but a source of disquiet to them. My
mother felt torn between her religion, her husband, and me, and
was eaten up by bad conscience and remorse, while my stepfather

was a victim of mistrust and jealousy.

At that point, I promised myself I would disappear with my baby when I left the hospital, to make sure my mere presence in town wouldn't cause them any further pain. Had it not been for Tata Roz, my maternal aunt, I don't know where I would be today. Throughout the time I was staying with my baby with his sick lung, she brought food every day, and kept me company—all night long, at times—while she told me her life story. That is how I came to also know my other Aunt Roz, whose strength of character was at least as great as that of her namesake, my paternal aunt. Character is the crucible in which destiny is created.

• • •

Long before her sister married my father, Tata Roz had lost her own family. She had struggled to have her one son and had been clearly told she couldn't have another child. Her husband was suspected of having "sacrificed his wife's womb" through his sorcerer's practices for the sake of gaining greater powers and growing wealth. Moreover, since her health was frail, a persistent rumor claimed she would die young unless a great healer soon released her from the spell.

Her mother had come up with the idea of telling the couple that she was on the brink of death, and asked her daughter to come back to say farewell. In fact, it was her way of making her daughter leave home without inviting her husband's wrath. But as soon as Tata Roz was gone, he sent her a message that their only son had died and was buried because his mother had abandoned him. He let her know she had no reason to come back to him anymore, accused her of having betrayed him, and said she was responsible for the loss of their son. He threatened to cut her into pieces with a machete if she dared to show her face again. It caused Tata Roz a great deal of suffering, and she didn't really regain her equilibrium until she could invest all her motherly love in her nieces and nephews. This was why she devoted herself so aggressively to fighting my father, in the hope that when the trials were over her sister would get all her children back before she, too, was told they had died. And all of them would live an exciting life together, women struggling in solidarity for their children, with no men underfoot!

But the trial had barely come to an end when my mother had found nothing better to do than remarry! And why?

"Just because the man's name was the very same as your father's, do you realize that?" she said to me heatedly, still incensed at what her sister had done.

Then she pulled herself together and went on: "This way, at least, she solved the problem of her identity: Madame Njokè all her life, and always the wife of one great love, 'whatever the birds of misfortune may say,' as she tells me at times."

And so Tata Roz had to resign herself to letting go of her beloved sister.

"I envy her for possessing this immortal love, ready to brave anything and survive every vile act. But still, I can't help but find it pathetic, and not very easy for her! Your mother deserves not only respect, but compassion as well, and I really wish you would forgive her," Tata Roz kept repeating to me in the maternity clinic, convinced that I must be terribly angry with her.

The truth was that I wasn't angry with her. I just wanted to understand. . . .

"Why, Tata Roz, do you say that my mother Naja is the wife of one great love, when in court you said she had taken as many lovers as my father had mistresses?"

"You believed that? At court we were at war, and we had to rattle the pride of your father, that madman. And look how she manages to sustain that one feeling inside her head. That is why I'm asking you not to be too hard on her: Her battle is not easy to justify or understand; not even I as her sister am able to do it, and it often sickens me. So if you, too, get involved . . ."

"Don't worry, Tata Roz, I'm not angry with her; I love her, or at least I think I do," I told her. "All I ask is to understand."

"But is that really what it is, love, the thing we all talk about," she responded. "Perhaps you don't have, or share, the same feelings as the rest of us in the family. If so, how do you explain the absence of any reaction when you're faced with events one-tenth of which would require a variety of expert healers for other people? No, you're not . . . how shall I put it? Normal? No, simple. That's it, you're not simple."

Tata Roz's problem was that their joint religion was really beginning to test her nerves.

"I think that my sister is now using it as a little fortress against every personal reflection or scrutiny, to the point of occasionally destroying her common sense and her survival instinct. Obviously, she found this new husband of hers in her religion, but so what? Is that a reason not to see the flaws in your partner and at least try to keep them at arm's length or change them? Is that a reason to refuse to even talk about them? Because of that man, I'm starting not to like my own religion anymore, and I'm staying with it just to be close to my sister."

This is why Tata Roz decided to find herself a husband as well, but from outside her religion—a husband who would be like a shield when she feels the need. For this reason, she calls on him a week before I leave the hospital.

Tata Roz's husband catches live crocodiles! They say he has four eyes and sees things that ordinary mortals do not. He has a kind of disturbing power that makes those around him fear and respect him, including my mother and her husband.

Tata Roz's husband has a dream in which his brother-in-law is supposed to receive me into his home, on pain of disaster. Although Jehovah is the only savior, a dull fear creeps in, which my aunt feeds so thoroughly that my mother ends up by convincing both herself and her husband to take me in . . . and they do, reluctantly.

Of course, there is Njokè, and then there is Njokè. This one is not a Lôs, far from it, but he does come home every night. He doesn't drink, doesn't bring home any co-wives or droves of children born out of wedlock. He doesn't always come back with bruises or in handcuffs. He certainly doesn't cause any impatient jitters when he is late, and no anxiety either. As a man he is not exciting, but he isn't a catastrophe, either. What's more, every morning before he goes to work he leaves money for the daily needs. Three hundred African francs and a shopping list. He, at least, knows what he wants:

Njombi: 100 francs
Sapac fish: 100 francs
Tomatoes: 25 francs
Chili peppers : 10 francs
Onions : 15 francs
Oil : 50 francs

With some small changes, it's the same list every day.

When he comes home he checks it, makes sure there's some onion, some oil, and perhaps some chili pepper left. If so, the next list may contain a few specialty items, such as:

Bandjanga: 20 francs
Mbongôô: 10 francs

But it's always the same bearded *sapac* fish, always the same red tarot, also known as *njombi*.

Since Tata Roz has succeeded in getting me back into my mother's and her husband's house, the door has also been opened to my two youngest sisters. One is plump as a ball, the other down-right skeletal. And both of them are always famished. Indeed, the daily ration ought to be increased, but that's not in my stepfather's budget. My mother decides to open a little doughnut business to earn the rest, the need for which is more cruelly tangible every day. As a result I inherit her share of the household chores. In addition to running the house, there is now everyone's laundry and ironing; I have to go to the market and do the cooking as well. It certainly doesn't bother me, as I am hoping that my mother and her husband will finally have the chance to appreciate me for what I'm worth, at least in this area, which I believe I master very well. Unfortunately, I have to work under the strict scrutiny of the husband, who always finds something to criticize: A crease is his pants isn't straight enough, a shirt doesn't have enough starch and must be soaked again, a piece of furniture needs more polish, a corner of the floor is not sufficiently waxed and will have to be redone before dinner—it goes on endlessly! My training as a good housekeeper is inspected with a fine-tooth comb; all that remains to be done is "placc" me. . . .

To this end, a good brother in their religion must be found to marry me. They want me to stand out. I have to study the Bible and preach. My attendance at the Kingdom Hall must be as regular as the most zealous among them. I have to wake up at four in the morning every day in the hope of getting everything done and getting to bed before midnight.

Eight months later, someone notices me, and a candidate presents himself to ask for my hand. My stepfather agrees without asking my opinion and certainly not my mother's. After all, since she is considered as one with her husband, it would be unthinkable that she might have a different view. He only suggests that the suitor wait a little longer so that my baby will be walking, at least. Until that time he is to help me become better acquainted with the Bible. At times he must accompany us when I'm preaching to check my progress.

The young people to whom I preach seem to be more intelligent than I am. They always have very sticky questions that I cannot answer. And my suitor seems dumber than I, for he not only lacks answers, but comes up with such ludicrous arguments that I'm ashamed of him. When he becomes so ridiculous that the students turn into the preachers, he grows angry and always ends by saying, "In any event, the devil will soon be locked up for a thousand years."

For the last period of my Biblical studies, he no longer comes with me. He always has some important errand to run and joins me only at the end of the session. Yet he notes down the same number of hours spent preaching as I do, the liar! But bad luck can have a good side: I discover my own creativity. I invent answers the way I see them. Sometimes, I use the answers of the madwoman Némy, trying to push her logic a little further.

I speak of an eternal God because he is eternally evolving. Of a tolerant God because he is understanding and generous to everything in existence, even that which they call "evil," because he himself has created it. I speak of a loving God who sacrifices himself for the life of his creation through Christ, who is his personification and the manifestation of his love of the flesh, of matter, and of the forms created by him. I always find a solution for anything that seems problematic to them.

Then I realize that I am more and more convincing to them—or at any rate, I make them eager to continue studying twice a week. I begin to believe I may convert at least one of them. That is enormously exciting to me, and gives me great courage. I no longer feel my fatigue. I reread the Bible from cover to cover to find better answers every time. Sadly, though, I often have the impression that by saying what is written in religious texts you run the great risk of preventing people from believing in God. In fact, you might be surprised at the limitations of the sacred word in history and space. I tell myself that if I'm offended by it—I, who am so open—then others could be completely hostile to it. The outlook needs to be widened, liberated, and surely God must be allowed to grow and transcend these shackles caused by the limitations of the transcribers. I am determined to be an effective Christian, converting dozens of young people like myself and devoting every day of my life to this effort.

Now a whole pack gathers, my contemporaries and some a little older, impatiently waiting for our Bible meetings. The following session is to deal with final questions. I'm about to cut them off when one of them asks me an embarrassing question about the sexuality of couples. I stutter that, um. . . .

"The couple . . . becomes one flesh and . . . eh . . . you make children. . . . That's what Matthew says, unless it's in Genesis, um. . . ."

"Yes, but what about pleasure? In the eyes of your religion, is a couple allowed to experience pleasure?"

"Eh . . . I suppose that in order to make one flesh out of two, you should . . . um . . . but I don't want to tell you silly things, and I'll ask Kingdom Hall to give me additional information on the subject, which as long as I've been here has never before been raised . . . eh . . . I'll bring you a satisfactory answer next time, believe me."

"Here, take a look at this book entitled *Sexual Relations in the Home*. Read it and compare it with the answers your church gives. The next time we'll delve into this topic exhaustively, as it's our last point of concern before we can convert."

I put the book in my bag, together with the Bible, just when my suitor arrives. The only word he's heard is *sexual*! But it's enough to get him started on a real interrogation before a "council," to have me resign from my preaching the next day, and to hand it over to "a more experienced team." They send me to a new district with a team of driveling old fools. I am extremely frustrated and rebel against my failure to make my first convert. Nevertheless, I'm determined not to give up. I confide in my brother, who is now living with our uncle while he continues his studies at the high school. He asks to see the book and promises he'll read it in two days or less, summarize it for me, return it to me, and help me find incisive answers so that I can successfully realize my dream of converting someone, even on my own. In any case, I decide never to marry that fool who tried to make my faith and efforts a failure. Since then, in my memory, I envision failure as his wizened, stupid face with the twisted, drooling mouth, and his chapped hands with their bitten nails.

My brother does not return the book to me. We don't discuss it further, and because I am being watched by old preachers in a district far from my new friends, I end up forgetting about them. But they don't forget me. Recognizing that I won't be back, and especially that what I have preached to them is not compatible with what the "more experienced team" is telling them, they dig in their heels and demand their book back.

The emissary who comes to retrieve it runs into my stepfather, who calls to me, matter-of-factly, "Halla, come here and give them back their book!"

My heart jumps. I have a foreboding of disaster. I had forgotten about that stupid book. And I don't have it. So, trying to show maximum calm, I answer that the book is at my brother's, and invite the young man to come with me to pick it up.

"Go back to your chores," my stepfather orders. "I'll send your little sister to get it. Wait outside, young man."

My little sister leaves. The young man will get his book back outside the house, without my stepfather seeing it and imagining who knows what. More fear than misfortune, I tell myself, and, feeling more tranquil, I go back to my chores. I don't know how much time goes by, but my head has already let go of the incident when I hear that metal voice again, rasping my name: "Hall . . . llla!"

How I despise the way he calls me. One day I'm going to render him voiceless—or else I'll change my name!

"Hall-la! Come here! The book is not at your brother's. I ask you to give this young man his book at once. Why are you lying and claiming it's at your brother's? He says he doesn't know what book you're talking about! What is this all about?"

"I am not lying, believe me! My brother took the book on the same day it was given to me to read. He promised to read it quickly and help me come up with effective answers to the questions that came out of my preaching. Unfortunately, they put me in another district, and it was no longer up to me to respond. So I forgot to give the book back simply because I didn't have it. My brother didn't give it to me as we agreed. I'll go and remind him myself, then he'll give it back to me without fail."

"You're not leaving here. Tell me the title of the book and your sister will go and remind him so that he can send it to its rightful owner who's still waiting here."

"The title? I . . . I don't remember. But you can ask the young man to go with the little one."

"Young man! Come in and tell me the title of the book since Mademoiselle doesn't seem to remember it anymore."

The young man undoubtedly senses danger, as do I; he says he doesn't know the book's title because it belongs to his older brother.

He has only been sent to get it back and didn't expect to have to come up with the title.

My sister goes off on the new mission but again returns empty-handed. My brother won't give the book back, saying he misplaced it. The young man leaves, coming back an hour later with his older brother in tow who demands his book. He refuses to mention the title, which exacerbates the suspicions of my irascible stepfather, who forbids me to set foot outside "until this business has been cleared up." I beg him to let me go and look through my brother's things by myself. After all, it concerns me more than anyone else, and even if I can't remember the title I will recognize the book when I see it. Unfortunately, my stepfather calls two of the neighbor's very burly sons and asks them to keep an eye on me while he straightens out the business with my brother. In the hands of these two lechers, to whom I have shown nothing but indifference as my only defense strategy, I am a prisoner of my destiny's next page, apparently already written and sealed.

The outcome is that a mother of three children—one dead, one taken away, one living—several times engaged, is held down spread-eagled by four strapping guys, one of them Guéyè, the biggest hulk in the area. They whip her—fifty lashes on the buttocks with rattan twigs. Why? Because she held a book with the title *Sexual Relations in the Home*, whose pages she has never opened. And all of it done in the name of the Jehovah's Witnesses and the purity of their religion.

For years I wonder why my brother chose to give the book to my stepfather rather than to me. Surely he must have known the trouble he was unleashing. Why did he aggravate the tension, bound to draw suspicion to me? What kind of tortuous desire did he feel to hurt me? What kind of obscure grudge? Even now, as I remember these events, I catch myself suspecting my brother of never having forgiven me, perhaps unconsciously, for our childhood quarrel. Maybe he always kept it buried in one of oblivion's folds, which conceal the ravaged memories of our continent's origins, and fosters what they still call witchcraft.

In my memory, anyway, my stepfather and the religion whose features he will forever represent for me symbolize the "blocked" aspect of life. Surely that is why my memory has repressed the remainder of the time I spent in his and my mother's house before the final break. It is as if I fled that very day, although more time went by during which other anxieties were amassed, and they became a sort of lever greater than the fear of the unknown, the fear that in the end the religion and its representative had managed to infuse in me.

From the cataclysmic day of being held down and whipped, a new sensation almost carnal in its consistency awakened inside me: I named it refusal. In any case, misfortune is always good for something. And so I gained something very important from this hellish day: From then on, even when everything is a total mess, one thing remains very clear whenever it manifests itself in me, and that is my refusal.

My whole being knows instantly what it does not want, and recalls the watertight veil I place between my skin and my innermost being to isolate it from all violence on the fateful day when I was held down and whipped.

Viciously holding my legs, the boys assault me with their lewd looks and twisted mouths and count the blows to their public coitus to the rhythmic chanting of the bystanders—10, 11, 12, 13, 14, 15. . . .

My stepfather's sick gaze assaults me like corrosive acid as he frantically whips me to the point of a sadistic orgasm, like a rapist.

Resist, my veil! Resist, my refusal! Or else I'll die of shame instead of pain.

For this man is busy abusing me, brazenly climaxing in public, and all those present are benefiting by it, getting off with him as they count the lashes ever more relentlessly: 45, 46, 47, 48, 49, *ééééé*, . . . *and* . . . fif-ty.

Then he immediately withdraws to his room and hides. He knows he's been seen in his pornographic, orgiastic public act, clearly seen by everyone. He won't ever mislead anyone in this district again. He is sweating from his despicable exertions, sweating from shame and fear above all.

I remember that during one of our nocturnal chats in the hospital, Tata Roz said to me: "After orgasm every loveless sexual act always shows its ugliness to the one who has committed it, because the sex organ is intrinsically one of the ugliest parts of the body, and a loveless sex act is what is most bestial in man."

I imagine my stepfather in the throes of that experience as he wonders which attitude to take to pull the wool over our eyes. I catch myself making a bet: "He'll have to be rigid and even more distant; add balm to his voice; be immaculately dressed in his superstarched khakis, ties more tightly knotted than ever before; it's the least he can do, for he has been seen, very clearly seen," I tell myself and rejoice over it in the depths of my heart.

"Only sadists are immune to visions of ugliness and go on feeling pleasure no matter what the act has been," Tata Roz used to say. Thus, from that day on I must have become such a vision to my stepfather. I stand up as if nothing has happened, my back straight, readjusting my clothes without any solemn or provocative gesture! Enormous pleasure fills me as I think: "I've won, I've resisted their attacks, and it is they who in their flaccid state look pathetic."

I snub them with my unruffled look: Everything all right? Are you finished? Very good.

Even the witnesses are ashamed, and I'm delighting in the elusive and baffled looks. I do not need to hide; they are turning away one by one, deserting the place, hanging their heads. I stay a moment, straight as a queen, then finally leave, feeling my impeccable cloak of refusal beginning to slip from my shoulders. I rush through the living room to my bedroom before someone discovers me only half dressed in the dignity of my refusal.

Do sadists weep after their warped pleasure?

I wept long and quietly. . . .
Oh! How suffocating it is to weep quietly.
It tightens the nerves and flays the skull;

It compresses the brain
And pulls the entrails into the throat;
It contracts like an imminent delivery
And soon a scream will be born.

The scream we hear is my mother's, cloistered in her bedroom: "I beg you, Brother, not that, not today, not after her! No, noooooo!"

Surely he wasn't going to rape her, too! In the hospital, Tata Roz made it known to me that my mother Naja had already been abused twice in her life. The first time was by a cousin of my father's, one desperate night when the latter had pushed her to the brink of insanity again and, getting drunk first, she'd fled to the bush planning to kill herself. Disgusted and ashamed, she hadn't dared complain about it. The second time it was a fisherman on the island where Tata Roz had taken her to look for another place to live. The result was the pregnancy that had made my mother crazy for a time, when we almost lost her. Fortunately, there was the ritual and my father's return, whereupon she created a version of it that made her survival acceptable.

How many times in one lifetime are women raped? How many times and how many mother Najas are beaten up before admitting that it was better to be alone than in a bad partnership? How many times before they find the courage of an Aunt Roz to take responsibility for themselves in a different way?

"Nooooo!" my mother Naja screams again as she beats on the door with all her strength.

I close my ears and my entire brain.
I don't want to know anything, hear anything, understand anything;
I want no further answers or questions.

Resist, my blood, resist, my belly;
Persist in being tombs to the uproar in my veins,
In the craters of my throat,
Tombs of the pandemonium inside of me. . . .

The door opens with a crash; my mother comes out, and dashes into the kitchen.

I quietly stop crying, and just as quietly start to collect my few things and put them in the small cardboard suitcase my older sister has given me for the maternity clinic. I don't know how much longer I'll be staying in this house, but I do know that I refuse to live here for the rest of my life and wait for my stepfather's new schemes to possess me or for some salutary marriage he will try to arrange.

Tata Roz takes my child on his first birthday, and says to me: "If you still want to, this is the time for you to go and find yourself elsewhere. Don't worry about the child; with the grace of God, nothing bad will happen to him, certainly not by my doing."

I write my mother a letter asking her to forgive me for having brought her nothing but further troubles when what she needs is profound peacefulness. I slip the letter into the bottom of my suitcase and put it back underneath the rickety bed.

31

The next page of my destiny opens one lazy evening. I finish all my chores with time to spare now that I have no baby clothes to wash or meals to prepare for my child.

It is meeting day at Kingdom Hall, and a special day because my stepfather is to give a lecture. For the occasion my mother has come home from the market early. Both of us are ready and waiting for the return of the master of the house. His bath water is warm for him in the washroom, his afternoon snack carefully placed on the table.

A lazy and extraordinary evening. My mother has spread a mat on the veranda and is lying down to get some air and rest her back. I sit down beside her. What an exceptional moment! We have so many things to say to each other that we don't know where to begin, and especially where and how to end. The master of the house will soon arrive and, without ever having mentioned it, we know he won't like to see us close. One of us will have to get up at any moment, as we normally do quite spontaneously when the hour of his return approaches so that he won't find us together. Today, though, neither of us feels like moving. On the contrary, the intense conversation makes us forget the time and all precaution.

An indolent, bewitching evening . . .

I lie down next to my mother on the mat. She puts her arm

under my neck like a pillow. We are so comfortable. . . .

"Mama Naja, do you think my son will be all right over at Tata Roz's?"

"Of course. Your aunt has always been good at raising children. At this time in his life your son couldn't be in better hands. You see how little I am available to you and you know how that bothers me. Let's thank Jehovah for having softened your aunt's heart enough to help us. Everything will be fine, you'll see, don't worry."

"And you, Mama, will you be all right?"

"Calm yourself and don't worry about me. Only God knows how to reward our efforts. When he considers them sufficient he'll help us out of our trouble. And then we'll see things clearly, we'll understand everything, and we'll find our balance again. . . ."

"Aha! Because you lost it, and where might it be, that balance of yours, dear ladies. . . ." He thinks his humor is irresistible, the hoarse voice of the converted brute.

Startled, my mother springs up.

"Ah! Hello, Brother. You're early. You must be nervous. Your water and snack are waiting for you. If you hurry up we'll even have time to listen to a practice reading of your lecture, just us, so we can give you some feedback. That way you'll feel more relaxed when you're there, what do you think?"

Instead of reacting to all her attention, he attends to the one person who pays him no mind, and that is me.

"And the other rude 'grand lady,' isn't she planning to move?"

"We're both ready, just waiting for you, now," my mother says hastily to avoid a squabble.

"She's ready to go with her hair all a mess like that? Get up and do something about that hair. . . ."

At that very moment I believe we all knew the irreparable had come knocking on the door. I feel my veil of refusal cover my entire body, suddenly heavy as a stone. My mother moves forward and tries to get her husband away from me, but he pushes her roughly and plants himself on his two legs like a fishwife expecting an answer from a fellow gossipmonger.

"What's the matter? Are you deaf? I'm telling you to get up and do something about your hair. Didn't you hear me?"

"And what's wrong with you?" I hear myself reply. "I thought the lecture was about 'greatness through tolerance.' Did the subject change—was it replaced by a different one about my hairdo?"

My voice takes us all by surprise and, truth be told, scares us with its calm gravity. It sounds like someone else's voice. We're all wondering who spoke. Of the three of us I am the most astonished, for I am casually lying down as if I weren't the one being addressed. On the inside I tell myself to get up and go to my room to defuse the situation, at least, but unfortunately my body won't listen anymore. It is completely under the control of my refusal, now as hard as marble.

Mama pulls her man to their room like an obstinate mule and locks the door behind them. I leap up, intending to pick up my suitcase and flee into the city before he finishes his bath and food. Just at that moment, however, the "fiancé" shows up, smiling from ear to ear: He is bringing me a present that is both useful and nice. "An umbrella for the stormy season," he says, looking inane.

I manage to hide my bad mood and accept the gift in a friendly manner. I open it right in the living room and try to entertain him with mimicry and silly postures, as a way of thanking him. He laughs loudly, but comments that I have a funny look. I tell him I'm hungry. He gives me ten francs to go and buy doughnuts. Just as I'm about to close the umbrella, the stepfather's voice comes at me in volleys, instantly deflected by my shield of refusal that I hadn't yet lowered completely. I stand motionless, in the center of the living room with the fully opened umbrella.

"What kind of sorcery is this, opening an umbrella inside the house!"

"Come now, Brother," says the fiancé in greeting, "that's just a superstition. She was merely trying it out. I just gave it to her as a present."

"Well then, she'd better close it or try it outside!"

I don't know how, but I find myself outside with the umbrella that had suddenly become the embodiment of my refusal. When my stepfather, dressed to the teeth, finally and ceremoniously appears to read his lecture on the veranda, I stay under my umbrella. He can't bear it: He's hardly begun reading when he interrupts himself and orders me to close the umbrella.

"I don't see why; we're outside now, it's my present, and I'm already on my way to Kingdom Hall. Besides, there I'll hear what the umbrella might keep me from hearing of the lecture you're giving now, which in any case wasn't planned and isn't even obligatory."

Then he tells me that if I care about going to his lecture I must close the umbrella and go inside to do my hair. Mama and the fiancé have the courage to state that they frankly don't see why my hairdo is so important, but he categorically silences them: "I make the decisions here! Either she changes her hair or she's not going to the lecture!"

"Fine! I choose not to go to the lecture."

"Why?"

"Because I already know every word you're going to say; I've heard it all many times, forgotten it all just as fast, and never seen you put any of it into action or make it into living examples in this house. So, I promise to be a good girl and wait in my room, using the time to read the last issue of the *Watchtower*."

"Oh, no! If you're staying here it will be outside. That will teach you to taunt your elders even though you don't even have a home of your own yet. Besides, who'll guarantee you'll ever have one? Disobedient as you are, you're certainly going to spend a lot of time wandering around outside. Maybe you'll starve to death or have an accident on some sidewalk where dogs will eat part of your body and the firemen will barely rescue what's left, leaving me in charge of a disgraceful burial."

He spills his guts, vomits his hatred and curses, gesticulating wildly as he starts all over again for the benefit of the neighbors and onlookers who have started to congregate. My poor mother has once again withdrawn to weep alone in her room. The fiancé, totally undone by the intensity and scope of his anger, barely manages to once or twice stammer a dismayed, "I don't understand, Brother."

The presence of a public, enabling him to feed me to the lions once again, makes me explode, and for the first and last time in our lives my stepfather sees and hears my rage.

"You have no right whatsoever to curse me. You are not my father. I've worked for you with great devotion without ever getting anything in return—no consideration, no respect, not the slightest salary to give me some dignity. You will never bury me. At the hour of my death people will have forgotten your name and your existence. For always wanting to belittle each of my efforts and initiatives, remember this day when you're about to preach on the topic of 'greatness through tolerance.' From this day forward my efforts will start to bear fruit, for from a single dry kernel of corn a huge cornfield can be grown. They will beg me to come and open the door to let you out of the door you are now closing in my face, the prison you are bound to be locked up in one day, and they'll have to jump through hoops to have you set free. . . ."

And to get him out of my life, I left.
Like a joke, a gag,
As if to frighten us all;
I headed for my destiny with
Ten francs in my pocket and an umbrella in my hand.
I left for a world unknown,
Prepared to live a life without a tomorrow. . . .

• • •

Passages from my stepfather's prison journal:

How many lawyers does it take to intervene in this affair? How much money has she already paid, that Fitini Halla, who will never be my daughter and who apparently won't leave my life until I'm dead? What magic spell binds us somehow? Why did it have to be she who has to get me out of prison?

After all, wasn't she the one who cast the evil fate on me, predicting I would go to prison? Let her figure out how to get me out of this, or else she'll never have any peace! It must torment her, otherwise why would she go to such great lengths? She'll never like me, she has way too much contempt for me. This I know; I've always seen it in her eyes. And with the business that sent me here, I'm nothing more than a common thief to her as well. As if they don't know who the real thieves in this country are! Why did I have to get caught, anyway, and go to jail, just for a few meters of lace, some little bags of buttons, and a few other odds and ends! And all that while the tax collector has been diverting tons of money for decades and getting away with it.

I fell in a trap. A trap set by the Baffi, past masters in the art of settling accounts, falsifying books, and gradually spiriting away receipts, one cent at a time, without attracting anyone's attention. And to think that I never paid any mind to the small amounts of missing money, the intangible pennies that in the end, after two decades, make holes of several million.

I've seen that Baffi tax collector with his gang of cousins and nephews sweep offices, cart away boxes of garbage that were, in fact, merchandise carefully swiped from previously delivered packages. I saw them in the market unobtrusively replace the merchandise at lower prices, earn tiny amounts of money, acquire "shopping carts" and patiently make these yield a profit, one cent at a time. I've seen a small organization make fortunes, like termites in an anthill, each member of a large family of them methodically doing his small part for the success of the group.

I've admired the skill of others, appreciated their ingenuity, solidarity, and patience. I've wanted to act like them. But all I took were old packages, already opened, that had been there for who knows how long. Surely the sender had died. Moreover, the tax collector made it very clear to me that he was getting ready to liquidate any packages that had never been claimed and had no return address. He practically donated them to me. I told myself that I, too, would start a little business, adding a penny at a time every day for as long as I had until my retirement, which was eight years. I fell into a trap set by the Baffi, for they were the ones who rushed off to the police, who caught me red-handed.

What lousy luck! I had entrusted the merchandise to my nephew Benoît so that he could unload it quickly in the market without leaving any traces. But the good-for-nothing chose to keep it, claiming he was going to open a shop! Everything was still around when the investigation began. I can't help but think of that very peculiar Fitini Halla, although she would certainly have been more efficient and discreet if I had handed the business over to her. But just seeing her has always driven me crazy. She's a witch, a seer, an evildoer, and a sexual poisoner who in some impulsive and unpredictable way makes you forget God and religion. You hardly have the time to realize what you're doing before the harm is already done. She's not a woman; she's a genie or a seductive devil.

I can't believe I'm in prison just because of that wretched package, and they gave me twenty years. The Baffi asked for the death sentence, showing that during my twenty years of service I had filched several million! Me! What would I've done with it? Their investigations couldn't bear it out. The trap is as big as a house, but the judges still sentenced me to twenty years!

The truth is that the curses of that witch brought me bad luck. And to top it all off, she has to be the one to fight to get me out of here. She must be elated that her spell worked. Everything she predicted on that fateful day that she rebelled is actually happening to me, but I'm not done with her yet. We'll see what happens when she meets the witch-doctor spy, who was in our cell and was set free by the president yesterday. I've made arrangements for him to meet her. He will turn her luck around. She must lose her husband and then . . . he who laughs last laughs best.

32

In those days a young Jehovah's Witness did not read newspapers or listen to the radio, and, had there been television, would not have been allowed to watch it. He would have been spared from the latter temptation, however, by the president of the republic who couldn't stand seeing himself on the screen. They said that when he was in the so-called developed countries and saw his face on the screen there, he would fly into an uncontrollable fury, and they'd be forced to keep a close watch on him to make sure he didn't smash any TV sets to smithereens. A young Jehovah's Witness would only go out within the perimeter of his preaching terrain and would know nothing else about the city. So what he knew about the world and current events was merely what he read in *Awake!* or the *Watchtower*, the only officially authorized publications, which definitely truncated global events.

That was the life I led throughout the time I lived with my mother and her husband, Njokè Number Two! It was so limited that I no longer even remembered the direction from which my older sister and I had come fourteen months earlier.

So when I decide to leave the perimeter of my preaching area, I have a moment of true panic. It is my impression that the world beyond will be a battlefield, an Armageddon! I roam around for a long time, going in circles, afraid to take the plunge, and aware that if I step across the threshold it will be for good.

How will I manage without any material or intellectual baggage? What assets do I have? A quick overview nearly dissuades me from leaving, but my refusal to turn back is stronger. So I review everything I can do to survive with dignity, and draw up a kind of curriculum vitae with an eye to my future job search.

- "Housekeeper, all-around maid": housework, laundry, cooking, child care (superior level, great experience).
- "Nurse's aide" in clinics and rural hospitals: dressing wounds, giving intravenous injections (medium level).
- "High-level agricultural worker" both in privately owned fields and industrial cocoa, coffee, and palm oil plantations.
- "Agent" capable of serving where a good level of reasoning and discussion is needed. Expresses herself articulately and knows how to present convincing arguments.

I'm tempted to put "Jehovah's Witness preaching experience" between parentheses, but I'm afraid I'll run into someone like myself whose reasons for not yielding would be too personal and who would use them to make me "pay for the sins of my fathers" well beyond the number of generations required by Jehovah himself! I come to the conclusion that from now on I'd do better to present myself under my own label and learn to convince others with my own words. First I need to know what it is that I have to say, and to whom. And I won't know this by going around in circles in my usual shackles. First I have to cross the Rubicon!

As soon as I've passed the "street of two churches," I stop looking back and thinking about the past. Fear melts away, as do feelings of sadness and fatigue. I walk with a light step, humming, "Take my life, oh, Lord God, and let it be in thy honor. . . ."

I'm not looking for a destination; I just walk, and that's enough for now. I take streets because they're clean and attractive—the color of the houses, their light, their architecture. Time is completely expunged from my memory, and I don't recognize that the day has come to an end.

On my right a train whistles. I look up and read "Harbor Station." There's great excitement; people are running in every direction, some with suitcases or bags in hand, on their back, or on their head. Children are rushing forward with baskets of peanuts, sticks of manioc, coconuts, hard-boiled eggs, and all sorts of other things. I'm caught up in and carried off by the whirlwind all the way to one of the gates.

"Your ticket!"

"What ticket?"

"Aren't you traveling?"

"No! I'm picking someone up."

"Well, where is your platform ticket?"

"Where do I get that, and how much is it?"

"Over there at the window, ten francs!"

I go to the ticket window and without a word put down my ten francs for the agent. Just as silently he hands me the platform ticket. When I finally get to the platform there's a train about to depart. I barely make it in, and don't know its destination.

MOVEMENT NINE

33

SONG 13

True, there is not necessarily a destination for each step,
But walking every day until the next one comes
Inevitably leads to our destination, our one true place, which is our
        destiny;
And in my heart and in my head I walk
Without seeking any longer to distinguish dream from reality,
Without wanting any longer to plan something at all costs.
Someone is waiting for me;
I know it and I feel it,
Though I don't know where or when;
All that I must do is walk toward her or him,
And if I fall, or fall asleep, then it will be he—
He or she—or even death, who'll come to me,
And quietly, I'll open my arms in welcome.

Bayard, you were neither death nor life,
But you were at least one of its stages,
An obligatory but oh-so-beneficial passage.

● ● ●

The train is jam-packed with *bayam-sellam*, the "women who buy and resell."

The *bayam-sellam* overrun every aisle of every car with their bags of unlikely merchandise, chirping like veritable magpies. They wind up monopolizing my thoughts. . . . Ah, these fighting women who nourish the country!

Every day at five in the morning they're in every marketplace throughout the land. They bring in what the interior lacks: medications, refined oil, smoked cod and other fish, soap, all kinds of fabric, books and notebooks, preserves. . . . They supply the rural women, whose agricultural produce they buy and take to town, contributing to a flow of energy that brings the country some equilibrium, no matter how slight.

"Really, these women should all be decorated," I say to myself. "They are the country's true development agents, and I wonder how we'd manage without these nameless women who do enormous work for our survival every day."

I find all of them beautiful, the plump and the pudgy, the slim and the muscular, those who stand like solid tree trunks, the tiny ones who move like ping-pong balls, lovely, amusing, and brilliant. Although most of them are illiterate, they've always been mistresses of microeconomics with their balls and burlap and other mutual aid fundraising. In our district near the great market I occasionally used to observe them, but never really had time to think about them. If I were a village chief, I tell myself again, I'd find some way to bring as many of them as possible to my village, and make them my principal development agents.

All of a sudden I'm pulled out of my sweet dream about the economy's draftswomen when I see the conductor approach with heavy step, striding across the bags like a somnambulist tightrope walker. He looks like my stepfather, in his stiff khakis with their buttons like the nails on a crucifix. Backing away, I attempt to hide behind the biggest of the vending women, trying to put a maximum distance between myself and him.

"With a bit of luck," I say to myself, "we'll reach the next station soon, and I'll be able to get off." My heart is beating like a water drum in my huge effort to keep my evasion unnoticed; I'm breathless and afraid I'll faint. A firm hand roughly pulls at me, and then I'm sitting in the lap of a young man in a shirt covered with buttons as large as medals!

Good heavens, another conductor, I tell myself, slumping in arms that hold me as if I were a baby. I am comatose and slip into my black flight of oblivion.

When I come to I feel enormously stupid. I don't know where I am and don't remember how I got there. The tall young man in the shirt with the thousand medal-like buttons is leaning over me, and he smiles. The rumbling of the train merges with the snoring of the many passengers who are asleep on bundles of bags. There are women vendors who have slid beneath my feet and are snoring loudly. I have a lump in my throat. Daybreak begins to show on the horizon, but it is still dark. I close my eyes again without being able to release my tongue.

"You can sleep some more if you want, especially if you're going to the last stop. There are only two more. Actually, where are you getting off?"

I can't get out a word.

"Very well, the last stop, just like me. Sleep then, and I'll wake you when it's time."

"Thank you."

"Ah, so you're not mute, after all. Thank God! Sleep now."

"I'm awake."

"Good. Where are you going?"

"I have no idea. Where is this train going?"

"To Mfoundi, of course! Don't tell me you caught a train without knowing where it's going."

"Yes, I did."

"Well, now! Fine, sleep some more. When we get there I'll take you to my sister's. Perhaps you'll want to confide in a woman."

I immediately feel reassured. The lump in my throat vanishes, and I tell him about my escape, which now surges up in my memory, intensifying my anxieties and waking me completely.

"They'll go looking for me, I'm sure," I say, trembling and clasping him. "They didn't think I'd be capable of fleeing since I didn't know the city and had nothing with me. But when they recognize I'm not coming back, I'm sure they'll go looking for me, and I don't want them to find me! Please, help me!"

He seems to be deep in thought, then says: "When children escape from the paternal home the parents can go to the police and file a missing person's report, an arrest warrant, even."

"An arrest warrant? What does that mean?"

"It means that anyone who recognizes you may arrest you and take you to the police to have you sent home. Often parents promise rewards to the people who find their lost children."

"Please, don't report me to the police, don't take me back, I beg you. Besides, if you do take me back, they won't give you anything because they're quite poor and, what's more, they don't love me. As it happens, they're quite happy to be rid of me and are only waiting for me to die and have dogs eat me!"

"Whoa there! Easy does it! I didn't say I would take you back, and anyway, no warrant for your arrest has been filed yet. So while we wait, I'll hide you at my sister's house. And if a warrant for your arrest should be filed, we'll take it from there."

"How will we know, though?"

"All you have to do is check with the town hall or the central police bureau. These things are posted."

I am mortified. I imagine my picture in every town hall and police station. I imagine people recognizing me in the street and arresting me to take me to the closest police station. They will take me, handcuffed like a thief, to my stepfather, who will call back that brute Guéyè and his gang to hold me down and whip me again!

Suddenly my heart settles down: I know that won't happen because I refuse. All I need to do is forge ahead.

• • •

"My name is Bayard. I'm in my fourth year at Saker High School. I'm on my way home for Easter vacation. I'm a prince and *yéyé*! And you?"

"My name is Halla, but they usually call me Little Mother. And I'm nothing special. What is *yéyé*?"

"Where do you come from that you don't know what *yéyé* is?"

"I come from the self-contained district of Jehovah's Witnesses where I used to preach, and I've never heard of *yéyé*. What is it?"

"I'll tell you later. Now let me think about what I'm going to tell my sister so she won't be suspicious. I don't want her to think bad things about you."

We find Bayard's sister on her doorstep, about to leave, with her children, for a vacation to their native village.

"My husband is away on assignment and the only one here is the caretaker to watch the house," she tells us regretfully. "I've already reserved and paid for our bus tickets, so I really can't stay here with you as I would like to do. Wouldn't you rather come with us?"

"No, not just yet," Bayard answers. "I've got to take care of some things here. We may join you later. Just let me write a quick note to the family."

We stay in his sister's house for five days. Bayard leaves every afternoon and is gone almost all night. He sleeps all morning and wakes up just to go out and buy bread, milk, or sardines in oil. Sometimes he gets fruit—avocados, mangos, tangerines—and then we eat the only meal of the day. He turns the radio on and gives me a running commentary on the *yéyé* songs—the rock 'n' roll music—they play. He tells me that he doesn't really know when the *yéyé* movement got started or who started it. But he thinks the sixties will turn everything that humanity has known until then upside down, and it's more than likely that the exclamation "yeh, yeh!" expressed a recognition and acceptance of these upheavals and new lifestyles. And he's a *yéyé* because there's nothing more modern and liberating than that. Africa is independent, and so is he; men are walking on the moon, and he feels prepared to go and live on Mars with the Martians, because he is *yéyé*, yeh!

A *yéyé* has to be unequivocally recognized as such—his bearing, his manner, everything—yeh! And, of course, it has its costs; you need plenty of the right connections. Later he'll teach me to become *yéyé*, but right now he has other things on his mind. Besides, we have to wait and see whether my parents will try to find me.

In the middle of the afternoon Bayard leaves again until well into the night. I toss and turn without falling asleep until he comes back. I read everything I can put my hands on and listen to the radio until they sign off for the day. I struggle to visualize my future, but it's no use; my imagination fails me completely. My only plan for now is to wait for Bayard's sister to return and beg her to hire me as housekeeper or nanny for her children. Perhaps I'll find a husband one day and have my own home with children of my own whom I will be able to keep and care for, whom I won't throw out, not even to get into heaven. I'll live with them until they're grown and have their own families. I don't feel in the least bit *yéyé* and don't see myself living on Mars with the Martians, whom I've never heard about before. They must be the demons whom God himself threw out of heaven, and who went straight into the abyss with the Devil for another thousand years, right after Armageddon.

After Armageddon, I shall not be among the hundred and forty-four chosen by God to enter heaven, or among the thousands of faithful who shall inherit the earth. Since I'm no longer preaching and haven't the slightest ambition to do so, and since I haven't obeyed either my father or my mother, it is obvious that I'll be swept out of God's memory and forgotten by everyone. Religion provides me with only one consolation: It does not have a hell other than total removal to oblivion. As far as I'm concerned, I already live this oblivion, halfway at least. My hell won't be any worse after I'm dead.

The first three days seem like three months to me. The nights are too long and boring after the radio goes off at midnight, and the days are unbearable in their intensity. Every sound might be an informer, a policeman, or who knows what. As soon as Bayard is gone the minutes drag on like lazy tortoises making long stops. I have the feeling that time comes to a halt altogether because the minutes don't take their feet off the clock's brake anymore, and the hands on the watch stay fixed on the dial.

The fourth day comes in a rush.

Early in the evening Bayard arrives like a cannonball, out of breath, and tells me that my picture is posted at the town hall and that my parents have a warrant out for my arrest. It is imperative that we leave town before anyone recognizes me and has me arrested. He'll work it out so that we can go within two days, but he has to think of a good hiding place first.

At dawn on the fifth day he comes home and finds me watching for his return through the keyhole.

"We're leaving. I'm taking you to my mother in Tchékos where no one will look for you. And when they're tired of searching and take your picture down, you can come back to town to try to find work. And who knows, maybe between now and then you'll learn to be *yéyé*, and we'll understand each other more and get along better. . . . Come on, hurry!"

• • •

What is it that inspires and introduces a new style? What is the word that sets it off, what gesture or inspiration, what genies coming from which waves drive such echoes across the world, with multiplying responses and repetitions, and then in just such a way that that they're suddenly accepted as the right thing.

At the time, the style was known as *yéyé*, yeh! You had to have pants that hung from the lowest part of your behind with bottoms as wide as elephants' feet, shirts that were wildly flowered or else riddled with buttons, even on the back of the collar, and manes of hair.

Children of the poor did almost any kind of work, day or night, just to be stylish. Rich kids learned to rob with their father's weapon in hand. Dockworkers passed themselves off as students, and students became dockworkers at night to earn what they needed to buy square-tipped shoes.

Planters' children stole sacks of coffee or cocoa, cans of palm oil, and even cattle to be secretly sold so they could buy what they called *yéyé* clothes. Civil employees, unbelievably, passed themselves off as students so they could go on being *yéyé.*

Some styles arrive, stay on the surface, and you know they won't last. Some change everything so much, including the visions of the world, that you think they'll last forever; but they vanish, slowly but surely, and then are totally forgotten as if they never existed. Yet, so much havoc is left behind, so many deeds committed in their name, that they continue on in the realm of absurdity all alone.

Style is precisely that—passing absurdity.

Bayard was totally in style as a *yéyé*—in the way he talked, walked, ate, and breathed, yeh! He was in the city for his studies and had failed several times to be admitted to the sixth grade. He was beyond the age when he could enter public high school, so his parents had been forced to pay a high fee to enroll him in a good private high school and give him the opportunity to obtain at least the minimum secondary-school certificate. They hoped to turn him into an educated man, able to take up the traditional chiefdom to which he was heir and bring it into the modern world. He was the youngest of nine children and the only boy. Needless to say, he cost his family a great deal, and they overprotected and spoiled him.

But Bayard had other things in mind than continuing a small chiefdom, which in his eyes stood for nothing more than folklore. He just wanted to be *yéyé*, yeh!

The only important thing about the chiefdom, as Bayard saw it, was that it still had a few hundred planters and growers who turned over the tithe of their produce to the throne out of respect for their traditions. His uncle functioned as regent, waiting for him to finish his studies and be enthroned. He sent Bayard a solid share of the tithe, which he used to live well beyond his means. Since no one else in the chiefdom had an education, the entire family made sure that Bayard lacked nothing so that he would pass his exams. The previous year, when Bayard failed his seventh grade entrance exam, his oldest sister had gone to Wouri to meet the school principal, and had managed to straighten that out. She didn't regret it, because Bayard rewarded her by passing his entrance test for the eighth year. By focusing a little on his work, Bayard should have been able to get promoted to ninth grade. His family was prepared to do anything it took, and Bayard knew it. As a result he requested plenty of new books, tools, medications, and so on. Since he was completely immersed in the *yéyé* world, there was no doubt that he had abused their generosity. In the village they were beginning to wonder what Bayard was actually doing in Wouri with all the money they sent him.

Since he was on his way home for Easter vacation, Bayard was certainly wondering what he might come up with this time to squeeze the maximum out of his parents. That was when he noticed a young girl moving backward in his direction, clearly very frightened by something or someone. He stretched his neck and saw the conductor. The young girl approaching him was reeling; he pulled her down firmly, convinced it was the *yéyé* gods themselves who sent her to him. She turned around and collapsed into his arms like a ripened fruit on the verge of dropping. He gently kissed her forehead, and the girl fell asleep.

"Sleep like that comes from fleeing or dying," Bayard said to himself, and decided, "so be it, my lovely one's will be done. I want you to consider yourself dead to the life you've lived until now, to be reborn into a life that will belong to me, Bayard. I really like you, you know. The only problem is that, at first sight, you're not really *yéyé*! But never mind, you look like a thoroughbred and you'll certainly please my parents. If necessary, I'll know how to change you into a *yéyé*, when the time comes."

● ● ●

We arrive in Bayard's village on the bimonthly market day. It seems that everyone has already sold everything, or bought what they could afford. People are strolling around waiting to feast before heading home.

Then we hear the sound of ululating, and dozens of women come charging at us, soon to be overtaken by a group of young people who throw themselves at Bayard. He turns and points at me, speaking Lemandé, a language I don't understand. Right away the group picks me up and puts me on a *tipot*, a kind of stretcher, the sort used to carry chiefs, and hoist me onto their shoulders.

An uncontrollable panic comes over me. My God, why hasn't it occurred to me before? I had landed in the hands of a cannibal! That's why he's been so kind to me, asking nothing in return—because he and his family are going to eat me.

I start to call for help in my mother tongue, asking if there is anyone there who understands my language, Mèè, and can save me from the cannibals. A young woman right beside the *tipot* tells me to calm down.

"I am Bassa as well and speak Mèè like you. You can rest assured that you are in no danger whatsoever—on the contrary! Prince Bayard sent a message that he was coming with his fiancée, that her parents had dropped her off at his house and requested immediate redress for having slept with her before marriage. It's perfectly normal that his cousins and nephews should carry you to your connubial home. I envy you for having hooked the last Lemandé prince, who's been coveted by every girl of good family here. I welcome you and congratulate you, lucky princess."

I am thunderstruck! As it turns out, by the time we arrived in his home town that first day on the train, Bayard already had a plan, and had asked his sister to deliver the message to his parents. We stayed in Mfoundi just long enough for his family to prepare for our arrival.

Bayard is walking far ahead of me, leading the procession. I can't talk to him—and anyway, what could I say? All I could do now was wait. Since I am his "fiancée," we are bound to end up alone together somewhere, and he will explain.

As I wait, I relax and try to enjoy this incredible means of transportation. It is the first time, too, that I had see the savanna, its interminable horizon and magnificent valleys with their golden undulations, flowering shrubs, and alternating cocoa and coffee plantations. It is a marvelous view, and I drink it in. And so, it is as a young girl newly "deflowered" and very much out of her depth that I arrive at the court of the Tchékos chiefdom.

My "mother-in-law" receives me like a princess: She has laid out several velvet *pagnes*, some printed with Java wax, so that my feet won't touch the ground. She herself washes my feet while I'm still being carried, and finally they put me down carefully on the sumptuous *pagnes*. After the words of welcome, they take me to the back of the courtyard, where a special bath has been prepared for me. Three of Bayard's young nieces are assigned to wash me, massage my back and feet, and rub me down from top to toe with shea butter perfumed with ylang-ylang flowers and other unfamiliar scents. They wrap me in different velvet *pagnes* and bring me to the uncle-regent, next to whom a special stool has been placed for me. When Bayard arrives, more than a hundred people file by to greet us, all close members of the family or the chiefdom.

Then we move out to an inner courtyard, where a gigantic meal has been set up on raffia carpets. It is very late at night before they bring me to the wedding chamber. I expect that Bayard is postponing for as long as possible the inevitable moment of confrontation, when we'll look each other in the eye for the first time. But protocol obliges him to join me, and there he is, in the doorway like a bas-relief in a frame.

It is the first time that I look at him the way a woman looks at a man. Until then he has been a savior, a benefactor, to be looked at with eyes lowered. And he has introduced himself as my fiancé, the first man in my life. I wonder whether I would have loved him if he'd wooed me and asked for my hand. I look at him calmly. He looks down, comes in, and sits on the mat instead of the bed.

He is a handsome prince. Under different circumstances he would certainly have seduced me, but tonight I feel nothing but cold anger. He has conned me, he has lied to me. He invented tales of arrest warrants and, from his superior position, treated me as the ignoramus I was; you cannot love someone who treats you as if you are an inferior. He didn't even consider courting me, and even less talking to me about his plans, which would at least have implied some trust. I was an object for him, a potentially good match for his status.

"Please forgive me," he finally stutters. "I wanted to tell you, but it was a little complicated, and I really preferred my family to see you first so that I would know how they'd react. In case it was to become serious, you see—I mean, in case I were to fall in love with you. I couldn't marry a woman my mother didn't love. But before getting to that point, I needed a strategy."

Then he told me how the idea came to him. He claimed that I carried myself like a princess, that I would make a very good impression on his parents and would persuade them to give him all the money he'd ask for, in order to pay off my own parents. We would share it all and, if things didn't work out, we'd say goodbye, no harm done. But if we fell in love we would decide together what to do with the money. He was ready for anything that suited me.

What was he trying to do? Although he didn't say so, the only thing on his mind was the *yéyé* movement. It was the only thing capable of stimulating his intelligence and creativity, the only thing that motivated and justified his actions. It held his entire being captive and, in some way, I envied him for having something that solid and all-consuming in his life. I felt a certain irritation, perhaps a touch of jealousy of the thing that managed to occupy such a dominant place, while I . . . I was undeniably too much of a nothing and deserved whatever I got. Never mind. It was time to change, to stop being and appearing so irrelevant. I decided that from this very instant I would make people reckon with me.

"All right, I understand your arguments. You're a fast worker, and I congratulate you on your achievement. Let's talk about the rest now, since we're not in love."

He looked at me as if he were seeing a new person.

I have often wondered what to make of his astonishment. What did he expect? That I'd throw my arms around his neck to tell him I loved him? That I'd protest in some way, and he would have to calm me down with flattering words? What did he expect? I'll never know. He was silent for a while, didn't react, and then seemed to get a grip on himself.

"Fine! We'll wait for the parents to confer and give us whatever they decide. Then we'll go back to Wouri and we'll share the loot there."

"Out of the question! We're not leaving here unless I have my share in hand. How do I know that you'll give it to me once you're no longer afraid of being exposed to your parents?"

"Hey there! Take it easy. I'm not a robber, after all!"

"That's what you say."

"Don't be any nastier than you have to. Haven't I treated you with respect until now? If I'd wanted to take advantage of you, what would you have done?"

"There's nothing you could have done to me, for I am protected, which you are not, with your one exposed flank. If you have any doubts, let's make a bet that I'll ruin all your plans immediately."

He glances behind himself fearfully and begs me to lower my voice.

"You see you can't try anything to oppose me. So let me in on what you thought my share would be."

I've really scored a point. The young gentleman has discovered a new person, when he thought he knew her through and through. I'm just as surprised as he is. Except that I'm exultant with the girl I've discovered inside me—capable of strategizing, being courageous, and calculating to save her hide—while he is devastated to have caught a panther instead of a kitten. That is when he remembers he's a man and I'm a woman, and that he can talk to me of love! But for me, it's too late. It's not a young man I'm dealing with any longer, but an imposter, someone who steals another's trust and swindles his parents. With such a person you have to be very strong, or anything can happen.

For the moment, I'm the stronger one. Negotiations ensue, and we decide to stay calm in front of the family, play at being young fiancés, and wait through the time his parents require to collect everything needed for my "dowry." But in the privacy of our room we remain the strangers we've been so far. We are to share everything fifty-fifty before we leave the family.

A period begins that I shall always consider as my first great initiation into womanhood—the discovery of the almost complete array of temptations and inhibitions to which women are subjected sooner or later. This is on a small scale, of course, but large enough to specify my approach to life in a decisive manner. I'm convinced that if I had not experienced this I would have been a very different person.

The first thing revealed to me is the value of water. From my native forest to Wouri, and passing briefly through Mfoundi, I had not yet realized that you could suffer from a lack of water. Thus, I wasn't aware of the importance of water and even less of what it might represent in life. Every day they placed a huge basin of water in my bathroom here, for my personal use and my laundry. I was beginning to find it annoying and wanted to dive into a river, the way I did at home, to swim and make music drumming on the water. But every time I mentioned it, the only response was discrete smiles, and the next day they would give me an extra large quantity of water.

On the fifth day after our arrival, I was so insistent about going to the river that my "mother-in-law" decided to accompany me herself. We walked for such a long time that I was getting worried, wondering whether she wasn't taking me somewhere other than the river. The truth of the matter was that there was very little water in Tchékos. It had to be brought from a distance of almost seven kilometers, drawn from a small hole that filled up rather slowly and only when it felt like it, so that some people might have to wait for a long time before the fickle hole would be willing to hand over its precious liquid, while others could literally watch it overflow as soon as they came near.

Each person brought the largest container she could carry because the trip could be made only once a day, and some people arranged that they would only have to come every two or three days. Water was so precious that it was used very sparingly.

Once I discovered how hard it was to find water in that region, I understood how highly the family rated me. I noticed that every other villager used hardly more than the contents of a soup tureen for their daily ablutions. What had I done to deserve so much more? I decided to be like everyone else, and saw in the eyes of others that soon after I'd done this I'd climbed a few notches in their appraisal.

I experienced how a home can be run and an entire family fed with so little water at their disposal. Until I left Tchékos I never spent a moment without being surprised; I was in admiration of the miraculous art of living the life that God had entrusted to women. Ingenuity magnified by generosity makes her the master of adaptability—just like water! What is more adaptable than water, which weds the shape of every container, evaporates or condenses as temperatures alter, refreshing oases or flooding whole areas as the weather dictates.

For the first time in my life, I made the connection between different kinds of water and women: women like Grand Madja, women like my mothers Naja, women like my aunts Roz, so dissimilar and yet so alike. Who among them were the springs of my native forest, certain their destiny was original, nurturing, and inexhaustible, concerned only with their lasting forever? Who among them were the turbulent waters of the great rivers, where you thirst for the absolute without ever controlling it, forced to play around the obstacles—winding, fleeing, burrowing, and crashing, as long as there is no break between them? Who among them were the waters that form the springs of the savannas, finicky and selective, doing only what suits them, even if it means they seem sterile or parsimonious, yet constantly renewing the challenge to persevere in being precious and necessary as survival demands? I didn't find an exact answer, but I was sure of one thing: Woman and water issue forth from an identical symbolism, as that first week in Tchékos made clear to me.

I feel like a contained body of water. I don't know whether I'll flow lazily or spurt out like a geyser, but I feel ready to assume my new situation and adapt to my new family. No one recognizes that Bayard and I have a problem. He is certainly telling himself that time will take care of everything, and even I am beginning to think that way. The only trouble is that I still don't feel like being intimate with him. Something prevents me from going all the way in my adaptability, and I tell myself that the real reason for my rejection of him will become clear to me in time. There's no rush. If we are meant to be together, nothing will stand in the way. Yet nothing should force us, either, if a true urge does not come from the depths, like water. . . .

Time speeds up in the second week.

The oldest daughter of Bayard's family is married to a wealthy and important chief of a neighboring region. She has heard the news of our arrival. She is shocked to learn that I came with empty hands because I'd been thrown out by my parents as a result of what her younger brother had done. She arrives with some thirty servants who bring ten bags of cocoa and coffee, as well as a dozen palm leaf packages with fowl—chickens and ducks—and pigs. Goats and sheep are kept on tethers and arrive grazing on yellow-green grass. A suitcase filled with all kinds of *pagnes* is the last item on the list of wedding gifts.

The illustrious "sister-in-law" tells me that all this is mine. I may keep it, or I may sell what I don't like at the market and then buy what I would rather have.

The third daughter in the family is also a queen of one of the eastern regions. She sends a delegation bearing a dozen tubs of palm oil and ten bags of cocoa, with the same message: Sell what you don't want on the next market day and replace it with whatever pleases you.

That evening Bayard figures that we have a minimum of two hundred thousand francs just with the cocoa, coffee, and oil alone, not counting the cattle, which would be enough to start a breeding herd. Moreover, neither Bayard's father, the Regent, nor his mother has as yet contributed anything, and he says that he can smell millions.

The temptation is enormous! I have never had so much that is mine, and perhaps I'll never have it again. They love and respect me here, and here I would have a place that is mine through my very own doing. If I so desire, I could spend the rest of my life here without any of my relatives ever knowing. I could afford a prosperous marriage, and be luxuriously endowed in a way that would buy me the honor and respectability my own family seems determined not to give me.

I would start my own family, have my own house, and turn my stepfather into a liar, since he said I would never have any of that! I wouldn't have to be a maid anymore. I could work to help my husband assume his responsibilities to his traditions. Our encounter could be seen as a godsend.

The temptation of an easy and predictable life is a great trap. It's the need for material goods and safe connections that always ends up nailing a woman down somewhere, even when her feelings aren't very strong. Fortunately, I felt doubly creative and even adept at making a stable home built on objective choices. But first and foremost, I had to be capable of creating feelings of love.

For Bayard, our union was blessed by heaven itself, which had made us cross paths. All we had to do was love each other and we would be the most *yéyé* couple of all *yéyés* ever! I think that for me that was the word he should not have uttered: Something had recoiled inside me. It was the fact that such generosity on the part of his family still could not change his plans to cheat them!

My grandparents had taught me that I would first have to deserve the trust placed in me. All we owe other people is trust. It is a heavy debt that can be paid only by returning that trust. Bayard could not be my husband, for he had no sense of honesty, and even less of responsibility. Paying debts is incumbent on the father of the family. A man who has no sense of his debts won't know how to establish a family, because he will expose his wife to almost anything, I told myself firmly.

Without any great commitment by their son, I could not assume the debt of trust the family was about to place on my shoulders. I believe it was then that I decided to leave.

34

Market day came again two weeks after I had arrived in Tchékos on the *tipot*. For two days young people brought all my merchandise to the chiefdom's depository, the market's central place. Consequently, Bayard and I were quite empty-handed and very comfortable when we went there that day, together with all the young members of the ruling family.

My "mother-in-law" is surprised to see me dressed the same way as when I arrived, although I could have worn one of the beautiful *pagnes* they had given me. I cite my lack of ease in wearing a *pagne* when I have to do a lot of walking, and ask them to give me some time to get used to it. I sense her disappointment. She would have liked to see me carrying myself proudly in one of the lavish velvet *pagnes*, which would have called greater attention to my quality as a princess-like figure about to be married; it would have increased the standing of her son, the prince, for the couple's first outing. But in the end she accepts my argument.

My heart is pounding wildly. The night before I wrote a letter to the uncle-regent in which I explained the truth and asked him to forgive both Bayard and me. When he comes back from the market he is bound to find it in plain sight on his work table. In the letter I ask him to hold a family meeting and a purification ritual and blessing for Bayard so that his conscience will be changed, and he will accept his destiny. I have decided not to come back again, and implore him to apologize for me to his family, all of whom have been generous to me. If there is nothing I retain from all they have given me, it is not because I lack gratitude or am disdainful, but I deem myself unworthy of their trust and would feel like a thief if I accepted it, given Bayard's and my circumstances.

I work it so that I am the last one out of the house, which I lock, and then I give the keys to the uncle, who walks up ahead of us; I know I can no longer stop him from finding my letter when he comes back. I don't feel prepared to face the family, and so there is no question of my returning.

In the marketplace I am all eyes and my senses are sharp, in search of a way to disappear unnoticed. But I am surrounded! Male and female cousins, nephews and nieces, and innumerable servants compete for my attention with a thousand little gestures. One wants me to see a small shop, another shows me a certain corner of the market, while yet another wants to introduce me to an aunt, a great-uncle, and so on. How do I extricate myself?

I will have to wait for the time of the sub-prefect's speech.

Ah, yes! The long-awaited moment, the most solemn moment of all the festive celebrations in the country's interior regions. This is where the government's authority is confirmed and hierarchies are recognized: The sub-prefect represents the prefect, who represents the governor of the province, who represents the minister of the interior, who is the representative of the head of state himself. In short, here the sub-prefect represents the head of state, whom no one dares to ignore!

The sub-prefect is flanked by the commander of the police brigade and the police commissioner. Their seats face those of the mayor and deputy, who are in turn surrounded by the chiefs of the various villages.

Two kinds of notables face each other: the "governmentals" and the "traditionals." The former occupy the central positions, some hiding behind the sub-prefect, others behind the commander of the brigade or the commissioner. These are the shady product buyers, their interests linked to those of leading candidates. They are Baffi, Lebanese, or Greek, and have a solid grasp on the attaché cases that invite you to speculate about their buying power. This is the governmental court that decides the price of the merchandise before it's purchased.

The other court consists of the village notables of the different chiefdoms, each close behind his respective chief; they look timid, almost embarrassed, probably wondering how they will be swallowed up. A court of figureheads and folklore will have nothing to say other than thanks and praises for the government. All they are expected to do is deliver.

Nevertheless, the various courts compete in signs of apparent respectability: *pagnes*, hats, fancy pipes, umbrellas and canes, attaché cases, and even cigars. . . .

Between the two courts, a bullhorn will be used to amplify the speeches.

Expressions of gratitude from the traditional dignitaries to the government.

Entreaties and grievances, and then a motion to support the head of state.

The sub-prefect's speech will be last, after the mayor and the deputy speak, should they wish to do so—which often happens only when election day is approaching. The sub-prefect's speech will contain references to the solicitude and benevolence of the head of state and will ask that people double their efforts for development. He will not neglect to mention the deterioration of the exchange rate, the courageous battle the head of state is waging to stabilize it, and the promise of a final victory should he be reelected for another term!

People listen with half an ear, since they could recite by heart the words, which are always the same, pronounced since the world began. The sun is blazing hot, and everyone is keen on just one thing, to hear the price the government has set for the merchandise this time before releasing its leeches on us—a price that can vary

from a hundred to a hundred and fifty francs per kilo from one market to another. Thus, you never know in advance what you will earn,
and no one is able to plan. Finally, it is only after this long-awaited
speech that calculations can begin at last. For, of course, there are
still the unforeseen events of rigged scales and quality evaluations of
the merchandise, solely at the discretion of the government's hench-
men. If they decide your cocoa is of C rather than A quality, you
might lose as much as two hundred francs a kilo. And there are the
poor chiefs busily bargaining, bribing the "evaluators" to rate the
sacks of their subjects or their own courts in one category rather
than another.

In the end, the market power of a chief is limited to trying to
have his subjects ripped off by fifty rather than one hundred percent, and then only if the quality of his product is truly the best. . . .
Oh, God, when will this stop? And how far will it go?

The sub-prefect is beating around the bush in an increasingly
unctuous tone. People are growing tense: The prices won't be good!
Everyone is so edgy that no one pays any further attention to me. I
back away slowly. At the end of the street I see a bus that is larger
than the one we arrived on two weeks earlier. I go over to it without
being noticed. I get on. The sleepy driver opens his eyes, so bloodshot
that I feel like running away, but my fear of getting caught and
brought back to the village is greater than my fear of the bulging eyes
examining me. I bend over so I cannot be seen from the outside.

"Good afternoon, sir. Can you take me to Mfoundi?"

"No problem, Pretty Little Miss, that's where I'm going. One
thousand four hundred francs a ticket. We'll leave as soon as the bus
is full, when the buyers have stopped buying."

"Can't we leave right now? There are many other markets on
the way, you can fill up there."

"Hmmm, you're running away, aren't you? How much will you
pay me if I leave right now?"

"How much do you want? I have no money. . . ."

"That's what I figured! But you have such beautiful eyes that it's
difficult to refuse you anything. All right, then, I'm perfectly willing

to leave right now and fill the bus with passengers in Bokito. On the condition that you sleep with me for two nights. . . ."

"Just two? A whole week if you want, but let's go right now!"

"Easy there, Little Sister! I said two nights and no more, understood? Don't count on sticking around with me in Mfoundi, eh! I didn't ask you to go there. Don't think you found yourself a husband, is that clear?"

"Very clear, Brother. I just wanted to thank you more. Let's go before people notice my absence."

Since the vehicle was parked at the top of a hill, he let it coast and turned the motor on when we were halfway down and out of sight. People were still tensely waiting for the crucial price that would cause them to explode with either joy or gloom, or else with withheld anger against something—or someone—that no one could really pinpoint.

I was on my way to the next ordeal.

We had driven for almost an hour and we were already quite a distance from Tchékos before I stopped looking in the rearview mirror. No car had followed us, and nobody was going to start worrying for a while yet. Before anyone would realize I had fled, we would be too far to catch up with. . . . God, how they would search for me! How Bayard's heart would jump! His mother would go especially crazy. Just thinking about her, about her pain and disappointment, made me squeeze my lips tightly to keep from crying and from asking the driver to take me back. Would he have done that? He paralyzed me with fear, that man.

• • •

Letter from Bayard's uncle to Halla Njokè:

Dear Little Halla,

After you vanished from the market, we looked for you everywhere and were very afraid. Fortunately, we found your letter when we came home. Without that, Bayard would surely have invented still more lies. Your note was a brutal awakening, but it was good for us, for it forced us to look truth in the eye, and we have made our decision: Bayard will not go back to Wouri. We will make him go into the sacred forest to prepare for his enthronement. He has to confront his destiny as chief! If he wants to transform his people into *yéyés*, that is what they will be left with, but at least he will have done something. By making him study things that have no relationship to our reality here and that are of no real interest to him, we were going to lose him.

Bayard's mother says she misses you. She says she will always see you as Bayard's first wife, even if nothing happened between the two of you. She says that all you needed to do was sell everything the family gave you and leave with that money; it was yours, for you suffered to acquire it. She says to tell you that she planted a shea tree in the middle of the courtyard that will be named for you so that Bayard will never forget you.

It is an educated brother-in-law who had just met you at the market who is writing this letter for us. We'll save it carefully. I know that one day we will hear from you, and I will do everything I can to send it to you, even if it takes ten years. But if you do not receive it, God will protect you and bless you anyway, because you are in our prayers.

The whole family sends you greetings.

(The letter would reach me through the intermediary of the director of the national radio three years later. When I participated in the public broadcast of a very popular program, Bayard's uncle heard me and sent his letter to the director of the radio station, requesting that he call me in and hand it to me personally.)

MOVEMENT TEN

35

I look at my rescuer a bit more closely. His bulging bloodshot eyes stare at me hungrily, as if I were a succulent dish served to a famished gourmand. Then I look at his hands. Are these fingers? Young manioc tubers? No, they are dwarf bananas or blood sausages. Yes, lively, constantly twitching blood sausages. In her own peculiar way of giving us sexual education, Grandmother used to tell us laughingly that it was easy to recognize a man's sex organ merely by looking at his fingers, then multiply their length and width by three to five, depending on his build. The driver's fingers already seem to be as big as an erect penis; even if you were only to double one of them, he would seem to be much too big for an inexperienced little girl like me. Judging by the lecherous way he looks at me every now and then, I'm convinced he won't hesitate to grow seven times as large, the monster! Surely he will kill me.

There is nothing left for me to do but send urgent prayers to Jehovah, Jesus, and the ancestors as well, to beseech all of them to save me from this new wasp's nest. Then it is as if I hear them answer me in chorus: "Your flight is not over yet. You'll have to keep running away many more times until you find the living space that both your body and your mind can endure and accept."

I agree with the choir inside me that I have to remain calm until they show me the right moment to escape, and inspire me with the necessary impulse and courage. Once this is decided, I do not even notice the rest of the trip going by. With my eyes closed, I keep focusing on my inner voices. My consciousness completely overlooks the various stops where passengers and freight are picked up, and even the stops made to give the Muslims a chance to pray.

Ever since that day, I remain silent whenever I'm faced with a problem. It has become clear to me that when you listen to your inner voice, you always find the right word or gesture at the right moment, for you only take those actions that the mind decides upon. How else can I explain the fact that my eyes do not open again until they read the sign telling us we have entered the town of Mfoundi?

Then I am completely aware of every sound and every word. Women are crying out to be let off here and there, but the driver says he will stop only at the terminal; after all, he can't start letting people off arbitrarily and go through the trouble of climbing on top of the vehicle, uncovering the rack, taking the bags of a given individual down, one at a time. They had better realize that he won't say it again and that he won't stop before the final station at Nkak.

Terminal of Nkak—the place where Bayard and I took the bus two weeks before. It's a crossroads and a transfer point. The direction in which my destiny had pointed me when I took the train to Wouri must now be abandoned, here at this bus station when I get off this coach. It's clear inside my head that the moment and place of a new flight have just been pointed out to me.

"Be patient for a minute, little sweetheart, I'm going to take down all the bags and drop off the cash receipts. Then we'll go home," the driver says, trying to be charming and reassuring.

His voice sounds like thunder to me, and all I feel is terror. He puts his forceful sausage hand lightly on my shoulder, and I freeze completely. He smiles and says: "I can tell you're numb; don't worry, I'll massage you and get your circulation moving again, you'll see. Wait for me here, all right?"

"Yes."

This was to be our second and last conversation. I watch him in the rearview mirror as he climbs onto the roof of the bus. I wait for a moment when he is very busy and open the door with tremendous care. All the passengers are looking up, anxiously waiting for their baggage.

The four streets that face the Nkak bus station are open to me. I pick the one on my left; I take a deep breath, count to five, and leave as surreptitiously as possible. I'm already at some fifty meters' distance when I hear his dreadful, gravelly voice booming from the top of the bus.

"Impossible! Do something down there, stop that girl, the one sitting near me in the bus, she's running away! She's a thief and must have snatched all the ticket money!"

"Thief, thief! Catch her!"

I take to my heels, and the witch hunt begins. Men, women, children, and even roaming dogs join the crowd to catch me. I get off the main road and disappear into the shantytown. I run so hard it feels as if my legs are about to come off; I run between the hovels and puddles, almost slipping in the mud each time. My temples are about to explode, and I have no idea where I'm going anymore.

• • •

I take a narrow alleyway between two huts and find myself before an open door with a curtain. There is no other escape. I go in. Two young men are sitting in a tiny room on the only two available chairs, playing their guitars. A metal double bed stands behind them covered with a cheap bedspread that goes down to the floor. Behind me dogs are barking. I bolt under the bed. The two youths keep playing their guitars and singing, as if they haven't seen me. A man enters the little room and seems quite put out by the younger ones, who very calmly keep on playing.

"Excuse me, Brothers! Did you see a young girl bolting by here? She's a thief who . . ."

"Brother, are you blind or don't you know the difference between a street and a room? When you are in your own room, do you see any thieves go by?"

"Excuse me, Brothers, but the children said she came this way."

"But you're not a child; and surely you know people can't go running through rooms. So out you go, see you later—can't you tell we're busy working?"

The man leaves. The barking of the dogs and the cries of the pack in full pursuit continue as background to the sound of the music inside, and it seems to me that an eternity passes. Then the two stop playing. They go out and lock the door. I wonder if it's possible they didn't see me come in. I am getting myself ready to try something when the door opens and closes again: They're back.

"It's OK, Sister, they're gone; they've left the neighborhood. You can come out now."

They raise the bedspread, look at me, and laugh. They're younger than I had expected. They must be about my age, or just a little older. I feel reassured and come out from under the bed, with some difficulty. My legs are shaking, and my teeth are chattering with delayed and uncontrollable fear. I collapse on the bed. The boys are watching me, curious and surprised, but with a hint of compassion as well, which I find touching. Apparently, they also expected someone older. They hold a little conference in a language I don't understand or recognize. After a long while, when my shaking stops, the taller one speaks: "Good! Have you calmed down now? Take out your stash, we'll share it, and then you're going."

I look at him in astonishment. So that's the situation: They really believe I've been stealing and actually didn't redirect my pursuers for my sake, but only to get a piece of the take. I find them very bright for having seen their own gain so quickly and managing to keep calm. Girls would have screamed and not thought of such an opportunity right away. I'm in awe. Besides, their expressions are kind and without malice.

"Thank you so much, Brothers, for saving me from that horde! But I'm afraid you are about to be disappointed: I didn't steal anything and so have nothing to share. I'm really sorry about that. I would have loved to share with you; it would be a nicer way to thank you for what you did."

"Hey, Little Sister, don't think we're idiots! We made some

inquiries and we know you went off with all the cash from the bus from Tchékos! Without us they would have caught you and taken it all back. With us, you'll give us what you decide to give, and if you're good there'll be no trouble. Otherwise, we'll frisk you and we'll be much less nice about it, you see?"

"So, Little Sister, don't force us to be less than courteous with a pretty girl like you," the younger one adds, trying to sound intimidating.

"And you, boy, I'm not your little sister, don't go too far! I tell you, I have nothing. If you don't believe me, go ahead and frisk me. Look, I don't have a pocket or a bag. I even lost my umbrella."

"Fine, we'll do just that and more because you're a liar, too. Why should the whole world be after you if you didn't take anything?"

"You're right, I did lie a little. If they're after me it's because I didn't pay for my bus ticket. I had no money and so I promised to pay for my seat by sleeping with the driver for two nights. Instead I ran away while he was unloading the bus. But I swear to you, I didn't steal any money."

"My foot! What sort of a fool would dare chase a girl for a story that would make him a laughing-stock if the girl were caught? Stand still, put your hands on your head. Hemmil, stay by the door so she doesn't try to run away. I'll frisk her myself."

His hands begin to palpate me down to my pubic area, passing over my breasts, belly, and my neck beneath my hair. He takes off my underwear and even my shoes and examines them with a magnifying glass. They go so far as to check under their own bed, thinking maybe I've hidden the loot there and am planning to come back secretly to get it. Then they give up, recognizing that I truly have nothing, and profusely apologize to me before they tell me I'm free to go. But I refuse to leave. Thinking I won't go because I'm afraid to be seen and caught, they suggest taking me home when everyone has gone to bed.

"Thank you, but I have no other home than the very spot I'm sitting on. Besides, I'm so tired that I'd really be grateful to you if you'd let me sleep a little bit first. I'll explain the rest later."

"You're out of your mind," the older one exclaims. "Hey, miss, you've got to leave right now. Staying here is out of the question! My mother would give us a very hard time. She finally allowed me to play music in a bar on the condition that I keep up with my studies and be as serious as a priest. No alcohol, no girls, especially not here at home. If she finds you here, she might make me stop playing music altogether, and I couldn't bear that! I hope you aren't here to create any problems for us."

"Certainly not. So let's be quiet. Turn off the lights and let's go to sleep before your mother hears my voice. I don't want to create any problems for you, but I can't leave here right now."

"No way, you've got to go right now. Soon our mother will be here to check up on us as she does every evening," insists the younger one, who's getting on my nerves with his bizarre need to play tough. Furthermore, he keeps turning my panties over and over on the corner of the table where he put them down, and is trying my sandals on for the twelfth time.

"I'm telling you that I can't—don't you get it? I cannot leave right now because I have nowhere to go, and it's already dark! Tomorrow we'll figure it out. Don't insist; it's no use; it will only cause you problems, you understand? If I keep talking your mother will hear my voice and come to see you, and I've a pretty good idea what she'll think when she sees you and that boy over there fiddling with my panties and shoes. Let me get some sleep, and I promise to be as unobtrusive as I can."

"Well, back under the bed then, right away, for that's my mother's voice you hear. She's coming now. . . ."

36

No sooner said than done. I dive under the metal bed for the second time that afternoon, my heart pounding. The mother must not suspect my presence or she'll throw me out or call the police, I'm sure of it. My little power struggle with the boys won't work with her, and I don't know what would happen to me then. Something tells me I have to stay here. So I hold my breath and stiffen my body to keep from making any movement at all.

The boys have shoved my things under the bed and pretend they're doing their history homework, something about the French Revolution. Someone knocks on the door; the younger one opens with noisy greetings and tells her what good grades they got in math. The mother seems pleased. She congratulates them on the neatness of their room and on the fact that they're studying rather than playing music. She says she's worn out and wants to go to bed early; she just wanted to make sure they were there. She tells them to get some food; she has kept it warm in the kitchen because she hadn't heard them come home. They shouldn't forget to close all the doors tightly and they shouldn't go to bed too late. She wishes them goodnight.

"And don't forget your last evening prayer or the first one in the morning," she adds.

I'm amazed at all these reminders and attentions for such big boys. Obviously, when you've been raised as if you were an adult from the age of nine on, it's difficult to understand the state of mind of parents and children who put so much weight on adolescence.

After the mother leaves, I come out from my hiding place, lie down on the bed, and fall asleep like a baby without exchanging another word with my hosts, who don't dare address me anymore but prefer acting like good little schoolboys.

I wake up first and can't get over it: They're both asleep curled up against me like little sparrows! They snore softly, completely unaware, completely innocent. I feel years older than they are; I feel like their mother. In spite of my overfull bladder I don't dare move for fear of waking them too roughly and scaring them. I wonder what time it is—six or seven o'clock, no later, I think. I wait like this for another half an hour and then the older one wakes up. What I see successively in his eyes is first astonishment, then a fleeting panic, then awakening memory, and then, once again, the compassion that seems to be characteristic of him. He smiles at me and sits up. We look at each other in silence. My free hand strokes the younger one's hair as he wakes up startled and stares at me in fear.

"Good morning, children," I say in a whisper. "You're finally coming up for air. Did you have sweet dreams in my arms or perhaps nightmares, judging by the crazed look in the eyes of this little weird one."

They both burst out laughing.

"Well, to tell the truth, I haven't slept this well in a very long time," the older one says. "But now I wonder if I'm really awake or still asleep and dreaming. Is it true that you came in here like a ghost last night, that you refused to leave and imposed yourself on us by falling asleep on our bed, that we must have joined you there and slept in your arms like babies, even though we have no idea who you are or what your name is?"

"I dreamed that my mother came back," the younger one adds, "that I was a little baby again, nursing while she massaged my head. It was nice!"

"Well, get up now, the dream is over. I'm not your mother, even if I had to rub your head a little to wake you up gently. I really have to go to the toilet before my bladder explodes, and your bed won't be as comfortable then for your next dream."

"There she goes again! You think you're just going to leave here in bright daylight, go straight to the bathroom that everyone else in the family uses, so they can see you, and then calmly come back here again?" the little one asks nervously.

"And you really think I'm going to hide out here all day long without emptying my bladder, without washing up or brushing my teeth, just so you won't get yelled at by your mother?"

"I'm afraid you have no other choice but to stay here until it's dark. You can't be seen, but we can help you get cleaned up without you going out. I'll see what I can do. By the way, my name is Lorrent, and that is Hemmil, my first cousin. And you?"

"You can call me Little Mother or Ma Fitini, and you can do whatever you want, but I really have to pee, for god's sake!"

They both rush out the door. Soon the little one returns with a big old tin can, puts it in a corner, and goes back out in silence. He turns the key in the lock. I am a prisoner, but my bladder protests so much that I can only think of emptying it.

I hear several voices outside. Apparently it is a densely occupied compound. They're making small talk. It seems to be the weekend: They're all delighted that they can sleep late and relax a little at home. They exchange the latest news. Was the little thief caught yesterday? They have a lot to say about the delinquency that ensnares even young girls, turning them into tigers and vampires. They wonder whether, in these times we're living in, the dead themselves are coming out of their graves to grab some of the money. In any event, they say, the girl has vanished like a ghost. Even the dogs have lost her scent.

"She must have been a ghost. It seems that no one heard her voice during the entire trip and that she was hiding her eyes!"

In short, people are comfortably gossiping at home. I am not prepared to leave because I'd be spotted at once, and so I have to accept the shame of living all day long with my pee in a can!

Just imagining that the boys would come in sooner or later, smell the pee I have held in too long, and perhaps even see its color, makes me want to vanish beneath the earth. I swear that if my hosts hadn't been careful to lock the door from the outside, I would much rather have run the risk of leaving and having to flee all over again. I have to find a way to avoid the unpleasantness of such shame.

Searching everywhere for a rag,
I find the leg of an old pair of pants,
And use it to create a cover of my own making,
And conceal my pee can, a gift-wrapped present
That I hide in the farthest corner under the bed.

With the bit of fabric I have left I sweep the room clean and collect all the sand under my can. I make the bed, straightening the spread very neatly before hiding underneath it again, just to be sure. And a good thing, too, for the key turns in the lock, and I hear the mother's voice: "It's not possible! What little genie has come through here since yesterday? Thank you, ooooh my God! These people know how to sweep and make the bed before leaving, and without any arguments or sermons! Lord, please send the same genie here every day, ooooh, if that's who inspires them and imprints good manners into their brains! Perhaps I'll only have to deal with the littlest ones soon. Ah, it takes boys so long to grow up!"

Quietly she shuts the door again and leaves. I thank my lucky stars and every genie for having encouraged me to clean up. She would surely have wanted to do it herself and . . .

At that point I didn't know yet that I would be playing the good genie under the bed for more than a month; what's more, I didn't know that throughout my life I would be increasingly seen as a genie, and a genius, too.

Lorrent and Hemmil come into the room every now and then, slip something under the bed for me to eat, and then go out again. They do homework, read out loud, take turns being on the lookout while the other goes out and empties my toilet-can. They even bring me a moistened towel to daub my face and a bamboo toothpick. My recent stay in Tchékos comes in handy. I use the towel so meticulously that I feel completely washed and refreshed. I read everything I can get my hands on and dive beneath the bed at the slightest sound. By evening I have the feeling I've been flattened by a tractor!

Still, I have to continue living under the bed because my hosts are now going to work. They explain that they play in a dance bar for three hours a night on weekends, before canned music takes over. This allows them to earn a little money and make progress in their music while still keeping up with their studies, something their parents absolutely insist on. During their absence their mother usually comes into the room to check that they've cleaned up properly, or to put down food, laundry they'd left hanging outside, or a clean sheet. All of it, I tell myself, to keep an eye on them without appearing to do so. My new friends also warn me not to fall asleep on the bed and get caught there!

I spend almost all weekend under the bed. It is an inescapable situation: I don't know the town and wouldn't be able to make it through a single night there, while during the day I can't show my nose outside the door without putting my hosts in danger. How and when will I manage to get out of this?

I have to find a way out! Late that night, when they come home, we cannot sleep because we keep examining the situation from every angle: my own abilities, their options to find me something to do or a shelter to hide in. They don't want to throw me out because they wouldn't know what would become of me. They already feel a bond with me and feel it is their duty to help me.

Since they don't play Monday night, and it is three weeks before school begins again, they lock us in early to recover a little from the unusual weekend. Then suddenly Lorrent jumps up from the bed, all excited: "I have a brilliant idea! Can you sing?"

"Eh . . . yes, a little!"

"Whose songs can you do? Sheila, Vartan, or Hardy?"

"Excuse me? I don't know who they are; I've never heard of them. I only know songs about Jesus Christ. 'Take my life, oh Lord, that it may be lived in your honor. . . .'"

"Excuse me, too—that's not what you'd sing at a club!"

"At a club? But how and why sing at a club?"

"Are you for real? You're not joking? Can anyone really be this dense?"

"Now you're insulting me! And since I'm so dense, explain what songs they sing, and why use a club?"

They both laugh out loud.

"Excuse me, Little Mother," Hemmil then snickers, "you're too much. We didn't know there were people so out of it in this day and age that they don't even know what a club is, have never heard of the singers and the songs that even babies can hum. Where have you been? Are you sure you're part of this world?"

"Ah! Because your pursuers said you were a genie from another place. We'll get the whole story at last! Actually, Lorrent, did you tell her about the visit of your friend from the P.J.? Here, why don't you show her the document he left you?"

Lorrent gets up, goes through the pockets of the pants he wore during the day, and hands me a carbon copy given to him by a friend who works for the criminal investigation department. Amidst their steamy commentary and bright laughter, I finally understand that, within the framework of his investigation, a policeman friend of Lorrent, having heard of the disappearance of a Mamy-Wata genie near his house, came to see him in the hope that Lorrent, with his sense of observation, could give him some precious information or at least a more detailed description.

"I made fun of all this nonsense," Lorrent continues, "but my friend was eager to convince me with supporting evidence that female genies most certainly exist, that they travel all over the country, going so far as to swipe money using magic tricks and give it away to their flesh-and-blood lovers, as the following deposition attests, which he got especially for me! Read it yourself. . . ."

Files of the Criminal Investigation Department of the Mfoundi Police:

Minutes of the complaint lodged by M. Bidios A Mian, bus driver of the Mfoundi-Tchékos line—

Against Mademoiselle X, around 15 or 16 years old, height approximately 1 meter 75. Light skin, golden eyes outlined in gray, heavy roll of braids down the neck—Wearing a sky blue skirt and a white sweater—

For theft of the total cash receipts for the Tchékos-Mfoundi itinerary of Friday, 13 September—

The plaintiff claims that the thief boarded the bus in Bokito and that he told her the price of the ticket. She allegedly paid without a word and sat down beside him in the front. She presumably spoke not one word during the entire trip and vanished after being chased into the seedy section of the Briqueterie district, as numerous witnesses saw. Even dogs allegedly lost her scent almost immediately and began to howl loudly.

All the ticket receipts supposedly disappeared from the driver's cashbox and, according to many passengers, their own money disappeared from their bags as well while they were in pursuit of the young woman.

M. Bidios confirms that many passengers noticed the thief's gray-and-golden eyes and came to the same conclusion, namely that they were dealing with a genie or a ghost who presumably took everyone's money, mixed it in with her magic money, undoubtedly with the purpose of granting the wishes of her mortal lover. He states that he wrote down the passengers' addresses so they may be summoned to appear in court in case the thief is found.

The total amount of money gone comes to more than two thousand francs.

Remarks by Officer Messi who took the deposition: N.B.: It is the fifth case of this nature in less than a month.

All bus stations need to be alerted to the one detail they have in common: golden eyes encircled in gray! It certainly concerns one and the same bandit!

"And so? What did you make of it?" I ask Lorrent.

"I recognized this was about you and was very surprised at people's imagination and inventiveness when it comes to making some easy money. What a windfall for your suitor, the driver, to keep all the money himself and claim to have been robbed by a genie! Although. . . ."

"Although what? Finish what you're thinking."

"The truth is that I'm not so doubtful anymore about your being Mamy-Wata or some other genie like that! Even though your eyes aren't golden and outlined in gray, who knows, their warm light brown may have created some confusion when the light hit them at a certain angle. As for me, I'd be willing to sell my soul if you could love me as your mortal lover and help me become rich and famous. . . . Would you want to try?"

"Enough bedtime stories, boys; let's get back to reality. Lorrent, you were saying just now that you have a brilliant idea, and since then we've been talking about nothing but nonsense or clubs," I mutter, beginning to lose my patience.

"That's right, the club, my idea! If you were a bit more with it and knew how to sing, we could nominate you to be the singer in the club of our bandleader's cousin. The girl who used to be there left for France and there aren't many singers around. It would be a dream come true for you."

"First explain to her that a club is not necessarily something to be used for beating. Look at her bewildered face! She's never heard of any nightclubs, those fancy bars where drinks cost ten or twenty times more than they should and where affluent people go to have a good time. The bands that play there earn enormous amounts of money."

"Why aren't you jumping at the chance, then, since you're so up on things?" I ask.

"We don't have the time because we have to go to school. And besides, to be honest, as musicians we're not good enough yet. But you, with your royal bearing and spunk, you could grab the slot if you could sing a little."

"I've never heard of any nightclub, that's true enough, but now that you've finally explained it to me, why don't you teach me to sing instead of talking so much, and then we'll talk about spunk."

"You're not at any loss for words, are you, Little Mother? You're bound to have pluck as well! But what we probably won't find are records and a record player for you to listen to the popular songs of the day," Hemmil says.

"What's a record player?"

"Just drop it, it's not important! Let's go to sleep, the night will bring new insight. Cross your little genie fingers, and let's pray for something good to happen this week," Lorrent says and turns off the light.

We had become a real team that week, if not actually a family. I slept between two boys who cuddled up against me as if next to the breast of a mother or a very loving mistress, and yet there wasn't the slightest manifestation of any sexual desire. We each did our best to be as gentle and attentive to the other two as possible, and I made every effort to be as useful as I could. The mother had stopped checking up. She apparently was reassured. Nevertheless, I remained watchful and was always ready to hide.

On Wednesday my hosts managed to borrow a record player as well as some records by Sheila and Hardy. We spent most of our time copying and memorizing songs. They helped me as much as they could because I wasn't used to such nasal sounds and I had a hard time understanding the lyrics. Besides, we were forced to keep the volume down as low as we could, which didn't make things any easier.

By the end of the second week, I was already fairly comfortable singing four of the songs. On Saturday at dawn, my hosts succeeded in getting me out of the house for the first time. I waited for them in front of a small shop where they had some friends. At nine on the dot they joined me there and took me to the flea market. They had me try on various clothes; it was a wonderful day. We all agreed on a bright red corduroy miniskirt and a white short-sleeved shirt with a Peter Pan collar. Ankle-high red boots and white hose provided the finishing touch. We went to friends of theirs in a far-off area of town where they redid my braids. I was completely made over. Toward five in the afternoon, we went to meet the owner of the club for my audition. My heart was beating a mile a minute. I felt so odd in the miniskirt that I expected to see my mother Naja or her husband appear any minute and scream bloody murder! It made me forget the key of the first song.

In spite of it all I managed to hold the owner's interest, and he was willing to try me out. Unfortunately, when he heard I was sixteen he told us that he was not allowed to hire anyone under eighteen! All our hopes caved in. My hosts were already counting on my earnings, with which we would rent a small studio where we would be free to rehearse as much as we wanted; and they had started looking for a name for the group we would form. What now?

Another week of hiding under the bed and rehearsing at night passed before Lorrent and Hemmil decided to let me do an audition for their own boss. Obviously, that would pay ten times less, but it would at least be a start.

Hemmil suggested I do one of the songs by their boss, who considered himself a writer and composer and would be pleased. This required another week of study and rehearsals.

All in all, it took a month and a week, to the day, from the time I arrived to find work for me. On the day of my audition, wisely ending with the song composed by the bar's owner, the man hired me and provided me with a room above his bar, as well as a salary that was four times greater than that of my friends. It was high time, too, because Monday they had to go back to school, and we were beginning to worry how I'd manage all by myself in their little room all day while they were gone. The gods were with us, and our dreams slowly started to come true. . . .

They always came by after school, and we rehearsed as often as we wanted. We were going to make big strides forward and use their next vacation to launch our group. We were going to be a new kind of African-style Beatles or Surf.

The first months were marvelous. I went through every song of every singer I could get my hands on, and my friends went out of their way to accompany me as best they could on the guitar and in the refrains. Our repertoire grew stronger, and the boss was as pleased with us as the audience was. The name Ma Fitini began to be chanted in the streets of my quarter when I passed by, to the great pride of my friends. I divided my salary into three parts: one for them, one for my expenses, and the third I saved so that we would have a small fund with which to launch our group. It wouldn't be much, but it was better than nothing, and would help us take our first steps and make contacts, at any rate.

However, one day the mother came to visit me instead of the boys, and asked me to stop "leading her children astray." She forbade me to encourage them on the road to moral degradation; she also threatened the bar owner that she would file a complaint against him for corrupting minors, and he was forced to hire other, older guitar players. I didn't see my friends for the rest of the school year, but continued to put their share aside, telling myself that during the vacation, when they were free, they would come to see me to develop our plan. Nothing and nobody would get in the way of our dream, certainly not I.

But our paths would soon diverge, and for good. Lorrent, under his mother's pressure for him to study and find a "normal" job, got so exasperated that he decided to become a train conductor in the government-controlled railroad system. Hemmil failed his probationary exams twice and his final exams three times. In defiance, he left Mfoundi and went looking for me in Wouri when he heard that I had become a well-known singer and guitarist there. Sadly, he came too late to create the group we'd dreamed of, for he discovered that I'd grown discouraged and left the world of music to go back to my mother, who needed me after her husband's arrest. Hemmil was to become a very mediocre singer in clubs, and would leave them entirely when he turned into a complete alcoholic. Years later I heard about his sad situation at the same time that I found out about Lorrent's accidental death; his train had had a collision while he was at the wheel. I would search in vain for Hemmil to help him work his way out of his predicament, but without success.

I was very angry with myself for not having been Mamy-Wata and loved them and helped them become rich and famous, as Lorrent had wanted. For it was they who had forged my destiny, opened every door for me that I used through the maze of art. And for a long time I felt that I had done nothing for them, that I had completely failed to return the favor. It was like a sickness that frequently made me seethe with rage, from which I recovered only when I learned to accept one fact: Gratitude doesn't always go directly to the person who helps us, but rather to all the anonymous hands of God.

MOVEMENT ELEVEN

37

As I wake up with a start this morning, I find Auntie Roz stretched out on the Senufo bed as usual. She always has that serene look of the wise, those people who are reconciled with every aspect of their lives.

Maybe today she will be willing to talk about herself a little, I say to myself as I approach her, careful not to startle her the way I had just been startled: That is bad for us at our age.

Maybe today she will talk to me about her relationship with knowledge. For instance, how and when did she learn everything she knows: languages (she speaks at least four); professions (she knits and makes extraordinary beaded hats; she is a seamstress and certainly creates the finest traditional gowns, *ngondos*, that any Douala woman would love to wear; not to mention the fact that in her time she was secretary general of the women's sections of Mpôdôl's party). How did she learn so many things when she'd never been to school?

Above all I'm hoping she'll speak to me of her relationships with men. I have only known her to be alone, without a man in her life. How did she come to that point, with all the men she must have met?

I come very close to her and hold my breath. I am pondering my many questions deep inside myself; I am looking at her tenderly, then she quietly opens her eyes, smiles at me mischievously, and says, "And you, where are you with that memoir of yours? How and when did you learn everything you know, and why have you been living alone in Laguna all the years that we've been here? How did you come to that point?"

I stand open-mouthed for a moment that seems like an eternity. Could this woman read my mind, or was this just a "coincidence"? Were we perhaps on the same wavelength, with the same anxieties at the same time? Were we the same kind of women? And for that matter, where did I fall in the classification I'd begun at the spring on the Tchékos savanna?

"When I woke up this morning," Auntie Roz continues, "I said to myself that maybe you'd forgotten me, had given up on 'paying tribute' to me as you announced early this year. And since you haven't said anymore about it, I wanted to get it off my chest. Now I'm reassured."

"Reassured? By what? I haven't told you yet whether I started my project or not. . . ."

"Your face told me when you found me here this morning. Come, sit down, we'll pray together. I'm very busy today and I can't stay with you as long as I'd like to."

An enigmatic prayer this morning, almost abstruse.

Auntie Roz recommends my household to the God of gods again,
Beseeches him to prevent us from vain drifting and intellectual verbiage,
To grant us the true serenity of faith.
Above all, the youngest ones who are enticed by a thousand illusory
traps;
May the God of gods make sure above all else:
That all the rustling of the awakening conscience of the children of this
suffering earth does not fall back into the usual apathy,
But continues its gurgling
Until a veritable song of inner liberation dawns.
In the name of Jesus Christ may it be so, Amen.

"You know, I wouldn't like to find myself in a kind of 'movement of women agonizing over their country,' just because it's fashionable," she adds and gets up nimbly from the Senufo bed, as if she had suddenly been called away by a very urgent matter.

As she leaves she throws me that mischievous look again, after pressing a gentle kiss on my forehead.

"You will tell me, won't you? I mean, you will read to me the next time, won't you? In any event, I hope so. . . ."

And she leaves me there, stuck like a scarecrow in a millet field! I'm deeply touched. It makes me forget my schedule for the day; I find myself automatically in front of my desk, and sit down with a thud. I'm envious of Auntie Roz, who appears to be as light as a bud on a dewy morning, while my bones hurt so much that I can neither get up nor sit down without softly groaning.

A movement of women agonizing, did she say? "A rather old-fashioned movement," I say to myself, laughing this time, but all by myself, for I don't know a single woman my age who comes across as lively as Auntie Roz, although she is much older. Probably that comes from always having to carry the world—by nature, by choice, through pressure or oppression—which gives us the appearance of heavy but precocious maturity, despite the serenity of our faces. A women's movement at our age? We'd look pretty strange. . . . My eyes sparkle with some unidentified delight, my fingers, already stiff with age (or from unfinished sleep, I say as an aside as if to justify myself), play the keyboard of my computer and fling my thoughts in a different direction.

"Not just because it's fashionable," Auntie Roz had said.

• • •

The *yéyé* movement goes on, in full swing. Various streams are born, and people don't know to which saint to offer their devotion, or which star to grace with their idolatry. New ones are born and die every day. The young tirelessly repeat foreign songs, mimicking the Beatles, Rolling Stones, Johnny, Antoine, and who knows who else, without ever listening to African music. Singing any song other than what's *yéyé* and popular amounts to marking yourself as backward.

That is when, to my great displeasure I discovered how thoroughly I couldn't bear the style anymore. To love what is in style simply means to love being with and like other people. In short, conformity is one way of loving harmony. It is social and sociable, comfortable, logical, and normal. He who doesn't like what is in style is in some way asocial and abnormal. I was completely astounded to find out I was like that; I had always thought of myself as the most normal person around.

I caught myself despising everything my women friends did, what they wore, how they spoke or danced, what tunes they hummed. As a result, the songs they said were hits bored me intensely and wore me out. Only songs that were hardly known and came from various places in Africa were captivating to me—songs in Yoruba, Bambara, Ashanti, or Lingala, languages I unfortunately didn't understand, but whose sounds excited me enormously. I also discovered songs by old jazz and blues singers, and even songs by men that I thought would be marvelous when sung by a woman. I don't know what made me think that both the musicians and the club owner were as bored as I, and that they would be glad to have a different repertoire as a change of pace. How wrong I was!

The musicians refused downright to get involved with outlandish styles that seemed difficult to play, from the viewpoint of the *yéyé* movement. The style of the moment is what makes the world go round, and is the easiest to handle.

My boss didn't hide his surprise that anyone would want to distance herself from what was in and pleased the public. To him I was nothing but a madwoman, or else pathologically arrogant. I was warned to come back to my senses or else I would be fired.

Every musician, bandleader, drummer, and guitar player shamelessly suggested they help me rehearse my repertoire to convince my boss of the validity of my approach, but on one condition only—that I become his girlfriend!

With how many men is a woman expected to sleep in one life in order to reach her goals? When a man wants to possess a woman, does it ever occur to him that there was someone else before him? Certainly not, when he thinks he has a chance to possess her at a bargain price, without any commitment or responsibility.

I had to find musicians who shared my sensibilities, like Lorrent and Hemmil, not demanding sex before anything, but wanting to dream, work, and create with a woman—true partners with whom to form a group to show the owners of nightclubs and bars a primarily African repertoire. There were bound to be patrons for this kind of music.

I left Mfoundi to follow a bunch of boys who had just begun their own group and were going off to conquer the public on the coast. They were looking for a singer, and I joined them without a second thought.

I searched pointlessly, worked with various musical groups, and lost battles before they were even begun, never to find another Lorrent or Hemmil again. My hopes for a change in the public taste had to wait for "big names" such as Fela Kuti to arrive before African music was able to energize every entertainment site, including those at the top, before it could be solidly established in the popular mind. As far as man-woman relationships were concerned, all I ran into in those days were men who demanded sex even for a few simple rehearsals. What would they require to hire or produce me, promote me, or broadcast my compositions?

"What else can you demand from a woman when you've already had her body?" I bluntly asked of Mama Dora, a kind of old madam who worked in the new club in Wouri and treated me a little like a granddaughter. "Her heart? Her soul? Can those things be negotiated?"

"Yes," she responded just as openly. "Sooner or later you're made to let go of one or the other. But you have to know how to gain time, make them wait, so you can at least choose the 'lesser evil'! Otherwise, in this environment, you know, a woman may be bedded down by an average of two hundred men or more."

So I learned to gain time by talking and getting men to talk. I learned rather quickly that a man is not satisfied with having only a woman's body; he also wants her heart and her soul. So he could wait, come and go, learn to be patient in a certain noble way, if he thought that by doing so he would reach his goal and attain overall possession of her. Failing this, he might even lose that famous physical desire! When a woman knew that she was holding a fine trump card in the negotiation, that would allow her to safeguard her dignity. She could then attain the greatest serenity even as she endured turmoil of all sorts, and, above all, live without being afraid of men, without hatred or contempt. In any event, in those times that was still a valid strategy.

I drew the conclusion that the woman who cared about her dignity and wanted to avoid too much pressure, bargaining, and negotiation had to choose one from among the most powerful of men, and stand resolutely behind him as if he were a shield.

Constantly exposed to all these pressures and the blackmail of sex, I decided to pick the most highly placed of all the suitors of the moment, a magistrate, a federal prosecutor—and he was tall, handsome, and rich! He was, of course, also the most threatening, and often had me picked up by the police because I was still underage and too young to work in such places. But he didn't intimidate me in the least. I chose him because he knew the owner of the nightclub where I'd just been hired with a group, the Zouaves. The boss would go out of his way to greet him and insisted on serving him himself, lowering his voice and using all kinds of honeyed tones, with "Master" here and "Monsieur Prosecutor" there. As long as he was in the club, the band had to play his favorite songs. I figured that if I were with him the others would leave me alone, out of respect or fear; above all, I would definitely be able to build up and insist on a repertoire that was intrinsically my own.

It was a good move, for many bands had to rehearse with me, more by force than by choice. It became a veritable saga! Nonetheless, working and making progress was a laborious affair with every one of the bands; I was constantly juggling problems and ploys, while standing steadfastly behind the "great shield" the prosecutor had become for me.

When the band leader began to overstep the limits of the business deal to try to get his hands on me, too, his Zouaves quickly seemed too inept to Monsieur Prosecutor to properly show off the new progress "his" singer was making. The Prosecutor had the club replace them with the Red Carters, who, he decided, were more experienced. The new repertoire began to attract customers in ever-greater numbers, to the great satisfaction of the club's owner. Unfortunately, however, the owner couldn't resist the temptation to demand his share of the woman as well. He had just transformed his space into a "spot that was right for Monsieur Prosecutor's little star" when Monsieur hastened to find me a place in a high-class club where the famous Rebels of the Red Ball reigned supreme.

But the new bandleader didn't seem to recognize that the excessive amount of smoke in his club was causing monstrous allergies for my "godfather." Imagine the poseur rushing onto the dance floor to be the first to dance with the singer right after she finished her set, a fat cigar in his mouth, as if to attribute her success to himself, which irritated the "real" proprietor immensely. Monsieur Prosecutor then arranged for a new club to be opened outdoors for his protégée, the "state-of-the-art" nightclub of the moment, which offered dance performances around a swimming pool to the music of the highly celebrated Red Devils.

When the owner of this last club in town and his new band began to push their luck, I couldn't help wondering where I would be going this time. Did I have to spend my whole life hiding behind my prosecutor-shield, even if it would mean cheating like Mam Naja?

Whatever his power and beauty, however much comfort he may provide, a shield was never more than a hideout, a place where the protected person shrank, and thus validated her own fragility and fear: all unacceptable for the long duration!

Furthermore, my shield was not really offering me any great comfort. Of course, Monsieur Prosecutor assured me an enviable home in a fancy area, a more-than-pleasant lifestyle, beauty and health care, a pretty little Mini-Minor car, the dream of every young girl. Although I was too young to have a driver's license, he had a temporary one delivered to me after I proved to him I knew how to drive—thanks to you, Father, who gave me that opportunity through many plantation roads.

I found this shield, so obsessively jealous, clinging, and demanding, quite onerous and tiring. He was married to an absolute tigress who continuously "hunted" him by scent, like a quarry. She followed him everywhere: to movie houses, piano bars, nightclubs, and chic restaurants. And when she tracked him down, she took him under her arm like a purse, and all he could do was follow along in silence, eager to avoid a scandal. In our club, though, he resisted, tried to cajole her by offering her champagne, so that she began to enjoy coming there more often.

During such times I was obviously not supposed to know the gentleman. Still, he watched my every move and, when he deemed it necessary, had my boss call me to order immediately. He frequently asked the owner to join him at his table, playing the gentleman, and slipping him a huge tip that also included my drink. It was a tacit agreement that obliged him to serve me as a consolation a kir royal or any other classy drink that I enjoyed. He would whisper to me that it came "with the compliments of your Monsieur."

He'd say things like: "Stop dancing so frantically with that person; he seems much too vulgar and forward; and stop looking in Monsieur's direction; you might attract the attention of Madame."

For now, those were the rules of the game, the bargain, and it was viable. But the weight of the shield began to be much too taxing when Monsieur Prosecutor got it into his head that he was deeply in love with "his little singer, that she was becoming much more than window-dressing or a piece of costume jewelry." He started to spend more and more time with me, taking time out from work or his life at home to drive me to the beach or the movies. It wasn't long before the relationship became the talk of the town.

I was called in by the governor of the province, who advised me to be discreet and moderate in my relations with a highly placed state functionary. They were asking me, a minor, to control the impulses of an adult of his standing, and one in a high-level public position, at that. I rebelled and decided to break it off. But he had me picked up by the criminal investigators and locked up for three days in the cell of a prison, where his cousin was police commissioner. The latter came to plead with me on his behalf, trying to convince me not to break up with him and asking me whether I was aware of my responsibility.

"My cousin needs you like the air he breathes, to keep him stable, to do his work right, and to help the country advance—in short, to live a happy life. He begs you not to drive him to the edge by refusing him your heart. . . . He's afraid of doing the worst!"

"What is the worst?"

"Anything! Suicide, murder, the death of one of you or maybe both, I don't know!"

Here we were—blackmail! As soon as I was let out of prison, my house became another prison. More opulent, perhaps, but more oppressive as well, for now Monsieur Prosecutor lived there half the time. He arrived as soon as he was through in court, loaded down with new personal items. He had his own set of keys and let himself in as if he were at home, whether I was there or not. He washed up, changed, and had the maid whom he had hired—and who acted as my new jailer—serve him his favorite drinks. His clothes, his colognes, his shoes, and even one of his magistrate's robes turned my house into a conjugal dwelling, while in my head I was still totally unattached and free.

I tried to explain to him that such behavior was proof of a lack of adult responsibility and professional acuity; that a functionary of his status shouldn't allow himself to live a double life so brazenly. He told me he agreed but insisted that only marriage would straighten out the situation, and asked me to please marry him as soon as possible.

At the time, polygamy was still officially permitted in many African countries, and here the law didn't even set the limit at four, as does the Koran. Here a man had the right to marry as many women as his means would allow; it was simply a financial question. It was therefore quite normal that a person of his rank would take a second wife, a spouse who was barely eighteen years old.

I took the liberty of reminding him that I wasn't in love with him; that he never gave me enough time to feel a single emotion; that he imposed ways of conduct and a rhythm of life that were too stressful for me to imagine spending my whole life with him.

"If you don't agree to marry him, his life and career will be at stake, for he is completely prepared to abandon everything for you," his father told me. "My wife and I beg you to agree to this marriage, if only just long enough for our son to calm down. Then we'll help you get a divorce if you still insist, and wholly in your favor, as it will mean a great deal of money with which to remake your life with a boy your own age. You're still young enough to take on such a profitable adventure without any great risk, while you wait to find love. . . ."

I don't really know why I became so furious. Perhaps it was out of jealousy, when I saw what some parents will do for their children. Here were these respectable old people going through such trouble for their son, who was at the very summit of society. Just to guarantee his future, they were ready to buy my morality, my dignity, and my youth. My own material, financial, and even my filial situation—oh, Father, oh, Mother!—placed me in a position to accept the offer, for there was no one on my side to protect me. My fury with my parents was about to explode, and I knew his parents would think it was intended for them. I got up and left the house without being able to say a word; my throat was too constricted.

When I came back late that night, Monsieur Prosecutor had moved in completely. He had set up his office: Two new wardrobes and packed suitcases were waiting to be emptied. I no longer knew what to do. . . .

Of course, I knew that by leaving him I would lose my place and put my developing career in jeopardy. But, I felt capable and ready to set out on a new adventure. Surely I would find another benefactor, but who was to say he wouldn't demand even more? At least this one loved me; I had proof of that now. He respected me and my profession, too. Another person of his standing would find it ludicrous that his girlfriend could display herself so inanely as a little singer for a miserable salary, a sum he would spend in a single evening just for a bottle of whiskey. Perhaps it was the need for security and the fear of the unknown that influenced my decision to stay with him, but the key was his love for me. His tenacity and resolve, his permanent presence and truthfulness, far outweighed any awkwardness. It was thrilling to be loved this much. We then lived in perfect harmony.

When he was called on to explain why he'd left his marital home, he replied that his private life was his own business and suggested he would resign if this posed any problem. No one insisted upon this because at the time the government still needed its new elite, which had graduated from the best European universities, justifying its demagogy and rationalizing its pride.

As was to be expected, the news reached his wife. She came to the club one evening with a well-sharpened machete, determined to split my head in two. If she didn't succeed, it's only because heaven wanted it so. The boss was always on guard when she appeared. That evening he grabbed her arm just in time before she went for my neck. I didn't recognize what was coming, because I had completely focused my singing on a group of people who had asked for a specific song, and who were looking at me with such interest that they, too, had not seen the danger. The owner ordered the bouncers never to let this woman into the place again or allow her to wander around the area.

She then began to stalk us. Going to the club became a veritable obstacle course, as we had to make sure that no one was following us. Finally, we secretly moved. For weeks, she didn't give up; on the contrary, she included everyone she could in her project—brothers, sisters, uncles, cousins, and nephews—and in the end they found the new house to which we'd just moved. Fortunately, the watchman was a second cousin of Monsieur Prosecutor and wouldn't let her in. She spied on us unwaveringly, and one day crept out from the hedge around our house like a bird of prey, lunged at me with a can of gasoline, and set fire to my little car.

I barely managed to come out of it unharmed, and threw myself at her with all my might, fighting with her like an Amazon. I won easily, tearing her straightened hair out in bunches, ripping her clothes so badly that in order to protect her dignity, she called a taxi driver she knew, who took her in his car and drove off at full speed.

When the prosecutor heard the story that night he decided we had to leave town for a while, retreat to a town on the shore to think things through calmly and make decisions for the future. He phoned one of his trusted men and instructed him to reserve seats and buy the tickets for us, not recognizing that by doing so he was delivering us into the hands of a traitor.

• • •

Early that morning we check in and board the plane, together with a teeming crowd, as large as in a bus station. At take-off something very serious happens: Madame, having alerted every authority in town, has arrived with her three children and stands in front of the plane, demanding it run them down so that her husband will be free to lead the new life he's chosen—at the cost of theirs! She declares that she's thrown something in one of the motors. Whatever the truth, it needs to be checked out, and all the passengers have to disembark.

When she sees us, she plunges headlong into complete hysteria:
She shakes and drools as if in an epileptic fit;
She chatters in a shrill voice and gesticulates like a puppet in the wind;
She crashes like a ball against each obstacle, and cracks her teeth.
Firm hands get hold of her and immobilize her, serving as a shield
    for us.
A wall of policemen separates us from her crazed looks and from the
    children.
Insults rain from her bleeding mouth, rushing like a torrent,
Splattering us and sweeping us right into the heart of torment.
The bystanders mutter, whisper, and point all the way to the waiting
    room,
Where relatives wait for us with worried and reproachful eyes.

We are surrounded by every personality Madame and her family have
   notified;
All of them berate us, preach to us, shout until they're hoarse, trying to
   outdo each other.
They speak to us of betrayal, recklessness, lack of judgment.
They order us to end this impudence.
Wordlessly, we look only at one another.
He reassures me, protects me from this bonfire.
He truly loves me more and more, and does his very best.
It's my turn to do something for him, my turn to love him—
For the first time, since we've been together,
To think of him, and not just of myself, and it makes me tremble,
How truly willing this man is to give up everything for nothing,
Just so he can love and disappear without a trace;
Just because he crossed my path one day.

SONG 14

It is my turn to love and protect him now: I must set him free;
I must relinquish my security and perhaps my work as well;
I must put a little balm on his heart
And, more than that, return some of his ardor.
I tell him that I love him from the bottom of my heart,
That at this moment his happiness alone matters to me;
From every pore in my body, I tell him that I love him,
And that for now his life is my most precious treasure.
Our eyes are locked, and I believe profoundly in our shared
   understanding.
For once there is no further fear or doubt, no separation,
No hiding behind a shield; there is only the fusion
Of one heart with another, of one being with its fellow.
We bathe in inexpressible affinity; we feel the everlasting
And discover freedom and the path that we should keep for all eternity.
Hands pull at us, move us apart, thinking they can separate
What is now a sealed union, the miracle consummated.
We smile at one another, we wed, and the invisible connects us.

In this moment, we give each other everything; we end our life of
   pursuit;
We're freed from our desire, and all we hear is the song of the wind.
We have rounded the corner, we have climbed the wall of time!
And when, oh Lord, I manage to leave this airport,
I'll rise above all this; saved from a dishonorable death,
My heart will not be drowned in shame and sorrow,
Facing these women and these children whose
Eyes are boring into me.
By granting me love and compassion at the crucial moment,
   you have blessed me,
And I promise you, my God, that I'll get back on my path, I'll not waste
   time
As I did two years ago; without shield, without umbrella,
I will leave all bitterness and all desire far behind;
I will hand myself over in full to the next stage,
Where God alone is knowledge and is power,
And there I'll patiently wait for him to guide me. . . .

38

Letter from Monsieur Prosecutor
(delivered to my mother Naja, where I found it six months
later):

My dear little Halla,
   I know, everything has already been said between us,
everything done and consummated;
   I cannot see anything more or better we could have
done.
   Yet, I am weak enough to desire you still,
   After, at the airport, I discovered your love.
   Yet at the same time I don't think I want to see you
anymore—
   I'd be too afraid not to see that same look in your eyes,
the one that made all my troubles so worthwhile;
   There is no other look of yours that I could bear again.
   Still, I can't resist the longing to speak to you one final
time,
   To tell you, in simple and clear words, what I feel,
   And especially how I am living since our separation.
   I hope this letter will reach you as late as possible,
   When all the floods have ebbed.

I will deliver it to your mother. One day, sooner or later, you'll go back there and read it.

Little Mother of my heart, incapable of facing that "what-will-they-say," that many-headed monster in terror of which I was raised, I thought I would live in an emotional underground all my life, for what I loved was always unpopular in my milieu. You made me confront and conquer this monster, and I know how to love differently at last. I know how to accept another person completely for who she is and have her be part of me, inside myself, past all fear. Today I could lose my job, my family, all the honors I receive, and I would still succeed in starting a new life, finding a new mission. So I went back to my family, not because I was giving in to the pressure, not out of fear of anything or anyone, but out of love for you and for her.

I know now that your destiny is not in my home. It was an obsession of mine to want to possess you from the first day I saw you. Don't be so surprised; it is the truth. I recognized you the day I followed you to the nightclub where you had just been hired. I always hesitated to tell you this, though I'm not sure why. I will tell you now.

The first time I ever saw you was in the courtroom of Wouri. Your parents were in appeal over a paternity suit and custody of the children. A blood test separated you somewhat from many of your brothers and sisters. While all of them were crying, you alone kept calm, and that really struck me. As young as you were, you seemed to be the one element to appeal to and calm the others, even your parents, who were mad with anger and rebellion.

It was the first case I tried; I was then the youngest prosecutor of the republic in my region, having just returned from my studies in Europe. My head was spinning with pride, and I felt as if I were living a fairy tale in which you were the elf. Do you remember pulling at my robes? What spell did you cast on me there? I'll spare you all the fantasies that went whirring through my head. Later, only your face clearly stayed with me—so much so that when I saw you in the bakery buying croissants, I thought it was a miracle, and the fear of losing sight of you impelled me to behave in the way that so astounded you. . . .

Do you remember? I shouted at you and asked you to remind me of your name.

"Since I haven't told you yet, how can I repeat it?" you answered with a smile and left serenely, as if the problem was resolved once and for all.

I followed you in my brand-new car, insisting on dropping you off.

You looked at me compassionately, as if I were a sick man, and went on your way.

I crawled along without daring to speak another word for fear you would vanish. If you didn't do just that it is only because you had a specific goal and nothing was going to deter you from it, especially not a skirt-chaser. I felt very ashamed. I couldn't imagine a girl in Wouri refusing a chance to be that comfortable, and instead going the whole distance on foot without being diverted, for they all love luxury and comfort. And the "irresistible womanizer" I thought I was found himself to be totally ineffective!

You can't imagine my joy when I saw you come into the restaurant-club where I was a regular. When you disappeared through the backdoor, I asked the owner, whom I knew well, why there was a minor present in his club. His fear proved to me that I had him, and I wouldn't lose sight of you again. Heaven was with me and had sent me the elf of my dreams.

Obviously, you turned my life upside down, and I was already lost to my family. But you knew how to be a sister and friend and, thank God, everything straightened out in my mind; my family is happier than ever before. I reminded my wife that it was thanks to you. If you had wanted me for yourself, she couldn't have prevented that.

Now I feel able to think about our country and what is going on there, to reflect on the battles that everyone could fight individually, starting with self-conquest, which is in my opinion the hardest to conceive of, take on, and succeed at in our current situation.

My parents gently chide my wife because of all the scandals she caused, and, surprisingly, she laughs at them, she who was so crabby and intolerant before. You have left your mark on all of us. My oldest son asked me what it was that you had that his mother does not. She was the one who answered him: "She has an older soul."

When I think about it, I realize that you've remained an utter mystery. In the end, I'll never know what you thought of me, what I stood for in your eyes. What did you say to yourself when you left me at the airport? I felt ready to crush anything that might come between us and set fire to it. But you had the same conciliatory look you had in the courtroom years earlier, and I understood then that we had to drink our distress down to the dregs, and in that way alone would we come out of it as greater and better people. So I hope it has been the same for you as for me. If I write you this final letter, it is to assure you that I am fine and wish you all the happiness you deserve. But above all, I wanted to tell you this so I can be at complete peace with myself.

To you, forever, your "supreme shield" as you called me then.

Dan Minlo

• • •

And you, Auntie Roz, did you have a love this strong, this beautiful, if only for one day? Did you decide then not to settle for a bland and boring love like that of your namesake, my Aunt Roz, you who were not tied up with a disastrous brother you could not abandon without feeling you were killing his mother? Or was your first love just as hurtful as that of your other namesake, Tata Roz, so that you decided not to waste your time again with other, risky encounters, but rather to favor more people with your love, more broadly and impersonally—to earn love as Christ did, *ad vitam aeternam*—for all time? What happened to you? What happened to all my aunts Roz?

39

SONG 15

To move like the earth, like life,
To move like pure energy,
Without any other purpose but to progress,
Irrespective of polarity—
To move without any thoughts, just to move.
The only true place of thought and destination
Is moving itself as the ultimate action,
Moving as essential, vital activity.

And if we sometimes turn in circles,
It is because life is not ready yet for a rebound,
So move, move, move, and go around;
Keep going until destiny comes prancing back between a thousand loves.
Mother Dora, you had turned around and were there for the rendezvous,
Great opener of doors onto new and mad pathways!

● ● ●

I didn't even realize I'd made a made a full circuit of the town, taking the small interior road, and felt as if I'd come from another planet when I heard a voice calling out at me: "Halla Njokè, why are you jogging at high noon? Can I drop you somewhere, my girl?"

Mother Dora, the old madam from my earliest club! Where was she coming from, and what was she doing there at that precise moment? Why she and not someone else? From then on it was clear she was the instrument my destiny had chosen to show me a new direction.

I wanted to talk to her, but my voice didn't work. I was too far away and had not quite come back from the journey of my nomadic self. Soon, when my mind was completely back in its temple, the tongue obeyed, and greeted her and thanked her for being who she was, for being here.

• • •

Trembling, Mother Dora comes out of the car, opens the door, and helps me in as if I were ill. The gentleman at the wheel looks at me as at a strange phenomenon. I wonder what I look like, glance in the rearview mirror, and recognize I'm drenched with sweat as if I have just come out of a shower, my clothes clinging to my skin, and my eyes strangely staring. I must be scaring them because no one talks now. I do my best to smile, and we drive off.

"I apologize, Mpessa, but you need to take me back home; I'm going to take care of the girl; she's in bad shape," Mother Dora tells her friend. "We'll do your errands later, if that's all right?"

"Of course. You're right."

When the car turns the first corner, I notice we're in front of the airport I left five hours before! I certainly have made the rounds, of the place and of the issues at hand. It is time to look elsewhere. I close my eyes and let myself be driven.

There is a kind of mental void that isn't all that empty. It's a mental void that does not consist of an absence of thoughts or perceptions, for these are located at a very high level and in such a mysterious register that objective memory cannot record them. There certainly is a special corner in memory, in the brain, where these "extrasensory" perceptions are recorded, and are then transmitted to objective memory under specific conditions or on special occasions. There can be no other explanation for the fact that we can spend so much time in objective mental inactivity and suddenly, at a given moment, find ourselves with great numbers of already assembled thoughts that flood the consciousness, as if we had been living elsewhere, taking our time to articulate them this way—unless you believe it's heaven-inspired, the way prophets receive the word of the divine.

I don't remember having gleaned a single active, objective reflection from that entire day. I don't remember any of the faces I saw, any possible incidents or events on the way, and yet I went some thirty kilometers between seven in the morning and one in the afternoon! No memory of places, or even of the cars that always threaten to crush the poor pedestrian. Did anyone hit me? Did I stop at a red light? None of this is recorded in my objective memory. But a thousand thoughts emerge from my brain when I wake up at Mother Dora's late in the afternoon. Surely they were shaped during the walk and were put aside, waiting for the mind to be liberated during sleep so that they could be imprinted in areas more accessible to the objective consciousness. As I wake up, some of them do, indeed, stand out clearly.

First of all, I don't want to be beholden to anyone anymore just so I can sing. Either they'll accept me on the basis of my intrinsic abilities, or else I'll change professions. Second, I have to learn different ways of expressing myself, different skills. We are taught that there aren't any fools, just limited individuals. In the event that I do not sing again, I can always work as a waitress in a restaurant or a nightclub and be paid in percentages, as I've seen dozens of girls do for a living. I feel ready to embark on an entirely new activity without rejecting anything out of hand, except prostitution. I know I would like most of all to go back to the village and work the soil beside my namesake. Strengthened by these resolutions, I slowly surface from my "mental void," well rested and receptive to hearing the suggestions of Mother Dora, as if she were a new Aunt Roz.

I had not seen her in more than a year and thought she had lost some weight, but she was still as positive, energetic, and pugnacious as always. She told me her boss had asked her to find him a singer who knew enough standard pieces to sing with soundtracks, rather than a live band, two hours on weekend evenings. We left early to try out a few songs, and she introduced me to the boss before the place opened to the public.

It was the only place where I ever really enjoyed singing, and if I am still singing six decades later on the edge of my grave, it is surely in memory of my times at the Domino. There, my repertoire actually depended entirely on my aptitude alone. If I did well in setting lyrics and melodies to the tracked music, the song would automatically become part of the repertoire, and they would give me a small bonus for each new piece.

When my time was up, I could accept drinks from the customers, and even if I didn't drink, I received a percentage of the ones offered to me. It improved my salary considerably. Moreover, the clientele at the club was particularly select and friendly. People came to hear music at a low enough volume to have a pleasant conversation and dance if they felt like it. At last I found some men who didn't feel they had to chase after every woman they met!

I honestly believe that the Domino satisfied me, with the happy experience of singing by myself in an atmosphere where I could perfect my personal art, with the complete respect of my small audience.

Is that not how you, too, must have learned things, Auntie Roz—at the mercy of your innumerable steps, stops, junctures, refusals to go forward that sometimes come over us, just like a donkey? You think you've come to a halt, while the real move has only just begun—Destiny is advancing.

But I have to admit that if my singing was not totally transformed into a symbol of hardship, it's because of the first "intellectual" I have ever met—Ndiffo, the builder, the creator through thought; Ndiffo, the Pure Spirit!

40

Sixty years later, I still think of him. I think of him whenever I see a bald man! Undoubtedly, this is because it was the first time I'd ever seen someone so truly bald: His whole head was completely bare down to where his neck began, his scalp so smooth and bright that it caught the reflections of the club's lights and seemed to return them as a mirror would.

I also think of him every time I think of tenderness.

Since then, the word "tenderness" evokes in me the feeling that his smile and his gaze produced, and also the feel of his bald head. His smile had a way of spreading like a soft nightlight with an almost voluptuous sweetness. His gaze rested on people like a soothing balm. And in the end, one always gave in to the desire to touch his extraordinary bald head, where your hand would stay as if magnetized, trapped.

I also think of him each time I feel like dreaming while awake, out loud, undoing and remaking the world, imagining future ordeals, then inventing tricks and solutions to confront them successfully. For he is the first person I saw being and living in that way.

With his velvet voice, he could design whole cities, all through the night, installing and moving fountains, statues, and monuments, public parks, and bridges.

His cities had the peculiarity of boasting prestigious and generous governing authorities, who walked the pedestrian streets and wrought miracles, solving every problem that the population laid before them. As a result, the streets occupied a large part of his designs, all ending in superb squares like the spokes on a wheel of fortune. How could I have known that such dreams could never be realized? How could I have known that governments would amputate all the creativity, inventiveness, and imagination from their elites, and most of all refuse them the means of making their dreams come true? Had I known it, I would have foreseen the wretchedness that at millennium's end would bring the people down. Perhaps I would have foreseen what the famous Armageddon would look like, the one that the religion of both my mothers Naja mentioned so often. Had I known it, I would have devoted more time to Ndiffo, to help him realize even one of his visions. At the very least, I would have helped him better formulate the concept of his "cities of responsible people."

Regrettably, I listened to him with only half an ear, preoccupied with my worries about earning a better living. He then made an even greater effort to make me understand his brilliant dream. He would take a gold pen from his pocket and scribble some outline that he'd explain to me at length. When the lights went down in the club for the languorous slow dances, he'd light his lighter and keep on drawing his vision by the spark alone, as naturally as if he could see in the near-dark. Nothing could be allowed to stop the flow of his inspiration, least of all myself. I would have felt like someone who refuses to come to the aid of a person in danger. And besides, if I rose, suddenly aware that I was there to earn a living and not to dream and that it would be helpful to increase the drink orders to raise my percentages; or if I went to greet new customers, he would cling to me as to a lifebuoy, begging me not to break his train of thought. He reached a point where he would pay my boss for ten or fifteen drinks each evening, provided I stay and listen to him and ask my naive questions. So each time he came to the club, three or four times a month, after I sang my sets I was wholly absorbed in a purely intellectual and aesthetic activity that, in addition, made me some money. I became more and more interested in the professions connected to this pursuit. He told me about teaching, journalism, commercial exploration, literature, and much more—new possibilities for me, as long as I worked hard. He began to give me a new book each time he saw me.

After a while I was completely immersed in careful listening and voracious reading. From then on, sharing his exhilaration was like a drug. I found it fascinating that just by thinking alone you could come up with so many ideas and images, and know how to transmit them so effectively that the public was able to feel it had actually experienced them! I lived in these imagined cities, knew their streets and monuments and even their inhabitants: innately rich people full of generosity toward their fellow citizens, people who were always prepared to recreate their own world, constantly correcting and improving not only the structures and infrastructures but their own habits and customs as well. Soon I couldn't tell his cities apart from those in the novels I devoured. It would be wonderful to sing in cities like these, where all people participated in never-ending renewal using their own tools. For me, those tools would be lyrics and voice, since I didn't know how to design as well as Ndiffo, whom I now saw as my master.

Decades later, I still hold on to the conviction he inspired, which is that we create hell or heaven through deliberate thought. Thank you, Master Ndiffo, for teaching me and giving me your blessing.

SONG 16
Often I think of Master Ndiffo, too,
Every time I graze despair,
Every time I have dark thoughts,
Thinking about my father, about the masses of creators
I met after him, and all the intellectuals
I saw who had to fight to no avail,
Fight the monstrous epidemic of despair
Come crashing down on all Africa's intellectuals,
For three decades running, without a shred of doubt,

Endangering the education, the future, of several generations,
So that in the end they drowned in it, became inured,
Threw in the towel, had no self-protection, not even to remain immune,
Depending only on humanitarian aid;
Yet each time, my dear Ndiffo, I remember, too, that you were
The first to be affected, or so I think,
And that is why my compassion for you is now rekindled,
And so to you I say, as to all lost generations, that
We, divine, must find ourselves, inside our spirit, once again.

41

The more I read and learned, even though I didn't always understand it all, the more I felt like trying something other than singing in nightclubs. An unexpected opportunity arose.

One evening after I finished my sets, Mother Dora told me there was a gentleman who wanted to offer me a drink. To my huge surprise, there was my Uncle Noël sitting quietly in a corner. He was the son of Grand Madja Halla's youngest sister, and thus my father's first cousin. I used to meet him at the Kingdom Hall of the Jehovah's Witnesses. Whenever he and my mother were alone together, he frequently seemed to be arguing with her, but as soon as someone approached, they pretended to be chatting about odds and ends. As a result I was always a little afraid of him, and seeing him there at the nightclub made me very suspicious. A thousand and one scenarios flitted through my head, one more alarming than the next. He must have guessed what I was thinking, because he stood up very cheerfully and asked me to join him.

He most graciously offers me champagne. In a place where the price of one bottle of champagne equals the salary of four employees, my boss wants to meet the customer who's making such a fuss over his little singer. Papa Noël, looking a little tipsy, I thought, introduces himself to my boss as the founder of the largest school in his district and a great producer of industrial products. He tells him unashamedly that I am one hundred percent his daughter, the first drop of blood conceived in the belly of a woman, his cousin's wife, alas, but everyone knows what youth is like: It heats your blood, and you don't know what you're doing. He claims he always wanted to take care of his daughter, but they had continually prohibited him. Now that he has finally become a wealthy man, he has been looking for her again. Hearing that she was hanging out in bars, he is here to see for himself. No, he's not angry with the club owner, he need not worry. On the contrary, he thanks him for having kept an eye on her so carefully, but a situation like this cannot go on forever. I don't dare say anything, afraid of unleashing some unpredictable reaction. My silence is taken as an acknowledgement of the facts, although it actually stems from my memory of Tata Roz's confidences about my father's cousin having abused my mother.

My boss is eager to show how happy he is for me. He almost has tears in his eyes: A reunion such as this—a newly wealthy father who suddenly reappears—is like a magic wand at work. The future of his favorite singer seems guaranteed, without a doubt. Nevertheless, he'd like the father to know how talented his daughter is—that she manages extremely well, and with great dignity. He wonders if it might not be better for the father to support his daughter's career, which has gotten off to such a fine start.

But it appears that "the father" in question wants his daughter to try different things before making a final choice. I insist my boss tell him I must finish out the month so that he has a chance to find a replacement for me, and also so I can prepare myself, for I have no such plans in mind. In fact, I want to confer with Ndiffo, but he won't be back until the end of the month.

When he returns, Ndiffo advises me to accept my uncle's offer, but only on a trial basis, for a maximum of three months and without resigning completely from the club; he promises to convince my boss to hold my place open. I will work part-time and sing part-time at night, so that I won't have anything to regret, just in case. . . .

I have to confess that I don't question the veracity of my uncle's words, having heard so many similar allusions during the courtroom sessions of my childhood. What I do know is that, as my father's first cousin, Papa Noël is my father as well, and for this reason I have to call him Papa and behave as his daughter, in any case. He has the duty to take care of me, but also the right to forbid me any activity he deems unworthy of the family. He may even beat me if I disobey, for I am still a minor.

So I agree to play the role of model daughter, but inside myself I refuse to reconsider the problem of blood relationships that have suddenly resurfaced in my life. In my own mind it is clear that I have only one father. Having been forced to wonder himself, he emptied his blood in my belly to seal it once and for all, and the tests confirmed it. In spite of everything and whatever it may cost me, I shall never hark back to this again.

Another reason why I don't feel like arguing issues of paternity with Papa Noël is my deep desire to leave the nightclub world and live more of a daytime life.

Under his guidance, I devote myself body and soul for three months, without taking any time off, to an overhaul of his school. Although I never went to high school, I begin as a teacher, move up to general supervisor, and finally become assistant director. Taken aback by such a rapid promotion, I ask Papa Noël for an explanation.

"My main problem these days is one of ethics and trust. It's hard to find people who have an ideal of their own or are willing to share someone else's. A new sickness I call 'financial shortcuts' is corrupting every sector of the country, sparing no one. Everybody is eager to cheat the one person who's unlucky enough to depend on his little bit of power. The school is having a hard time becoming the institution I dream of. But I can count on you; you have your own world vision and personal ethics that stand as an antidote to our corrupt society. I'm counting on you to keep this school going after I'm gone, and if I'm speeding up your training, it's only because I don't think I have much time left."

Another dreamer, just like his cousin my father—the only difference being that this one tries, day after day, to make his dream a reality with the same obstinacy but without any violence. I'm quite proud of him and feel close to him in his thirst to make his ideal come true. Unfortunately, the experience also leads me to discover that I am not cut out for conventional pursuits.

The only thing that guides me is my passion to create, at my own speed and in my own way, without depending in the least on other circumstances. I want to be able to work day and night for as long as it takes to arrive at a result. I know that there is not much I can change within the system we have, and I cannot make a permanent commitment to him, knowing that I'll disappoint him later.

At the end of my trial period, I explain this to him, and for a long time he looks at me in silence, as if to dig deep down inside me for the reasons for my refusal. I am scared he'll be angry because his disappointment is great; we really have worked very well together in a good atmosphere, and the school is on the right track. Will he understand? Will he accept my position, and will he forgive me? Finally he speaks, a touch of nostalgia and pride in his voice: "I understand; for me it would have been too good to be true, but for you it would be too limiting. Your dreams go much further than mine, and that is as it should be. Children have to go further than their parents. You have given a lot to the school in a very short time, and I know you have a lot more to give to children—but that will come later, for you can't help but love them, and helping them will be a priority for you. When your time comes, your own school will be much more significant than this one. You really are my daughter, and I am proud of that first drop of blood of mine. Go then, my daughter, and may God protect you."

I don't understand what people see in me when they talk this way, but I want to believe them with all my heart, just so that God will hear them. I kneel down before him in a gesture of humility and gratitude, thanking him for his fatherly forbearance and understanding.

He spits in his hands, rubs them together vigorously, and places them warmly on my forehead. He prays silently for a long while, hugs me briefly, and then helps me up. I am deeply touched. A father's blessings, whoever he may be, can always be helpful in life and are a good thing to take away—especially for people like me, who are exposed to all kinds of surprises.

Even today, I believe these blessings continue to protect me and kindle my energy, both in what I initiate and in the difficulties I face. All we need to do is believe, and anchors such as these nurture and fortify faith.

The other reason I didn't accept Papa Noël's proposals is that I intended to make my living with the artistic creativity I had already chosen as my mode of expression, even if I didn't yet quite see what form that would take. In the meantime, I had more appealing practical training possibilities in which, I was told, my creative choice would blossom more fully, and also offer me a more rapid climb up the social ladder. As such prospects would demand greater availability from my end, I couldn't keep juggling part-time positions.

During the three months I had devoted to my uncle's school and the small children, I continued singing at the club three times a week. Because I felt more at peace, my voice and approach to singing improved. The clientele grew more and more interested in me, in a more respectful and more generous way. As an expression of congratulations and encouragement, the audience gave their huge tips directly to me—tips that were sometimes larger than my base pay—and they never expected anything in return. This also bolstered my choice of a possibly artistic career.

Another unusual thing was that some customers, people new to my life, began to offer me collaboration in new areas of work. They said that I expressed myself very well and had a good way with people, which was bound to open many doors. Newly affluent African entrepreneurs and Western immigrants offered proposals in the areas of journalism, publicity, and insurance. In order to persuade me to accept, they said that the work would enrich my culture, reinforce my character, and equip me for an artistic career. They were absolutely right, and I still thank them for this today. Some of them contributed significantly to what I think of as my training in "the school of life." Artists should always be educated in the most eclectic manner possible to perceive and interpret effectively the diverse aspirations of their society.

● ● ●

Auntie Roz, who always went to sleep around nine o'clock, arrived one night at a most unusual hour—almost midnight! "What's going on, Auntie, that you're here at a time like this? What calamity has happened now?" I could only ask.

The last time I'd seen her like this was when my mother Naja died. That time she arrived around ten, sat down on the eucalyptus stump in the garden, and kept vigil in silence until morning. We called her in at midnight to light the five candles of our mother Naja's star and place them on the large Lobi deathbed in the living room. Then we—my sister, her family, and all the grandchildren who were present—watched the candles burn down in order to determine the final signs of how Mama had departed and send energy to the weakest points, so that she could present herself in a more balanced state, as she sparkled before the narrow gate.

The candle at the "body point" of her star literally burned out in barely half an hour. Her emaciated body had given up quickly, even before she had realized emotionally and intellectually that the end had come. Then the candle at the emotional point flickered out before an hour was up. How sad she must have been to see herself so helpless and diminished. The pain of her infected bones must have driven her mad. The candle at the intellectual point lasted more than two hours. She must have taken time to make peace with herself and think about each of us. On the telephone, my oldest sister had told me that our mother had been able to summon her and ask her to alert my youngest sister and me that she was waiting for us to say a final farewell, although her clinical death had already been confirmed.

The last two candles, at the points of will and conscience, did not burn down until five hours had passed, and then they went at the same time. She had waited for us for three days in a coma, and had come out of it only to ask whether my youngest sister and I had arrived. During those three days, we were standing around at the airport, where a strike was keeping every flight from taking off. Precisely those same three days! Will and conscience must have been in a rage when they left a body already long abandoned by all the subtle facets that once had kept it alive.

"That's what they call dying in despair, dying of woe, dying in decay," my sister said, breaking down and sobbing. "That's where submitting yourself to bad choices gets you. To prove what? What did you prove, my mother Naja? For whose benefit did you suffer so much, Mother—tell me, whose? Why not admit that you made a bad choice, that you were wrong? Why not forgive yourself and give yourself another chance? Why not start over again? Why couldn't you have loved us instead of that damned man, Mama, the way our grandmothers loved their children more than their men! And now you have left us for good, and for nothing!"

We went out into the garden, and Auntie Roz took both of us in her arms. I was trembling from head to toe because no word would escape from my mouth, though I had the feeling that my words were pushing their way out through my sister's lips, so similar was our anger.

"Don't blaspheme, my girls," Auntie Roz said, gently but firmly. "Your mother would have explained it had you been there in time. And had you been there in time to help her body, she would still be alive, for you can see how she willed herself to hold on! At last, she was prepared to live for you and with you, but heaven did not want it so; the airport strike did not allow it. It is fate; it was the end of her road. Calm down now, and let us bring her star some strength before you have to get back to the airport. You must absolutely be near her for the burial. Don't forget, Fitini Halla, you are not to go to the morgue or the grave, agreed?"

Seeing Auntie Roz here again at such a late hour made my heart leap, and I told myself that another one in the immediate family must have departed. . . .

"No, no, look here, I'm not always a bearer of bad news," Auntie Roz cried out, seeing my alarm. "I'm not the only messenger of death, and so it's not my role to announce every surprise attack. True, I was at a wake and I need to go back there. But I really wanted to know where you are with your writing in 'tribute' to me. . . . Well, I want to be alive to see it. You yourself suggested it; I didn't ask you for anything."

So I read her the chapters on Ndiffo and Papa Noël, sure that she would tell me she didn't see the connection to her, and perhaps finally decide to tell me something about herself. But all she said was: "That's good, you're on the right track. That is how you learn, you see; that's how I learned, too. It probably wouldn't have pleased your mother very much to be reminded of certain people, but she would have liked your respectful approach. I'm sure that I will recognize myself. And you see, I had forgotten about Dora! Keep going and hurry, now; I'm eager to read the beginning and the end. . . ."

42

The first proposal I accept after leaving Papa Noël is the one from Monsieur Diaw, founder-director of a pan-African monthly magazine. He suggests that I write a few articles and explore publicity. "Press and P.R.," as he likes to say, is a new empire to be conquered. The articles would emerge from investigations of my nightclub environment and deal with social facts, unusual encounters between men and women, youth and its particular problems in this milieu, prostitution, delinquency, moral disintegration, the stampede of new scourges such as vice, sexual perversion, drug addiction, and so forth. He's keen on telling me that I can publish under a pseudonym to spare myself possible attacks.

Right from the start, they offer me huge benefits: three-star hotels, a car and driver, meals, a bonus for each article published (depending on its importance and to be negotiated before it appears), plus twenty percent of each advertiser I attract.

"For a girl who's just eighteen and lacks any special qualifications in the field, it's a bit excessive," I tell myself. This kind of situation creates powerful needs for what are essentially useless goods, and are certainly at the root of several of the ills my new boss wants me to explore. I have the feeling that I'm already in the middle of my first investigation.

Very excited and eager to begin, I agree to sign a contract for a three-month trial period, after my "master" and friend Ndiffo has checked and approved it. He, too, finds such expensive hotels a bit bizarre, but he tells me that they will be the safest places for me, especially since he has to absent himself for these same three months. On the whole Ndiffo agrees with me: It's all too good for it to be honorable. But he is counting on my intelligence and my great sensitivity to help me raise some interesting issues and truly awaken the vigilance of Wouri's youth and, indirectly, of all Africa, which has been tied hand and foot and handed over to the onslaughts of a corrupt civilization.

My first research project comes out of my new way of looking at the world. In the almost seven months I've been at the Domino, I never wondered seriously about the lavishly dressed girls who frequent the place in the company of Western men. Night after night I've been preoccupied with doing my musical sets in the best way possible, and spending time with those customers who invite me to their tables afterward, which I was happy to do because they were considerate. Our conversations were refined and respectable, and even infused with a great deal of humanity: attentive listening, proper responses, patience, and good humor. The customers seemed to appreciate these relationships enough to return again and again.

But I never recognized that other people thought my behavior was odd because it kept them from propositioning me in a way that was apparently quite common. I thought the club's approach was different rather than my own. I really didn't know that all nightclubs are hunting grounds of every kind, and that the fabulous young women I saw did nothing other than chase after luxury.

One night I decide to follow one of these young women, who has come in by herself. She goes over to a lone customer who has been sitting forlornly in a corner for quite a while, sipping his drink and looking miserable. I am determined to get at the truth, and sit down at the same table as if I were waiting for someone. I hear them negotiate their love relationship in a way I would never have thought possible between human beings.

The girl agrees to make the gentleman's fantasy come true in the place of his choosing and for the length of time required, between one and four in the morning, in exchange for a hundred thousand francs. He insists that she must remain silent and that any word or sound coming from her will bring the contract to an immediate end.

I leave the club without saying goodbye to my boss, get into the back of my business car, and ask the driver to get ready to tail the car I'm about to point out to him, for if I've understood them correctly, that will happen soon.

Less than ten minutes later the couple comes out, and they get into a rather ordinary vehicle, compared with what I expected. They drive along the bank, cross the bridge, and leave town. If I were by myself, I would never have dared to continue my pursuit. We keep a safe distance so as not to arouse suspicion. At the exit just past the first suburb lies an enormous cemetery. The car leaves the highway and takes the main lane between the gravestones. My driver goes a bit farther, makes a U-turn, and parks just in front of the entrance, headlights off. He tells me not to expect him to go into the cemetery at such a diabolical hour.

Uncontrollable shivers of fear run down my spine. Still, I cautiously get out of the car and crouch down as if to urinate, waiting for my eyes to get used to the dark. Then I recognize that a light shines weakly from way down in the back of the cemetery. The light, no doubt, belongs to our infernal couple, who probably don't want to be in total darkness.

I slip quietly down a lane running parallel to where the couple is, two lanes over. I creep farther into the field of tombs and come out behind them. Thank God that on this side the mausoleums are quite grand, and I can easily hide, moving forward toward the scene—which almost makes me cry out in horror!

The girl is completely naked, and her hands are tied to two cement posts around a grave. Her slightly parted feet are also tied to heavy stones that obviously were brought along for this purpose. It leaves the girl in a bestial position that seems incredibly humiliating to me. The man is on his knees in a sort of invocation. Every now and then he puts his hand into the girl's vagina, takes it out and places it on the tomb, continuing his invocation in an increasingly mournful tone. Suddenly two other, almost identical men emerge from somewhere and sit down next to the first one. The three go on together with the invocation and then a large wolfhound appears. He is wearing something like red underpants from which his enormous penis protrudes. The dog mounts the girl as if she were his usual bitch and begins to have rough sex with her, yelping hideously. The man who had brought the girl takes the gag out of her mouth and pushes his penis in. The other two grab her breasts with their teeth. The poor girl moves as if in a trance, and I sense that if these bastards were to climax she'll never survive.

It's more than I can take. I feel my ghastly scream come from deep inside my bowels, just as it did when they were lowering my grandfather's body into the grave. The two men, who seem like apparitions to me, and their hellish hound begin to shriek and shake as if they were caught in an electric trap. They finally pull away from their victim like leeches, crawl behind the mausoleums, and vanish into the night. The other one pleads with her: "Please, I apologize, I'll untie you, just don't kill me!"

I realize that because he hasn't seen me and doesn't know where the scream came from, he believes he is dealing with a girl more fiendish than himself. He sets her free, takes a wad of banknotes from his pocket, and throws them in her face.

"Here, here! I'm paying you, and that's where our contract ends! I never want to see you again!"

He rushes to his car and takes off, leaving the girl behind. She drags herself up, gathers her clothes, and puts the money in a pocket. She staggers off down the lane, looking in every direction in boundless terror. I think even she had no idea where the scream came from. About a hundred meters on, she faints.

My scream stops when the thug takes off, but then it's the silence that terrifies me, freezes me to the spot, because I suddenly remember that I was forbidden to enter any cemeteries precisely because of that scream. Terror tears me out of my rigidity, and I take to my heels. I find my driver in a state of total panic. He tells me he heard the screams of wild animals or demons and begs me to get into the car at once so we can leave this cursed place. He saw the White man flee by himself and thought he'd killed us both, but hadn't dared go into the cemetery to check. He was just about to leave and call my boss for help, he says. I beg him to give me a hand to carry the unconscious girl to the car; before he agrees, I am forced to threaten to bring charges against him for failure to assist a person in danger. We take the girl to the car and surreptitiously leave her behind the nightclub. I steer clear of drawing the driver's attention to the wretched, so bitterly earned money the girl has on her. I know that when she wakes up she'll need all of it just to get cleaned up. There is nothing else I can do for her, since I have no intention of getting caught on my first investigation, and even less of being mixed up in a story that could cost me my life.

With my first investigative experience I have plummeted straight into hell, and I wonder whether I'll have the nerve to recount such a tale, and whether the boss will agree to publish it.

In addition, I wonder whether it's advisable to report on such horrors—to what extent it's useful to make innocent minds aware of the kind of horrors that will only encumber and sully their consciousness. Certainly, awareness is essential, while ignorance is the mother of all evil, as they say. But maybe there's a certain kind of knowledge we could well do without. After all, there are some sacred texts that endorse the idea that death is born from the coexisting knowledge of good and evil.

I'm deeply troubled and shocked by what I've just discovered. Neglecting my musical set, I devote two whole days to taking notes, ripping them up, and starting over from scratch, without being able to find a way to formulate a piece capable of truly reflecting what I saw. I decide not to write the article or ever mention the story to anyone at all.

So it's a great surprise when a week later I see the same girl, even more dolled up, sit down in the same spot and begin her hunt all over again, as if nothing happened. It takes my breath away.

Then I decide to ask her some questions and see how she'll react. I sit down at her table and greet her as if we were friends.

"Ah, there you are! What about your husband, didn't he come with you this evening?"

"My husband? Who do you mean? I'm not married."

"Oh, really? The gentleman you were with last week at this same table isn't your husband? What a pity, you made such a special couple."

"What was so special about us?"

"Your way of being. From another world, as if you were extra-terrestrial."

"Amazing, are you clairvoyant or what?"

"Sometimes. But don't take offense. It's only because the gentleman interested me, and since he's not your husband, I'll speak more freely with him the next time he comes."

"You see him here often? I'm looking for him, too, but I doubt he'll be back here again."

"Why? Did you scare him away?"

We both laugh. I suggest we have a drink to our good health and become better acquainted. By the end of the evening she gives me a telephone number and begs me to call her if the man should come to the club. As she leaves, she says: "Above all, do not go out with him because he's a devil. If you think I'm lying to you, just open those clairvoyant eyes of yours."

Every now and then, later, I use the argument of clairvoyance to tell her a few truths, and in the end she reveals a good part of her prostitute's life to me, including her tricks and methods. But she will never speak of the cemetery incident. It is another piece of consciousness locked away, just to survive—survive a dog's life!

I write two articles based on the material gathered from her. My boss is pleased with me, and even before publication he pays me an unbelievable price for each article: double my former monthly salary, including tips, and far more than the contract stipulated. In addition, he presents me with a lighter, a gold cigarette holder, and a carton of extra-long, corn-colored cigarettes with golden filters—

real gems, although my boss knows I don't smoke. I see no reason for such a gift unless it's to create needs that are likely to force me to want to earn even more money, and thus be prepared to do anything to that end; in my head, that much is clear.

My third article deals with these new and artificial needs, which are fashioned from start to finish in the minds of youth: senseless needs that become veritable traps or prisons, and are at the root of social disintegration and a corollary of vices. I accuse the wealthy, Africans and Westerners alike, who don't know what to do with money and use it to corrupt their power, which seems to be their only pleasure—in comparison to the lack of power of the so-called underdeveloped nations. My boss congratulates me as if it all has nothing to do with him, and pays me the same fee again. I do notice, however, that not one of my articles is ever published. When I express my concern, he makes it clear to me that our relationship first needs to move toward greater trust, intimacy, and friendship.

By the end of the three-month trial period, I've written a total of ten articles, not one of them published, but all of them royally compensated. Accompanied by my boss, I have learned to canvass for advertisers among the executive directors of important companies, to whom he introduces me as a collaborator and protégée; but not a single one of those contracts is made in my name. I receive gifts on a regular basis—dresses, shoes, perfumes, and expensive cosmetics. I have obtained my regular driver's license and no longer need to have a driver day and night. I look more and more like a fashionable doll when I go to these appointments with my boss to drum up advertising. I'm expected to offer a cigarette and light one for myself in my cigarette holder, then place the golden lighter ostentatiously on my leather purse. In short, I have learned how to appear as what I am not. Moreover, this particular man makes me feel that he'd be happy to exchange me for a good cover ad. The way he introduces me to his future clients sometimes reminds me of my father, and I am always on guard with him.

In spite of all the good results, I'm not integrated fully, but am granted only an extension of the trial period. The boss again brings up the progress of our personal relationship and reminds me of the huge investment he has made in me—in every aspect of my training, my comfort, and my social image, which is no longer that of a mere nightclub singer, but of a journalist. I answer that I'm not a journalist, since none of my articles has ever been published in any paper. He assures me that from the moment I belong to him, my articles will appear as he sees fit, since it is his job to schedule them. The first thing he wants to be sure of, however, is that he won't be launching me on behalf of anyone else.

This boss and I will never see eye to eye, and therefore we can never love each other. His bargaining shocks me profoundly and constantly reminds me of the practices of the girl at the club, which one dark night transformed her into a bitch in a cemetery. When I return to the hotel I pick out all the things the man has given me, fill two suitcases with them, and have these deposited in his room, along with the car keys. I gather up my personal belongings and walk out. I leave without a farewell or any regrets.

43

SONG 17

We should taste the yes and the no of our own experience—
Yes and no, day and night—and in coexistence
Straddle the tank of our consciousness, always about to take off
For the eternal dwelling of luck,
As in the fairy tales of our childhood:

"Once upon a time there was a voyager of the past
Present in the future like a fiancé,
Anointed with scented boa grease,
Awaiting his already finely adorned betrothed.
'What do you desire?' he asked her.
And the fiancée subtly answered:
'To melt away in the Unique and be only That,
Past, present, and future all at once,
That is what I want and what I can do!'

"And once in her lifetime she was
That voyager of desire,
Who could discover and savor life
With all the commitment of her own existence."

What game do you make your creatures play, oh, God?
Raya and Raye cosily taking turns
Or violently cavorting on their path,
Angel and devil each in turn.
Could you really not sanctify or
Demonize us once and for all,
To be done with it, just to be done with it!

• • •

I no longer wanted to follow the course that seemed to be imposed on me—a course made of artificial, easy options that depended neither on my talent nor my hard work, nor on any of the strengths I would have proudly displayed. More and more, I was surrounded by a new and improbable group of people, crumbling under the weight of false needs known as "what's in." They used language full of Anglicisms and bombastic words that people caught like a virus, pushing their snobbishness so far that they monopolized the same license plate numbers on their big fat high-priced cars, using every letter of the alphabet: 555 A, 555 B, C, D, all the way through Z. To prove what and to whom? What difference did it make to themselves, their families, or their country? I didn't see or understand it. All I knew was that I didn't want it, not even as a gift. I categorically refused to take that direction; in pursuit of my destiny, I wanted to go elsewhere. Besides, I'd had enough of following my destiny so passively. Just once I wanted to decide on a direction myself, and bring it to a positive conclusion or else pick up the pieces on my own.

Since my return to Wouri and throughout the time I was singing in nightclubs, I had made regular visits to my mother Naja and my Tata Roz, trying to be as useful as possible to their whole family. My mother had accepted nothing from me, however, and still less from any of my friends—no money, no gifts, not even a drink or a meal—because, according to her, the money from my dismal milieu could only be dirty and dishonorable. An unmarried girl who sang in places of perdition couldn't possibly be an honest worker!

"To find out whether you are truly on your own path, get off it every now and then; break with what seems impossible to lose without losing your life in the process. And if you find your conscience is better because of it, that means you weren't really on your own path. On the other hand, if you yearn for it, if everything seems blocked, and you can find no reason or strength or joy in continuing, never hesitate to turn around and go back to your former path, for you'll have the proof that it was right."

Remembering these words, which Tata Roz had said to me before I fled my mother's house, I decided to alert no one, to say goodbye to none of the people I knew, not even to Mother Dora or my boss or my dear Ndiffo. I was thrilled with the experience I had gained, of course, but I wanted to go back to the point of departure, to the crossroads where I had taken one fork, and wait a while. I resolved to go back to my mother, who was quite alone and in trouble since her dear "husband-brother" had been imprisoned. In fact, I recognized that my first and primary preoccupation was still to be the pride of my parents, and especially of my mother, who, it seemed to me, had not been given much of a chance. I wanted to live with her, thinking that without the inhibiting presence of her husband, I'd find a way to prove to her that creativity doesn't inhibit honesty, and that she could count on me. Furthermore, it was time for me to provide modern artists with the dignity that the great poets of the past had enjoyed. If this were truly my path, I would succeed—I was sure of it. If not, the future would be sure to give me the wallop I deserved: As Grand Madja always said, we can never run faster than our destiny, and even if we go past it, it will always catch up with us sooner or later!

•   •   •

One evening, during a very animated conversation with customers who had stayed late at the club, we were complaining about the ever-increasing negative perception of the work of artists in general, and of women artists in particular. A gentleman by the name of Oron drew my attention to certain areas in the creative arts in which a woman's respectability was guaranteed because she was less exposed. He suggested that if I truly felt at odds with the environment I was in I should seek my new form of expression in sculpture, painting, pottery and ceramics, or literature.

Taking into account what I'd already learned, it seemed obvious to me that, having begun my pseudo-journalism career those past few months, writing would be the logical next step for the new life I was planning, on the condition that it be outside of the circles I wanted to abandon. I was going to try writing poems, songs, and maybe even novels! I would submit my songs to great singers and publish my novels with famous publishers such as those I had discovered through Ndiffo; I would live off my royalties and enjoy a more select and subtle fame. If my mother still had any objections, well, that would be too bad for both of us. I was even prepared to marry the first candidate she would consider serious, as long as he'd be tolerant enough to accept my situation as an artist and help me convince my family that it was an honorable profession.

With my program clearly defined, I arrive unannounced at my mother Naja's house. Here I find a new woman, open and feisty! Delighted with my decision, she tells me of her plan, which she hopes I will share with her: Get her husband out of prison, get him away from the plot against him by proving his innocence, and rehabilitate him in the eyes of all the "brothers." In pursuit of her objective, she grows more attentive and watchful, and becomes better informed about the country's politics by listening to the radio I brought with me, although she's shocked each time by "so much injustice and senseless violence."

Clearly, some marriages mark the end of daring and creativity in women. Alone and free, my mother in no way resembles the timorous woman I once knew, and it is a true pleasure to share this undertaking with her. A perfectionist in search of the absolute, she does her part of the job boldly, meticulously, and with great imagination.

We put our money together to purchase the clothing stock of a second-hand shop run by an expatriate about to go home, and we reorganize the running of it. Each of us spends half a day selling from our little counter in the market while the other busies herself with personal affairs or administrative and legal steps to be taken on behalf of the brother-husband. When my mother is at the shop, she irons the clothes that have been tried on, arranges them as if they were brand new, and cannot stand any small spot or crease, a missing button or a hole. She readjusts, mends, dyes, and, better yet, she produces new outfits with her own hands from the good pieces taken from worn items. Her fingers, like a fairy's hands, transform pumpkins into royal carriages, and it doesn't surprise me later on when I find my own fingers always hungering to touch, knead, and recreate shapes.

My mother is involved with her preaching or Bible studies as before, but she does not impose them on me. I take advantage of this to write everything that comes into my head, a kind of automatic writing that I do without attention to rules or laws, without seeking mastery or aesthetics, simply putting down as faithfully as possible my sensations and feelings, no matter how chaotic they might seem. At night I read her some passages while we prepare food together for the next day.

When it is my turn to be in the shop, I use the time to put what I have learned about advertising into practice, connecting with the clientele as much as possible, which rapidly brings us a loyal and diverse patronage.

This is how we collect a tidy little sum of "clean savings" and manage to retain a lawyer for my stepfather's defense. Although we both know that the accusations brought against him are true, my mother is eager to believe in his innocence, as if her faith and confidence could transform her guilty spouse.

"Do you know the importance of what we call 'names of bravery' in our tradition?" she asks me, when I have too overtly shown surprise at her obstinate "belief in her man."

"I don't see where you're going with that," I reply, confused.

"When you call your child 'Mountain Lion' or 'Dry Seasons' Lightning' to celebrate his nobility or fearlessness, you don't do it because you think he's really like that, do you, but because you wish he may become that way."

"Yes, but . . . I still don't understand what you're trying to tell me: We weren't talking about children, but about your husband, who has been convicted of unscrupulous acts."

"First of all, my girl, men never grow up. Even when he's very old, your man will often remind you that he's still a child. So you must always keep that in mind if you want to live with him until the end of your days, and you must take it into account so that you will be able to love him over and over again. I lost your father because I didn't understand that soon enough. But let's get back to names of bravery. Giving a child a brave name means declaring love and respect for him, but more than that, faith and confidence in him. For if someone has no confidence in you, you owe him nothing. When my husband comes out of prison, what I would like is for him to be convinced that my trust in him never left me for a single moment. I don't want this for what's past, but for the future, so that he has a name of bravery to cling to, and can believe in the possibility of a new innocence."

"I understand, Mama, but I'm afraid it's this lack of blame, this false trust, that encourages impunity and supports our men in their refusal to look themselves in the face and question themselves."

"It's not a question of encouraging impunity, my daughter, but of always allowing belief in redemption and rebirth."

"Monsters are reborn, too, Mama; but I hope I'm wrong. And I promise you that I'll do everything in my power to release your husband from his twenty years' sentence. I hope he'll get out as quickly as possible so that we have time to look truth in the eye together."

Those few months spent with my mother, struggling along on only what we made ourselves, and for our own ideas and choices, were like a drink from the fountain of youth. I felt renewed, with a new self-confidence as a woman and a mother. Most of all, I was fearless and without contempt, without resentment toward either of the mothers Naja, or even toward my father or stepfather. I felt certain once again that fear made people malicious, and that they needed compassion rather than condemnation. I had my stolen childhood back and I felt full of dreams and momentum. In addition, my creative choices had been reinforced, and it made me very happy to discuss those with my mother.

"Mama Naja, I want to tell you something that is very important to me before I go to Mfoundi to take the needed steps to get your husband out of prison. I now know, with greater certainty than before, my future path, and if it should inevitably lead to disgrace then I was born for disgrace. It is my destiny but, fortunately for me, also my choice: All that I have to do I will do through artistic creation, and I would be so happy if you could accept me that way. . . ."

"Do you still doubt that? Didn't you accept me with my crazy affiliations? Of course, there will always be things we disagree about, and that is as it should be. Be yourself and be happy, my daughter. I love you."

MOVEMENT TWELVE

44

Three years after leaving Mfoundi and my friends Lorrent and Hemmil, I am back there once again, filled with apprehension but with new hope as well. I arrive in a new state of mind and with very clear plans concerning my professional and family life. I am here to organize my first concert with songs I wrote—in the end I can't give up singing—and submit my first set of lyrics to a national publisher to get at least one opinion, as well as to meet individuals who are likely to help my mother and me with my stepfather's case.

I immediately go to the Copyright Society and deposit copies of everything I've written before setting out to find a concert hall. I have come here with you, Amanyun, my new friend who loves my poetry so much. You and I are almost inseparable.

We find a cute little studio and pay six months rent in advance to make sure we won't find ourselves on the street. Then we start job hunting so we can live with a minimum of dignity while we wait for our dreams to come true. Each day we cover many kilometers on foot to find work, each on her own, and we don't meet up again until noon or the end of the day to talk together about possible appointments together. Between looking for better professional opportunities and trying to make effective contacts to set my stepfather free, the appointments begin to pile up, and we're becoming veritable joggers.

While our efforts to free my stepfather from his hole will have no success for another three years, professional and personal movement comes quite rapidly: Amanyun, you immediately find a secretarial job, while I have to wait a bit longer, but achieve the ultimate solace of meeting the love of my life.

On that particular day we are forced to walk in the blazing sun. I feel as if my whole life is ebbing away in a steam of sweat that is bound to kill me; in my mind I am already back in the protective shade of our little studio, and my body walks on, driven only by the goal of getting to it. Mere survival instinct guides me between cars, bicycles, and other pedestrians equally crazed by their desire to find some shade, so that I don't notice that Amanyun has met someone and stopped.

I hear her voice far behind me, shouting my name, and I turn around, a ghost coming from a different world, bewildered and already drained by the thought of having to backtrack. She is motioning at me wildly to join her, her face expressing such pure delight that she no longer seems to feel the stifling heat that just moments before slowed down every reflex.

An equally delighted young man is touching her as if he can't believe his eyes. I join them reluctantly and stay off to one side, next to a streetlight in a pointless search for shelter. My friend is so wrapped up in the memories her reunion evokes that she doesn't even see me anymore.

"Enthusiasm is so wonderful! Magical enough to forget this oppressive heat, but I'm sure that it could be marvelous, divine in fact, if we let it bloom accompanied by a glass of fresh juice somewhere in the shade," another young man says to me with a comic look, vainly trying to find shelter under the same streetlight.

"Oh, excuse me!" the excited young man says to his friend. "I almost forgot about you, and myself as well, so that I didn't even introduce Amanyun, my childhood friend, to you. . . . This is my friend and classmate at the university, Albass."

"Pleased to meet you, Amanyun. But please, don't start introducing my streetlight partner until we're away from this oven, for I can tell already that I won't want to forget her name for anything in the world." Our "comedian" goes on looking at me with his slanting eyes, so full of mischief that it makes me oddly uncomfortable.

"Right. Well, let's head for the Red Donkey, then," Amanyun says, taking me by the hand, wild with joy, and pulling me along like a recalcitrant mule.

As we go to the bar, my thoughts are registering nothing around me. They are preoccupied only with the sensation provoked by that slanted gaze, which I could swear I've seen somewhere before, though I can't for the life of me remember where. My thoughts review my short life three times over without managing to find the slightest reference point. And yet, the less I remember the more the feeling of déjà vu increases, exasperating me.

Mother Dora once told me that the average woman in the milieu we live in had about two hundred love encounters. Ouch! In my short life, where the record doesn't even add up to the number of fingers on one hand—and that already seems extraordinary to me—surely I haven't reached a point where I can't recall who has been with me! Why am I so plagued by the feeling of having already "lived" with this strange character? I say a quick prayer, asking to be spared from reaching the numbers Mother Dora mentioned, lest I get lost in an appalling mess.

Once the fruit juice is served, Amanyun makes the introductions: "Bobitang, my best friend. We were in the same class from sixth through ninth grade and then, unfortunately, we lost touch. What a thrill to find him here, as if we had seen each other only yesterday! Bobitang, this is Halla Njokè, a dear friend, a sister, but my idol as well; she is a poet and a great artist."

"That's exactly what I've been telling myself ever since I laid eyes on her," the forward young man retorts. "Poetry, poetic, artistic—and words began to fail me, until I found the most fitting one yet: This is a goddess, and I—I am no longer Albass! From here on in I am a true Albatross, meant to laud her gracious divinity to the greatest heights. At your service, divine Halla!"

"I've never heard such nonsense before, Albass, but I'm delighted to see you again," I hear myself say.

"Oh, you already know each other," Bobitang exclaims. "Look at you!"

"In a previous life, long before I became such a 'Holy Joe' as I am now, I was her guardian angel, her savior, her guiding light. . . . Please, my friends, ask her to give me another chance and let me transport her to the summit of her life!"

"I bet those are lines from a play! When and where are you performing? I'll have to come and see you since you're so deeply involved in your rehearsals, you're obviously bound to be fabulous," I can't help saying with a laugh. He is very funny and emphatic, both in his postures and his voice, so that even Amanyun and her friend begin to applaud.

"You're quite right: he used to do theater at the seminary he just left, and when he's flustered he starts acting again to put up a good front because he's actually very shy; I can only ask you to forgive him. Though I do understand, my very dear friend, because your girlfriend here really is very mysterious."

And so we live through three days of comedy and farce, day and night until Monday morning, because we stay together without a break. They come to our studio with us, where we cook and eat together; and together we go to the market, the movies, and even to church on Sunday! We visit their apartment as well, read my poems, passages by Genet and Gide, material from their Black African literature courses, and much more. The first two nights we spend in our studio, they in my bed and Amanyun and I in hers. The last night we go to their studio, using the beds in the same way. The four of us listen to each other intently, soaking up these shared moments as if we've been thirsting for them all our lives and are afraid we would soon be deprived of them. The return to class on Monday is like an ax falling, and we all hold hands, not wanting to let go.

For two months we live this poetic and platonic dream before other feelings and desires emerge—two months in which the feelings of a previous connection grow stronger with each passing day. Although we speak of it often, neither Albass nor I can figure out when that might have been, as if our memories live in fear of something dreadful and so bury it ever deeper inside each of us. Therefore a certain embarrassment begins to develop. As long as the four of us are together, everything is perfectly fine, and we try to share all we've done during the day. As a way to review their studies, Bobitang and Albass take turns lecturing us, even mimicking their professors' voices. We tell them about the progress or results of the steps we're taking, relating details of our encounters and trying to imitate notable people we've met, as well. This playful way of doing things, inspired by Albass's quest for spontaneity, always creates an atmosphere of complete openness.

But as soon as Albass and I are alone together, a false modesty curbs the earlier spontaneity. I understand that our sexual desire is irresistibly awakening, and although practically nothing stands in our way, we aren't able to admit it. Why, then, can we no longer get a word out of our mouths or look each other in the face, and why can we not touch each other? Suddenly I decide not to sleep at their place again, and one night I even refuse to have them over to our place, which triggers the first clash ever between Amanyun and me.

"Will you just tell me what's wrong with this boy in your mind, or in both your minds? I can't tell what all the contradictory attractions and revulsions are for either of you, but I can tell you that it's really beginning to get on my nerves!"

"Nothing's wrong, I assure you—nothing in particular, anyway. It's just that we're sure we've met before, but where and under what circumstances? It's driving us crazy not to remember something that important. If it's true, then we must have been so bad together that our consciousness doesn't want to go back there, you see? And that thought is becoming more and more unbearable to me. So as long as I don't remember what happened before, I don't want this boy anywhere within one square foot of me, that's all!"

"That's a crazy story! Only people like you have problems like this."

"What do you mean 'people like me'? What am I like?"

"A little strange, you can't deny that! I wonder whether there isn't a bit of madness in you at times, if you're not possessed, if you're not perhaps a genie, squeezed inside the body of someone you once took over in a trance."

"Here we go again! That's what you think of me, too? But you tell anyone who'll listen that I'm your friend, your idol, and who knows what else. What game are you playing? Fine! Now that you know I'm abnormal, why not just join your normal friends and leave me alone?"

"You really are a genie: You even guessed what I was going to tell you. I really don't want to break with our friends because of your crazy whims, when we get along so well together. Besides, it's Christmas vacation, and I don't feel like hanging around here with all that business about your concert. So I'm going to leave you alone and go away with them. When we get back I'll move in with them. If you're more comfortable here, good for you! If not, you'll know where to find us."

Strangely enough, I feel relieved to be alone, facing myself, facing my memories but also my challenges, which are already on the backburner. Having all my time to myself again, I find a hall within ten days and schedule my concert, then start rehearsing with three musicians. I even organize a real publicity plan for the event, going around to meet journalists and broadcasters in person, and I find a sponsor. During one broadcast I also meet the director of a local weekly, who suggests I write some short articles on cultural events for a nice fee. Under my present circumstances, without any resources, this is a windfall. I'm beginning to believe that solitude is lucky for me, and so I'm not overjoyed when Albass shows up at my door one evening. I clam up right away, determined not to let anything from my past get in the way again.

"I can tell I'm bothering you, I'm not welcome, and you didn't expect to see me. Yet, surely you must have known it couldn't end this way, and we have to talk."

"I don't understand what you're talking about, not ending this way. We didn't start anything, had no plans together—not as far as I know, anyway. So what are you talking about?"

"The two of us, then and in the future."

"I'm not available for long discussions right now. I have to work hard to deserve the professional opportunities I've been given and to guarantee my own future. But if you promise to keep it short, I'm perfectly willing to let you talk to me about your 'in the future,' since it seems to mean so much to you."

"Thank you! In fact, it does mean a lot to me to talk to you about all this, just so you will at least know it, but I promise not to waste your time. Can we go in or would you prefer going to a public place?"

"Let's go in. We're here already, and it will save time."

I don't know why, but I'm annoyed. I have the distinct feeling that my destiny is once again going off on its own—that it is about to show me, or even impose on me, a new direction, and, again, I really want to say no and create a different path. . . .

Despite everything, I take the time to offer my guest some water, but he refuses. "No thanks, I'm liable to hold everything back again. It's better that on an open one-way road the passengers keep moving along," he says, trying in vain to look funny again.

"Fine, I'm listening. . . ."

"You see, if I don't talk about it with you, I'll be powerless for life. When I was in seminary, it happened that I met a girl one day, or rather one evening. And when I say 'met,' it is because I cannot find any other word, since I didn't really see her face or ask her name—and yet I possessed her brutally, and she was still a virgin."

"How so? You were afraid to tell her you loved her, and without finding out whether she might love you, too, you lay in ambush for her in the dark?"

"Don't laugh, please. I didn't know her. I was sitting quietly by myself in a corner of my friend's little house, waiting patiently for him to finish making love to his fiancée in his bedroom. That's when the girl came in and sat down beside me. I didn't even want to talk to her because she was extremely upset. But in the pale light of the storm lantern she seemed from one minute to the next to be transformed into a polymorphous genie, and aroused such desire in me that I couldn't resist speaking to her. I'd hardly said a word when she began to cry and, to console her, I foolishly took her into my arms. Then the devil himself grabbed hold of me, for there is no other explanation for the passionate attack I made on her—and so awkwardly, too, because it was the first time for me."

"Well, well, well—and then what happened?"

"Her sky blue skirt was all bloody, as if I'd slit her throat on top of it; my friend and his fiancée were looking at me as if I were a child killer caught in the act. And then? I don't know. I only saw her look for an instant as she left the little house, her skirt still steaming from the hot iron they used after washing it out. I'll never forget how much blood I caused her to lose, and she didn't even scream! I left the place with an enormous sense of shame that I can't get rid of. Even cloistered in my seminary for another four years, praying and begging heaven to forgive me, I couldn't find any peace. Clearly, if I couldn't even forgive myself, why should heaven forgive me? It occurred to me that I needed to see the girl again. If she could forgive me, then I might obtain absolution. So I went back to Wouri to look for her, but, alas, my friend's fiancée had died six months before, and he couldn't remember the name of the girl in question. He only remembered that his fiancée had once told him that her friend had a baby as a result of this affair, and that her father had beaten her to death. Did she survive? And the child? If not, then two people were dead because of me—all because I couldn't manage to control my first sexual encounter. Ever since then I've been stuck with the terrible feeling that I'm a brute or worse. I wonder if my next sexual act will unleash another disaster, and I keep postponing it."

"Do you mean that in the past five years you've had no sex with anyone?"

"That's right, five years to the day, and that's why it's so important for me to talk to someone about it today, especially to you."

"Why especially to me?"

"Because every time I'm with you I have the same mad desire I felt that famous night, and it goes right to my head again. And if I didn't come up with any ploy to stay away from you, I'm afraid I would jump you the way I did that night to that poor little girl. She was so alluring, although she was still a child, something I obviously didn't take time to recognize. It's important to me that you understand the reasons for my discomfort, and I'm afraid you'll think I don't care for you. But . . . how do you know it's been five years since this happened to me? I didn't tell you that before, did I?"

"Because it's five years to the day that I left a little room, my blue skirt steaming from a hot iron, after glancing briefly at a boy whom I knew nothing about, not even his name, although I'd just slept with him, and felt my belly should never be penetrated by anyone else ever again. I never wanted to have to make love again with any other man after that, for the rest of my life. All I remember is that he, too, was wearing sky blue, a sweater, and that the detail of the matching color has come back to my mind more than once."

"So it was you? But . . . but . . ." he keeps stammering.

"So it was you?" I say, equally stunned. "Why keep silent all this time, though? I wasn't angry with you, you know; it was my own fault. I was the one who instigated it all."

"You think I recognized you and kept quiet? I've only just realized it. But now I understand the reason for your discomfort. There had to be a reason."

"If you think that I knew, you're wrong. I, too, am just now realizing it. I had a very skinny boy in my head; how could I've made the connection with the big man you've become? In any case, our spirits knew it all along and were giving the warning signal. Now everything is clear at last."

"Tell me quickly, is it true you had a child from this madness?"

"Oh yes! One day at a hospital I ran into my friend from that time and told her the consequences of our encounter. She promised me she'd tell her fiancé and ask him to give you the news. But she was already very sick, and now you tell me she died. I never saw her again, nor did her fiancé ever visit me, as she'd promised."

"And the child? What's become of our child?"

"He's in Wouri with my aunt."

"My God, my God, my God! How great and merciful you are!

I shall praise you forever more. . . . Thank you, a thousand times thank you! Thank you for sparing me the misfortune of losing the first child of my blood carried in a woman's belly, thank you, too, for returning my first love to me."

And he begins to weep like a beaten child. I join him on the floor, where he has collapsed, and we weep together, rubbing each other's heads soothingly, caressing and kissing, finally loving one another freely, tenderly, so tenderly, although it doesn't keep me from bleeding. A little scared at first, in the end he holds me very tightly and calls me his eternal virgin. When I wake up it is daylight, and he's already washed and dressed. Leaning over me with a loving look, he smiles and to give himself composure goes back to his role as a comedian, the one he is so fond of.

"Get up, Madame, the day of glory has arrived: We're going to find our child."

"How can we? Your courses are starting again soon, and I have to rehearse for my concert. "

"Our child cannot wait another day! What can wait are courses and rehearsals and all the rest, for as long as it may take. Hurry up, or we'll miss the train. . . ."

And so I'm back on a train headed for an obstinate and incontrovertible destiny. We appear at my mother's house accompanied by brothers and uncles of Albass, who immediately arrange for the traditional ritual of asking for a bride's hand in marriage. My brother represents my absent father and receives his share of the symbolic gifts. Two of my uncle's oldest sons represent the maternal family, and everything runs with the swiftness of youth.

Tata Roz hands our child to his father, her eyes and heart filled with tears born of conflicting emotions: On the one hand, she finds it hard to be separated from the little boy, who already sees her as his own mother; on the other hand, she is deeply moved and happy for him to be with his real father.

The whole thing lasts a week—a week that completely changed the planned course of my life as it was then. My first concert would not take place for another five years, and my first book would appear two years after that first concert. But writing did not abandon me, and for years it continued to be my only paid activity, thanks to the weekly journal in Mfoundi, which subsequently opened many other doors for me.

In spite of everything, I was afraid the rest of my destiny would turn dreary or mildly tormented, the way I'd seen the lives of my mothers Naja become. Thank God, it was quite the opposite. Albass entering my life through marriage became a true platform for the plans and synthesis of everything I had learned. The need to write and express myself and earn my living in a dignified way without being dependent, literally forced me to share in secret the academic studies of Albass and his friends. Albass opened the door to new knowledge offered by university-level classes—a knowledge of the worlds of literature and art as well as politics and social and urban environments. These studies allowed me to experience the relationship between inner, personal evolution and collective, global consciousness. Albass entering my life was the beginning of the apprenticeship of the only great love that God anticipates as life's "grace" for every individual, the kind of compensation that justifies all sorrow, all trials and tribulations. In this incarnation, there is no denying it, Albass's love was my grace, and there are no words to describe that form of grace. All we can attempt to describe are its effects or manifestations. Among the most eloquent manifestations in my memory are a tenderness and respect that defied every taboo in our backgrounds, causing a thousand gossips to say that we had used magic to bewitch each other! We each had an immense desire to keep the other from suffering, which forced me to hide my previous history with my father and gave me the strength to bear the weight of a secret that could only have sullied his heart. This same desire to keep the other one from suffering was to make him divorce me later on, one-sidedly, when he felt that he had become something that limited me—whom, he said, he had always dreamed of as an "eternal upward force." Did he know that, by liberating me this way, against my will, he was obeying my destiny, whose time had been accelerated, as Grand Madja used to say? The love of Albass was an immense support on the road to my hermit's shelter.

What else is there to say to demonstrate the impact of this love on my evolution and on the rest of my destiny? Oh yes! I should at least mention a few of the encounters that gravitated toward our home like planets around a sun, attracted by our love. These were encounters with such intellectually or spiritually highly evolved personalities as Master Minlon and his friends Singa and Hino— avatars among the angels who had fallen into the heart of torment. In my eyes they deserved to live the eternal life for reasons other than their impact on Albass and me and on our love. They truly sowed fine seed on our whole generation, and genuinely awakened stars. Sadly, no one has yet stood back far enough to pay them this homage. So, although I no longer have all the passion and enthusiasm for writing of my earlier days, and although my memory increasingly diminishes as I move toward my final dwelling place, I have promised myself to try to celebrate at least Professor Minlon, through the links of my own tottering memory, either through song or through tears.

For as time passed, many heroes fell on the fields of interminable and impossible battles against the unrelenting underdevelopment of neocolonialism. Both material and moral despair dehumanized entire populations over several generations. But in my eyes Minlon, even from the very depths of his fall, continued to be an authentic guiding star in the firmament of this continent's memory.

45

Master Minlon, a firm teacher as affectionate as a father,
A knowing guide, unbeatable, exemplary, the father of whom you
  dream,
Rich in experience tested in the West and the East,
And speaking naturally both to children and the great,
With the same love and the subtle humor only serenity provides.

You were the professor, the grand master of the Chair of Literatures at the University of Mfoundi, which both Albass and his friend Bobitang attended. Unbeknown to you, Amunyan and I became your students, reciting your courses by heart, imitating your accent by mimicking our companions. In your comparative literature course you taught Plato and Socrates, Pascal and Sartre or Camus, along with Senghor, Damas, or Cheikh Anta Diop. Albass said your courses were syntheses of anthropology, sociology, philosophy, theology, and mysticism, all rolled into one. Through your courses, our heads swallowed the world in time and space, and there was no end to our aspirations to be more concretely present, faced with all the human monuments you would describe and unveil before our unfettered imaginations. We were thus able to identify with Isis or Cleopatra without feeling foreign to Juliet or even Madame de Maintenon! But were there any heroes closer to us, heroes who were like us?

You sent us off in search of greater knowledge about our oral traditions, looking for an evening recital of the *mvet* epic, the Sunkang or Essingan rites right in Mfoundi or its suburbs and surrounding areas. We were exhilarated to find the heroes of our dreams in our own tales, and to compare them to those of other worlds.

We were Ngok Hikweng Manyim, Children of the Light, initiated and prepared to penetrate the dark belly of an obscurantist, the many-headed monster, and to destroy him from the inside, at the very core of darkness. We were that child genius who spent twenty-three months inside his mother's womb, was born with twelve teeth and already speaking, calling himself Ndjambè Ndjambè Libénguè and explaining to his mother—a widow weeping over his father, who had died because of a plot—that he was destined to restore the Ndjambè dynasty. We were the heroes of a new era, with new masters and new knowledge stolen from Hilolombi, the God of Gods, by the God Um, who stole fire for the love of humans, who were so in need of it!

In the field we discovered professional researchers, and through our meetings with them we became amateur researchers. In their company we dreamed of stealing knowledge for all those who, like myself, had been deprived of it through marginalization, impoverishment, disorganization, and the decadence of our societies.

Thanks to you, Professor Minlon, I went back more regularly to Grand Madja with my little family to amass additional information carefully. We always came back with a greater awareness of the gaps and inequities, but also of the wealth of the imagination from which we originated, a way to open ourselves to essential questions.

I used the time with Grand Madja to give her my wedding dress, still filled with my perfume, so that she could wear it on the day she left to reunite with our very noble and deceased husband. I sensed that this reunion was approaching, in the same way you can hear the Nséguék, disciples of Um, coming from a distance: far and nearby at the same time, impetuous and vibrant, but oh-so-sweetly enveloping, irresistible. Deep inside myself, I heard his inimitable but so very recognizable cry, Grand Pa Helly's cry to his beloved; it was the mighty sound of the disciples of Um, his own Nséguék sound, the chant of inner knowledge. . . .

On the night of farewell, I held Grand Madja's hands in mine as we lay back to back, communicating through our spines, her favorite position of late. She said to me: "It is possible we will not see each other again. Your Great-Aunt Kèl Lam has chosen you to follow me. I told her that I thought it was a bit early for you, but she answered that you will be the right age when the time comes, that you would have to be—tomorrow, even, if need be! So be brave, because they are going to speed up your time: We need you."

I did not understand what she meant by that, of course; all I knew was that she and I had both heard the call, and that we would not see each other again. So I had to make the most of the present moment. I let her velvet spirit invade me.

It was a journey of inner rhythms that makes you forget all past pain. You heal; you are more quickly restored; you become almost transcendent! I left her late that night, full of ideas for restoring our traditions but also with a mad desire for my husband, as if I had a premonition that I was going to lose him, and that loss was related to Grand Madja's final words to me.

● ● ●

Since Albass and I had been married and living with our child, spending our impassioned life with each other and with our culture, I had again experienced forms of parapsychology, but this time in a most disturbing way. For instance, lightning would always strike the house when I was alone during a storm; consequently, Albass wouldn't leave me by myself when there was a tempest. Even if he had a class, he hurried home to protect me. The Ngangans had said it was just a stage that would pass quickly, and they had tied an alloy of three different metals around my left ankle. But Albass continued to worry.

One particular day I felt a storm coming, and, because I knew that Albass had a very important class with Master Minlon, I decided to meet him there so he wouldn't feel obliged to be absent and risk not passing his final exams. A neighbor agreed to pick up our child from school and keep him until we returned. I sat down in the back of the amphitheater, near the door, to keep Albass from leaving unnecessarily should the urge come over him. I saw his head five rows in front of me and kept my eyes riveted on his neck, as if everything I heard were coming to me via his mind. Every now and then he'd suddenly turn around, as if he guessed my presence. I would then slip farther down in my seat so he wouldn't see me and lose his concentration.

The class had been announced as a very important one in preparing for the final exams, and was so eagerly awaited that, as soon as Master Minlon came into the room, adjusting his robe, no one gave any further thought to the impending storm.

Master Minlon seemed even more extraordinary to me than Bobitang and Albass had led me to expect. Although he was of medium height, when he spoke, summarizing the previous class, he seemed gigantic. His arms looked like the wings of an enormous bird in flight, and one felt the presence of great knowledge. Yet his style was simple and pure, almost paternal. I listened with my whole being and also through the ears of all his students, who seemed to be drinking in his words, especially Bobitang and my Albass—who sat with his head back, the way I imagined Christ's disciples on the Mount of Olives!

"You may be disappointed, my dear friends, for I am not going to give you the class intended for this afternoon," Master Minlon said after he finished his review. "I am very moved and would rather share this emotion in the hope it will better prepare you for the class, which we will make up later. I hope you don't mind too much. Well, then: I saw an extraordinary show at the Grand Abbia last night, a complete theatrical spectacle in which music, dance, and words—sometimes sung, sometimes chanted—were sublimely interpreted by the performers, one as magnificent as the next. There are days like this when magic inhabits the artists on the stage and transcendence actually occurs.

"I thought I was hearing a fusion of the great voices that so influenced my development and stimulated my youth—a strange mixture of Mahalia Jackson, Myriam Makeba, Jessye Norman, and Lakshmi Shankar, but also the quintessence of the voices of the Baka or Aka Pygmies, the Australian Aborigines, and the traditional Gregorian singers. In short, what we were hearing made me think of an era of great planetary fusion, of which I sometimes dream!

"But it should also be said that the play was extremely beautiful in itself. It was a kind of opera, written in collaboration by three musician-poets, one African, one Asian, and one from the South Sea Islands, who spend their lives between their own continents and Europe or the Americas. It truly reflected the evolution of music since the beginning of the century, and managed to outline the 'global' music of tomorrow, which will be fed by all the roots of former civilizations while turning constantly toward the future. It will be a music that opens the whole of humanity's consciousness toward more spiritual dimensions, without inordinately etherizing its carnal power.

"The composers had agreed to make the singers push themselves as far as they could go in vocal technique and mastery of the musical styles that had developed over the centuries.

"The story, concerning a caravan of travelers and its various encounters, was so eloquently told that we felt we were physically present in the old jam-packed Dakar-to-Bamako train. In the small boat in the third scene, which brought the assembly from Mopti to Timbuktu, it was as if our skins were covered with the mists of Lake Debo. We were the group of traditional artists of various African origins preaching purity of styles and roots, the only ones able to bear witness to the artistic mastery of a given people as the heritage of all humanity. Surrounded by professors, students, entrepreneurs, and cultural journalists from the caravan, we then found ourselves on the other side, the group of 'modern' artists, wishing to impose a mixing of all styles in order to offer a variety to 'broader markets,' to encourage greater consumption. As if we were there, we were living intensely the colorful moments of exchange in Goundam about thorny problems of spirituality as a link between the human and the divine, via memory, in astounding oratory jousts between two seated Tuareg dances. . . ."

When he finished his description, Professor Minlon told us that recounting this journey had reminded him of another, though much less poetic, one—his own work during the years in which he had tried to awaken in his students the questing flame that would permit each new experience lived to liberate its share of divine perception, by way of an appropriate corner of the memory. For, he reminded us, as we all know, "When memory goes looking for dead wood in the bush, it comes back only with the firewood of its choice." He deplored the fact that politicians were in the process of reducing those years to nothing, by devaluing knowledge; he said he dreaded the negative repercussions and the delays all this would certainly engender, not only for our continent but for all of humanity as well.

I was listening excitedly, wondering what was actually happening because I hadn't quite followed the specific process of the devaluation of knowledge. I was so happy in my little world without television. For me, and for all Albass's friends, the knowledge of our teachers had supreme value, and I could easily see that they were all just as surprised as I was by Professor Minlon's alarming speech.

Recognizing our dismay, Professor Minlon briskly drew our attention to the reprehensible direction that education was taking, lambasting the idea of consumerism, which the authorities were trying to impose and against which we needed to fight with all our power. Otherwise we would see our countries revert to situations worse than what they had experienced during colonialism, since, he said, "the enemy will only become more and more indefinable and nameless." He blamed the "political authorities, infantilized by false needs and even more harmful to the young than the colonial enemy had been!" He also blamed our "youth already so attracted to what is easy, and unconsciously serving those in power." His wrath started to bubble like rising yeast, and I had begun to worry when suddenly he calmed down and laughed uproariously at a vision we were not able to share.

"You know, my friends," he then said, "in an earlier period I stopped my Tibetan studies, which had seemed extremely instructive to me and which I had pursued with great diligence until the day when I read in one of my books that the Black race was still in the infant stage. My pride stung, I threw the book and the rest of the studies away, over my shoulder. Several years later, observing the behavior of the other peoples of the world, I began to wish that the Tibetans were right, that our people really were like children, with the flexibility and adaptability of childhood that makes it easier for them to forget and forgive. What would happen if we actually remembered every single thing we suffered? Yesterday, when I was thinking about certain things this continent has gone through and still goes through, all of which was very clearly revealed in last night's show, I felt good in my childlike skin, actually finding deep inside me the peace and pure happiness that simple beauty provides: "Yes, we're lucky to still have works like these—works of pure innocence shot through with wisdom in a way that only children know how to combine. May you, too, write works like these and perform them as well—and why not do it for people who have become stultified inside their heads and hearts as adults, like the ones who govern us, so that you can be as beneficial as dew on arid soil," he concluded. "Any questions?"

"Yes, Professor, if I may. . . ."

Albass recognized my voice and turned around abruptly, ready to rush over to me, but Bobitang held him back by his shirt. Not knowing what was going on, the professor watched him sit down again, in awkward silence. He turned to me: "Speak, Mademoiselle, although I don't think I've ever seen you in my classes before, have I?"

"That's true, Professor, I'm your student, but only . . . covertly. But I'm very interested in what you said about flight in the face of our individual journey through our own memory. Those who can afford the luxury of pretending to be amnesiacs have their history already written, preserved in sound, images, and microfilm, and in all sorts of versions: subjective, doctored, reexamined, and corrected, profane, esoteric, sacred, and many more. They can always go back into them when the moment is right to attest to their time on earth and their humanity. Whereas we—we haven't articulated our experience enough to permit ourselves any amnesia. And besides, shouldn't remembering be a constant battle for us?"

"Certainly, Mademoiselle! But the documents you mention have helped us so well to erase our tracks, even into our inner selves. . . ."

He briefly recalled the harmful effects of various religions, of autos-da-fé, whippings, and other physical and moral tortures that would make anyone forget his name; he spoke of brainwashing and forced assimilation that would never be recorded. He said we ought to persist in reinventing new reference points to remember and to help us stay connected to the material reality of the civilization that was running the world, and would undoubtedly continue to run it for a long time to come. It was a civilization to which we were already connected, in spite of ourselves, like a caboose, and we seemed doomed to play the role of the world's tail end *ad vitam aeternam*!

"We might have preferred to develop our spiritual faculties and place our actions on a different plane, who knows! The prevailing civilization inflicts its choices irrevocably, and we find ourselves hooked by force, obliged to live in a way we didn't wish for or conceive of, and one we certainly didn't choose," he lamented.

A long discussion followed, in which many expressed exasperation with Africa's contradictions, procrastinations, and slow progress. Checking his watch intermittently and trying to stay calm, Albass was fidgeting impatiently. Finally, Professor Minlon concluded: "I often catch myself praying for things to move along more quickly and disintegrate more rapidly. Only then can we hope for a rebirth, that mythic return to a golden age or the lost paradise mentioned in ancient texts. Alas, the time of the gods differs from human time, and so we have no choice but to be patient, to live and let even the monstrosities live. But look here, you have completely altered the order of my class and taken me in another direction, Mademoiselle! In fact, Mademoiselle . . . what was your name again?"

"Madame, Professor," Albass called out as he stood up. "May I introduce Halla Njokè Albass, my wife. She has taken us all by surprise, and I beg you to please excuse her. She is obsessively curious and talkative once her passion is unleashed. And I do believe that you have succeeded in doing just that."

"Congratulations, my dear Albass, you have a veritable sorceress here; and I would be deeply honored, Madame, if you would continue to take my classes . . . how did you phrase it again? Ah yes, 'covertly,' if there is no other way! Well, it's time to go, my friends, and I promise to stick more closely to the syllabus next time."

He came toward me and greeted me. All the students were crowding around us, and I could tell I was going to have to greet each one individually and chat with this one and that one, which was bound to take a lot of time. All at once I felt totally worn out. The professor rescued me in the nick of time when he suggested to my husband that he drop us off at home, for the sky was threatening and a fine rain was already falling, indicating that a harder rain was not far off.

That is how this leading figure of our university came to share our meal for the first of hundreds of subsequent times, either at our house, at his, or sometimes in other places—always with the same simplicity and warm, almost paternal affection that cast an impression of immutability and eternity, even as everything around us was falling apart at a more and more frenzied pace.

• • •

Those meals. . . .

Ah, those meals with Master Minlon—how enormously exhilarating they were! Hard to believe that for some people preparing a meal is torture! Grand Madja was right: It is not given to everyone to make work pleasurable. Chores are the things you do without any pleasure, and that truly is the lot of slaves.

On the other hand, my husband and I felt we were growing as we made these meals. We used a maximum of creativity and imagination to receive our master as his rank deserved. It meant a great

deal to us to consider each moment with him a rite, the beginning
of the end of an initiation; and our own modest means did not limit
us, because we would go to the Briqueterie.

The Briqueterie was the neighborhood where everything was
possible, and every African town has one—places where anything
can be found, at a price for every pocketbook. The Briqueterie's specialty was its gigantic stoves, always functioning, every day of the
month and throughout the year, so that everyone could have *soya*,
skewers with very spicy beef or fowl, at any hour of the day or night,
depending on his purse and taste, but always enough to eat his fill.
Kidney or liver, filet, ribs, tongue, feet, skin or tail; poultry, beef,
mutton, pork, or even game—all were thinly sliced, perfectly flavored and spiced, and then grilled. Albass and I took turns purchas-
ing *soya* each time we expected Master Minlon. We would prepare
it in our own way, improve the seasoning, and present it carefully in
banana leaves, on skewers, or in crab shells, and we served it with
roasted yams, fried or steamed plantains, rice or manioc sticks that
we also bought there.

Master Minlon marveled at all the varieties that loosened his
tongue, as he put it. Sometimes he would surprise us, arriving with
mountains of hot *soya* and a group of his friends to whom he had
bragged about our specialties, and then we all participated in the
spontaneous festivities. And, indeed, tongues would loosen. One
day there was an argument with Singa, Master Minlon's "politician
friend," as he liked to refer to him sarcastically. Indeed, having been
part of one of our particularly successful festive evenings, Minister
Singa expressed astonishment that one could live this well on such
limited means. He attacked his government's mismanagement,
"organized merely to share the cake with their buddies, plunging
the people into misery and loss of dignity, leaving them less than
crumbs to pick up." Master Minlon rose like a cobra and asked him
tersely: "What do you mean by 'such limited means'? Does 'means'
refer only to money? And because my friends spend little, you think
they have limited means? How do you evaluate their work, commitment, hospitality, and their creativity? You make me vomit, all of

you! What I would like to see happen someday is doing away with money altogether, finding different symbols, different representations of worth!"

46

No sooner said than done.

That very evening, we planned on inventing a new system with new symbols of worth and new ways of acquiring and trading.

That very evening we planned the obliteration of money.

A true "Worldwide Organization of Nations" was to propose and achieve the obliteration of money by way of a planetary referendum.

First we would burn all paper money.

The real paper money of every affluent and every impoverished nation.

The false paper money of corrupting and corrupted countries.

But would the pollution it caused not asphyxiate every creature with lungs living on earth?

Perhaps we should invent machines to reduce all paper money, true or false, along with all bureaucratic paper with the exception of books, to powder or paste, and recycle it into fertilizer and give it back to the soil.

We would organize a huge consciousness-raising campaign to limit the gridlock caused by too many machines. The human would be given more value, so that a solid part of human work would come back to human beings, and—oh, miracle—we would see lines of billions of people at work, like the Egyptians in the time of the Pharaohs, handing each other rocks to build pyramids, or like the Chinese

when they erected the Great Wall—men, women, and children working together again to construct projects for their own use.

We envisioned a multiracial crowd of every origin, some on the
machines, others beside or behind them, renewing eroded and poor
soil, seeding, creating nurseries, transplanting fruit trees, growing
flowers, in short recreating paradise on earth. It was a magnificent
moment of exhilaration and great love.

We took on the destruction of all metal money.

Billions of tons of coins in gold, silver, iron, bronze, or copper:
We would melt all this metal in ovens that would be transparent like
urns; and we'd do it in public, like the barbaric spectacles of old!

Alone or with their families, people would arrive with food and
drink and material for do-it-yourself projects. They would sit down
around the ovens, commenting, painting, sculpting, and laughing
loudly. There would be a "something for everyone," drawing more
people than ever before. Even pregnant women and new nursemaids
would bring their fretful babies to the transparent ovens, where the
melting metals would stimulate the imagination and calm the nerves
with the beauty of the colors and sounds. Photographers of every
type would have the time of their lives.

With the help of various graphics and scale models, specialized
orators would be invited to explain how other forms of exchange
could be manufactured from all these liquid metals. Very special coins
would be worn around the neck or wrist. Coins would be put on the
wrists of newborns, who would keep them on for the first seven years
of their lives. These coins would symbolize the importance that the
community attaches to them. These values would allow their parents,
or relatives responsible for orphans, to feed and care for them, protect
them, and teach them all that they should learn. In addition, every
child in its first seven years would have the right to tenderness and
protection, for which the parents would remain responsible. Their
only duty would be to allow the child to learn. Every adult would be
requested to see it as a sacred duty, not to be ignored, to care for any
child who wears this coin, without exception.

The second kind of coin is to be worn by all children from their seventh birthdays on, a day to be celebrated as a generational mile-stone. All seven year olds, dressed in their best finery and surround-ed by their parents and entourage of whatever sort, would solemnly receive the coin, having first gone through a kind of initiation. It would be explained to the children that they must gradually come to deserve the coin through community service. In addition to learn-ing, the children would then begin to serve the community.

Every seven years, children would learn to distinguish between what is beneficial and what is harmful. They would learn what is scientifically, materially, psychologically, or spiritually dangerous in itself and for the whole community, so that they would no longer act out of ignorance, but rather out of fully responsible choice. Passed on from generation to generation, the new traditions would guarantee the interest of all through personal evolution. The first forms of creativity everyone would need to develop would involve the invention of better living conditions for all, greater possibilities for opening up or broadening both individual and collective con-sciousness. Of course, the coin assigned to children at this age would provide them with the right to be nourished to their complete satis-faction, to be cared for and taught without needing to present any documentation, until the age of twenty-one.

On their twenty-first birthday, all would receive a third type of coin, with equal ceremony; but this time would be worn for the next series of five seven-year periods. The third coin would be magnetic and registered as a credit card, the dividends of the owner's actions going to the benefit of individuals and the society, depending on the vibration of the aura. This credit card would be good for all acquisi-tions, trips, important achievements, designs, investments, research, initiatives, and more. Obviously, in addition to food, the care and costs of a child's apprenticeship would be guaranteed by the earlier coins. A fourth type of coin, purple in color, would allow for the results of one's efforts to be reaped more calmly, at the time of "retirement," limiting duties to the relaying and sharing of knowl-edge and experience for the rest of one's life.

For weeks on end, specialists would present and explain various models so that everyone could truly understand the new lifestyle about to be launched, and how to make it last throughout each person's lifetime. In this way, everyone would clearly have the same opportunities for at least the first twenty-one years. Any lingering differences would no longer flow from the inequalities that have dominated human life for millennia, but only from innate differences, not those imposed by administrations or politicians.

That same night, we also decided to put an end to false needs and values, if only in our dreams. We decided to destroy all toys.

We would take the tons of dreadful teddy bears with synthetic fur that invade homes, fill up trashcans, and saturate the earth, unable to absorb them; the mountains of little cars, dinosaurs, toy guns, monsters, and other metal or plastic "deadly weapons" that have emerged from the imagination of derailed minds, forced to invent whatever would sell, just to survive; all the toys of useless consumerism, damaging children by numbing and totally alienating them. We would pile them up, crush them, and turn them into a material as hard as steel, ready to be delivered in blocks like cement bricks, to be used for new buildings.

"Then, we must destroy all plastic. The little jet-black bags that have become walls and roofs in the shantytowns! The black bags that cover the bodies of millions of daily casualties, black bags, garbage bags, mysterious contraband bags! Multicolored wrapping bags, bags full of written words, the blue bags buried in the ground that keep plants from coming up again, baggies in every color caught on electric poles, trees, and shrubs in cities and villages, looking like vultures, scavengers, or other birds of prey.

"And, last but not least, we must destroy all weapons. The tons of scrap iron ready to blow up the world, the antipersonnel mines that mutilate the globe—human stupidity exploding in the faces of children!"

Ah, our discussions, our constant dreams, to be made reality according to our own opening up, our evolution. There was no problem for which our dreams didn't find a solution, no evil without a remedy, at least in the world of dreams.

We stand there together, in the living room or the courtyard, before or
*   after our ritual meals. . . .*
Not a dream we didn't share. Dreaming of values. . . .
The value of things, moments, and beings. . . .
Our life, an active dream we were building like a temple
With the fervor of our faith and the simple strength of our spirit!

• • •

Sometimes Professor Minlon managed to make us feel we were
playing such an important role for our country that we began to take
ourselves seriously. One particular evening, he spoke to his friend
Singa the politician as if to explain or justify himself.

"Since I've been coming to the Albass home I keep dreaming of
a new world. I don't know if it's in the spices Halla uses or in their
way of living together, but as soon as I'm with them or think about
them, something pushes me irresistibly toward different aspirations
or keeps me from burying my dreams as, I think, I was about to do
under the pressure of your government. Thanks to the two of them,
I feel I will die standing, shouting at oppression, proclaiming our
shared refusal to live in inner poverty. This I owe to them, and I
won't stop bearing witness to it, anywhere and at any time it may be
needed. . . ."

As a result, my husband got it into his head that our love was
the vessel of a great destiny. We were in service to rebirth. Almost
his entire class at the university felt invested in the mission, literally creating a movement. Together with the whole group, we
were becoming actual disciples of a master, whose great gift awakened an unquenchable thirst in us for ever greater knowledge and
action.

Certainly, we suspected that our dreams might not please everyone, but we didn't think we sounded like revolutionaries, more dangerous than men of arms. For us these were just dreams we tried to
formulate by writing poems or composing songs, to feel more positive and more valuable to those around us. We were hoping, in this

way, to influence the general development of our society—to change things not only in our own lives, but in the life of the world. Regrettably, we didn't suspect how much the rot had already eaten away— so much that the absurd had become the rule of life, specifically where the relationship of people to money was concerned.

Money—that colossal response to every exchange.
The most material spiritual symbol ever invented,
Its symbolic value completely distorted.

By now, we had the impression that money had to be amassed in equal quantity to the weight of the desired object. Would buying a house mean you had to find a container of money at least as large? People were stuffing their mattresses with it, piling it up in safes built into walls, filling chests they buried in the ground, though it did not guarantee them any dignity.

The president of one African republic even took the time to put his personal stamp in indelible ink on several hundred million American dollars—that is to say, half of his country's budget! Tons of money that could have fed, cared for, and taught millions of individuals who were gradually sinking into disaster were found heaped up in chests that followed him into exile. "After me, chaos," he liked to say.

When the deposed dictator fell seriously ill, members of his own entourage swiped several chests each and got away. Some were caught and killed. Others fled with their cursed chests into the virgin forest, where they buried them. When these thieves were finally able to open the supposedly impenetrable locks with acid, they found the stamped bills, which had been rendered totally useless. Until the end of the century, these people could still be found in various world capitals, still trying to find a specialist who might literally "clean" these stacks of money, erase the damned ink from the bills for which they had sold their souls.

Of course, these were only folkloric African flourishes, not comparable to the feats performed by cartels of thinking minds in the West, which in a matter of seconds seize the world's money with a few clicks on a computer keyboard.

Nevertheless, I wondered whether, with all that money, they were any happier, any closer to God. No? So?

So. . . .

Our evenings certainly were festive, but they were celebrations that ended in nights of anxious and feverish dreams rather than in the sleep of oblivion. Some nights Master Minlon literally crushed our naive enthusiasm by shoving our noses into the fact that our situation stood at a dead end. We could see no signs of progress; we no longer knew on whom we could count. As it was, the powerlessness of African politicians who were heads of state was increasingly deplorable, and all the more so because our leader was one of them. For simple budding poets like us, the objectives diminished with every passing day because of the population's growing illiteracy. As a result, our infrequent publications, which might have tweaked their consciousness, seemed very ineffective indeed, and doomed to failure.

One evening the party ended in a mournful mood, and Master Minlon's voice trickled away like a funereal chant. "When you come to power, your hands are already tied.

"Pacts have been signed by uneducated, if not totally illiterate, predecessors.

"The interests of the most powerful require unbelievable conjuring tricks.

"Corruption comes through bogus needs, and you are stuck in it up to your ears.

"Financially speaking, they have you, with money that isn't yours.

"Blackmail, pressures, partial satisfaction of your new desires, promises. . . .

"Philosophically and ideologically speaking, the traditional ideas have been so cheapened that it occurs to nobody to look to them for a solution to our problems, even though you and I know that, sooner or later, those ideas are the only way out!

"Spiritually speaking, you come from a race that has not had any 'Revelation.'

"You will not be saved either by your culture or the color of your skin.

"Your ancestors have never known any 'True God.'

"Your redemption depends on revelations and saviors that hail from elsewhere.

"So, verily I say unto you, if Christ himself came back to earth today and wanted to help Africa out of its hole via politics, he would not even have a cross on which to be crucified, but would be shamefully stoned instead, like any adulter of his own era! And I ask you, who would want to wear common stones in his memory?

"How else, then, can you feel like the son of God except by going 'undercover'?

"How can you convince anyone to be the creator of his own destiny and responsible for it?

"Merely with our words and scribbles, without being thought of as mad, as a traitor, or anything else equally humiliating—without dying more than once?

"All of this to tell you, children, that for now, shockingly, it can still cost you your lives if you want to offer ideas that allow Africans to believe in themselves, through avenues liable to liberate them from the stranglehold of those currently in power! If I am lying, take a hard look at me, and you will see what will befall me, for I still intend to keep trying, to speak up loud and clear anywhere there's a need, even if no one will publish me. . . ."

• • •

We did, indeed, witness how those in power plotted against these "pseudo-masters of knowledge, who set fire to the minds of the young, just to strengthen their hold over them and better negotiate their privileges," as the communiqué stated that dismissed every professor from his academic position, requesting that his car be turned in and the house assigned to him be vacated within forty-eight hours. . . .

And you, who so wanted human worth not to have any price:
The politicians put a price on your head,
Offered a job to anyone who would humiliate you,
An endowment for anyone who would ensnare you and drag you toward
    immoral or illegal actions.
And plenty of people came running to destroy you. . . .
You resisted so fiercely that you lapsed straight into indigence, and we
    were outraged!
In your fury, you decided to become a merchant: They ruined you.
You decided to become a parliamentarian: They shouted you down and
    poisoned your life.

Nothing had any value anymore except money, and everyone ran after it like a donkey after a carrot on a stick attached to its head, while poverty came pelting down ever harder on the whole world, and human beings became rabid beasts again, senselessly tearing each other to pieces in civil wars and fratricide.

Yes, Master Minlon and all you intellectuals like him, we witnessed the intolerable humiliations inflicted on you, and the youth who idolized you lost their desire to learn. Under our thunderstruck gaze, knowledge became a symbol of futile efforts and a source of pointless frustration, so that only some colorless functionaries and a few vile careerist politicians emerged from our entire generation, which had been so hungry for knowledge and so creative in our dreams of new worlds. The few unrepentant souls were condemned often to a lifelong exile.

It was then that a string of reproaches and regrets galloped through my head like an incoherent old tune, and deprived me of all desire. A despairing old refrain from my Aunt Roz inspired me to write this song:

For want of any great faith,
We have wasted a great deal of time,
And here is our bygone generation.

We wrestle and tussle;
Misery brings the generation back again.
We race and compete;
There is no recourse left.
We buy and resell;
Bankruptcy waits in the wings.
Alcohol bonds us like glue,
As do cigarettes and cigars.
Fat joints undo us;
Misery has no solution.
We eat, we drink, we go to bed, we sleep,
And wake up at the door of death.
On the horizon, only six of one, a half dozen of the other;
Here and now, always and everywhere, more of the same.
Please let me have one great dream, just one more,
Or else offer me an alternative, at least,
Gbagbo, Zadi, the system makes us desperate and bogs us down, oh dear!
Have our masters really fallen permanently silent?
Must sorcery decimate each chosen figure?
What do our genies say, the righters of wrongs, Ngué Ndjông and Oum
    Inkora Intong?

My heart was leading me astray, and I had the impression that
everything I did was foolish.

"Catch me before I go insane," I heard myself shriek, though no
sound would come from my hopelessly clogged throat. . . .

And so I fled!

• • •

Yes, I fled!

What else can you call the deliberate wish to fade away, to vanish from your own sight—in other words, to withdraw because you
don't want to go forward any longer? To refuse the changes and the
successive moments of which eternity is made? Believing, for example, that you have everything you want, that you want nothing else,

or that you are so miserable it cannot possibly get worse, you're convinced any further effort is pointless. Is that not the same as the wish for life to stop moving, to die, to flee?

On the one hand, I was much too fond of my little home, my little bit of personal happiness, which I didn't want to lose for anything in the world. On the other hand, I was angry with all my friends, Albass included, and with myself for not having done anything more for our dear fallen masters. I felt we had surrendered, that we had already been crushed like yam stalks without stakes; and an untenable sensation of failure—or worse, of betrayal—was tugging at my insides.

No one in our group spoke of dreams anymore. No one wrote poems anymore, or organized "nights of imaginings," as we had christened our meals. The team stopped all its research in the oral traditions, which had always driven us to question ourselves. Progress now only implied an unimportant administrative job one could pursue, some political person one could bribe for a less punitive assignment. All our words and gestures seemed insipid and ineffective, and to me it was as if a closing parenthesis had been placed behind the progress we had so coveted, as if we had been devoured by a multiheaded monster and been turned into zombies by its saliva.

The most depressing thing was that no one spoke about it, no one complained about anything at all. We were all doing our best to live as if nothing had happened, hauling our existential anguish around in muffled silence. Women retreated imperceptibly into an artificial quest for luxury: They tried to dress more expensively, show off their cars, their new complexions flogged with photographic developer, chemical whiteners, even if it meant arranging for secret and devious little trades to obtain them. Men grew bigger bellies because of the thousands of types of beer they tried, and equipped themselves needlessly with pipes and cigars as large as their sex organs. We found ourselves in a kind of indescribable mire, all of us disgusted with ourselves and yet unable to admit it.

I fell ill without quite knowing what was wrong, and had to go through several operations in which I lost important organs, never understanding why each surgery caused more harm than the previous one; in the end, they had to evacuate me to the West. And so, like a coward, I departed on a stretcher, leaving behind everything that was dear to me; I left for an exile of no return and without any farewell.

But as you, Grand Madja, used to say: "The secret of the eternity of life is that everything has a beginning and an end! Everything must die to be reborn."

MOVEMENT THIRTEEN

47

The morning that I read Auntie Roz these notes from my memory's wanderings, riddled with holes though they were, tears suddenly began to flow from her still mischievous eyes. How strange to see her so shattered—as if she were an awkward psychic, who had dropped her mask during a sacred ceremony. I took her in my arms, and one of Grand Madja's old lullabies began to well up from my throat, cautiously, as if I were afraid to be indiscreet.

Tears never fill a bottle,
Or else I would have a trunk full of bottles filled with tears.
I have wept so much over being caught off guard,
Wept so much over seeing betrayal on the face of the beloved,
That my trunk should be full of bottles filled with tears.
Alas, tears never fill a bottle.

"Oh my daughter, my dearest niece, how deeply you have touched me! How you have pierced me by bringing it all back to me! But then, it couldn't have been otherwise—I was but the mold into which you were to be poured; I was but a guinea pig for your future experiences. All you did was meet the people who had put their mark on me before. All you did was take the path I had to clear, since there weren't millions of individuals who had new dreams and struggled in a different way. In my time, too, everyone who made progress, teetering on slopes like these, inevitably encountered the same monsters, the same angels. Ah! Dora, my friend Dora, after all you suffered, in seeking redemption you spread your love to children heading for trouble, and were also able to take care of my niece!"

I hardly dared to breathe, afraid to break the stream of trust that had opened up. Auntie Roz stretched, turned her back to me to cuddle up closer against me, and kept talking, almost to herself.

"Just like you and your friend Amanyun, Dora and I ran away to Wouri, determined to serve the country side by side with Mpôdôl. 'To the devil with marriage and the swarms of children that will only increase the number of sheep in the colonist's herd,' we used to say at the time. True, we were not among those first women to be educated then, not having had a chance to go to school, but we wanted to be among the 'First Female Resisters to lead the Political Battle for the Liberation of the Country,' at least. Women's patriotism would be the footing for the new nation, as advocated by Mpôdôl, and it seduced us more than the love of a man and the desire to have a family. Besides, what man of the time and milieu in which we lived could possibly have awakened the same kind of enthusiasm in us? Our thirst for the absolute made us more demanding, while our men were too busy trying to ape the White man! Feeble shadows or pale copies that they were, they had become invisible to our eyes. You see, it was an extraordinary period: Everything was new. Anyone who wanted to could be first at something: the first to be taught, the first to be an executive, prime minister, and even the first to be a traitor to his fatherland—the possiblities were there!"

"And you and Mother Dora, did you become the first free women activists, unencumbered by husbands and children, and utterly devoted to the struggle for independence?" I couldn't help but ask.

"Yes. The 'Amazons of Modern Time' is what Mpôdôl himself named us. Ah, what an honor, what happiness! And so when he had to go underground, it seemed impossible for us not to follow him and at least to serve as his ears, mouth, and third eye—in short, to be his link to the outside world. You quickly had to learn languages, guile, secretiveness, and lots of other things, because it could save your life. So the mothers and aunts called us to tell us that time would be speeding up for us. It's a phrase you, too, have heard. . . ."

"Yes, but what does it actually mean?"

"Didn't I tell you we've had the same life? So why are you asking me questions again?"

She turned around and looked at me, her face wet with tears, then finally smiled as she wiped her eyes to chase away the burdensome shadows.

"Oh, I know why you don't understand 'the speeding up of time'; you have been blessed by the gods; you already were a mother when you were chosen. . . . A woman should always hurry to have her children while she's still young and innocent. You never know what will happen later. Dora and I, having been as good as gold, were caught up in other things before becoming mothers, and we had plenty of time to question ourselves. When they tell a young woman that 'time will speed up' for her, it means she'll have to undergo an initiation before her time, which normally wouldn't occur until after menopause, when she can't have children anymore. You know what that does to you when you're twenty? You immediately want to have everything that is forbidden, even that which you had willingly refused. It was then that we fell in love, longed to have children, wanted to make a home like everyone else—but no! Anyway, you know what it is, you who have escaped death so many times through your sheer obstinancy in wanting another child to strengthen your home, although you could do nothing other than lose it!

"It is true that my beautiful love physically lasted only nine years, the ultimate number prescribed by our initiations. But these nine years were so intense that they gave us a feeling of eternity that has never left us, even though our communal life came to a chaste close, like a final parenthesis, as if to help me face the more solitary quest that seemed to impose itself on me, and guide me to a kind of hermit's shelter that in the end was transformed into an exodus, an exile. . . ."

"But at least you had that beautiful love. You have been a complete woman, fully happy, for nine full years. What more can you ask for in life? In the end you've had everything, just as your grandfather predicted: all things female, all things male! While we . . . and especially my poor Dora . . ."

Her voice shook a little, and she got up, as if she were annoyed that she couldn't remain as calm as she wanted to be. I used the time to serve her some water, then brought the glass back to the kitchen so she could pull herself together, but she took my hand and followed me, as if afraid to be by herself. It was the first time she showed her age: her spine compressed, her shoulders hunched as if she were very cold, which gave her a slight hump and made her look exhausted. Ah, what a rough time she must have had, like all my aunts Roz. . . .

Auntie Roz took me to the back of the garden, between the roots of the great rubber tree that had emerged from the ground like rocks. Leaning her back against the tree in Grand Pa Helly's favorite position, she reminded me of him. I thought the flow had dried up for today, for it didn't look as if Auntie wished to keep going. She scratched at the roots, picked some grass and shredded it between nervous fingers, then threw it to the wind like seeds of her tattered story. All of a sudden, she straightened up, took my head in her hands, and, looking me straight in the eye as if she were facing facts that had always escaped her before, she said: "Other than your childhood loves, such as Yèrè and your former husband, do you know that all the mature men in your story have also crossed my life in one way or another? Do you know that your Uncle Kon, the murdered prefect, was the great love of my friend Dora, who was expecting his child and followed him everywhere, even to that monster Bitchokè, where he was cravenly assassinated, and no one will ever know by whom? Dora was in such shock that she had a miscarriage. Do you think he died just so she wouldn't have the baby, or did she miscarry so she wouldn't have to know what it was to be a complete woman, because it had been decided one day that her 'time as a woman had to be speeded up' and made to serve the Bassa cause?"

"Auntie Roz, you're frightening. How can you say such things? And what might that remarkable cause be, that we've never even seen? Where are the Bassa today?"

"Who knows! Still, those are questions we can't help but ask, regarding the kind of iron grip of solitude that hounded us all, forcing us to abandon everyone we loved or to watch them die violently before our eyes! Do you know that Dora managed to find funds for a young man who was hanging around her to study in Europe because she was afraid she'd fall in love with him, just to have him move away from her and so protect him from what she now thought was a bad fate, if not a downright curse? That was Ndiffo. She was irresistibly attracted to him and decided to channel the impulse by making him into a son instead. When he returned to this country later on, she began to love him by proxy, and put him in contact with every girl in whom he showed even the slightest interest. She loved him through you, I tell you, for she literally threw him into your arms by continuously bragging to him about your qualities. When she told me this later, I didn't know it was you. . . ."

"Really, Auntie, you know an awful lot about me! And now you tell me all these things about Mother Dora. But when do I get to hear something about you?"

"Ah, me—you know, it's better to spare you my epic tale. All you need to know in the end is that I had to give up on Minlon so that he could be treated for some mysterious disease that was eating him and about to sweep him off in broad daylight. Otherwise he wouldn't have been able to finish his studies, and that would have been a terrible waste, don't you agree?"

"You're absolutely right! It would have been an unthinkable disaster, for who else would have sown the little hope in us that keeps on lighting a few sparks here and there for a possible future? Truly, Auntie, your sacrifice was worthwhile, as I see it. But then what happened?"

"And then? Well, in the end we forgot each other, time passed, and we recognized we had to love in a different way, and only to the extent of our own strength, faith, and creativity. Still, I had to leave; I don't think I could have resisted if I had stayed there. . . ."

"Actually, Auntie Roz, you should each have been declared a Lôs! Did anyone ever hear of a female Lôs? Still, that is what you were, even if it wasn't said."

"No, we weren't Lôs. The function of a Lôs is not bestowed upon you; you become one by yourself. We were given a mission. They decided to sacrifice us, sacrifice a large part of ourselves, the female part of our creativity."

"But you ran away yourselves to find greater exhilaration, and activities that involved the world more than a mere household could! The fact that you were selected was just an effect, while the cause came from your own aspirations and your own choice! That is being a Lôs—forcing nature and destiny. In the end, you have also succeeded, and I'm not the only one blessed by the gods!"

"Perhaps, but not as much as you. I didn't find my Minlon again! I didn't smell his scent or hear him whisper in my ear again. I never had those incredible shivers that ran along my skin, flooded his, and then came back to me like the backwash of a wave at high tide. We didn't embrace each other again, to form a lightning rod against the thunderbolts of stupidity that subsequently wreaked such havoc and caused a tidal wave across the entire continent! Whole generations sacrificed . . . every value flouted . . . whole fields of knowledge forgotten, forever lost! What purpose did we serve? Sometimes I tell myself that if I had at least held on to my Minlon, if I'd married him, he might have died but done so happily in my arms! Instead they killed him through despair, exhaustion, and bitterness . . . and he departed all alone!"

48

Auntie Roz had been forced into exile and drained by no longer being allowed to dream. It was here in Laguna, where I arrived as an exile ten years later, that I came to know her. My mother Naja had accepted my invitation to visit me here and, still the good Christian, she was looking for information on places of worship and practicing Christians when someone told her about Auntie Roz. As soon as she heard the name she wouldn't stop looking for the woman, whom she said she hadn't seen in at least twenty years. In order to find her, she let everyone know, including the national radio.

Their reunion was a geyser of emotions, a river where memory went on an eclectic fishing trip. They talked for hours on end, laughing and crying, twittering like birds or whispering like naughty little girls. Why didn't I think of listening to them, of recording them? No doubt because I wasn't aware of what they would awaken in me later on, and therefore I wasn't ready to connect to their stories.

My mother had only just made a fresh start when she lost her husband. Although he had come out of prison with all the names of bravery, faith, and trust she had invested in him, he couldn't prevent himself from showing his true face: that of a common, petty, run-of-the-mill man. God might have spared her the cruelty of such a truth, but no—the women of my clan will never feed on illusions. Lucidity will always cling to their skin, like leprosy, like the traces of an illness brought on by breaking a taboo, incest, or a criminal disease. The women of my clan are condemned to see every truth for what it is and bluntly contemplate the dark side of the gods! He went away, the brother-husband, without paying what he owed her for her trust.

He went away, the namesake of her great love, when it was too late to backtrack or find another. But the women of my clan are creative. My mother Naja had doggedly gone on finding new names of bravery for the next generation, her eternal children, reinventing the ideal image of her love by busying herself in a search for traces of his great feats in the prison journal, when death took her by surprise. . . .

SONG 18

I have been so sick at heart, my mother!
Hunched over, you departed, twisted like game in a gamekeeper's bag.
My nerves were trembling for you, who used to stand so straight.
Come back and give me some advice, one last time;
Come back and tell me what is good, what is evil, what renders one less
*   proud.*
Guide me on the road to eternity:
The light has been extinguished, the doors are closed.
Where is the exit and where the entrance;
Where do I sit and where do I stand, my mother?
How do I tell the story and to whom?
Ah, what a pity!

I have been so sick at heart, my mother, my nerves trembling.
Look how I seek your mother, Ngo Nuga Bassogok.
Who will prepare koki for me, and nkônô, if I want them;
Who will cut hikok for me, who will dig up the yellow yam? . . .
The old things bring on yearning, and when you yearn for them
And cannot be satisfied—
Oh my mother, you know, do you not—
That is when you think you'll die.

Help me Grandfather! Grandmother, I am shivering;
I am struggling in vain, and, oh, so far away,
While behind me all my people perish.
The next year my father, too, departed, deserting me forever,
Never having set me free from the seal of our secret.
I have shivered and been so very sick at heart.

• • •

Auntie Roz has slid down against the rubber tree, forming one body with its huge roots, which emerge from the ground between her legs like an interlacing of rock and rattan: She seems to have found her place in the eternity of nature. My heart jumps: as long as she doesn't die here like that! I look at her more closely; she is breathing. . . . If you listen carefully you can hear her breath, like the light whisper of a deflating tire.

On her Senufo bed, when she refused to talk about her life, forcing me to go digging through mine in order to understand hers, I hadn't recognized that she only wanted to let me know we were not all that different. Yes, like myself, she was a simple woman, but one who had been asked to rise above her physical state, to serve the world and the gods, without fully enjoying her womanhood and, above all else, like all the women of my clan, without complaining.

You, my auntie, had no children, and I know what it costs a woman not to nurture her fertility: She is doomed to mortal solitude unless she creates—with her own hands, the clay of her own heart, and the water of her own lymph—thousands of children where two or three would have been more than ample! Solitude must have been hard for you. And you must have slaved away, like all my aunts Roz, to produce all the children you have around the world! And how courageous you must have been not to let yourself be snuffed out in anonymity, like my mothers Naja.

Auntie Roz is a personality here: She is known to every rung of the social ladder in Laguna, from the lowest to the highest, known as the mother of every ravaged heart that seeks new strength for a pure rebirth. . . .

She did not become rich financially, and I know what financial poverty costs a woman, unless she infuses every material strand she touches with the breath of a different wealth—psychological, mental, and spiritual—to shelter her from prostitution and every other form of corruption. She must have infused and infused so many of them, my proud auntie, as all my aunts Roz have done, as brave and superior as a true Lôs, but cursed because as a female they cannot ever be a Lôs.

But she succeeded in broadening her horizons and pushing her limits to the infinite. She, who never attended school, taught other teachers, of every background, everywhere she went. There is no place—including the Wailing Wall, to which she invited me last year—where she doesn't have a follower. She, who never had children or a husband, founded hundreds of happy homes and baptized thousands of grandchildren and great-grandchildren in the name of the Father, the Son, and the Holy Spirit, for ever and ever!

I compare my little life to hers through my scattered, skimpy memories, through my poor feelings gone astray in time and space, and tell myself: "Like her, may we let sorrow escape and fade away. Let us keep silent about the anger that refused to show its face, be named, or described, like all the anger of all my aunts Roz."

I think of the millions of hardworking women, like the *bayam-selam*, who tirelessly make the wheels of the emerging continent turn, all oblivious to their painful and unfortunate personal histories.

Then I want to take hunting horns and trumpets to strike up a hymn to the glorious mothers Naja and aunts Roz, for all the epic silent battles that, beyond all despair, have caused this tortured continent to remain the continent of all possible tomorrows for all of humanity.

Why should I lack serenity?

Why should I be unhappier than my mothers and my aunts?

I look at Auntie Roz, and my thoughts fly up to my joys and my finest aspirations, the ones that have allowed me to hold the road in spite of everything, and I want to believe again, sing of love again and again.

I want to sing for all my children, all the hundreds of children that I, in turn, on my own small scale, have produced across the world.

Like my mother Naja, I would like to give them thousands of names of bravery in the name of "Ultimate Knowledge"—self-knowledge; knowledge of one's own little life, which may be harmful or beneficial to the rest of life on earth; knowledge that we have a choice and that we are therefore responsible. . . . Yes, grandchildren of mine.

Diyilem, "Knowing the Customs";
Yi Tep, "Knowing How to Choose";
Yi Baï, "Knowing How to Shine";
Yi Art, "Knowing How to Unite";
Yi Ning, "Knowing How to Live," "Knowing How to Produce";
Yi Num, "Knowing How to Be Great";
Yi Ba Banga, Yi Hè, "Knowledge, Where Are You?"
For these, and for all the others I haven't named,
You and all your descendants are—let me say it again—
You are responsible.

From the heart of my land, set aflame by the fratricidal war of the poor, let me name you again and again, all of you so close to my heart, let me sing of you one last time in memory of my mothers Naja and my aunts Roz,

Before my voice falls asleep.
Why should I lack serenity?

I want to sing of you as well, Albass, my first beloved,
For whom I felled the large banana tree in the backyard,
Sacrificed the largest rooster in our farmyard,
And cooked the yellow sweet potato ready to serve it with a laugh,

So that you would come and visit me without a middleman.

Pay a visit to our only son, the only stalk of wheat, from which an entire field will grow.

No, I am not unlucky!

Oh, I know, the day that everything must come to an end,

The hour when you must die,

The source at which you quench your thirst flows over to drown you,

Even your friends help to spoil your business,

And within your own fence you find a serpent to bite your fingers.

Yes, I would have liked you to come and visit me, my first desire,

To see the work of the Oldest Love, the spirit offspring I have given you,

Like so many stars in the firmament, like a field of anthills,

Each one adding from the earth to the earth,

With your name embroidered on each glory.

What does it matter that you did not come?

I did my share and explored every angle of our design.

I dream of walking on again, moving forward to a last love, new dangers, and . . .

I hear you cry: "Another love at eighty years of age?"

And I answer you: Why not, if this one could

Refuse renunciation and compromise.

I still feel ready for a quest for a last absolute,

A last supremely proud love that, at the slightest word to counter his power of resistance, of survival of eternity, would unleash a whirlwind from his eyes, his nose, his mouth, his blood—blood like a volcano whose lava cannot burst forth.

No sweet word, no caress, no enamored look could channel it!

His blood a torrent, a hurricane bolting to strike everything down.

"Will he not strike love down, too,

Will he not crush himself, too, forever?" you say.

"Yes, but should a hurricane be tempered? Should one try to influence the weather?

I who am not a Lôs as in olden days—

Why should I fight to slow it down or speed it up, fine-tune it over time?

Can we and should we make blood quiet down?

May I worship it as my Pope;

May the whirlwind of his blood howl like the ocean;

May it raise the waves of all my impulses and thrust them against the rocks of my desire, to smash them and lay them out with all their froth like a languid backwash, to be tossed against my desire for him, and give me just one wish: to love him tenderly until I reach my final dwelling place, my ear against his heart, my lips in the hollow of his neck.

Should my eighty-year-old heart be dissuaded, when eternity is all I want to believe in anymore?

Alas, I hear a grave requiem dragging on the heels of my dehumanized men, who tear each other apart for scraps of what looks like power, but lacks any divine conscience—a power worse than that of the jungle, a power that devours without the duty to perpetuate life, that kills for the sake of killing, on command, a robotic power. And I fear an even greater oppression for women, my daughters, if every Aunt Roz were to vanish completely, without memories, amputated, full of holes. . . .

A return to trading of a sort that maliciously hides its muzzle behind words that no longer mean the same things.

You must remember, if not your mothers, then at least your aunts, who were able to kill evil with silence, and whatever will be will be. . . .

12 July 2002, 11:22 a.m.

GLOSSARY

Baffi: A pejorative term used by the Bassa for all immigrants.

Bambombock: See *Mbombock*.

Bandjanga: Small dried crayfish, considered to be the food of paupers at the time, similar to the *sapac*.

Bassa: A people—and their language—of Central Cameroon, belonging to the Bantu group.

Bayam-sellam: The women vendors in the markets, possibly pidgin English that comes from "buy 'em-sell 'em."

Bikagang: The mound that remains after palm oil has been extracted, which is then carefully piled up for growing mushrooms, or else is used to rapidly light a fire, for its is highly flammable.

Bissimè or *Bissima*: See *Sima* or *Sime*.

Bissoumè: See *Soumè*.

Bon Ba Long: Literally the children of the land, a term meant to refer to the nobility and deep-rootedness of patriots.

Fula: Ethnic group also known as the *Peul*; they are West African nomads who have moved well beyond those boundaries today.

Hikok: A climbing shrub whose leaves are among the toughest in the forest, which are used to make one of the most-refined and best-known sauces in the Bassa region, for special occasions only.

Hu: Generally refers to the spiritual and brilliant potential of the human being, but has a more pejorative connotation when this is used to harmful advantage.

Kindak: Female title; the equivalent of *Mbombock*; literally meaning the "Mistress of Recommendations."

Koki: A local dish, such as *nkônô*.

Kou-Bilim: A two-headed serpent that heralds disaster.

Lan: Oil extracted from the center of palm pits, known for its therapeutic values, especially on the fontanel of babies, and for its cosmetic property; used as sacred oil in certain rites.

Lemandé: A Cameroonian people of the Mbam Department, as well as their language.

Lilan Liliaceae: Plants of the Lily family.

Lobi: One of the Voltaic horseback-riding peoples in Côte d'Ivoire, Ghana, and Burkina Faso; also the name of the art they create.

Lôs: Powerful men who get their power from natural or supernatural forces because of their own strength of character, and who impose themselves as leaders and guides of their people without necessarily having been chosen or appointed.

Mamy-Wata: The water spirit that can be either benevolent or malicious depending on the individual with whom she deals.

Man Nyu: Literally a "child of the body," that is to say an orphan who has lost both parents.

Masso: A yellow sweet yam.

Maoum: Comes from *Oum*, a very esoteric part of the *Mbock* initiation.

Mbock: The Universe that contains the major philosophy and all the subdivisions of the areas of initiation of the Cameroonian Bassa people.

Mbombock (plural form: *Bambombock*): An initiate into the wisdom and sciences of the *Mbock*.

Mbongôô: A kind of highly aromatic pepper from Guinea, used in the preparation of a very famous black sauce, today considered to one of Cameroon's national dishes.

Mbu: The air, the spirit; the soul; the divine and immaterial part that stimulates all material creatures and allows them eternal renewal.

Mèè: Literally means "I say." The Bassa use it to refer to both their people and their language when they want to show their pride in the philosophy, wealth, and wisdom it contains.

Mintets (plural form: *ntet*): a kind of container made of woven palm leaves to hold game, fowl, and other domestic animals when traveling.

Mvet: A xylophone.

Naja: A venomous snake that spits.

Nding: A female section of the *Mbock* that deals specifically with dance, choreography, and other symbolic physical expressions of initiation. It comes from the verb *téng*, which means to tie or knot. The author therefore tends to translate the term *Nding*, which includes the initiation dance, its songs, and its philosophy, as "dance of the symbolic knots."

Ngangans: Great initiates and therapists who treat both natural and mystical sicknesses.

Njombi: A well-known tuber, whose red variation is called Macabo in Cameroon.

Nkônô ngond: A dish made of crushed squash seeds.

Nkus: Widower.

Nséguék: A powerful sound used for its forceful vibration.

Ntet: see *mintets*.

Oum: In the ancient hierarchy it was a stage to which no one under the age of fifty could gain access.

Pagne: Straight yardage of usually printed or batik cotton fabric that women wear tied around the hips, or sewn as skirts and dresses; also worn by men, particularly for special occasions or at ceremonies.

Safoutier: Fruit-bearing tree; the fruit, known as *sas* or *safous* resembles black plums, except that it is oily and needs to be either braised or steamed before eating. It is very rich in vegetable protein and is wholesome for the young especially in times of food shortages, when it protects children from malnutrition. The *sas* or *bitôrô* is a very famous dish in Central Africa in general and specifically in Cameroon.

Sapac: Originally the name of a brand of imported frozen fish that ended up becoming the name of a small bearded fish imported under the same name, the cheapest on the market so that anyone and everyone could afford it. By extension, the term also came to refer to the cheapest prostitutes that anyone could afford to pay.

Senufo: One of the Voltaic horseback-riding peoples in Côte d'Ivoire, Ghana, and Burkina Faso; also the name of the art they create.

Sima or *Sime* (plural forms: *Bissima* or *Bissimè*): Spirit, genie.

Simgang, yôp, e badjôb: These trees are considered to be sacred and magical, able to heal all kinds of physical as well as mystical maladies. The non-initiated are not always able to see them.

Soya: Skewers with very spicy beef or fowl.

Soumè (plural form: *Bissoumè*): Trafficker in human bones.

Tipot: A kind of throne for chiefs and later for the colonizers that would be carried by burly men during ceremonies or official trips of a formal nature.

Um: See *Maoum* and *Oum*.

Yéyé: Rock-and-roll music.

Yik: Widow.

AFTERWORD

A memory marks us more than the act itself. The act is not what's important, it's the remaining trace of the event that is. . . . As for me, [to write this novel] I went about digging deep into my memory. And what I found in my head [was] very, very violent. But as I say, no one lives the same thing in the same way. Other family members do not have the same recollections that I do, although we experienced a certain number of these events together. What becomes obvious to me is that Africa has a suppressed memory. Why is there so much silence in Africa? If African women started remembering all of the violence they've experienced, well, it would set off an explosion. Is this really a good thing? I'm not so sure. I believe that one succeeds in killing the event through silence, and perhaps in our case it's for the better.

—Werewere Liking, "Aesthetics of Necessity"

With *The Amputated Memory*, her fifth novel, francophone Cameroonian artist Werewere Liking confirms her great lyrical talent while probing into a collective and familial past, making an incursion deep into her own subjective memory. Published by *Nouvelles Editions Ivoiriennes* in 2004, the work has been nominated for a number of prestigious literary prizes—including the francophone *Prix des Cinq Continents* (Five Continents Prize)—and in 2006 was named recipient of the Noma Award for Publishing in Africa.[1] Written roughly between 1996 and 2002, the novel took six years to complete, while the author continued to run her fifty-odd person Ki-Yi Arts Cooperative and Foundation in Abidjan, Côte d'Ivoire. While writing, she was then also mounting multiple productions for the stage, tending to the many social causes she embraces—particularly providing assistance to African youth—and continually seeking material means for survival in the ongoing climate of fear and insecurity that Côte d'Ivoire's undeclared civil war had imposed.

A reflection of what Werewere Liking calls her "aesthetics of necessity," writing and publishing *The Amputated Memory* became a historical imperative for the author. The novel permits her to inscribe her minority voice into written African history, and in the process enables her to challenge the legitimacy of official versions of history that have completely neglected or avoided the complexities, particulars, and especially the silenced victims of Cameroon's traumatic "events of independence," the country's bloody struggle in the late 1950s to become free of France's colonial yoke.

Salvaging African women's memory is clearly part of Liking's larger project to redefine African history in general in her constant negotiation with non-African intellectual paradigms. Remembering ("re-membering") becomes a necessary step for the author to claim narrative subjectivity and historical agency.[2] Precise historical conjunctures have led Liking to this necessity, for in the postcolonial context rethinking their story has become the primary means for Africans to tangle with the challenges posed by Western history and the written archive. From the 1960s on, the imposition of exogenous histories and colonizing master narratives made the process of transcription and transmission an ethical necessity, part of a quest of remembrance to "decolonize the mind."

Like its multifaceted author, the saga related in *The Amputated Memory* stands at the crossroads of genres and traditions. Somewhere between poetry, traditional African ritual song, essay, autobiography, and historical narrative, Liking's novel takes on the destiny of an entire nation through the life of the heroine, Halla Njoké. Halla's dizzying trajectory, which includes the lessons of her grandmother, Grand Madja, allows entry into the ancient knowledge of the Bassa people of south-central Cameroon. We might see the novel as a progressive unfolding of the heroine's initiation into womanhood: Halla's encounters with violence and adversity are experienced as signposts along an ever-accelerating initiatory path.

The female members of Halla's clan provide the spine of the novel, linking together in the narration an analeptic voyage amalgamating beginnings and endings, joys and tragedies, and the destinies of old and young women. From Halla's stunningly intelligent grandmother Madja to her victimized mother, Naja, to her calculating stepmother, also named Naja, to her three aunts, all named Roz, the intertwined story of the older generations creates a panorama of women's life in Africa that takes us from a forest village to the booming city life of Douala. The women—sometimes distorted, sometimes complementary mirrors of each other—fight with the Cameroonian resistance, make and lose babies, exercise professional skills, and often find themselves in thrall to unworthy men.

Halla's story, which she narrates, eventually joins up with that of her old Auntie Roz. The many "coincidental" parallel experiences of Auntie Roz and Halla position these women as female avatars of the Lôs, considered in the Bassa cosmology as supernatural figures of male power. In the novel, such Lôs are represented specifically by Halla's passionate and brutal father who defies "laws and destiny" by his very nature. Halla and Auntie Roz, however, prove to be the true centers of supernatural wisdom and strength. The discovery and mutual recognition of Halla's and Auntie Roz's inextricably linked fates simultaneously stir up and explode the immense, unfathomable, and solitary silence imposed on the women by years of difficulties, deceptions, and doomed or disappointing love. These heroines defiantly challenge lost female memory, while at the same time recognizing the crucial importance to survival of selective silence.

The Amputated Memory thus positions silence as a primordial indicator of African women's history and of women's power over the continent's destiny. But it also sets in motion the dialectical necessity of telling one's life to unleash what the silence has held back. For if Africa has been excluded from the archives of Western "history" due to its oral traditions, its unsung women's lives supply the stuff of writerly possibilities. Halla muses about this tension as she faces her own old age:

> Let us keep silent about the anger that refused to show its face, be named, or described, like all the anger of all my aunts Roz. I think of the millions of hardworking women . . . who tirelessly make the wheels of the emerging continent turn, all oblivious to their painful and unfortunate personal histories. Then I want to take hunting horns and trumpets to strike up a hymn to the glorious mothers Naja and aunts Roz, for all the epic silent battles that, beyond all despair, have caused this tortured continent to remain the continent of all the possible tomorrows for all of humanity. (422)

LIKING'S SINGULAR TRAJECTORY

The Amputated Memory can be loosely and cautiously qualified as autobiographical. We see in it clear parallels between fictional incidents and what we now know about Liking's life. In particular, the last section of the novel, the least metaphorical, articulates Liking's lessons about life. What the narrator gleans from her experiences are the kinds of moral precautions Werewere Liking teaches to the young arts students who populate her Ki-Yi Village.

Born in the village of Makak, located between Douala and Yaoundé in Bondé, South-Central Cameroon on May 1, 1950, into a family of the Bassa ethnic tradition, Werewere Liking-Gnepo (*née* Eddy Nicole Njok) was initiated early on into her ancestral traditions by her paternal grandparents, who designated her with the coveted position of "priestess" of the Bassa philosophy and ritual practices. Her paternal grandmother, Ngo Biyong, assisted her grandfather in bringing her into the various Bassa secret societies normally reserved for males, where she received traditional teachings and the sacred knowledge of the cosmos, or the Mbock.

The year of Liking's birth marked a significant turning point in her country's history, the end of a decade of world war and the beginning of the anticolonial, Maoist-inspired revolutionary movements, such as the Mpôdôl and the UPC (*Union des Populations du Cameroun* or Union of Cameroonian Populations), under the leadership of the charismatic and later martyred Ruben Um Nyobé, also of the Bassa people. The nationalist independence movements that were to sweep across Africa during the entire decade of the fifties began in Cameroon, the only colony of France in sub-Saharan Africa to take up arms in its struggle for sovereignty—as had Algeria in North Africa and the island of Madagascar, off Africa's southeastern coast. Liking directly bore witness to the forces of change leading to her country's independence in 1960, and her writing has continually reflected the tensions and paradoxes inherent to the fraught exchanges between Africa and the West, between an ancestral wisdom and a modernity offering new forms of subjective and collective identity. As she explains, "I am myself a postcolonial product. I was taken into the bush, in hiding, during the resistance movements and struggles for independence. My writings therefore necessarily carry with them all of the contradictions stemming from this period" (2002a).

Liking has been selective in offering specific information about her formal education, and as Irène D'Almeida notes, Liking "has deliberately chosen to blur biographers' charts, especially in regard to her private life and academic training" (2000). What has been pieced together from interviews, articles, and other exchanges is that Werewere Liking is essentially self-taught.[3] She completed at least three years of elementary education, and then was taken out of school by her father. By age twelve she was married according to traditional custom; before her thirteenth birthday she gave birth to a daughter. By age fifteen she had begun to write poetry. Around October or November of 1966, Werewere Liking began to earn her living as a featured singer in Douala's nightclubs. The name "Werewere," which became her stage name, given to Eddy Nicole by her parents-in-law at age twelve, is in fact a distorted reference to the English adjective "velvety." It was meant to reflect how her person embodied the qualities of the fabric's pleasing softness and prized beauty.

The writer's whereabouts between the mid-1960s and early 1970s remain unclear, but we do know that she had a son, Lem, with a second husband, Albert Liking, that she launched a successful musical career in the urban music scene, and that she began to associate with Cameroonian intellectuals of post-independence Africa. By 1968, Liking had begun to paint, thus beginning a fertile, genre-crossing career. Between 1969 and 1971 she worked as a journalist in Cameroon, and during this period she was also invited to organize various exhibits of her paintings. The year 1974 marks the beginning of Liking's research on oral traditions and traditional theater techniques in Cameroon, Mali, and Côte d'Ivoire, specifically exploring the didactic techniques used in the initiation rituals of various ethnic groups in these countries.

As Irène D'Almeida notes, Liking was born at a time "when it was finally possible for women to write, to break the silence culturally imposed on them" (2000), and the 1977 publication in Paris of her first book of poetry, *On ne raisonne pas le venin* (There's no reasoning with poison), places her "among the first Francophone African women to come to writing" (xi). This early endeavor is the first indication of Liking's direct contact with the French capital. During the period 1976–78 she spent some time in France where she exhibited her paintings in Parisian galleries and met other artists.

When one thus places Werewere Liking alongside her African sisters and fellow writers, the exceptional nature of her career becomes more readily apparent. Not only is her first book of poetry only the second such undertaking by a woman of Cameroon—following Jeanne Ngo Mai's elegies, *Poèmes sauvages et lamentations* (1967)—it also places her, along with novelist Lydie Dooh-Bunya (*La Brise du jour* 1997), as the fifth Cameroonian female to publish a literary work.[4] Liking is the only woman writer from Cameroon who did not enjoy the privilege of some form of higher education, whether in Africa or Europe, and, unlike her compatriots, she did not set foot in Europe until she was well into her twenties.

Liking explains that such a markedly precocious career—by age eighteen she was already a poet, singer, painter, and mother of two—is a fundamental aspect of her native culture, which nurtures a natural proclivity for artistic proficiency and creativity. She comments: "I always lived in a milieu where traditional poetry, ritually chanted by great bards in my grandparent's courtyard or sung by the traditional *Mbée*, *Nding*, or *Koo* priestesses, was the stuff of childhood lullabies" (2002a). With *On ne raisonne pas le venin*, Liking produced an initial articulation of what were to become trademark *topoi* of her writings. These include: the word as an instrument of combat; the call to action of African youth; the need to regain harmony within a space of cosmic chaos; the importance for Africans to recognize and cultivate their sacred ancestral past; the parallel need for a modern, syncretic African society that has undergone a healing process; and, finally, above all, the need to grant Africa a voice, to fill in its voids (1997).

The politically repressive and culturally stifling atmosphere of Cameroon in the 1970s under Ahmadou Ahidjo—who had a history of imprisoning those writers and intellectuals not representing his government's perspective—prevented Liking from returning there to live following her travels. Fieldwork on ritual practices in Mali and Côte d'Ivoire with French ethnographer Marie-José Hourantier led her to study and cultivate what would become her trademark theatrical genre, the *théâtre-rituel*, a theater practice meant to help cure a community of its moral or psychological illnesses. The two women went on to publish over seven collaborative works together (drama, oral tales, and essays), notably *A la rencontre de. . . .* (Upon meeting . . . 1980) and *Orphée Dafric* (Orpheus of Africa 1981). The first puts Africa and the West in conversation and the second adapts a Greek myth to the initiatory voyage of an African artist. Liking and Hourantier later moved definitively to Côte d'Ivoire in 1978, where they have remained ever since, each one now directing her own theater company.

Liking's first two solo novels, *Elle sera de jaspe et de corail* (1983a; trans. *It Will be of Jasper and Coral* 2000), and *L'amour-cent-vies* (1988; trans. *Love-Across-a-Hundred-Lives* 2000) are arguably her

most significant contributions to women's writing and are break-
through novels in her trajectory as a writer. In both, she uses poly-
phonic writing, juxtapositions of divergent styles, and linguistic
invention to refashion African history and question gender.

Upon her 1978 arrival in Côte d'Ivoire, Liking began to teach
and train students in traditional African theater at the University
of Abidjan. By 1985, however, she left the university setting to
focus all her energies on the artistic leadership of the Village Ki-
Yi, a Pan-African arts collective she had founded two years earlier
with Hourantier. From that point on, Liking began to mount
multiple large-scale productions for the international stage, an
activity particularly intense between 1987 and 2002, when the Ki-
Yi's productions were presented to critical acclaim in festivals
across the globe. While at least a dozen dramatic works have been
published in multiple languages in Europe, North America, and
Africa, several of her theatrical works remain unpublished,
although all were well received. Liking's creative activity was at its
peak between 1979–1984, when she was able to turn out three to
four texts per year while simultaneously staging performances of
her plays. With the full-fledged creation of the Ki-Yi Village
cooperative, Liking's written production took a back seat to the
performing and visual arts.

Over the past decade Werewere Liking has begun to receive well-
deserved recognition for her work, as contributing to literature and to
society. In 1991 she received the French *Prix Arletty* (Arletty Prize)
for her work in the theater and the same year was named *Officier de
l'ordre culturel* (Officer of the Cultural Order) in her adopted Côte
d'Ivoire. The following year Jack Lang, then the French Minister of
Culture, decorated her as *Chevalier des Arts et des Lettres* (Knight of
Arts and Letters), and the African Literature Association granted her
its 1993 Fonlon-Nichols Prize for Literary Excellence. In 1997 she
was appointed member of the prestigious international francophone
organization, the *Haut Conseil de la Francophonie*, and in 2000 she was
selected as laureate of The Netherlands' Prince Claus Fund for Cul-

ture and Development, whose website describes her as "galvaniz[ing] the cultural scene in Abidjan."[5]

ON EXCAVATING SILENCES

Werewere Liking's pioneering work in Francophone literature and theater bears witness to a centrality of oral traditions and also to the recovery and enactment of African memory. Both are evident in the structure of her ritual theater, in the creation of the Ki-Yi Pan-African Village as a site of cultural education and production, and in her systematic study of African epics and their integration into her plays, as, for example, *La puissance de Um* (The Power of Um 1979); *Sunjata* (Soundjata 1989); *Waramba* (with Koli 1991); *Sogolon Kedjou* (2002c). In these plays, she reworks the myths fundamental to West Africa's sense of self and emphasizes the central function of women in enacting such myths. Her novels foreground especially the crucial nature of female remembering. Whether in *It Will be of Jasper and Coral, Love-Across-a-Hundred-Lives,* or *The Amputated Memory*, Werewere Liking scrutinizes African women's memory mainly through the figure of the grandmother, Madja, a figure recalling her own ancestor. When asked about the intertextuality of familial memory in her novels, the author concedes : "One may establish an intertextual link [in my novels] in terms of family memory. The character of the grandmother, whether she is called Madja as in *Love-Across-a-Hundred-Lives* or Grand Madja as in *The Amputated Memory*, is always the guide. And there are most likely scenes which have the same historical source, even if I can't think of a precise example . . ." (2002a). The grandmother is thus a guiding matrix, a "before" and an "after" through which all memories and cultural references flow. She affirms the interconnectedness of generations of women, their deep appreciation for each other.

In many African cultures, a child's destiny is perceived as directly linked to the name he or she is given. Liking is her grandmother's homonym or namesake, and thus regarded as predestined to fulfill certain ideals that her namesake embodied. The writerly enterprise from this perspective involves a certain ambivalence. Her emblematic connection to an illiterate grandmother—presented as markedly intelligent—and by extension, to that of her ancestral oral tradition, simultaneously provides a powerful motivation for the act of committing memory to writing, and certain reservations for doing so. In *The Amputated Memory*, Liking repeatedly points to the potential for the treacherous distortion of writing and of the written archival tradition imported to Africa by colonial empires. This is illustrated in the novel by comments about the hegemonic force exercised by the repressive regimes of newly independent African governments :

> And the thickness of the layers of silence became shamefully tangible, since the governments had total control over the records and made sure that every trace of every deed that disturbed them disappeared. (7)

Increasingly aware of the unsettling silence she encounters as she excavates personal and historical moments from memory, the narrator in *The Amputated Memory* seeks to transform responsibly what she sees as a "collective aphasia" into a constructive reassessment, a process of "piecing together" to come to grips with the past.

Yet the "silences of Africa" of which she writes indicate the impossibility of any return to traditional oral culture. "Spoken" memories cannot, in today's Africa, function as before, when they served to create an unproblematic common frame of experience. With writing understood also as a means of tyrannical subjugation and coercion, of censorship and corruption, it is clear that any writing must also self-consciously examine its own motives, its own tendency to lie.

WRITING AND TRAUMA

Coming to writing was for Werewere Liking, as for the heroine of *The Amputated Memory*, Halla Njokè, an excruciating and ambiguous experience. Learning to read and write and entering into the world of letters did not come without costs. Life-writing offers a means of retracing experiences, of reactivating the remaining imprints of rapidly-disappearing memories, and of making a new inscription on the palimpsests of personal and collective memories. In Liking's case, as in the case of her heroine Halla, writing is as destructive as it is creative. It enables her not only to embrace the past openly, but also to *wear* traces of the past, like iconographic scars of those losses incurred by coming to writing—loss of her childhood innocence, her virginity, her oral upbringing, traditions, and more. This has created Werewere Liking's unique conceptualization of memory as something incomplete, truncated, *amputated*: memory carries manifest traces of the past without being able ever to reproduce it fully or faithfully. By observing that memory is an "imprint" or "trace" that remains after the event, the author significantly discerns its distorted, defective, and incomplete nature. What's left is a "stump," that which is left over after the limb of personal history has been amputated by time and erasure. In psychoanalytic terms, we might say that when, upon its violent return, repressed memory forces doors open, it gets mangled in the process.

MEMORIES IN *THE AMPUTATED MEMORY*

The Amputated Memory draws the reader into the memory-scape of Halla's coming-of-age tale in 1950s Cameroon, when the colonial tides were turning with the buildup of the Mpôdôl underground resistance movement and the birth of nationalist consciousness. The tumultuous struggles of the Cameroonian freedom fighters and the disappointment of the post-independence era help establish the road to Halla's female subjective identity, an identity in which the competing worlds of "tradition" and "modernity" emerge as brutal reckoning forces. Seemingly trapped in between, Halla must undergo a multitude of adversities, most often perpetrated by male characters, as necessary stages in a progressive ceremony of initiation to the truth of the world.

The novel's form, Liking's signature *chant-roman* reminiscent of the style found in *It Will Be of Jasper and of Coral* or *Love-Among-One-Hundred-Lives*, illuminates the ongoing tension between traditional orality and modern writing, a tension felt in the aesthetic practice of many African writers. The *chant-roman* style grants significant space to song and lyricism in its attempts to forge an alliance between ancient musical forms originally sung in Bassa and based on mnemonic techniques (involving work and repetitive gestures) and a modern narrative written in French. The free form of the *chant-roman* enables the author to address many different ethical and personal issues while always coming back to a central plot line—as a main structuring element. The process suggests the workings of memory, particularly the process of recollecting information and relating it to a live audience.

Like Liking's other novels and plays, *The Amputated Memory* is divided into "Movements," which are in turn divided into numbered chapters, many of which include songs (chants). This structure reflects a certain temporal progression as well as a reliance on learned traditional mnemonic techniques. In *The Amputated Memory*, as in her 1991 play *Singuè Mura* (Simply Women), for example, "Movement 0" indicates the beginning of narrative action and situates the reader in the immediate present. However, from this temporal standpoint all action will recede into the past. It is the primordial time of all beginnings, the alpha and omega, the pivotal moment when in traditional storytelling the storyteller opens with the spoken and gestural word to set the pace for the following Movements—other key chronological moments—to unfold and develop.

The eclectic style of the novel and its polyvocal, multilayered lyricism enable Liking to elaborate those questions that require processing or working through. The problem of writing brings to light a problem of reading, a haunting predicament for Liking—as well as for all African writers of her generation and beyond, since illiteracy handicaps well over half of the continent's population. It is indeed another one of the reasons why memory in the novel is disfigured or amputated. Halla recognizes the value of writing as a tool of memory in a process of historical bricolage or reconstruction, in which one is obliged to fill in silences and disparities as best one can. And yet, as for the traditional bard, the *griot*, or the Bassa *hilun*, songs are crucial in stimulating recollections. Songs thus are also central to recalling the traditional forces of historical memory. They complement what "writing memory" cannot show. Halla/Liking acknowledges that hers is an imperfect means of recording the past. She knows she disfigures, mangles, or amputates part of the whole picture. Yet in a postcolonial world that is "beyond orality," without writing, memory of African cultures becomes obliterated.

It is perhaps the unabashedly pro-French stand that Liking's father actually took in the suppression of the local resistance movements that created her own silence around the subject until she began this novel. Reckoning with her deceased father's legacy of collaboration and betrayal most likely has provided the author with ample questions about writing and distortion. The eighty-something-year-old character Halla is able to confront her past in writing by measuring the descent of her father into decadence against the rhythm of her own progression, the "acceleration of time" that she experiences as she discovers writing. Like the heroine of a bildungsroman, Halla enters into successive phases along her initiatory path toward "enlightenment," each moment bringing a new form of self-knowledge. Each step along this epistemological journey nevertheless carries with it a destructive component involving her father, the enigmatic Njokè, an unpredictable energy field, a dangerous superman.

Njokè's supreme transgression of the universal taboo of incest comes through in Liking's prose and song as one of the most poetic descriptions in the novel, a long-repressed and amputated memory that steadily emerges from the secret waters of the river where the incest occurs onto the page. Like the knife that Njokè would use to mutilate himself, like the penis that he would force into Halla's flesh, Liking's memory emerges brutally and definitively. Vivid, dramatic, keenly attuned to surroundings and precise detail, the memory recounted here appears representative of those traumas that maintain a life of their own, coexisting in parallel with more prosaic, episodic memories. Permanently "branded" by her father, Halla cannot undo his fatal act, nor can she prove its actual existence through writing. She can limit its tyranny, however, by recognizing herself as an amputated stump and by embracing the defective part of herself that remains. Halla's indictment of her father is, in fact, an underlying indictment of certain African traditions and male-dominant social practices in African culture. Liking equates Halla's experience with that of other African women, and with that of an allegorical "Mother Africa": seduced deceitfully, colonized, raped, pillaged, and thoroughly diminished.

Writing and "re-membering" enable Halla to fight back against this legacy and regain her dignity. If such an approach can help those myriad African women whom Liking claims to represent, then the amputated memory may be assumed to contain (and hence to rewrite) their histories as well. *The Amputated Memory* thus elicits an ethics of compassion: Memory acts differently on different people, much as it emerges differently for those who remember—or forget. By framing events and experiences within the parameters of the incomplete and amputated memory, one reconsiders one's own subjective need to remember, and one also assesses memory's impact on the present.

Werewere Liking is part of a generation of committed contemporary African authors (such as Tierno Monénembo, Tanella Boni, Boubacar Boris Diop, Angèle Kingué, Patrice Nganang) who have questioned and explored the workings of memory and orality, and in the process deterritorialized or "recoded" the domain of the African writer. A pioneer among Francophone African women writers, Liking's interest in memory, tied to questions of female trauma and silence, has been observed in the writings of a number of female contemporaries—from Senegalese writers such as Ken Bugul and Fatou Diome to Algerians such as Assia Djebar or Malika Mokeddem. Delving into childhood recollections and collective female memory has provided a means for these women to invest in a reconstructive effort, where memory holds the keys to the contradictory worlds they attempt to absorb in a mutating culture.

A WORD ABOUT THE TRANSLATION
Marjolijn de Jager has accompanied Werewere Liking's work since

the late 1980s. She has now translated three of Liking's densely poetic novels, working hand in hand with the author to find English equivalencies of cultural terms and practices specific to Liking's particular ethnic group or creating the right images to best capture Liking's experience among differing African cultures. De Jager has also visited The Village Ki-Yi and tirelessly promoted the humanitarian work Liking carries out there, forming new generations of African artists from children who have little or no access to education and training. De Jager, who also translates from the Dutch, has translated several other major Francophone writers; including Assia Djebar, Ken Bugul, and V.Y. Mudimbe.

Michelle Mielly
Grenoble, France
April 2007

NOTES

Many thanks to Judy Miller, for her invaluable expertise and help in putting the finishing touches on this Afterword.

1. The Noma Award for Publishing in Africa was created by and named for the founding president of the Japanesepublisher Kodansha, and is granted under the auspices of UNESCO. According to the Noma Award web site,

Werewere-Liking's novel or—*chant-roman*—is a truly remarkable achievement, illustrating the potential of African literature to renew and regenerate its forms. Through innovative and fully successful use of traditional songs, praise-naming, lullaby, letters and myth, the novel is unique in its form. Halla wants to write the biography of her admired aunt, and through this process searches her own memory: a memory dislocated, with parts of the past seemingly lost forever, but seeking to reconstruct itself. This is a deeply felt presentation of the female condition in Africa; and a celebration of women as the country's memory, and feminine patriotism and wisdom as central to the question for the self-determination of Africa.

2. This authorly impulse could be seen as a process similar to what Deleuze and Guattari describe as *déterritorialisation*, a form of "re-appropriation" that combats a dominant territorializing impulse common to Capitalist culture: "*[L]e livre assure la*

déterritorialisation du monde, mais le monde opère une reterritorialisation du livre, qui se déterritorialise à son tour en lui-même dans le monde" ([T]he book ensures a deterritorialization of the world, but the world carries out its own reterritorialization on the book, which then deterritorializes itself in the world) (Deleuze and Guattari 1980, 18; my translation).

3. See Liking's interview with Sennen Andriamirado for additional commentary on the subject (Liking 1983b). John Conteh-Morgan explains that "At a time when many Cameroonian girls of her age were being initiated into the mysteries of Western culture through formal education, [Liking] was instead being initiated into those of the many secret cults of her Bassa people. It was much later, rather like the Senegalese novelist Sembène Ousmane, that she taught herself to read and to write in French, skills which she subsequently used to explore for the stage those myths and ritual ceremonies that were such a vital part of her early experience" (1994, 211).

4. The previously published literary works by Cameroonian women were Marie-Claire Matip's *Ngonda* (1956), Jeanne Ngo-Mai's *Poèmes sauvages et lamentations*, Thérèse Kuoh-Makoury's *Rencontres essentielles* (1968) and Tabitha Yonko Nana's *La reine* (1972). Lydie Dooh-Bunya's novel *La Brise du Jour* (1977) was published more or less simultaneously with Liking's first book.

5. See http://www.princeclausfund.nl/source_eng/news/2000_were.html.

WORKS CITED

Conteh-Morgan, John. 1994. *Theatre and Drama in Francophone Africa: A Critical Introduction*. Cambridge: Cambridge UP.

D'Almeida, Irène Assiba. 2000. Introduction. *It Shall be of Jasper and Coral* and *Love-across-a-Hundred-Lives: Two Novels* by Werewere Liking. Trans. Marjolijn de Jager. Charlottesville: UP of Virginia.

Deleuze, Gilles, and Félix Guattari. 1980. *Capitalisme et Schizophrénie 2: Mille Plateaux*, Paris: Ed. de Minuit.

Liking, Werewere. 1977. *On ne raisonne pas le venin*. Paris: Editions Saint Germain-des-Près.

———. 1979. *La puissance de Um*. Abidjan: Ceda.

———. 1980. *A la rencontre de . . .* Dakar: Nouvelles Editions Africaines.

———. 1981. *Orphée Dafric*. Paris: L'Harmattan.

———. 1983a. *Elle sera de jaspe et de corail: Journal d'une misovire*. Paris: L'Harmattan.

———. 1983b. "La femme par qui le scandale arrive." Interview with Sennen Andriamirado. *Jeune Afrique* 1172 (22 June): 68–70.

———. 1988. *L'amour-cent-vies*. Paris: Publi-Sud.

———. 1989. *Sunjata. L'Épopée mandingue* (unpublished).

———. 1991. *Singuè Mura : Considérant que la femme*. Abidjan: Editons Kiyi.

————. 2000. *It Shall be of Jasper and Coral* and *Love-Across-a-Hundred-Lives: Two Novels*. Trans. Marjolijn de Jager. Charlottesville: UP of Virginia.

————. 2003. "The Aesthetics of Necessity." Interview with Michelle Mielly. *World Literature Today* 2:3 (July–September): 52–57.

————. 2002a. Personal interview with Michelle Mielly, in French. 2 June. Trans. Michelle Mielly.

————. 2002b. Personal Interview with Michelle Mielly, in French. 2 December 2002. Trans. Michelle Mielly.

————. 2002c. *Sogolon Kedjou, l'Epopée panafricaine, ou la vie ordinaire d'une femme épique* (unpublished).

————. 2004. *La mémoire amputée: Chant-roman*. Abidjan: Nouvelles Editions Ivoiriennes.

Liking, Werewere, with Souleymane Koli. 1991. *Waramba, Opéra mandingue* (unpublished; written with for the Kotéba ensemble).

Noma Award for Publishing in Africa. 2007. "Werewere-Liking Wins 25th Noma Award for Ground-Breaking Novel." April. http://www.nomaaward.org/press2005.shtml.

Prince Claus Fund for Culture and Development. 2007. "Werewere Liking: 2000 Prince Claus Awards." April. http://www.princeclausfund.org/en/what_we_do/awards/2000liking.shtml.

The Feminist Press at the City University of New York is a nonprofit literary and educational institution dedicated to publishing work by and about women. Our existence is grounded in the knowledge that women's writing has often been absent or underrepresented on bookstore and library shelves and in educational curricula—and that such absences contribute, in turn, to the exclusion of women from the literary canon, from the historical record, and from the public discourse.

The Feminist Press was founded in 1970. In its early decades, The Feminist Press launched the contemporary rediscovery of "lost" American women writers, and went on to diversify its list by publishing significant works by American women writers of color. More recently, the Press's publishing program has focused on international women writers, who remain far less likely to be translated than male writers, and on nonfiction works that explore issues affecting the lives of women around the world.

Founded in an activist spirit, The Feminist Press is currently undertaking initiatives that will bring its books and educational resources to underserved populations, including community colleges, public high schools and middle schools, literacy and ESL programs, and prison education programs. As we move forward into the twenty-first century, we continue to expand our work to respond to women's silences wherever they are found.

For information about events and for a complete catalog of the Press's 250 books, please refer to our website: www.feministpress.org.